NIGHT ROSE
WORLDS OF THE POLEAXES
BOOK ONE

J. C. COOPER

Formatted with Vellum

For anyone trying to find themselves in a world that doesn't value them for who they are, only for what they can do

CONTENT WARNING

This story covers topics of physical violence, murder, and implied abuse, as well as alluding to sexual activities, which are off-page. Please read with caution.

BELRUNE

 THE FOUNDERS

MONTCLAIR

VEROWEN

ISA

NALARAN MOUNTAINS

DEADLANDS

SEKADAN

DEADLANDS

SRILA

DEADLANDS

CHAPTER I

BRIATTA

B riatta Belrose wove her way through the bustling streets of Montclair, a bag slung over her shoulder, looking for all the world like just another young woman heading home or meeting friends for an evening drink. It was precisely what everyone else was doing at that hour, which meant no one would question her presence.

A young man with dark bags beneath his eyes passed by, bearing the Ardor-mark of an Air Ardorist on his temple, just visible beneath the shadow of his white headscarf. Briatta noted that, and a furrow appeared between her brows. The strain on Ardorists was growing with every passing cycle, and there had been noticeably fewer luxurious uses of it in the city. Once, fountains had bubbled brightly on every block, trees had bloomed with inedible, functionally useless flowers, and winds had wended between buildings to help keep the people of Montclair cool. Now, only edible plants or bioluminescent flora were planted and nurtured, and water was limited to what was drinkable.

A familiar ache of yearning bloomed within, and Briatta's

mind wandered to the lifelong hope she would soon also receive a tattoo, the same as every Elfean in Belrune if they were lucky enough to manifest their Ardor during their Choosing ceremony upon turning twenty-one. Not only because it had been her lifelong dream to follow that path, but because she desperately wanted to help her people thrive again. They could only do that with more Ardorists.

Above the biodome encasing the city and protecting the Elfeans from the unhealthy atmosphere outside was a sky perpetually such a light shade of blue that it was nearly white, always visible except when the biodome darkened for bionight, as it did now.

Briatta glanced up at the larger, yellower Polar Sun, still visible on the horizon of the wastelands beyond the biodome. When it was high in the sky, the biodome—the physical manifestation of combined Ardor protecting the Elfean people— would remain clear because the fiery sphere was farther away and less harmful.

Briatta had never seen the smaller, hotter sun that rose when the biodome was dark—the glowing giant that was dubbed the Nocturne Sun.

Aside from the suns, the sky was never filled with anything else because there was no weather outside the biodome except for the occasional desert storm where sand and dirt were whipped violently around.

Just as the biodome darkened completely and bionight had officially begun, Briatta paused, allowing her eyes to adjust, and pulled the cream-colored headscarf she'd been wearing like a hood from her head, letting it fall around her shoulders instead. The mushrooms dotting the ground beside where she walked glowed pink and orange, and the flowers on the tree above her shone a faint purple onto her cheeks. All around, lights of Ardor-manufactured nature blinked to life to illuminate the city. Only when she could clearly see again did Briatta continue.

Five houses away from the one that was her target, a familiar presence fell into step beside her. Briatta glanced up at Neven, her lifelong friend and the one with whom she most often went on missions for the Night Roses. His blond hair was cropped short and brushed back to reveal his still-healing Ardor-mark. When he glanced down at her, briefly meeting her gaze with his piercing blue eyes, the corner of his mouth slanted up in silent greeting. Her chest warming, Briatta smiled up at him. Rolling his shoulders and cracking his neck, Neven looked straight ahead again; he was more tense than usual, but it was expected, considering their destination.

"Binding 'til burning," Briatta whispered, then.

"Binding until burning," Neven echoed, and the back of his hand brushed hers. It was something most commonly said in Founders Halls to signify life since the Binding until they all passed and burned in the end, and it had become a familiar saying between Briatta and Neven as they started a mission.

One house away, Briatta stepped off the road and slipped into the shadows of the neighboring building while Neven continued without her. When she reached the back of the house, she set her bag down and pulled off her dress, revealing the black suit and leathers she wore only on such missions. Quickly, she pulled her long brown hair into a braid, tucking it behind her softly pointed ears, and then pinned it in a tight knot at the base of her head. Then, she wrapped a black headscarf over her features—similar to the pale ones she wore during the bioday to protect herself from the Polar Sun—and secured it at the top of her shoulders.

Tucking the dress and bag behind a large bush, Briatta quickly scaled the structure's wall and plucked a glowing pink flower from the adjacent tree. Then, she wiggled on her stomach across the roof, making as little noise as possible to take her predetermined position near the edge. From there, she could see into the master bedroom of their subject's home, while also being hidden from the street.

Briatta's eyes immediately sought Neven, who was disappearing around the corner of the target house, having also changed into his fighting clothes, blond hair now safely hidden beneath a similar black headscarf. Catching the glint of the blade strapped around his back as he vanished, her heart clenched in her chest, both with the usual nerves that came with this job and her fear for Neven's safety.

Briatta, trying to distract herself from the nerves coming to life in her heart, kept her eyes glued to the bedroom window, as she mentally reviewed every single detail she could recall from the case file she and Neven had pored over in the headquarters of the Night Roses.

The Night Roses had been formed centuries ago by a Belrose ancestor during a series of brutal murders that the city officials could not solve. Fearing for the lives of her family and friends, the ancient Belrose matriarch took up arms herself, and from that moment on, there were Night Roses standing vigil at all hours. Many terrible people had been stopped by the covert organization, even when the Weilers were unable to find sufficient evidence to bring such criminals to justice.

The Weilers, who were named after a guard animal that had been documented at one point during the expansive Elfean history, were the official soldiers of the crown. King Novak, the current ruler of the kingdom of Belrune, could not publicly condone the actions of the Night Roses, but he had never done anything to try and stop them.

While the Polar Sun had set, it was not yet considerably late, so it was no surprise that Mr. Bern was not home when Briatta and Neven arrived to settle in and wait. In fact, it had been planned this way. Through the bedroom window, Briatta watched Neven slide into the room and disappear behind the large desk in the corner.

Slowly, the minutes ticked by, and the sounds of people returning to their homes for the bionight diminished. A few streets over, loud, drunken shouts came from the popular bar near the city's center, and someone giggled so frequently and loudly that Briatta considered the consequences of leaving her post to knock the senseless woman out. Briatta's hearing was sharp, and though she couldn't distinguish what they were saying at this distance, the repetitive sound was quickly becoming disruptive to her job.

A sand owl hooted somewhere to Briatta's left, and she imperceptibly tilted her chin to turn her attention in that direction. Sometimes, bird calls were signals. Most of the time, they were just birds. However, sand owls were native to Vernona, and they rarely came this far north, preferring instead the even hotter climate of the southern reaches of Belrune—both kingdom and continent. Not that it was much cooler here. With two suns and the increasingly thinning atmosphere, most of the planet of Carceron was brutally hot these days.

Briatta kept her eyes on the window, but her ears remained trained in the direction from which the owl's call had come.

As the air cooled infinitesimally within the biodome—thanks to the protection that the darkness of the shield offered from the Nocturne Sun—Briatta's sweat finally began to dry, and she pulled leather gloves from her pocket, shoving her hands into them. The gloves were probably Briatta's favorite piece of gear; they had been imbued with a small amount of Ardor so they would never leave a traceable mark, and her hands would never be too warm so long as she wore them.

Still, she preferred to avoid placing her damp palms inside them.

After an hour, Briatta finally heard the telltale sound of Mr. Bern's black leather boots and, more notably, his cane rhythmically tapping the stone of the road as he slowly approached. He came into view moments later wearing a black bowler hat and an unbuttoned grey trench coat, the hem swaying with his lilting, painful step. Mr. Bern's leg had been broken in his childhood and allowed to heal poorly, and though the records didn't state how it occurred, he'd been estranged from his father since the moment he moved out.

Briatta couldn't help but curl her upper lip at the sight of him, and not just because of his atrocious taste in hats.

Tearing her gaze from Mr. Bern, Briatta looked back to the window where she knew Neven would be watching for her signal and opened her fingers, the glowing pink flower she'd plucked falling over the roof's edge and drifting to the ground.

Mr. Bern neared the front of his home and stopped on the porch, leaning on his cane as he searched his pockets. His hand reemerged with a key, and he unlocked his front door to step inside. Briatta held her breath as she waited for him to appear in his bedroom doorway as he had done each time she'd observed him, studying his habits. Today, though, it seemed Mr. Bern had other ideas in mind.

Briatta wasn't sure how much time had passed as she strained to hear anything from within the walls of Mr. Bern's house, but there was nothing. Suddenly, Neven jumped from behind the desk and darted into the hallway.

Shit. This wasn't the plan. What was he doing?

Torn between maintaining her post and rushing to help Neven, Briatta hesitated for only a second before hurriedly creeping back to the end of her roof and scrambling to the ground. As soon as her boots hit the dirt, she ran towards the rear of Mr. Bern's house to where she knew Neven would have left a key—copied meticulously by a Night Rose locksmith—for her should anything unexpected occur.

Well, Briatta would definitely classify this as unexpected.

Cracking open the rear door after silently turning the lock, Briatta paused to listen. It was absolutely still within the house, and she didn't understand how that was possible. Neven wouldn't have abandoned their plan for no reason.

As far as she could tell, this was a perfectly normal house that had the unfortunate lot of being owned by a terrible man. Regardless, she touched her fingers to the walls and felt for any hint of Ardor that might mask sound. Still, there was nothing.

Even before an Elfean manifested their own Ardor, they could feel when it had been used. It was a skill taught early in life because there was so much Ardor in their everyday lives that it was important to recognize when it was absent.

Briatta pushed the door open far enough to slip all the way inside and closed it gently behind her. It was deathly quiet with no audible noises filtering in from the street outside either, and Briatta had the eerie sensation that she had stepped into a mausoleum.

Then, a loud thud came from somewhere below her, and she quickened her pace, searching for the entrance to the basement. The main floor of the house was fairly open, with the entryway, dining room, and parlor all on the right side. They were clear, so that left the kitchen and the office. Every room Briatta passed was sparsely furnished and so clean that it was hard to believe someone actually lived there—a detail she fixated on due to her training.

The second Briatta entered the office, she spied the secret door. It was wide open, behind a large desk, and had been previously disguised by bookshelves. She hurried to it and peered down the staircase leading to the basement. Neven was halfway up the stairs, wiping blood from his sword. He glanced up and met her gaze, his expression grim.

She raised a questioning brow.

Instead of speaking, as voices could be identified, Neven finished cleaning his sword, sheathed it, and then signed with his hands. All Night Roses were required to learn this language to avoid leaving traces of themselves behind on the job, including what they sounded like.

"Intel is correct. Man downstairs. He went for him."

Briatta's stomach churned with understanding then, and she felt an overwhelming sense of gratitude that Neven was the kind of man who would risk exposure to stop another death from happening. Neven tucked his cleaning rag into his breast pocket and gestured to the hidden door, his own expression piercing.

Shaking her head in answer, Briatta dug into the smaller satchel she carried on every mission, strapped to her chest. She withdrew the Night Roses' evidence regarding Mr. Bern's links to a series of cases, all of the older men found dead, and spread it over his desk in chronological order. The pictures and paper trails they had found were freshly printed and clean of fingerprints, and Briatta had only touched them with her gloves. When she finished, she took a small square of paper from her pocket and quickly sketched a black rose.

The signature was the one hint of themselves that all members of the Night Roses left behind. Part of the reason was so the Weilers would know the Night Roses were responsible and consequently avoid looking for other culprits, potentially apprehending innocent people in the process. The other reason was to surreptitiously show the Weilers how their job should be done, especially with cases like Mr. Bern.

Briatta took the small drawing to the front door, checked that the street was clear, and pinned it dead in the center just below the heavy brass knocker. The black rose emblem was recognized throughout Belrune, and whoever approached the Bern house first the following morning would know to call for help.

With the scene set and proof arranged neatly in clear view, Briatta nodded to Neven, who had followed her. As they passed the office on their way to the back door, Briatta looked towards the basement stairs. It was maddening that protocol stated she and Neven could not free the man trapped down there themselves. The Weilers would have to be the ones to find him and take credit for his rescue.

Briatta breathed a sigh of relief as she passed through the doorway and into the warm bionight air once more, the normal sounds of Montclair nightlife reaching her ears as if she'd moved clear of a soundproof room. It truly had been unnaturally quiet inside Mr. Bern's home, and she shivered as she looked back at the house while she waited for Neven to check that, aside from their additions, the building was otherwise as they'd found it. When he was done, he gave her a thumbs-up before heading to retrieve the clothes he'd left. Briatta returned to her own things and pulled the dress over her black suit, stuffing the black headscarf into the bag alongside her cream one, removing the pins to free her braids.

Then, she walked back onto the roads of Montclair and made her way towards headquarters. A couple of blocks later, Neven joined her, throwing his arm around her shoulders and grinning down at her.

"Hey, Bria," he said as if he'd just caught up to her and was greeting a friend. She returned the smile.

"Nice job tonight," Briatta told him quietly, turning forward but watching him from the corner of her eyes. He ran a hand through his hair with his free hand, blowing out a puff of air.

"It could have been smoother. And we're late," Neven replied, pulling away and giving her a sidelong look as he shoved his hands into the front pockets of his pants. His blue eyes glittered under the Ardor lights lining the city's streets, small balls of pure light set into glass casings to illuminate Montclair through the bionight.

Briatta rolled her eyes. "It wasn't our fault."

"Still, we missed our chance to get noodles." Neven's tone was serious, and Briatta fought the urge to laugh. Their favorite noodle restaurant, Noodlegeuse, was only open until the middle of the bionight, but Briatta wasn't sure she could eat noodles at the moment, anyway.

"We'll get noodles tomorrow," Briatta promised, flashing a genuine grin. She liked their tradition of doing something together after missions as a way to ground themselves and return to the normalcy of life in Montclair.

While it was not required of Night Roses to deal death blows, someone who would be willing and able to was always sent on missions—should the need arise. Despite being skillfully trained, Briatta had never been able to end someone's life, even when the person on the other end of her blade had committed the worst crimes. Because of her hesitation, Neven became Briatta's permanent partner in the field. He would do anything to protect her, and together, they were a formidable and unstoppable force.

"You did well tonight, too," Neven said into the silence, his mouth curling up at the corners.

"The only circumstance that would result in my not doing well is if I were distracted by food," Briatta replied, sinking into her haughty mask of self-assured vigilante and smirking at her friend.

It was Neven's turn to roll his eyes, and his shoulders visibly relaxed. "You are a glutton."

They reached the street corner where Neven, when he'd been younger, had often waited for the Belrose family when they walked to headquarters from their home, climbing up on the old fire escape to watch for them. As they passed, she glanced up at metal stairs where now, she could often find him reading on the days they had missions, waiting for her to pass underneath so they could walk into headquarters together. Once, she'd gone up with him, and though she hadn't found the same solace in the spot Neven did, it at least offered an excellent view of the southern half of Montclair.

"Pray to the Founders for my redemption," Briatta quipped back, grinning as they crossed the road to the newspaper building that was the front for the headquarters of the Night Roses. They walked around to the side of the building and opened the door leading into the employee break room. Everyone working for the newspaper were also Night Roses, so they never worried about walking in on someone unawares. That bionight, though, the room was empty. It was well past normal working hours.

The room's back wall was painted a light-cream color and appeared completely unassuming. Briatta ran her hand over it, feeling more than looking for the spot that was smoother than the rest from years of being touched. She pushed gently when her fingers located it, and the seamless door swung smoothly open.

Briatta and Neven stepped onto the wide landing of a staircase and descended together into the underground warehouse from which the Night Roses operated.

The common area was smaller than expected because most of the building had been converted into living spaces that members could use under extenuating circumstances. Though the housing was meant to be a temporary solution, Briatta knew a few members who had become permanent residents. Before his Choosing, Neven had been one of them.

There were also conference rooms, training gyms, and armories, leaving little space for anything else.

A tall young man with red hair and freckles lounged on a black sofa by a large, red fireplace with a heatless, Ardor-made fire burning merrily inside. When Briatta and Neven stepped off the stairs, he looked up from his book, blinking at the interruption.

"About time," Rory Donal said, setting the book face down on the couch and rising to greet them. Then, he moved to the little front desk and hauled a huge logbook onto the counter from somewhere underneath. "Did everything go as planned?"

"No, the target was late, and I was forced to intervene before he...killed another man," Neven said roughly. Briatta reached out and took his hand, giving it a gentle squeeze.

Rory nodded grimly, scratching something on the page he'd opened to.

"Our informant was correct, though," Briatta added.

"Alright." Rory frowned slightly as he made more notes in the logbook. "Did anyone see you?"

Neven shook his head. "It was dark. And I was silent."

"Good. Well, that's all I need for now. Full review will be with Zora sometime tomorrow. Go home and get some rest."

Briatta and Neven turned to leave but paused when Briatta spied Owena seated on a sofa on the opposite side of the common area. She hadn't looked in that direction when they'd entered, and Owena had been still as a statue. Glancing up at Neven, Briatta raised an eyebrow, and he shrugged. He hadn't seen her either, then.

"Owena," Briatta walked toward the sofa, trying to mask the surprise in her voice. Already, she knew she would receive a reprimand for exercising decidedly poor awareness. "What are you doing here at this hour?"

It wasn't unusual to find her aunt at the headquarters during odd hours, but she hadn't been there when Briatta had checked in before heading out with Neven, and that had already been quite late in the day.

"I had my own mission tonight, and I thought I'd wait for you. You're later than I expected." Owena stood to join them, a brow arching as she waited for their explanation.

Neven crossed his arms. "We would have been later if only Noodlegeuse were open."

The corner of Owena's eyes crinkled as she smiled and gestured for them to go up the stairs. "Then I'm grateful it wasn't."

As the three Elfeans exited the building, Briatta could hear the rushing of the river Ravolo, which flowed a good distance behind their headquarters and was considered Montclair's eastern boundary. It had been running lower recently, so hearing it flow with such veracity again was comforting.

Owena ushered them back across the street, and they headed north toward the Belrose Estate. When they reached a crossroads, Neven peeled off from their small group and melted into the shadows with a nod of goodbye, heading west toward the poorer parts of the city where he moved after his Choosing.

A while after he had left, when Briatta and Owena passed the Founders Hall local to the neighborhood where the Belrose Estate was located, Owena said, "That boy cares for you."

It was something she said often these days, and Briatta knew her aunt was gently probing how Briatta felt about it. She wasn't ready to think about that yet though, and she avoided directly answering.

"We're lifelong friends," Briatta replied, her stomach twisting uncomfortably. "Of course, we care for each other."

Owena stayed silent for the remainder of their walk home, apparently unwilling to argue her point. When they reached the big, beautiful home that Owena had inherited from her parents, Briatta found herself once again marveling at how the building simultaneously appeared intimidating and welcoming. It was painted a shade of blue that sometimes seemed grey depending on the light, with white trim and large windows in every room. Big white pillars supported the overhanging roof of the front porch and the upstairs balconies.

Briatta's favorite part of the Belrose Estate was the two large, ancient trees framing it like living statues. Owena had allowed plants to flourish on her grounds with the help of a Flower Ardorist she hired year-round, and there were flowering shoots of every species and color entangled with the railings of the porch and vining up the walls, trailing into the magnificent gardens.

When they entered through the big white front door, Briatta's younger sister, Ellery, jumped to her feet.

"How did everything go?" Ellery tossed her book carelessly on the chair she'd occupied and looked eagerly between Owena and Briatta, the latter of whom was fighting the urge to pick the book up and gently bookmark the spot Ellery had saved, perhaps even apologize to it for the treatment it received from her sister.

"Everything went as expected. Why aren't you in bed?" Owena demanded, though Briatta could tell by the tone of her voice that she wasn't upset.

Ellery rolled her eyes. "I can't sleep when it's just me here."

"Isn't Aden here? He's supposed to keep watch when we are both out," Briatta said pointedly.

"He went to bed hours ago." Ellery gestured in the direction of Aden's old room, the first door on the right at the top of the stairs. Their older brother had moved out when he started working for the city after his Choosing ceremony, but Owena kept his bedroom the same even after he left.

Fire Ardor had awoken in Aden during his Choosing, and he had been called to work for Montclair's fire department shortly after, working alongside those with Water Ardor to put out fires around the city. Briatta knew he also had mundane tasks such as lighting small fires for the cold-blooded creatures of Belrune who chose to live within the biodome when it grew too chilly for them during the bionight. For the people on the continent, it was still hot. Briatta only understood the concept of being cold from learning about those scaled animals in school; she'd never experienced it herself.

"I'm exhausted," Briatta announced, even as Owena opened her mouth to ask Ellery another question. She knew if she didn't excuse herself, Ellery would keep them up the rest of the night with questions about their missions and complaints about how Aden had left her alone.

"Yes, we should get some rest," Owena agreed, moving to the base of the stairs, just behind Briatta.

"Wait!" Ellery cried, snatching her book from the chair and hurrying after them. "Tell me more!"

Ellery was a member of the Night Roses, just like Aden and Briatta, but Owena held firm that none of them would go on missions until they were eighteen. For Ellery, that was very soon, as she would come of age in a couple of cycles of the Nocturne Sun around Carceron, each thirty days, and she was eager to learn as much as possible to best prepare herself.

"You don't need to expose yourself to more of the world's horrors sooner than you have to." Owena's tone was soft and placating, but Ellery wilted.

"Fine," she sighed. "Goodnight." The youngest Belrose

disappeared into her room, which was directly across from Briatta's.

"Get some rest, Bria," Owena said from her bedroom door. "Tomorrow will be a long day."

"You, too." Briatta smiled to herself. The next day would be long because they would begin their preparations to visit the Palace of the Founders, the site of the twelve Elfeans who had saved Carceron and all of its inhabitants from death. They stood eternally as statues, and it was the only place where Ardor could be awakened.

Briatta's twenty-first birthday was coming up, and with it, the Choosing.

CHAPTER 2

The following day, the only reason the Belrose women woke on time was because Aden knocked loudly on all their doors.

"I'm up," Briatta groaned when he paused his incessant banging. "For the love of the Founders, stop!"

She rolled onto her back and stared at the ceiling, the exhaustion from the previous night still heavy in her bones, but the excitement of what was to come fluttering in her chest. As the shock of having been abruptly yanked from deep sleep faded, her eyes adjusted to the light seeping through the cracks in her curtains. Settling into her chest was the surreal feeling that came with the arrival of a day she'd waited for all her life.

"Good. Preida already has breakfast ready for you lazy lot," Aden responded, his voice muffled by the wooden door.

Briatta rolled her eyes and pushed herself out of bed.

The Palace of the Founders was thankfully located close to Montclair, which was convenient for the Belrose family but less so for the Elfeans who traveled from all over Belrune for their Choosing ceremonies.

"Well? Are you coming?" It was Aden again.

"For Founders' sake," Briatta said under her breath as she stood in front of her wardrobe, deciding on what to wear.

"Bria?" Aden prompted.

"Yes," she called, sighing.

Aden's footsteps moved away from her door once she answered, then she heard him knock on Ellery's door a moment later. Briatta pulled on a pair of green pants and a long-sleeved white shirt before cracking open her door to watch, knowing just what Aden was risking by banging on their younger sister's door. Ellery was, after all, seventeen and still filled with pent-up feelings she wasn't good at processing just yet.

"Aden! Why!" Ellery cried predictably, flinging her door open to find Aden with his fist in the air. He calmly pocketed his hands, lips quirking with amusement as he looked down at his baby sister.

"I *told* you to go to bed instead of waiting up," he said dryly, glancing over his shoulder to where Briatta was standing in her doorway. Without another word, he headed down the stairs, leaving Ellery glaring after him, her hair still mussed from sleep.

Owena opened her door at that moment, already dressed in her usual unrestrictive attire. She always chose pants and a top, though they varied in color and style. Of all the Belroses, Owena was the most accomplished fighter, and those who knew to look for them saw the hints of her training glaringly apparent in her everyday life.

"Are you girls nearly ready to eat?" she asked with a warm smile, noticing her nieces standing at their doors and staring at her. "We've got lots of shopping to do today."

"Ugh," Ellery grunted and slammed her bedroom door closed.

Briatta's eyes widened, and she met Owena's gaze with a knowing grin. While typically sweet and gentle, Ellery was definitely not immune to the effects of being a teenager.

"Well, I'm ready," Briatta said, even as her hands instinctively checked the knives she'd worn on her body since the day she'd been old enough—and competent enough—for Owena to allow it.

"I'll meet you at breakfast." Owena retreated to her room after observing Briatta's subconscious hand movements.

In the dining room, the family cook—Preida—had prepared a fantastic spread of honey, jams, and cheeses to pair with sour bread alongside oats, cream, and berries. With her mouth watering, Briatta poured a cup of tea and added a splash of cream, joining Aden at the table where he'd taken a seat after having invoked the wrath of the youngest Belrose woman. He smirked at Briatta, one brow lifting and slightly wrinkling the Ardor-mark on his forehead that declared his status as a Fire Ardorist.

It was said that Elfeans used to naturally develop tattoo-like markings on their faces when their Ardor manifested, but that wasn't the case anymore. Over time, it became the custom for the appropriate rune to be inked onto the temple after the Choosing. Briatta was skeptical that the symbols had ever appeared on their own; she suspected there had been an ancient way of creating the things, and there was evidence in her school's history books to back it up. She'd read about old needles stained with a dark substance that had been found in the homes of long-dead Elfeans, though many believed they were used to create traditional, more personal designs, on people rather than Ardor-marks.

Aden was the only Belrose to bear a tattoo, and it was the swirling rune for flame in an old dialect of the Elfean language, done in fine lines and with the deepest black ink. Although the people no longer spoke this language, the glyphs were still used to identify the Ardor that each Elfean possessed. It was a point of extreme pride to bear a mark, especially living in a world as hostile to its inhabitants as Carceron.

Briatta couldn't wait to manifest her own Ardor and attend her tattoo appointment. Everything was already scheduled—or at least tentatively reserved. Many of the people who performed standard post-Choosing services were no longer guaranteeing a time slot, considering the number of Elfeans who left their rituals without Ardor these days.

"Bold of you to awaken the beast so early," Briatta commented with a wry smile, her gaze flicking towards her brother as she slathered butter onto a slice of bread.

"She'll never make it as a Night Rose if she can't wake up when she needs to," Aden said with a deadpan expression before taking a long drink of water. "If you think about it, I'm doing her a favor."

Briatta chuckled, swapping butter for brambleberry jam and scooping a generous amount from the jar. "Ellery doesn't see it that way."

Aden's eyes sparkled over his breakfast as he picked up the newspaper that Preida left on the table for them every morning, always propped neatly against the vase of flowers in the center. A moment later, footsteps sounded in the hall, and Owena appeared.

"El's on her way down," Owena said with a warning look to Aden, who glanced up from his paper, smiling innocently.

While Aden and Ellery constantly clashed, Briatta was amicable with both her siblings. She seldom played intermediary because she didn't want to accidentally nurture animosity, but she could usually see the humor in their disagreements. They were rarely serious, and arguments were usually forgotten within minutes.

"There's another report of an activist attack," Aden said, his eyes flicking back and forth across the paper. "Happened between here and Seradan."

The kingdom—and continent—of Belrune was home to many cities, each encased in their own biodome. While Montclair was in the northwestern corner of the kingdom, just east of the Palace of the Founders, Seradan was farther south and bordered on the east by the Nalaran Mountain range.

Owena sighed, moving to the tea selection. "King Novak really ought to fight them with a harder hand."

The Kalaiden rebels claimed that their planet, Carceron, was slowly dying and King Novak wasn't doing anything to stop it. Even if the world *was* dying, Briatta didn't see how the king could make a difference, and she thought that the attacks were cruel and resulted in an unnecessary loss of life. Not even the most potent Ardorist could stop a force of nature like a dying planet, so why did they insist on perpetuating this fight?

The citizens of Belrune didn't know who to blame, and so it fell on King Novak. There was no way to know if there was anyone else out there, because of the way Belrune stood like a pedestal on the surface of Carceron. There was nothing around it, and though there was *something* beneath and around the continent, it was too far away to make out clearly. No one came to them, and no one left. They were, to their knowledge, alone.

Shortly after Owena finished preparing her morning tea, Ellery breezed into the room. She was beaming as though nothing had upset her, her cheeks as rosy and fresh as if she'd awoken hours ago and had spent the entire time between then and now applying creams and taking restoring walks in the garden.

"Good morning, family," she said brightly, picking up a teacup and examining the three teapots Preida had brewed.

The options were Rose Breakfast, Lady Grey, and a green jasmine blend for Aden, who did not care for black teas.

"Morning, El," Briatta said, taking a bite of her bread, now satisfyingly covered in butter and jam. Ellery selected the teapot containing Rose Breakfast, filled her cup, then moved to the table and pulled out the chair beside Briatta.

"Are you excited to pick up your ceremonial attire, Bria?" Ellery glanced at her as she pulled her seat back, settling her napkin on her lap.

It was Seren, the sixth day of the week. Carceron weeks lasted six days, and for the other five days, people went about their daily lives, working to provide for each other and to support the fragile life within the biodomes. Seren was the day of rest.

Each cycle was six weeks long, and there were six Cycles of Silence alternating with the six cycles of each of the six Ardors.

No documented moment in Carceron's history identified why the Elfeans of old had chosen to mark the cycles or weeks in this manner, but it had been irrevocably ingrained in their way of life, and aligned nicely with the orbit of Carceron around the Polar Sun.

In the previous cycle—the Cycle of Air—the family tailor, Naius, had taken fresh measurements for the costume Briatta would need to go before the status of the Founders, and today was the final fitting. If Naius needed to make any last adjustments, he would have a week to do so, because after this Seren, there would only be six days left in the second Cycle of Silence. The start of the next cycle would be the Cycle of Flame, and its first day would be Briatta's birthday and her Choosing.

However, Naius had not made a mistake in all the years—each twelve cycles long—that Briatta had known him. She already knew that the clothing would be ready to go.

"I am," Briatta said, swallowing her bite. In truth, she

could hardly wait, but she did her best to contain her excitement. Briatta knew she would be heartbroken if she did not manifest any Ardor during her Choosing, so she was desperately trying to remain unaffected by twenty years of anticipation.

Every Elfean wanted to manifest Ardor and play an essential role in their society. After all, they wouldn't be able to survive on Carceron without it, and this year in particular, there had been terrifyingly few Elfeans leaving their Choosings with Ardor.

Anxiety swirled in her gut, and Briatta's foot tapped of its own accord as she drenched some oats with cream and berries. Her eyes flicked to Aden's fire rune, stark against the pale skin on his temple, and she privately prayed to the Founders that she would soon bear a similar mark.

It didn't need to be fire. It could be anything. Any of the six Ardors, and Briatta would be happy.

After what felt like hours, the rest of the Belrose family finished their breakfast, and Briatta fought the urge to leap from the table and drag her aunt and siblings out of the house. She forced herself to lean back in her chair as if she were bored and looked around the room as nonchalantly as she could manage.

"Are we leaving soon?" she asked, pretending to yawn.

"Bria, you can cut the act. You're practically vibrating with energy." Aden smirked, setting his fork across his plate and standing.

Scowling, Briatta flew to her feet, nearly knocking her chair over. "I am not."

"You are," Ellery chimed in, fighting back laughter. "I've never seen you try so hard not to rush us."

Owena smiled. "We're ready to leave. No need to antagonize your sister."

Ellery and Aden rolled their eyes, united for once, and everyone filed from the dining room and exited the house. At the front door, Aden hugged Briatta. Despite it being Seren and the day of rest, Ardorists didn't get as many opportunities for rest because they were considered essential as a first response to certain scenarios.

"I'll meet you at the Founders Hall," Aden promised, then, with a wave of his hand to the rest of the family, set off to work, pulling his headscarf on as he walked out the door. As with all young citizens of Belrune, once Aden had graduated at twenty years old from general education and gone through his Choosing at twenty-one, he was assigned a job based on his Ardor after he'd mastered it. It was all heavily regulated by King Novak's administration, and the only people who were free to choose their careers were the disgraced Ardorless, those who couldn't wield the power of their world.

Since Aden worked with the fire control team of Montclair's fire department, there were rarely days when he had time off, especially considering the dry heat within the biodome. Water Ardorists tried to generate some rain every day to mitigate the risks, but the intensity of the two suns was difficult to counteract, and it remained arid despite their best efforts.

Petyr, the Belrose family groundskeeper, was waiting on the street in front of the Belrose Estate with a traditionally white carriage—most in Belrune were kept a light color to help ward against the heat of the suns—and a pair of silvery-white horses. The animals were nearly identical, except one had grey-blue streaks in its cropped mane.

Petyr and Preida, who had been hired separately years ago by Owena, had since gone through the Elfean bonding ceremony and were partners for life. Now, they stayed in a small guest house above the stables on the Belrose property, and they were practically family.

When they'd all piled into the carriage, Petyr climbed onto the driver's bench and picked up the reins, urging the magnificent white horses forward. Parkette Street, amid the bustling market district of Montclair, was the home of Naius's tailoring shop, which he'd fondly named Mont-Clothes. It was technically close enough to Penrose Avenue, the road that the Belroses lived on, that they could have walked, but it would have taken more time than they had.

"It's going to be another hot day," Owena observed, looking out the carriage's window. Fighting the urge to roll her eyes, Briatta turned from her aunt, who sat across from her. Owena must have been highly preoccupied to make such small talk.

"It's always a hot day," Briatta replied eventually, because no one else had. Her leg bobbed restlessly, and her hand scrunched the fabric of her pants.

"I don't mind the sun," Ellery said distractedly, her hands playing with her headscarf in her lap. Everyone wore them when they were outside during bioday to protect themselves from the two suns, though the Polar Sun was the one they were most often exposed to. Only those traveling beyond the biodomes while the Nocturne Sun was in the sky would have to worry about that sun.

Briatta didn't answer, but she could practically hear Aden saying, *"Well, this has been profound."* She tried not to burst out laughing as the thought popped into her head, and she somehow reined it back into a very unladylike snort.

Owena and Ellery both frowned at Briatta.

Petyr stopped the carriage at the end of Parkette Street, which was permanently blocked on both ends for shopping Elfeans to freely wander without worrying about traffic.

Owena thanked him for driving them, and after a quick conversation about where to wait, she climbed down from the carriage and paused to allow Briatta and Ellery to follow suit. Once the door was shut and they were clear, Petyr pulled forward and out of the way.

Still trying desperately to maintain her composure, Briatta waited for Owena to start walking as she pulled her headscarf loosely over her hair. Being Seren, it was busy; there were many people out enjoying their free time, doing their weekly shopping, or meeting with friends. The hum of activity usually put Briatta into a hyper-aware state for anything that might go wrong, but today, she was anxious, and she fisted the fabric of her shirt, unable to keep her hands quiet.

Mont-Clothes came into view over the heads of the bustling crowd, finally pulling Briatta out of her misery. When Owena pushed the old wooden door open, the tiny bell above the door heralded their entrance, and Naius burst out of his back room in a flurry of fabric, pushing his crooked glasses up his nose as he beamed at them. Neither Naius nor any of his assistants were Ardorists, so their temples were all as smooth and unmarked as Briatta's.

"Ah, my most favored customers," Naius declared, setting his bundle of canary and aubergine-dyed cloth on his front desk. One of his many assistants was seated behind it and seemed conflicted about whether she should say anything or allow Naius to handle the Belroses. She apparently decided to remain quiet, because she astutely returned to her previous task, quietly removing Naius's fabric from her workspace.

"Hello, Naius," Owena greeted him warmly. The door closed behind them with a second little chime from the bell.

"Come, come," Naius said, beckoning them through the shop and into one of the fitting rooms. Already hanging on the walls was the array of white components that would coalesce into Briatta's ceremonial clothing, and excitement fluttered in her chest at the sight of them.

"I trust you know how to assemble them?" Naius asked Owena. When she nodded, he made to leave the room. "Just holler when you're ready."

Briatta first made Ellery turn away, then she removed her clothes and pulled on a tight white undershirt. She grudgingly allowed Owena to watch, but only to ensure she put the outfit on correctly. After the shirt came a pair of billowing white pants that were fitted only at the waist and ankles. Finally, Briatta slipped on the pair of solid white sandals that she would wear only to the edge of the Founders' circle.

She turned, looking in the large mirror Naius kept in all his fitting rooms, and admired herself in the white garments. A huge grin spread across her face, and she reached for the last piece.

"That's probably enough for Naius," Owena interrupted, holding a hand out to stop her. "He'll want to make sure the shirt fits before you put the robe on."

"Alright," Briatta agreed, her hand falling back to her side.

Naius reentered the fitting room with a strip of fabric hanging around his neck, which he used for measurements, and a pen tucked behind his ear.

"Ah, that's looking great," he said, his mouth splitting into a wide smile. He approached Briatta, checked the fit of the shirt and pants at her shoulders, chest, and waist, and then stepped back. "Does that feel okay?"

"Yes." Briatta nodded, her cheeks beginning to hurt from smiling. She was so glad to finally be nearing this monumental day.

"Alright, the robe then." Naius pulled the final piece from where it hung, and Briatta ducked for him to settle it over her shoulders. It wrapped around her neck and fastened on her right shoulder, leaving much of the fabric hanging in soft creases around her. Then, he pulled the hood up, and Briatta gazed at her appearance in the mirror with barely contained awe.

It wasn't that she thought she was anything special to look at; it was just that this was an outfit she'd dreamed of wearing ever since she was little.

The large hood rested loosely on her head, the extra length settling in folds just below her shoulders. Despite being ritualistic garb that she would wear for only one day in her life, Briatta imagined what it would feel like to hold her daggers and spar in these clothes. The robe, of which the longest point fell to her knees, would probably get in the way, but it would be more of a dance than a fight, anyway. At least, that was the way that Briatta envisioned it.

Naius stepped back, his arms folded as he admired his work. "I don't think I need to do anything else."

"This is perfect, Naius." Owena smiled. "As always."

"I don't want to take it off," Briatta breathed. She turned to Naius and hugged him. "It's wonderful."

"Oh." Naius laughed. "Thank you."

Briatta turned back to the mirror and admired the clothes again before finally resigning to removing them. While she'd worn a similar outfit—in a pale clay color to signify she hadn't yet had her rite—for Aden's Choosing ceremony, there was something different about having her own white robes. Something special.

Owena and Ellery left the room, likely to settle the bill, while Briatta changed and then reverently folded the clothes, placing them into the waiting bag beneath the hangers. She would treasure these for the rest of her life. Always.

They signified that her life was changing for the better. She was sure of it.

CHAPTER 3

After leaving Mont-Clothes, the three Belroses found Petyr and seated themselves in the carriage again. Briatta held her bag of white liturgical robes protectively on her lap, still giddy from the joy of seeing her reflection in them. This was the perfect start to the best week of her life. The knowledge resonated in her bones like the soaring call of a bird would echo through the biodome.

In addition to the unique clothes Briatta would wear during the actual Choosing, they still needed to pick up the plain white standard shift that all Elfeans wore to their ritual baths the morning of their ceremony and birthday. She would get this article of clothing at the Seren sermon later today at their local Founders Hall.

Typically, addresses were given every two hours on each Seren, and families could attend whichever time worked for them. Today, the Belroses were on their way to an early address after their visit to Mont-Clothes so Briatta would be free to participate in Owena's evening lessons, which were required for the Choosing. It was the head of the house's duty to guide their younglings through the week leading up to the rite, helping them in meditation so they would be able to control their Ardor if it sparked to life until they were placed into training after their Choosing.

Briatta didn't understand why society waited until so close to the Choosing before preparing their children for it, but she was forever thankful that Owena had taught them the meditative techniques required for controlling Ardor from the very first day they'd arrived in her home. Everyone was required to learn this as they approached their Choosing, but it was still impressive that Owena retained as much knowledge as she did for not having manifested.

Both Neven and Aden had said that Owena's teachings prepared them better than anything else they'd been exposed to.

Petyr pulled the horses to a halt in front of the Founders Hall, located at the end of Penrose Avenue, and Briatta instinctively looked for their house in the distance. It stood where it always had, warm grey-blue in color and charming, just down the road. Petyr would return the carriage and horse team to the property while the Belroses were in the service, and they would walk home afterward. Reluctantly, Briatta parted ways with the bag containing her white robes, tucking them safely underneath the seat and ensuring Petyr knew to set them inside the front door as soon as he got home.

"Not to worry, Miss Belrose," Petyr said with a knowing smile. After all, he'd been through the Choosing just the same as every other citizen of Belrune. He was acutely aware of the emotional turmoil Briatta was experiencing. "I'll make sure your robes get home safe and sound."

Briatta watched the carriage until it parked in front of her house, where she could barely make out his form carrying her bag inside. Exhaling slowly, she wiped her sweaty palms on the fabric of her pants and turned to follow her aunt and sister into the Founders Hall.

Each Founders Hall was built with smooth white stone inlaid with twisting, swirling golden veins that wove through the material wildly, with no pattern. The solid walls formed a large rectangular building with a white stone roof, and the same smooth white and golden slabs that formed the walls also comprised the floor within. Even the pews, the altars, and the statues matched the rest of the structure.

Beneath the light of the Polar Sun, it practically glowed. Briatta knew that the granite was supposed to look natural— as if the structure had sprouted from the ground itself—but that was because it had been crafted by talented Land Ardorists. Anything that was a composite of the soil of Carceron, they could manipulate.

Briatta entered through the main doors to a circular room with twelve equidistant alcoves carved into the wall at chest level—the same that could be found in every Founders Hall. Within each cleft stood a small statue, an imitation of the corresponding Founder who stood at the original circle of the Founders, next to the Palace. That was where Briatta would be in less than a week for her Choosing.

As was customary, Briatta genuflected before the Founders when she reached the center of the vestibule. Then, she continued through the door directly across from the entrance and joined her family inside the great room of the Founders Hall.

"There's Sister Keirna," Owena said under her breath, touching Briatta's shoulder lightly and nodding to a young woman in priestess robes standing at the back of the room greeting people as they entered. "Go and ask about your bath dress."

Briatta joined the line of people waiting to speak with

Sister Keirna, who was fairly new to this Founders Hall and still trying to learn everyone's names. The population in Montclair was not large, so services were rarely full, especially because they had such frequent services. In fact, because there were enough Founders Halls that each neighborhood was reasonably localized, it allowed for much more personal relationships to develop between the priests, priestesses, and their congregations.

Owena and Ellery made their way to a pew near the back where both the exit and the front of the room were in view. Briatta smiled as she watched the austere woman who was her aunt sit neatly on her bench and carefully examine the room around her, thinking to herself that Owena would never truly be a regular citizen. The habits developed by her work with the Night Roses were too deeply ingrained, so much so that she kept watch even at the Founders Hall.

The line to meet Sister Keirna moved quickly, and Briatta bowed shallowly in greeting when it was her turn.

"Sister Keirna," she said, pitching her voice low so it would not echo in the resonant hall.

"Briatta Belrose, isn't it?" Sister Keirna said softly, her gentle smile setting her face aglow as she rose from her own bow.

"Yes," Briatta nodded. "I'm supposed to ask you about the bath dress I will need for my Choosing."

Sister Keirna brightened. "Ah yes, that's coming up. I saw one set aside for you in the back. I'll have it ready for you at the end of the service."

"Thank you." Briatta bowed once more before she parted ways with the young Sister. Within the Founders Halls, when greeting the king and other nobility, or at events where higher courtesies were recognized, it was common for the people of Belrune to greet each other with bows. Within these walls especially, everyone was worthy enough to be welcomed with honor.

Aden slipped in and followed Briatta as they joined their family at the bench, whereupon the sermon continued as was expected. The priests and priestesses wore white, floor-length robes cinched by golden belts with decorative tassels, and their shoulders were covered by a white shawl trimmed with more gold fabric. Each wore a golden necklace that hung to their abdomens, the intricate chain ending in a small golden figure. While she could not see them up close, Briatta knew they'd all taken a Founder as their patron upon swearing their final oaths, and they wore pendants of their patrons around their necks to guide them through life.

Some priests and priestesses had Ardor-marks on their temples, but not all did. If one wished to follow the vocation to become a cleric, it was the one occupation for Ardorists that the crown could not dictate.

Each service began with the head minister calling the people to prayer, and then they would read from the *Book of the Binding*, depicting the world-altering acts that the Founders had taken to save everyone. If not for them, Carceron would have died many years ago, and Briatta would never have come to exist. Now, the Founders were the only place where an Elfean could manifest Ardor, presumably because the concentration of Ardor and their connection to Carceron was so strong that it had fundamentally altered the way their world worked. Before they had existed, there was very limited information on how one could become an Ardorist; obviously, it was possible, because the Founders themselves were Ardorists.

Near the conclusion of the service, each person in attendance was called to the front, where they bowed to a larger statue—each standing in front of six unique altars to each known Ardor—of the Founder whom they required aid from that day. In this Founders Hall, there was nothing within the main body of the church to acknowledge the silent Founders. After that, the sermon was called to a close with a few songs composed in honor of the twelve holy Ardorists who had saved their souls.

For each of the next six days until her Choosing, Briatta would attend a Founders Hall and pray to one of the six named Founders. The other six were clouded in mystery, as no history had named them or their Ardor, and no tribute or prayer was given to them leading up to the Choosing. They were represented by the Cycles of Silence.

Briatta knelt before the Founder of Light, as her cycle came first in a Carceron year—followed by the six Cycles of Silence and the cycles of the other five Ardors in alternating order—and she would brighten the way for Briatta through this critical time in life. Since Briatta's six days hadn't officially begun, Briatta would come before the Founder of Light again the following day, but she figured that an extra appeal could only do her good.

When the service finally finished, Briatta led the way back to the rear of the hall and waited for Sister Keirna to return with her ritual bath dress. Sister Keirna appeared from the door on the side of the hall just as the last person filed out of the room, leaving only the Belrose family waiting there.

"Here you are," Sister Keirna said, holding a wrapped package for Briatta. "The instructions for care after the bath are inside. We'll see you tomorrow, then?"

"You will." Briatta smiled. Sister Keirna would be well versed in the rituals that took place prior to the Choosing.

Clutching her new parcel close, Briatta followed Owena out of the Founders Hall and blinked as they stepped into the bright sunlight. It was nearly midday as they walked home, where Preida would have food set out for them.

"Is it starting to feel real?" Aden asked as they walked, his grin cheeky.

"Hardly." Briatta laughed. Fluttering nerves seemed to have taken permanent residence in her chest, and every breath she'd taken since having woken was shaky. "I don't think I'll believe it's happening until I'm there."

"You'll be fine." Aden's smile softened to a more reassuring one, and he squeezed his sister's shoulder.

"I'm hungry," Ellery complained, her hand settling over her stomach as it rumbled loudly.

Owena raised an eyebrow and looked back at the little flock over her shoulder. "You can see our house from here."

"I know," Ellery moaned.

The Belrose house loomed large, that transient blue-grey color shimmering under the Polar Sun. A painted home such as theirs—which largely wasn't the color white—symbolized status because the residents could afford to keep it cool without lightening the exterior to reflect heat. While the shade of the house wasn't necessarily dark, it was something in-between.

With the year-round greenery that blossomed, thanks to Petyr, the house was a beautiful sight to behold. In honor of their namesake, Petyr had grown white rose bushes to vine over the house's walls, and the surrounding air was always heavy with the floral scent that emanated from them.

Preida had set out platters of finger sandwiches and sparkling juices along with freshly cut fruit from the property's greenhouse that Petyr also maintained. It was a simple lunch, yet everything was bursting with flavor and filling, leaving Briatta satisfied and refreshed.

After lunch, their aunt wanted to ensure the Belrose children could fit a sparring session into their day before Beginning Briatta's Choosing lesson.

She sent them downstairs into the basement, which had been transformed into a training space long before Briatta and her siblings had moved in. The walls of the entire bottom floor were bare of paint; instead, it was lined with weapon racks, shields, and relics of the Belrose family history. On the ground was one big mat.

Owena matched Briatta against Ellery, and the sisters each chose types of swords that they did not typically use. They circled each other slowly, but Ellery advanced first, which was precisely why Briatta consistently managed to beat her still. While her younger sister was talented and catching up to Briatta and Aden rapidly, she was still brash and overly bold with her decisions.

The fight quickly ended with Ellery on her stomach and Briatta's blade tapping the back of her neck.

"Kill strike," Briatta said, backing away.

Ellery grunted with frustration and pushed herself onto her knees. "I don't get it; what am I doing wrong?"

While Owena stepped in to review the session for Ellery, Briatta joined Aden, who was going through a series of exercises on his own with a longsword. This had been their lives from the day they had moved in with Owena after their father had sent them away. Owena had pulled them inside, fed them dinner, put them to bed, and the following day, she'd woken them all up before the bioday had begun and had them running sequences within a cycle.

Briatta would forever be grateful, because she couldn't imagine how her life would have turned out otherwise. If she and her siblings had remained in Srila—Belrune's capital, east of Montclair and of the Nalaran Mountains—with their father after their mother had been sent away, where would they be now? Likely still poor and living in a cramped apartment.

Briatta couldn't remember it very well, but Aden did, and he'd described it for her and Ellery many times over the years.

The situation had not been good. Briatta often wondered what had happened for their mother, Owena's sister, to have ended up in such poor health that she was institutionalized while Owena had done so well on her own in Montclair, as she'd been too young to remember. Why hadn't their father done more, she wondered? Once, she'd asked Owena about it, but the woman had remained tight-lipped where her sister Lila and her husband were concerned. She'd simply shaken her head sadly and changed the subject.

After hours of training, Owena finally declared they'd done enough for the day and that Briatta and Ellery would take it up again the next morning. The exercise helped clear Briatta's mind, and her breaths were coming easier. Founders, it was going to be a long week.

In the few hours left before dinner, Owena took Briatta into her office and closed the door. She sat behind her desk and settled in, steepling her hands as she looked across the polished wood. Briatta squirmed under the scrutiny and felt as though her aunt were examining her as if she'd never seen her before.

Owena's office had always been one of Briatta's favorite rooms in the house, second only to the magnificent library. The office was lined with shelves that spanned the entirety of the walls, all the way to the ceiling, and they were crammed with books and artifacts that Owena and other Belrose women before her had collected over the years. There were old metal figurines, tattered covers, and pens so worn it was easy to see where they had most often been held. There were also brand-new books and maps and tiny glass sculptures of the Founders arranged carefully in front of the books and on the desk.

The entire room smelled like knowledge, and Briatta loved it.

"I've already taught you much of what you'll need to know for the Choosing," Owena said finally. "What do you think I mean by that?"

Briatta considered the question, filing through the many years of constant work that Owena had put her through. There was the hand-to-hand combat, the weapons training, the meditation to center and ground herself when she was fighting and needed to separate emotion from her work, and so much more.

There were also the many tools that an accomplished Ardorist might use. She'd heard Aden complain about becoming more tired the more Ardor he used, and how much harder it was to focus when he reached that state of fatigue. And Neven, whose Choosing had been a few cycles ago, said that when his Ardor had awakened, it had felt like breathing when he'd never taken a breath. It was as though an integral part of him had been sleeping for all these years, and now he could not envision life without it.

Briatta imagined that the only way she would completely understand what she needed for using her Ardor would be for her to walk away from the ceremony with Ardor.

But...beyond that, internal discipline seemed necessary for an Ardorist.

"Mindfulness," Briatta finally answered. Owena quirked an eyebrow, nodding slowly.

"Exactly," she said. "When your Ardor awakens, you will need to separate it from emotion and use the concentration you've built over the years to control it."

Briatta noted that Owena said 'when' her Ardor awoke rather than 'if,' but she didn't point it out. Briatta's mother hadn't been an Ardorist, and neither was Owena, so when

Aden manifested Ardor, her aunt believed it was thanks to their father's genetic contribution.

"These lessons are meant to practice your self-reflection and prepare you for that moment," Owena continued. "But since you are already so well accomplished in that area, I am not concerned with wasting our time here. Is there anything else you'd like to talk about?"

Briatta tilted her head, her eyes drifting around the room and landing on the books.

"Do you have any advice for me?" she asked at last, the uncomfortable sensation of pressure returning to her chest.

Owena smiled, this time with sadness. "I wish that I did. But...my life is one that hopefully you will never know."

Her aunt didn't have to say that she meant a life without Ardor. A life of living between the lower and higher societies of Belrune. It was in the tone of her voice, the regret clear in the way her shoulders sagged, and her eyes clouded with some memory that Briatta would never be privy to.

Ardorists were the backbone of the kingdom of Belrune, the key to a comfortable existence. An Elfean without Ardor was barely more than a burden in the eyes of high society, and there were more and more Ardorless with every passing year.

Owena was one of few Ardorless women who maintained her position in high society, and it was only due to the whispered rumors of her connection to King Novak. Most of the time, a person who completed their Choosing without Ardor was gradually invited to fewer functions, even if they'd been raised in high society among other Ardorists. They were let go by their friends, sometimes even their family, and eventually forgotten altogether. The Ardorless were forced to work jobs that no one else wanted, and Briatta knew from her observations that despite working harder than anyone else, they were still punished for the one thing they couldn't control.

It hadn't always been this way, where Ardorists hated the Ardorless and believed themselves superior, but the growing strain of maintaining the biodomes and a livable environment was quickly worsening the division between the communities.

Briatta, Aden, and Ellery had been raised in the same liminal space that Owena existed in; they were not quite fully integrated into high society, comprised of Ardorists, but they were not quite associated with the low society Ardorless, either. While Owena had done her best to give her nieces and nephew everything she could, she had always refused their requests to attend more high society events than were required to show their face each year. Instead, she'd taken them to the poorest district in Montclair, D'ivory, and told them they couldn't return home until they'd each helped three people.

Then, Briatta had dragged her feet and wished she'd been dressed up and dancing with her friends from school. Now, she was thankful that Owena hadn't allowed her to become too comfortable with her life, especially as two entirely different paths stretched out before her, each just as possible as the other—though one was far more terrifying.

On one road, Briatta would leave her Choosing with Ardor. She would become a full-fledged member of high society and play an important role in the livelihood of her people. On the other road...Briatta would join low society, and her value as a contributor to their life on Carceron would plummet. She would slowly be pushed away by the friends she'd made in school, in which she'd only been able to enroll because she was related to Owena, and she would have no one.

No one but her family and the Night Roses.

Briatta told herself it would be enough. But as she stood, hugging her aunt goodnight, leaving the office and heading to her room, she had difficulty believing it.

She cast one last look at Owena, who was disappearing

into her own room. Briatta sometimes wondered if Owena had become such a skilled vigilante to compensate for the lack of power within. Her aunt had always maintained that power was subjective, and most people only chose to see it manifested as Ardor, firmly believing one would be a fool to disregard the unassuming.

Briatta just hoped she would be more. That people wouldn't even consider her unassuming in the first place.

CHAPTER 4

"Can we go to the market today, Owena?" Ellery asked the following morning after training, flopping into a seat at the dining table and quickly twisting her brown hair into a long braid down her back.

Each week, on the day after Seren, a market popped up in the middle of Montclair near Parkette Street. Because Ardorists needed to work every day of the week anyway, and most others had to work twice as hard to contribute to their survival as a whole, there wasn't a perfect day for a market, not even Seren. The market taking place the day after was the result of a long-standing tradition established by King Novak in Srila, and the one in Montclair was always bustling with activity, good food, and was one of Ellery and Briatta's favorite places to visit. Since school had ended along with the conclusion of the Cycle of Air two cycles ago and wouldn't continue until the Cycle of Water—which would come two cycles later, after the next Cycle of Silence—Ellery had more free time than usual.

"Sure," Owena said, smiling. They didn't have anywhere to be until Briatta's afternoon Founders Hall session, followed by pretending that she was having a lesson with Owena, so it was a good way to fill the day. Aden was not home anymore, as he'd returned to stay in his apartment near the firehouse until the day they would leave for the Founders.

They decided to go by foot for the long walk to the main square by Parkette Street, but before they left, Owena arranged for Petyr to pick them up later.

As they neared the market, Briatta walked past open storefronts with colorful clothes, plants growing in handmade and hand-painted pots, food stalls with sugary pastries behind glass displays, and people bargaining at every single one.

Vibrantly hued tents surrounded the perimeter of the town square. Each vendor hawking out their wares and inviting people to come and look. Briatta had seen this market set up hundreds of times, but her heart always swelled at the exuberant display of color and vitality. It was a bright sign of life amidst the deluge of end-of-the-world propaganda being spread by Kalaiden, the activist group.

"This is amazing." Ellery sighed happily. "I say it every time, but somehow it always gets better."

Briatta smiled and paused to examine a display of small wooden carvings, the most popular items seeming to be the Founders. She picked up a man who wore a long sword, the top half of his hair pulled back and braided down his back. This was one of the Silent Founders, and she examined him closely, wondering not for the first time what secrets he held that caused him to all but disappear into history.

Owena stopped to purchase a frozen fruit bar a few stalls ahead, so Briatta quickly abandoned the figurine and hurried to catch up, dodging shoppers as they moved sporadically between stands.

Ellery was immediately drawn to a display of jewelry,

exclaiming over the craftsmanship and holding up a little silver chain with a dangling blue gemstone.

Briatta followed aimlessly, stopping at the stall next to the jewelers, where tightly woven headscarves were laid out, and reached up to fiddle with the fabric of her own. She picked up one that was so light and soft that the lovely lilac material practically slipped through her fingers.

"How much for this?" she asked the seller, who glanced up from where she was weaving something new at her loom. The taut strings barely had any yarn as the project was still in the early stages, and Briatta couldn't tell anything about it other than the fact that it was azure.

"Thirty coppers," the weaver said, immediately returning to her task, fingers deftly working the shuttle stick through the tight threads.

Briatta considered the cost and decided it was completely reasonable for something handmade. She handed over the coins and joined Ellery and Owena, wrapping the scarf around her shoulders.

"Oh, that's nice," Owena commented, feeling the fabric. Briatta held up one end of the headscarf and grinned.

"It's my favorite color, too," she said happily, joining Ellery.

Briatta perused the jewelry, though she wasn't likely to purchase anything here. She alternated between her few simple gold necklaces, and it was rare to find anything that she liked enough to add to the rotation.

Ellery still held the first silver chain she'd picked and was debating with Owena about how she could pay her aunt back for it.

"I'll help Preida in the kitchen with dishes for a week," she swore, looking pleadingly up at Owena.

"Is that all my time and money are worth?" Owena asked with a wry smile.

Ellery started to argue, but Briatta was ready to move on. She pivoted, ready to offer the necklace as an early birthday gift to her younger sister when something caught her eye. She paused. Glimmering at the edge of her vision was a necklace that she swore hadn't been there the first time she had looked over the array.

Briatta turned back to the display and examined it carefully. It was a fine gold chain with a tiny timepiece, the little hands ticking around the face depicting a Polar Sun painted at the top and a Nocturne Sun at the bottom, though the Nocturne Sun was white rather than red as she'd been taught in school, which Briatta found odd.

Slowly, Briatta reached for the necklace and picked it up with her right hand, letting the chain slide through her left until the timepiece settled in her palm. It did not look like a new necklace; there was something aged about it, though it was in pristine condition.

"Where did you find that?" Ellery asked, interrupting Briatta's thoughts.

"Um, it was right here." Briatta pointed to the spot on the table where the necklace had lain.

"Really? I didn't see it." Ellery looked wistfully at the gold necklace.

"Let me see that," Owena said, taking it. Briatta felt a strange sort of loss as the timepiece left her grip, but she shook herself at the odd sensation.

"Beautiful," Owena commented, turning the little timepiece in her fingers. "It reminds me of a necklace I have at home. I'll have to find it when we return."

Briatta turned back to the jeweler, who watched the entire interaction with a puzzled expression. "What would you want for this?"

Taking the necklace from Briatta, the elderly gentleman

rolled the chain in his hands. "This is not one of my necklaces," he determined slowly. Then, after a long moment of silence, he added, "You may have it...it would not be right to ask you to pay."

Briatta accepted the necklace from the man and turned, wordlessly asking Owena to clasp it around her neck. It felt right somehow, as it settled on her chest, and she found herself reaching to play with the pendant as she followed her aunt and sister around the remainder of the market. Owena picked out a paring knife for Aden from a woman selling an assortment of kitchen tools—he was learning to cook now that he lived on his own—and then selected some spiced teas.

On the way to find Petyr, they passed a stall selling steamed pork buns, and at the scent of spiced meat, Briatta's mouth watered. As Petyr would be dropping her off at the Founders Hall to visit the Founder of Light without the chance to eat until afterward, Briatta decided to stop and buy a couple. Owena and Ellery each stole bites, much to Briatta's chagrin, but she allowed it on the condition they made sure food would be ready for her when she returned home. Full and each possessing something new, they made their way back to the street where Petyr would meet them.

A breeze generated by Air Ardorists picked up, so it would be good to be inside if a storm had been scheduled to blow through Montclair. Briatta tried to remember the weather schedule, but she'd been so distracted by everything else going on that she hadn't committed it to memory this week.

Above, flags of different, bright colors hung from a rope strung between gutters, fluttering cheerfully in the warm afternoon light of the Polar Sun. Music reached their ears as the designated meeting place came into view.

"Oh, is there a minstrel?" Ellery asked, her face lighting up. On the street corner where Briatta could see the Belrose carriage waiting, a young man was playing a lute and singing, the instrument's case open on the ground in front of him. Briatta frowned, wondering why he was playing here rather than in the market where there were more people.

As they neared, the playful tune grew louder. Ellery ran ahead, shoving her hand into her pockets and fishing out a coin to throw into the lute case before turning to Petyr.

"She *did* have money," Owena muttered as she hurried to catch up. Petyr climbed down from the driver's bench to open the door to the cart, where Ellery and her aunt disappeared inside together.

As Briatta drew closer, she also threw a coin for the musician before climbing into the carriage. But something made the hair on the back of her neck stand, and all her senses were suddenly alert. She hesitated at the door, one foot on the first step, looking over her shoulder and scanning the rooftops nearby to search for anything out of the ordinary. She didn't see anything immediately out of place, but she couldn't shake the feeling that there had been eyes on her. Eyes that were watching from somewhere they shouldn't have been.

"Bria?" Ellery asked, leaning forward in her seat. "What is it?"

Still searching, Briatta couldn't find anything.

She was tense from the impending Choosing ceremony. That was all.

"Nothing." Briatta shook herself and stepped in to join Owena and Ellery, settling into her seat with her new headscarf and necklace. "I'm just nervous, I think."

Owena gave her a sympathetic look, one corner of her lips pulling back as her brows furrowed. "I'll ask Preida if she'll make some chocolate cookies tonight."

Briatta smiled, appreciating the thoughtfulness of her

aunt. While Owena wasn't her biological mother, she was definitely a parental figure to them. "That would be wonderful."

THE FOUNDERS HALL had far fewer attendees, but Briatta stayed near the back anyway. She'd left her new headscarf with Ellery, asking her sister to leave it in her room, but the necklace remained around her neck. She fingered it absently throughout the sermon, and when she knelt to the Founder of Light, she held the timepiece tightly in her hand as she prayed to her.

That night, her lesson with Owena was the same as the previous one. However, they would be asked to confirm that they'd fulfilled this requirement on the day of Briatta's Choosing, and in order to be truthful, they had to at least meet every night.

The week continued in a similar fashion. Each day, Briatta rose and trained, then she attended the Founders Hall to kneel to each subsequent Founder. On the third day, it was the Founder of Flame, then on the fourth day, she prayed to the Founder of Water, and so on with the Founders of Flower and Land.

On the last day, when she left the Founders Hall after beseeching the Founder of Land to hold her steadfast in her decisions so long as they were the right ones, Briatta felt nerves like frenzied flutterflies—small glowing pink bugs with big white wings—in her belly. She swallowed thickly multiple times throughout the walk home, uncertain that she'd be able to go the rest of the day without either vomiting or fainting.

It was customary to stay in the Palace of the Founders the night before one's Choosing ceremony, and she could hardly believe that this day was here. That this was real.

She was so wrapped up in her thoughts that it took a long

moment for Briatta to realize she had stopped moving. Her fists were balled tightly in the fabric of her tunic, and her chest felt so tight she was hardly able to take a breath. Pressure was building in her heart, the nausea roiling in her belly, and she fought to suck in breath. Thankfully, she wasn't crying, but she could feel the tears burning behind her eyes.

Briatta stood there, gasping quietly. Outwardly, she tried to remain calm in case anyone passed her.

She'd only panicked once before—when she was very little —so she couldn't remember how she had pulled herself out of it. She was losing control of herself, her grip on her emotions slipping with every consecutive failure to take a full breath. Briatta desperately tried to think, to pull from her mind a way to stop this.

"Bria."

It was Neven. He'd appeared out of nowhere, as he normally did, and was by her side in an instant. The tattoo on his brow, the rune representing light in the ancient Elfean dialect, was still stark and fresh against his pale skin.

"Bria, what is it?" He grabbed her shoulders, standing in front of her and searching her eyes. She stared back, unable to speak, unable to breathe.

Understanding registered in Neven's gaze, and he pulled Briatta close, folding her head into his chest and taking deep breaths, lightly dragging his fingers through her hair and pressing his other hand to her back. She was stiff against him.

"Breathe," he commanded, his warm breath brushing the top of her head. He rested his chin there as he held her.

Briatta closed her eyes, safe in Neven's arms, and tried to obey. After what seemed like ages, she felt the panic slowly ebb away. At last, she took a deep breath along with Neven. Then another. With every full inhalation, her heart rate slowed, the tension in her shoulders fading. She wasn't entirely relaxed, but her body molded against Neven a little easier than it had before.

She breathed. In and out. In and out.

And then, when her mind was clear enough, she became acutely aware of how Neven was cradling her. While they had grown up as best friends and had always been attached at the hip, this was a line that they'd never crossed. The way his hand still trailed idly on her back was far more intimate than anything she'd allowed before.

An uncomfortable feeling replaced the anxiety in her stomach, and she pushed away from Neven, sniffling and patting her cheeks.

"I'm sorry," she said. "I...don't know what came over me."

Neven watched her carefully. "It's alright."

"It's just the Choosing. It's a stupid thing to panic over." Briatta was rambling, but she couldn't seem to make the words stop. "It'll be fine if I don't have Ardor. Other people have it so much worse."

She shoved her hands into her pockets and pointedly looked anywhere but at Neven's face.

"Bria, stop. You'll be alright."

"You don't know that," she said, her gaze stubbornly locked on a bush of iridescent mauve flowers.

"I do," Neven said firmly. "You are the most resilient person I know."

That wasn't really true. It couldn't be true. If anything, that honor should have gone to Neven. Finally, Briatta met his eyes.

"Well, now you're just making bad jokes," she said, and a small tearful laugh escaped her.

Neven shook his head but smiled and jerked his head toward the beautiful blue-grey house just down the street. "Let's get you home."

They walked slowly, Briatta watching the ground under

her feet as they moved. Neven was a quiet force beside her. She'd always felt safer with him, and while she still did, something had changed in their dynamic. His presence grounded her more than she'd ever realized. She swallowed thickly as she remembered how he'd held her while she'd centered herself, a shiver running down her spine.

They'd come so far from the scrappy young kids they'd once been, each orphaned in their own way.

Shortly after Briatta had turned nine, she'd been training in the headquarters of the Night Roses when Owena walked onto the training mat holding the hand of a dirty, skinny little boy.

"Briatta, honey, this is Neven. He's come to train with you," Owena had explained, sitting on her heels so she would be at eye level with the two children.

"Hi Neven," Briatta had said, pointing at his bare feet. "Where are your shoes?"

Neven had scowled, sending a reproachful look toward Owena, who in turn raised her eyebrows in silent consternation at Briatta. Shamelessly, the little girl had simply waited expectantly for a response.

Still frowning darkly, Neven had pulled his hand from Owena's and balled both into little fists. "Ain't got any."

Briatta had then kicked her shoes off, too—the little black ones she had only ever been allowed to wear on the sparring mats to keep them clean—and thrown them across the room. "Want to be my friend?"

Neven's blue eyes had widened, startlingly bright behind the dirt on his skin, and he had released his clenched hands. "Yeah."

From that moment on, Briatta and Neven were inseparable. He had integrated seamlessly into the lives of the Belrose family, frequently joining them at their house for meals, and he'd grown close with Ellery and Aden, too. In fact, when it had come time for Neven's Choosing, Aden was the one whom Neven had asked to stand in as his mentor and tether, with Owena's guidance.

Briatta had been confused and sad at first that Neven hadn't wanted her to be a part of the biggest moment in his life, but Owena had assured her that it had meant nothing against her. The Choosing was a deeply private, familial tradition for Elfeans. Neven had no family; they had abandoned him as a young boy outside of a Founders Hall, and he'd been taken in by the resident priest until the elderly man had died when Neven was eight. None of the others employed there had been able to take him in, and so Owena had found him a year later, huddled in an alley picking bits from a moldy loaf of bread.

While Briatta was his friend, Aden was the closest thing to a brother that Neven had ever had. Once that had become clear, Briatta had instantly felt guilty for ever having misunderstood Neven's intentions on with whom he made this step in life. She had gone out and sent a note to the location of the Founders, insisting that her brother send a message ahead on whether Neven had manifested Ardor.

When the missive had arrived the next day, stating Light Ardor had awoken within Neven, Briatta had planned a celebration to rival one of Owena's parties, surprising Neven with it when he and Aden returned from their stay at the Founders. She had hung dozens of clear crystals throughout the house so Neven could make the whole place sparkle with his new power.

Aden had complained for months afterward that nobody had thrown him a party when he'd received his Ardor, but he always spoke lightly and knew why Briatta had done it. Knew that Neven had needed that kind of support from someone who cared about him.

Briatta came back to the present when they stopped, standing in nearly tangible silence in front of the Belrose house.

Neven cleared his throat. "I came to wish you luck. I know you are probably about to leave, and..." He trailed off, seeming uncertain. "Well, you supported me more than anyone else in my life during my Choosing. So if there's anything you need, anything at all, let me know."

Briatta's throat constricted again as she gazed up at her friend. "Thank you," she managed to say, albeit thickly. "I will."

Neven seemed as though he wanted to hug her goodbye, but after what had occurred down the street, he only bid her farewell with a nod and turned back. Briatta watched him go, feelings of confusion and uncertainty swirling in her heart that she'd never before experienced around him.

CHAPTER 5

I t was late afternoon, and Briatta and the rest of her family were beyond the biodome of Montclair after passing through the biogate, traveling the gap of the deadlands between the city and the Founders thanks to the tightly sealed Belrose carriage filled with specially crossbred air-filtering plants. It wasn't far, so they would arrive at the Palace of the Founders in time for dinner.

Between the airtight carriage and the flora placed within it —developed by Flower Ardorists to clean air faster than any other in existence—travel was possible in the thin air beyond the biodomes. Of course, this was only feasible when Air Ardorists had confirmed desert storms wouldn't be happening in the near future that would consequently ban travel due to the dangers of the violent, whipping sand.

Sitting up front with Petyr was a designated Weiler escort, an Air Ardorist, so they could drive the horses across the dead-lands safely. Travel between cities was strictly monitored and regulated, but there was frequent need to go between Mont-clair and the Founders, so several Weilers were permanently stationed in Montclair to assist with the crossings as well as assist with city ordinance and protecting Lord Mallon and his family, the royal household designated to rule over Montclair in King Novak's stead.

When Petyr turned the horses, it revealed the smaller biodome where the Founders stood; it was so close that Briatta could see both the palace and the Founders themselves. The twelve massive stone statues stood in a perfect circle at the center of the biodome they dwelled beneath. While the carriage wasn't yet close enough for Briatta to see the details, every child of Belrune had grown up studying and worshiping the Founders, so she knew exactly what they would look like.

There had been an event, some sort of calamity that was not clear in the history books or the *Book of the Binding*. Some records told of a burning of the land that Ardor had been powerless to stop; it destroyed everything and everyone in its path. Others described a plague that had a one-hundred percent mortality rate across species as it swept across the lands and nearly ended all life on Carceron.

Regardless of the terrible incident depicted, the ending was always the same: The Founders were twelve of the most powerful Elfeans of the time, and they came together to place a binding spell on the world, shielding the survivors by halting the spread of the disaster. It had been thousands of years since, and these statues were now the only known location on Carceron where Ardor could manifest.

When they had attended a Foundling course—a class that would prepare them to attend sermons as adults—as young children, dropped off on Seren while Owena attended the main Founders Hall service, Aden had once raised his hand to ask what would happen if the Founders were to wake. The answer still haunted Briatta to this day: If the Founders woke from their eternal sleep as statues, the binding they'd placed on

Carceron would likely shatter, and the safety that they had enjoyed would disappear forever.

Carceron would then be destroyed, for the Founders had given their lives so that others might live, and one would not exist without the other.

The Founders formed a dodecagon, six ancient, powerful men and women alternating, equidistant from each other. Their original names had long been lost, so they were now referred to as the Founder of the type of Ardor they awoke within people.

There were only six active Founders—the Founders of Light, Fire, Air, Water, Flower, and Land—and it had been this way for as long as the known history of Carceron, despite the extensive research of many dedicated scholars to try and determine the purpose of the six Founders still shrouded in mystery.

Briatta couldn't imagine what the other Founders might awaken should they become active, because she knew of no other Ardor elements.

Petyr pulled the horses to a halt at the gilded arched biogate in the biodome ahead where guards waited for the arrivals of the Choosing. The Weiler on the left accepted the crossing papers from Petyr, talking to the groundskeeper more than Briatta thought necessary. Anxiously, she awaited permission for their carriage to pass, unable to hear the discussion as she tapped her fingers on her knees. Finally, the Weiler returned the stack of papers to Petyr and nodded his approval. The horse pulled their cart into the biodome of the Founders, and the flutterflies sprang into action once more in Briatta's stomach.

Owena took Briatta's hand, squeezing it gently. "Nothing to fear, Bria."

Briatta glanced at her aunt but couldn't do anything more than squeeze the woman's hand in return.

Petyr stopped the cart in front of the Palace of the Founders, which was a magnificent stone building that stretched into the sky. It had soaring buttresses and towers like the castle that King Novak lived in, of which Briatta had only seen paintings, but the palace was crafted of stone as close to appearance as possible as that of the statues of the Founders.

Aden opened the carriage door and looked at Briatta. They would allow her to exit before them, to be the first to set foot on the lush green ground below. This was her Choosing, her coming of age. What happened the next day would determine whether society would see Briatta as worthy. Swallowing hard, Briatta stepped down from the cart, breathing in the fresh biodome air and clutching her bag to hide her shaking hands.

The rest of her family followed, and Petyr took the horses to the stable.

"Welcome to the Palace of the Founders!" called a bright-faced young priestess clad in white robes with the typical gold brocade around her shoulders and belt as other Founders Hall ministers. She opened the door to the building, smiling broadly and waving Briatta and her family inside. "I'm Sister Mirana. Who are we celebrating during your stay?"

Owena placed a hand on Briatta's shoulder. "My niece, Briatta Belrose."

"Wonderful," the priestess declared, moving behind the stone front desk and running her slender finger, covered in gold rings, down the page. "Ah, here you are. You will all be staying for one night. Does that sound correct?"

"Yes, that's right," Owena replied, stepping forward to discuss payment and the details of their stay with the young woman. Briatta turned and admired the beautiful, massive lobby. Aside from Sister Mirana, the only other person in the room was a man sitting by the large fireplace reading a paper.

Briatta's gaze lingered on his back for a moment in curiosity before moving on.

Barely hearing a word, Briatta watched as her aunt handed over an obscene amount of silver coins along with one gold coin. Then, the white-robed woman handed two keys to Owena and Aden.

"...don't hesitate to ask if you need anything at all during your stay. Please have a wonderful, blessed time. It is an honor to meet you all." Sister Mirana bowed, clasping her hands in front of her, her short brown hair swinging forward with the movement. Briatta dug her nails into her palms, shaking herself slightly at the realization she'd been so consumed by her own thoughts, she hadn't heard the first half of what Sister Mirana had said. Briatta had been taught to be more aware than this.

"Thank you, the honor is mine," Owena said in answer, and Briatta and her siblings echoed dutifully, each inclining their heads. This was a very formal greeting that wasn't commonly used, but everyone knew of it in case it was needed. Before they left, Owena added that Petyr would be coming in from the stables shortly and was under their reservation as well. Mirana nodded enthusiastically and assured Owena he would be well taken care of.

Briatta, Ellery, and Aden collected their bags and followed Owena through the winding halls and staircases of the Palace of the Founders. It had been built not only in the likeness of a castle but in the size of one as well. This was done both to honor the Founders and provide enough space to house the number of young people who underwent the Choosing.

There were tapestries and paintings depicting scenes from the *Book of the Binding* along the walls they passed, miniature figures of the Founders standing guard at each turn, and Ardor lights lining the walls and ceilings. The building of this place had taken years, and Briatta knew the amount of Ardor and the skill wielded by the builders was nothing like the small kernels of potential that people today could brandish.

"This place is incredible," Ellery said, her voice filled with awe.

"It is a reminder of what the Founders can offer us and of how far we have fallen," replied Owena.

Aden glanced back at Briatta, his brows furrowing. Owena never hinted whether her lack of Ardor bothered her, but perhaps when surrounded by evidence of this one major loss, it might have disturbed her peace regarding the subject.

"What makes you say that?" Aden asked carefully.

"No one today could do this." Owena waved at the building and the finely carved details of the bricks, each textured lovingly by someone's hand.

"Maybe those activists have a point," Briatta muttered. Owena gave her a look of barely concealed surprise at her niece's mention of Kalaiden.

"Bria, you know there is no truth to their campaigns," Owena admonished. Though in truth, there wasn't a lot of accurate information on the Elfeans who comprised Kalaiden because they had done a shockingly good job of maintaining anonymity and leading successful raids when it was least expected.

Briatta, who had spoken only because she knew exactly how to shift her aunt's train of thought, smirked at Aden. Her brother's lips twitched, but to her annoyance, he agreed with Owena.

"How could you ever think well of the violence they stand for?"

"Oh, shut up," Briatta said, rolling her eyes at Aden. "I could be violent to you right now."

They reached their rooms at the end of a long hallway on

the third floor. A large window, facing west, overlooked the grounds where a wild, sprawling garden grew beside the stone walls of the castle. Beyond it stood the Founders.

Owena unlocked the room she would share with Briatta and Ellery, calling for them to freshen up before the evening meal. Reluctantly, Briatta tore herself from the window, though she found herself captivated by everything here, including the room.

The large room had three beds, each with a pale-blue canopy for privacy. A large sage-green woven rug covered most of the stone floor, thick and soft to the touch. Briatta set her bags on one of the beds, running her hands over the cool white fabric. It was so smooth against her skin, she almost didn't believe she'd actually felt it. She jumped onto the bed and sank into the comforter and mattress.

"Look at this, Bria!" Ellery exclaimed, and Briatta lifted her head to see where her sister was.

Ellery was in the bathroom, gesturing excitedly for Briatta to join her. Heaving herself from the feather-soft bed, Briatta joined Ellery in the doorway to the bathroom and gaped. There was a huge tub built into the floor of the bathroom, its lip sitting just a few inches above the same stone floor that continued seamlessly from the bedroom. There was also a sink, fluffy white towels, and expensive-looking toiletries on the counter.

"This is so lovely." Briatta sighed contentedly, her nerves regarding the Choosing temporarily forgotten.

"It is, isn't it?" Owena said, smiling softly. "I think it gets better every time I come back."

"How many times have you been here?" Ellery asked.

Owena considered for a moment. "This is my fifth time."

"Five times?" Briatta questioned, racking her brain. Briatta mentally sorted through the people she knew Owena would have traveled with. There was her mother—who was Owena's sister—Owena's own Choosing, and Aden. Briatta herself was the last and final person she could think of.

"Yes." Owena sat down on the edge of her bed.

"Who was the fifth?" Ellery leaned against the bathroom doorframe, seemingly having drawn the same conclusion as Briatta.

Something like grief passed over Owena's face. "A friend. Now, wash up before dinner. Then let's get your clothes for tomorrow and lay them out."

It was clear that the conversation was over, so Briatta and Ellery obediently did as Owena said, beginning the preparations for their too-short sojourn to the Palace of the Founders. However, if Ardor didn't awaken within Briatta tomorrow, she would most certainly think their stay wasn't quick enough.

By the time both Briatta's bathing shift and ceremonial robes hung from the curtain rod over the balcony door, and she'd washed her face and hands, it was time for dinner. Ellery was still patting her face dry when Owena jumped to her feet, having looked at the Ardor clock on the wall.

"Founders, we're going to be late," she said, smoothing her clothes and hair and poking her head into the bathroom. "Are you nearly ready, El?"

"Why is everyone in this family always rushing me?" Ellery complained, tossing her rag onto the floor and running from the bathroom, raking her fingers through her hair to comb out the tangles she hadn't had time to brush.

"We wouldn't rush you if you were on time," Owena snipped. Briatta's gut twisted uncomfortably at her aunt's rare display of animosity.

Perhaps Owena wasn't completely invulnerable to the feelings of inadequacy surrounding her lack of Ardor.

"It's alright," Briatta offered hesitantly, reaching behind

her to grip the edge of the dresser she leaned against. "It's just dinner."

Owena frowned at Briatta but didn't say anything more.

Ellery, for her part, wisely didn't add to the conversation. Instead, she shared a loaded glance with Briatta, and the pair followed Owena from the room in tense silence. In the hall, Aden waited with Petyr, both freshly washed and changed.

"Are you ready for your last supper?" Aden asked with a wink, slinging his arm around Briatta's shoulders and shoving his fist into her hair. Trying to escape his hold, Briatta jabbed her elbow into his side and reached up with her free hand to push his arm away.

"That makes it sound as if I am preparing myself to die," Briatta pointed out balefully as she put Ellery between her and Aden, having successfully freed herself.

"That's grim," Ellery agreed. "But to me, it feels like we're preparing to send you away forever and bring home a new version of Bria."

"If we are to take home a new and improved model, I'd like to have some say in the development," Owena joked. Just like that, the tension in the air diffused.

Ellery laughed with delight at the possibilities of that suggestion. "Could we request that she doesn't slam her books shut when we interrupt her reading? It always feels unnecessarily murderous."

Briatta scowled. "I don't do that."

"You do." Aden chuckled. "Why *do* you get so mad when we pull you out of your books?"

"I do not get mad," Briatta insisted.

Owena gave her a sidelong look as they rounded the corner of the hallway that brought them back to the stairs. As they descended, Petyr, of all people, chimed in.

"I think you should ask for her to like the vegetables that my wife cooks."

It was so unexpected that the entire Belrose family laughed uproariously, and even Briatta fought to hide her spreading smile.

"That would certainly make Preida's job easier, wouldn't it?" Owena gasped, still chuckling as they stepped off the staircase toward the dining hall.

"Owena used to make you sit at the table until you finished," Aden said, his eyes glazing slightly as if he were reliving the memories. "You were so stubborn that you'd stay up all night and barely eat half."

"You were definitely the most difficult child in that aspect," Owena said, smiling fondly at Briatta.

The group stopped at the entrance to the dining room, which might have been the great hall of a palace that was being used in a more traditional sense than this one was. A sign on the door asked that they wait to be seated, so the family formed a small circle while they watched for someone to help them.

"I wasn't that difficult," Briatta protested.

Aden and Ellery both laughed while Petyr looked skeptical.

"You were so headstrong, you could have rivaled the Founder of Land," Aden teased.

The Founder of Land was said to have been unmoving and steadfast in his decisions, which, of course, was meant to be virtuous but instead resulted in frequent comparisons to oxen in older texts. Briatta had never seen oxen, but they were in her history books as animals they had once known, renowned for their obstinate personalities.

Briatta hoped she might meet oxen one day, if only to see what they were actually like. Perhaps the animal conservationists and geneticists would be able to recreate them if the environment improved enough for more frivolous endeavors like putting resources toward creating more animals than they already had.

Even though Briatta typically abhorred being the butt of her family's jokes, for once, she appreciated it. The banter distracted her from her concerns about the Choosing and whether she would leave it as an Ardorist.

A young priest appeared and escorted their family to a table, where they were served a six-course meal starting with apple and cheese salad and onion soup, Briatta's favorite part of the dinner. All the dishes that followed were classic variations of vegetable puree with spiced meat plated with buns or grains. They were comfort foods, and Briatta knew she would eat so much that her belly would hurt by the time they were done.

And as most of the dishes comprised of vegetables in the forms Briatta actually liked, she made a point of talking about how much she enjoyed them, though she was met with four sets of rolling eyes each time.

Outside, the biodome over the Founders darkened, and Briatta blinked drowsily at the food still on her plate before finally pushing it away.

"I can't finish this," she groaned.

"Me neither." Ellery sighed contentedly, taking a sip of her white pear wine.

"Alright." Owena stood, setting her napkin on the table. "Ready to head up for the night?"

The table agreed, but as they reentered the main lobby, Briatta felt as though she needed to spend just a few more minutes outside to reflect on the night before her Choosing.

"I'll meet you upstairs," she told Owena and Ellery. They nodded and followed Petyr and Aden back towards the staircase.

Briatta pushed one of the big front doors of the Palace of the Founders and walked onto the large front steps. Above, the biodome was filled with twinkling Ardor lights depicting a scene from the *Book of the Binding* where the Founder of Light had put many little lights in the sky to help the people to see. They weren't there anymore of course, but they supposedly had been at one point. Some speculated the lights were simply not visible because of the two suns, but Briatta wasn't entirely convinced by that theory.

Across from the palace, closer than they'd ever been before, the Founders themselves were illuminated from the ground with an Ardor light in front of each one. Briatta's heart swelled with yearning. Their hands were raised in adulation, their heads tilted upward, their faces not fully illuminated by the Ardor lights.

"Beautiful, isn't it?"

Briatta whirled and saw a tall man with brown hair and slanted eyes the shade of kavfe—a dark and bitter drink popular among the Ardorless—watching her from where he leaned against the palace wall by the door. How had she missed him? She chided herself for once again not having paid close enough attention to her surroundings. That was twice in one day where she'd allowed her guard to slip, and that was unacceptable.

"Yes," Briatta said slowly.

"What brings you to the Founders?" the man asked, though there was only one reason why people came.

Briatta hadn't walked out here to talk to anyone—least of all a stranger—and annoyance flared in her chest. "I'm here for my Choosing."

She turned her back on him to look at the Founders one last time before she went back inside, though her hand hovered at her thigh where one of her daggers was sheathed as she walked towards the stairs.

"Good luck, then," the man said. Briatta heard as he pushed off the wall and listened for his footsteps as they receded.

Spinning on her heel, Briatta glanced in the direction she'd heard him go, but saw no sign of him. She hesitated for only a moment longer, puzzling over how he'd disappeared so quickly, before returning to her room and retiring for the night.

CHAPTER 6

On the morning of Briatta's twenty-first birthday, she awoke along with the Polar Sun as it rose and shone brightly through the window in the big, beautiful room she shared with Owena and Ellery. When Briatta had returned to their room the previous night, she'd found the heavy navy drapes had been drawn. Eventually, she'd convinced Owena and Ellery to use the canopies on their beds so she could rise with the sun on the morning of her Choosing.

So her sky-blue canopy remained secured to her bed posts, and the Polar Sun streamed through the window and warmed her cheeks. For a long, glorious minute, Briatta remained stretched out in her bed, basking in the morning light and sending a prayer to the Founders to bless her with a link to the Ardor of the world today.

As soon as Briatta swung her legs over the side of the bed and her feet touched the green rug, she heard her aunt and sister stir. They'd retired early last night as everyone wanted to be rested and clear-headed for the Choosing.

"Happy birthday!" Ellery cried, flinging aside the blue

fabric surrounding her bed and leaping out. She crossed the room and hugged Briatta tightly.

Owena moved more slowly than Ellery but was not far behind the youngest Belrose, smiling warmly.

"Happiest of birthdays, Bria. May the Founders honor you on this day," Owena said into Briatta's ear as they embraced.

Before anything else, Briatta would attend her ritual bath. It was an act of cleansing before presenting herself to the Founders for her Choosing. Every young participant bathed on the morning of their twenty-first birthday in the Founders' baths, washing away the parts of the person they'd been and emerging as the one they were born to be.

Briatta pulled on her plain white shift, wearing nothing else beneath it, not even shoes, and combed her fingers through her hair.

Unable to sit still and wait, she paced and checked the small viewing hole in their door over and over to see if the priestess who would escort her to the bath had arrived.

At long last, a knock came at their door.

Briatta hurried to open it. It was Sister Mirana, and she bowed at the waist in greeting.

"Good morning, Briatta. I am here to bring you to your cleansing."

Briatta returned the bow and nodded. "I am ready."

After glancing back at Owena and Ellery, who nodded encouragingly and each signed *"Binding until burning"* to her, Briatta followed Sister Mirana down the staircase and below the ground level, into the deep belly of the palace where there were no windows, and Ardor lights lined the walls instead. She kept a hand on the cool stone walls to center herself, as she was entirely on her own without her siblings or her aunt for support.

Sister Mirana guided her through a polished, glimmering

set of pearly doors—in a wall among many others like them —and they stepped into a hot, steamy room. There was a small, bubbling bath built into the floor in the same way the tub in her room had been, but the water here was illuminated from within, sending rippling caustics over the walls and the shining pearlescent doors. Twelve small versions of the Founders surrounded the bath, their arms stretched toward the water, the six active Founders each bearing a small cup.

Briatta was momentarily stunned by how beautiful the whole room was.

After closing the doors behind them, the priestess picked up something from beside the door and approached. It seemed this space had been prepared in advance for the ritual.

"Drink." Sister Mirana handed Briatta an opulent gold goblet filled with red liquid. Briatta obediently accepted the cup and held it to her lips. It tasted like an extra wine, though it must have been unusually strong, because Briatta felt the same heady feeling she typically experienced after several drinks despite having taken only one sip.

"Now, descend into the water." Sister Mirana gestured to the bath.

Briatta complied, stepping towards the bath, the stone warm beneath her bare feet. When she reached the edge, she carefully lowered her foot to the first step beneath the water. The bath was cooler than she'd expected, especially considering the bubbles. Sucking in a breath, she placed her other foot into the water and eased herself further into the bath. When she stood in the middle, she turned to face Sister Mirana.

The bath was small enough that Briatta would be able to reach Sister Mirana from anywhere within its waters, but deep enough to reach her chest.

The priestess picked up a brass pitcher with her right hand, supporting the bottom with her left.

"Pray to the Founders, that they might honor you on this day," Sister Mirana instructed in a low intonation. Briatta closed her eyes, thinking through all her requests for support and guidance for the Founders.

She nearly jumped when lukewarm fluid poured over her head but managed to maintain her composure and keep her eyes firmly shut.

The stream of water ceased, and Briatta ceased her prayers because she wasn't certain what came next. While every Elfean learned about this rite of passage in their Foundling courses, the exact details were never shared. Despite her constant pestering, Aden had never opened up about his Choosing ceremony, either.

"Keep your eyes shut," Sister Mirana murmured, her voice now much closer to Briatta's left ear. "Hold your breath."

Sister Mirana pushed Briatta backward with a hand cupping the back of her head and the other gripping her shoulder. Briatta yielded, sucking a quick, gasping breath as she allowed herself to be guided beneath the water. It was quiet beneath the surface, but she was only there for a moment before Sister Mirana tugged her back up.

Breaking through the water, Briatta reached up to push her hair from her face.

Sister Mirana stepped away, dried her hands on her skirt, and moved to the Founder of Light, picking up a small cup.

"I bestow upon you the blessing of the light," she recited, pouring glowing liquid into the bathwater. Replacing the cup, she walked to the Founder of Air and repeated the process with clear water. The Founder of Fire's cup contained boiling hot water, the Water cup was filled with blessed water, the Flower cup bore floral scented liquid, and the Land cup contained wet, red clay, which plopped into the water and splashed Briatta.

Once each chalice had been emptied into the bath and every blessing given, Sister Mirana dunked Briatta once more and then stepped back.

"From the Binding until your burning, may the Founders' blessings grant you an honorable path through this life. You may now exit the bath," Sister Mirana said formally, shaking a folded towel and returning to the entrance of the small pool.

Briatta emerged from the water, truly shivering for the first time in her life, not entirely understanding what was happening, as the white fabric of her dress clung to her skin. The bath had been cool, but soaked as she was, the underground stone room seem colder than it had been. She gratefully accepted the towel and wrapped it around her body, instantly feeling warmer.

If this was how cold-blooded creatures felt when the biodome darkened, Briatta had a newfound empathy for them.

"Congratulations." Sister Mirana smiled warmly, squeezing Briatta's shoulders.

As they returned to Briatta's room, they passed other young men and women on their way to or from their own baths, presumably through one of the many other pearlescent doors she'd seen. Each looked more nervous than the last, and Briatta tried to avoid dwelling on her own anxiety.

Sister Mirana opened Briatta's door for her and held it while she entered.

"May the Founders bless you on this day," Sister Mirana said, bowing before leaving.

Owena was braiding Ellery's hair when Briatta returned, and both looked at her expectantly.

"It was a nice bath," Briatta said, sharing a knowing look with Owena and winking at Ellery.

"Oh, come *on*," Ellery groused. "I never get to know anything."

"You will know when it is your turn," Owena chastised gently, pulling the last pin from between her teeth and sliding it into place in Ellery's hair. "That's part of what makes it special."

When she'd finished with Ellery, Owena helped Briatta braid her wet hair back from her face as well, twisting the final product into a bun on the back of her head in the same way as her sister's. Her aunt's own hair tumbled down her back, though it had been tamed into gleaming brown curls with the heated metal Ardor wand provided by the Palace of the Founders.

Looking into the mirror while Owena dabbed a small amount of makeup onto Briatta's cheeks, she tried not to turn her head when a knock came at the door. Ellery answered it and found Aden, clad in gold robes and looking even more put together than he usually did.

When an Elfean attended a Choosing ceremony, they wore gold robes to signify they'd already gone through their own, whereas Ellery was garbed in pale clay-colored ones like the dirt of the deadlands, indicating she had not yet undergone her own Choosing and was there for her sister.

Owena finished helping Briatta and went to the bathroom before emerging in her own gold robes and holding her small black coin purse tightly. Her hair fell over her right shoulder, pinned up on the left, and Briatta marveled at what a lovely woman her aunt was. Not for the first time, she wondered if her own mother had looked similar to her sister. With that thought, a small wave of unexpected grief swept over her, and Briatta's throat tightened. She longed for her parents to be able to see her now.

Aden walked at the front of the group back down the

hallway and through the main lobby, where they were greeted by a young priest at the welcome desk who bowed deeply upon seeing their robes and said, "May the Founders bless you on this day."

There, they waited to be seated at the doors near the front of the dining hall, as everything was done very formally at the site and Palace of the Founders, and the day of the Choosing was an especially proper day.

An older priestess noticed their approach and led them to a table that had been decorated with flickering blush pink candles in the center, set with shiny white stone dishes, the spaces between sprinkled with white flower petals. Briatta thanked the woman appropriately, clapping her hands and giving a half bow.

Breakfast flew by in a blur; Briatta tried to eat from the wide array of fruits and cheeses set before her, even adding some berries and cream to her porridge to make it more palatable, but her belly roiled with nerves. Now that they had officially begun their day, she was becoming steadily more anxious.

Finally, Owena stood, signaling the end of the meal, and they left the dining hall. Anyone turning twenty-one on this day would need to kneel to the Founders, and the ceremonies would be held one after the other to ensure everyone had the time they needed. In the meantime, the Belroses would spend the morning in the palace's Founders Hall, offering their time and prayers until Briatta was called for her Choosing.

According to Briatta's studies, it had taken a while for the tradition of the Choosing ceremony to be discovered after the Binding had occurred, and for several years, no new Ardor abilities manifested until someone stumbled upon a new method of awakening power. From her history books, no one even knew how anyone came into the ability prior to the Binding.

Upon entering the Founders Hall, Briatta took in the rows of stone pews and the smaller versions of the Founders that lined the sides of the room, each in their own alcove and each directly across from another, including the Silent Founders. The craftsmanship was remarkable, done nearly as well as the real statues. They were some of the best likenesses that Briatta had seen as far as she could tell from having only seen the true ones once before at Aden's Choosing.

There were already several similarly dressed families sitting around the room, and as the Belroses found a bench, an elderly priest entered the hall through a side door and called for the Liyettie family. A boy in white with olive skin and black hair stood with a group of people who were obviously his family as they filed through the door after the priest. He looked nearly as green as Briatta felt.

The hours ticked by and Briatta examined the tapestries displayed at the front of the hall to occupy herself with focusing on something other than twisting the fabric of her flowy pants. The handwoven drapery on the left was a depiction of the origin of the Founder of Fire, and Briatta belatedly connected that it was the first day of the Cycle of Flame, which was why he was on display.

On the right, the decorated fabric depicted the Founder of Fire becoming a statue, half stone and half man. His eyes were lifted to the sky as the roaring flames in the background turned the blue expanse of sky dark with smoke and ash.

Several more times, the priest returned to collect others waiting in the hall, until, at last, the side door opened, and the older man appeared once more. "Will the Belrose family please come with me?"

Briatta pulled her hood up, her hands shaking.

Owena rose, moving aside to allow Aden, Ellery, and Briatta

to exit the pew before following them down the hall and through the door. They entered a small chamber with a passageway, but the walls curved in such a fashion Briatta couldn't see where it led. The elderly man closed the door softly behind them and turned, clasping his hands and bowing towards Briatta.

"May the Founders bless you on this day, Miss Belrose." He rose, smoothing the front of his white and gold robes. "My name is Horace; I'll be guiding you through the ceremony. Please, right this way."

Horace turned and walked down the curving passage. It wound to the right and then to the left, and soon Briatta was thoroughly disoriented. She recalled this from Aden's Choosing and knew that it would open to the west side of the palace. From there, they would follow a path to the front of the building and cross the short stretch of ground to the Founders themselves.

As they stepped outside, it was just as Briatta had remembered, but her eyes had grown accustomed to the dim Ardor lights and candles within the Founders Hall and the passageway, and she had to raise an arm to shade herself as they adjusted to the brightness of the Polar Sun.

They walked along the side of the building with the gardens to their left. Soon, they reached the empty space between the palace and the circle of Founders as they quietly followed Horace over the stone path that still stood between Briatta and her Choosing. Ahead were six priests and priestesses, each standing behind an active Founder, their hoods raised and faces shaded. They acted as anchors.

As they approached the perimeter, the six clerics turned to face them and bowed simultaneously.

"We welcome you," they incanted as one. Chills traveled down Briatta's back.

Stopping at the edge of the circle of Founders, Horace smiled expectantly at Briatta.

"Only one will be permitted inside with you. Whom will it be?"

Briatta glanced at Owena, who stepped forward.

"I will."

Owena stepped inside, and Ellery reached out to squeeze Briatta's hand before she and Aden went to stand next to Horace.

Since Owena was acting as Briatta's tether, she remained beside Briatta.

Briatta took a deep breath, then a second, and then she stepped over the invisible line that separated her world from that of the Founders, clenching her fists and going slowly toward the middle. The exact center of the circle was marked by a small stone dais with twelve thin marble strips radiating outward to each of the Founders like a web, attached to matching platforms beneath their feet. Briatta hesitated for only one moment before stepping onto the circular stone and kneeling, placing her hands on her knees, palms outwards in offering towards the statues. She bowed her head and closed her eyes.

The Choosing, Briatta had been taught, was a straightforward process. For one to begin their Choosing, they only had to kneel on the stone and wait. If nothing happened within five minutes, then they were not Chosen. If they were Chosen, then their Ardor would reveal itself, and the next challenge would be to gain control over it. This was where the tether came in. Tethers were a member of the family who would assist, because things could become dangerous depending on the manifested Ardor and its power. If the person undergoing the Choosing did not have some level of restraint, the tether would help control the Ardor.

In case the tether failed, then the anchors were also present to help. There was always one anchor who had mastery over each active Ardor.

The silence pressed into her ears, and though Briatta had no way of telling how much time had passed—that was something that Owena would do for her as well—the seconds seemed to stretch on and on. The same uneasiness that had curdled in her heart flared its head once more; perhaps she was not meant to be Chosen.

Then, Briatta heard a faint rustle.

"Rise, Lady Briatta Analeise Belrose."

Briatta started at the deep male voice—and the use of a title she didn't have—and blinked her eyes open. Before her stood a shimmering, semi-translucent figure garbed in glittering dark regalia and strapped from head to toe in weapons. Twin shining black hilts peeked over each of his shoulders, daggers secured to a bandolier across his torso and on his thighs, and a small hilt was even visible from the top of his right boot. The man was tall with waist-length white hair, the top half of which was braided back from his face, and the rest allowed to fall in loose strands down his back. Though his clothing covered most of him, swirling black ink was visible at his neck and wrists, and Briatta's eyes caught on the designs; she'd never seen such extensive tattoos on anyone, even if they were mostly hidden. He blinked slowly at Briatta as she took him in, his piercing dark eyes making her feel bare.

Briatta rose to her feet, trembling, though she wasn't sure whether it was from fear or awe. This man radiated power, and she didn't recognize him. "Who are you?"

The man, whose hands had been clasped behind his back, swept his right hand around and gestured behind him, his head turning with the movement. Briatta leaned to see past him, her eyes widening as she looked at the statue there. Realization swept through her.

"How is this possible?" Briatta whispered, shifting her gaze back to the Founder who was somehow corporeal before her—one who had no known name or Ardor.

"We are here in spirit," the man said as though it were obvious and nodded to the space behind her. Briatta turned and, to her surprise, looked down upon herself, her body still kneeling with her eyes squeezed shut. She lifted her hands, fighting to remain calm as the same luminescence that engulfed the man surrounded her own hands.

"Who are you?" Briatta asked again, wondering if it was possible to throw up in her current state. Her heart pounded, and nausea coiled in her stomach.

The man ignored her question for the second time. "I am ancient. Who I am is of no consequence." He paused, silent as he gave Briatta a quizzical look as though he were carefully considering his next words. Finally, he spoke again. "Hear me, Briatta. I am bound just as you are, but I can say this much: You are the final key. The balance must be restored. Carceron is..."

He seemed to struggle to speak here, like he couldn't quite get the words out. He eventually settled with, "We are nearly out of time."

"What does that mean?" Alarm flooded Briatta's body...or rather, her ghost form.

"I am bound," the man said regretfully. "Do not be afraid."

"Please, what does that mean? What do I need to do?" Briatta begged, becoming frantic as she felt the hold on this world slipping, spinning away from her as if she were waking up from a dream.

"I only have one last thing to give." The man smiled. "Use it well."

The world seemed to shatter as Briatta snapped back to her

body, and the Founder vanished. Something cold like the bath and the room, but worse, filled and overwhelmed her senses, and Briatta spluttered, opening her eyes and falling forward onto her hands. Her hands, she could see now, from which cool darkness poured at a frightening rate. Briatta lurched onto her backside, scrambling to get away from the night black that pooled onto the ground and spread from her.

"Briatta," Owena said from where she stood, her voice firm and grounding.

Briatta, breathing hard, looked to her aunt, who had paled but bore an expression of grim determination. Owena glanced at the anchors around the statues and at Horace, all of whom appeared stricken and were backing slowly away.

"Briatta, to stop it, you will have to breathe. Gain control of your emotions, feel the part of you that has been awoken, and then you will to cease the flow. Remember your training," Owena said, her voice steady and reassuring.

Owena appeared shockingly calm given what was happening to Briatta, and that brought a small measure of comfort to her. She took a wavering breath. She could do this. Closing her eyes, Briatta fought against fleeing from the shadows spilling from her palms and breathed to slow her heart rate and clear her mind, as Owena had taught her when facing distress.

In pressing circumstances, remaining calm was the most important. It was panic from which the most mistakes were made. This familiar thought, something that Owena had said to Briatta and her siblings hundreds of times, brought Briatta crashing back to reality.

Having managed to regulate herself enough to think, Briatta ran through a mental checklist, internally scanning her body for anything that felt even remotely different. She stumbled across a...pathway of sorts in her mind that hadn't been there before. It was similar to the channel from which her emotions stemmed.

Slowly, Briatta worked to shut the steady flow of the *something* that emanated from that mental pathway, imagining herself twisting a mental cap onto it. When she finally opened her eyes, the darkness had ceased spilling from her hands.

"Very good." Owena sighed. Without warning, she ran forward and grabbed Briatta's hand, pulling her to her feet and dragging her, stumbling, to the edge of the Founders Circle.

"Quickly, grab onto me. All of you." Owena gestured urgently to Aden and Ellery, who stood slack-jawed and pale a few feet away.

"Hurry, I don't have much time," Owena almost yelled. Briatta's siblings jerked into action, closing the small gap between them. As soon as Aden and Ellery had their hands on Owena, their aunt raised her arms, and the entire world tilted.

This time, Briatta did hurl her entire breakfast, barely managing to spin away from her family in time.

When the ground stabilized beneath her again, Briatta staggered away from Owena, wiping her mouth. Dazed, she looked around, trying to determine what had happened.

The anchors and Horace had somehow returned to their original positions; a few of them stared at Briatta's vomit with open disgust, though none seemed to be afraid as they had been just moments before.

"W-what was it?" Horace squinted. "Sorry, I'm afraid I've missed it."

"No Ardor," Owena replied smoothly.

"Ah, that is a shame." Horace seemed truly disappointed. "It's happening all too often these days." He instructed the Water Ardorist present to clean up after Briatta and led the Belroses back to the palace.

"Have a blessed day." Horace bowed and waddled off to fetch the next family.

"What *was* that?" Aden demanded as soon as Horace was out of earshot.

"We will discuss this later," Owena's tone sharpened as she slipped into the leadership role that Briatta normally only saw at headquarters—or when she and her siblings were in trouble.

"Briatta, outside of the four of us, you were not Chosen. Is that clear?" Owena said.

"What? But—"

"I know you have questions. We will discuss it later. Ellery and Aden, you must second that Briatta was not Chosen. None of you will speak of what happened here today until I say it is safe. Do you understand?"

Owena's voice was uncharacteristically firm, and Briatta shrank into a younger version of herself.

"Owena, surely it can't—" Aden started.

"You will swear it. Swear it upon what is most precious to you," Owena hissed, her eyes gleaming dangerously in light of the Polar Sun.

"I swear it," Ellery whispered, her eyes wide with confusion.

"Fine. I swear it, too." Aden relented, folding his arms and glowering at his aunt.

"Bria?" Owena said, turning to her at last.

"I swear," Briatta said numbly, still reeling from the suddenness of the events.

"Bria. Not even Neven." Owena's stern expression scared Briatta, and she swallowed, forcing herself to nod.

"Owena, what did you *do*?" Ellery asked, still seeming dazed as she looked over her shoulder to where the Founders stood.

"Later," Owena snapped. And that was that.

CHAPTER 7
GALEN

G alen, dressed in stolen priest regalia and standing behind the Founder of Fire as an anchor for the Choosing ceremonies, thought it truly a tragedy the way these people existed. While Carceron was indeed a hostile world, there were better ways of living on it, and he pitied those who relied solely on the biodomes. What a waste of Ardor. Not that he didn't depend on it as well. It was just...more efficient, the way he lived.

Though the young brunette girl he'd been sent to keep an eye on didn't seem all that special, he would keep his word to his superior—to whom he was bound—and he'd followed her dutifully to the Founders for her Choosing.

He'd begun his watch on the young girl in Montclair, where she lived an admittedly interesting life. Galen had thoroughly enjoyed watching her and the blond boy, whom she seemed to favor, take down that awful man. The papers the next morning had been some of the most fascinating ones he'd ever read, especially because the city was apparently aware of the underground vigilante organization living amongst them, though they didn't seem to be concerned with making much of an effort to burn them out of hiding.

Then, the girl had almost seen him in the city market. He was excellent at his job, so it had surprised him. She evidently had a sixth sense when it came to being watched, and Galen had been extra careful from that point forward.

Knowing about the Night Roses, or whatever they called themselves, would at least make the time he'd spent following her worthwhile. Perhaps they could make use of these already well-trained fighters somehow. Perhaps...he was getting ahead of himself.

Maverik hadn't even bothered to share *why* he wanted Galen to watch the Belrose girl, though he was sure there was a good reason. There usually was with Maverik—if he cared to share.

It had been a long time, however, since Maverik had let Galen in, and despite having been very old friends, Galen was growing increasingly frustrated with the entire operation. He wasn't sure how much more he could take of being sent on these useless missions while Maverik did things that actually mattered and made a difference. It hadn't always been this way between them.

Galen had gone ahead to the Founders after discovering who the girl's aunt was; he didn't want her to think anyone was following them. It had been fairly late in the bioday when they finally arrived, and Galen had been cleaning his finger-nails in the lobby with a knife while reading a paper from the table while they had checked in. He had worn a light-grey cloak with a large hood pulled over his head so that the girl, Briatta, would not see his face and recognize him in the future. Maybe it had been foolish of him to engage her later that night, but he had been so bored, and the family had seemed harmless enough despite their occupations. After all, they only went after very bad people, and he was only somewhat bad.

Since Galen had Fire Ardor, he had pretended to be the Fire Anchor for the Choosing ceremonies. He'd knocked out the actual anchor and left him bound somewhere, taking his robes and keeping the hood low enough so no one would recognize that he wasn't who they would have expected.

The girl's Choosing had been uneventful, though he wasn't certain why she'd vomited, and he had a nagging feeling he'd forgotten something. That she'd thrown up was a little unusual, even with the obvious nerves and distress of not having been Chosen.

It was always a little strange to be here, to see the statues. Galen had avoided this place for as long as he could manage and had at first been resentful that Maverik had sent him here. Now, though, he felt only emptiness as he took in the stone figures. There was something about them that didn't feel right, and he'd never been able to figure out why.

Galen watched as the Belroses walked slowly back towards the towering stone palace. The old priest seemed to buy what they'd said, but something about the demeanor of the family seemed off. There wasn't anything unusual about not being Chosen, but Maverik had seemed so certain. Perhaps he'd gotten it wrong.

If only Maverik still cared enough to actually tell Galen why he was here in the first place. The only instructions Maverik had given were that this girl would manifest Ardor, and he wanted to know what it was without telling Galen why he was convinced the girl would have Ardor or how he knew.

Galen wished Maverik would at least explain why he'd started stonewalling Galen from the critical information and the interesting stuff.

He was truly done helping with Maverik's cause.

When they'd first started, it had been *theirs*.

Some small and vindictive part of Galen hoped that Maverik had truly been mistaken. It would have been nice to see Maverik get something wrong just once.

Galen had about thirty minutes before Horace would return with a new family, so he settled in for a long bioday of standing beside the Founder of Fire and fulfilling his job. Thankfully, no children had manifested Fire Ardor yet, though Galen would have been able to help if they had. Probably better than the actual Fire Anchor would have, but that was beside the point. He just didn't feel like speaking to anyone.

When the last family left their Choosing ceremony, the daughter having manifested Land Ardor, the Polar Sun had set and the biodome was darkened. Internally thanking the Founders that he at least had the cover of the bionight, and then feeling weird for doing so even though the saying was widely used, Galen hurried back to the copse of trees a short distance from where the Founders stood and stripped the clerical garb, tossing them to the ground beside the young male he'd stolen it from. The man was awake now, trying to berate Galen through his gag, though it came out as muffled grunts. He was curled on the ground in only his underclothes, his hands and legs bound. Galen kept his back to the man until he had his own clothes on, and his face was hidden by his grey headscarf.

"Sorry, brother," Galen said gruffly to the man on the ground, shrugging. Someone would realize he was missing soon, and they'd find him.

Galen ran to fetch his horse, which he'd left tethered on the far end of the grove. After he checked his tack to ensure it was still secure, he mounted and urged the beast into a quick trot to leave this place before all levels of atonement broke loose.

Reaching the translucent door at the edge of the biodome

that would release him back into the deadlands, he pulled his headscarf off so the Weilers would not think him suspicious as he held his papers out for them to check. They waved him through, and he breathed a sigh of relief. He put his Ardor mask—infused with Air and Flower Ardor so he wouldn't suffer the effects of the thin air—over his nose and mouth, keeping his back to the biodome so no one would see, and replaced his headscarf as he dug his heels into the gelding's sides. The animal launched forward in response, tossing its head in irritation before settling into a steady lope across the all-too-familiar red dirt of this cursed planet.

If Galen ever saw Shadrik again, he was going to kill him. It would probably be in the afterlife, as Shadrik was already dead, but Galen would do his damnedest to send him beyond that, too.

The return trip to Montclair didn't take long, especially as a solo rider no longer trying to hide, and Galen was grateful to spend as little time as possible under the Nocturne Sun. Something about the big red planet made him feel wildly uncomfortable even as the Weilers at the western entrance didn't give him any trouble. At least Maverik's forged papers were good.

Safely inside Montclair and free of the Ardor mask, Galen let his reins fall loose and allowed the horse to walk through the streets at its own speed. His checkpoint was at a tavern in the shopping district, and when it came into view, Galen exhaled.

He wasn't looking forward to it. Outside of the watering hole, he tied his horse to the post and loosened the girth of his saddle before heading through the large single door.

It was late enough that it was already fairly crowded, vibrating with a steady hum of voices as its patrons were well on their way to a painful, morning headache.

Sliding into a seat at the bar, Galen slid three coppers

across the counter at the bartender. "I'll have an ale. And whatever the kitchen is still serving."

The bartender took the coppers and filled a mug with ale the shade of piss, the froth sloshing over the edges as he slid it toward Galen, who took a long drink. It was terrible, just the way he liked it, and he had just started settling in to thoroughly enjoy himself while waiting when the tavern door banged open. A large man entered, nearly filling the entire frame as he pushed through.

Galen scowled, turning away from the door and sliding lower in his seat. To his dismay, a large shadow fell over him, and then the seat at his side was occupied.

He'd been hoping for a little more time by himself before talking to anyone.

"Hello, Galen," the man said quietly, pulling out his own coin purse and ordering a dark beer. "Thought you'd come straight to us, but it turns out you're just as rotten as I remembered."

Fury welled within Galen at the blatant accusation. He'd been told that this was the checkpoint. Had someone lied just to make him look like he wasn't doing his job properly?

"What the fuck, Lycus? How did you know to come here, then?" Galen demanded.

"Followed you when I saw you return."

Galen was so mad that he couldn't even look at Lycus. It was one thing for Maverik to no longer trust him, but another thing for someone within their crew to sabotage his social standing. Not that it wasn't already shit. Bitterness filled his mouth, and he took another swig of beer.

"We're all just barely delaying the inevitable. Don't see how whether some girl has Ardor makes a difference." Galen's tone was a shade sharper than he'd intended.

"You might have lost hope, but the rest of us haven't, and I won't let you speed up a wreck that we might still be able to stop," the man growled, accepting the stout from the barkeeper. "Pull your shit together, Galen."

"Shove off, Lycus."

"You're a real piece of work." Lycus peered down into his cup. After a long stretch of silence, he sighed. "You were my brother once. What in atonement happened?"

"I'd like to know the same thing," Galen retorted, still refusing to face Lycus.

They sat without speaking to one another for a long while. Eventually, the bartender returned with two bowls of vegetable stew, each served with a chunk of steaming sour bread. Galen was glad for the excuse to ignore Lycus further and dug into his meal. Beside him, Lycus did the same.

When their bowls were empty and their mugs at the dregs, Lycus exhaled slowly and leaned his elbow on the bar, rotating so that he was square with Galen.

"I don't want to fight with you." It was a quiet offering for peace, and Galen's heart clenched painfully as he watched drops of beer trickle down the walls of his cup.

"We're already fighting enough as it is," Lycus continued. "It doesn't help to argue with each other."

"This was the checkpoint," Galen said finally, nodding when the bartender asked if he'd like a refill.

Lycus huffed an incredulous laugh. "Who in the name of atonement told you that? The file lists the fountain in the city center."

"Don't know who told me. It was an anonymous handoff like it always is." The words came out as more of a growl than anything else.

"Well then," Lycus leaned back. "Report, I guess."

The barkeep returned with a full mug, and Galen took a long drink.

"It was useless," he informed Lycus. "Just like all the other missions that Maverik sends me on these days. Dead fucking end."

Lycus finished the last bit of dark beer in his cup and frowned down at the counter. "The girl didn't have Ardor."

It wasn't a question.

"No." Galen thought Lycus would get up and leave after the report—not that he'd shared much—but the big man lingered.

"Don't screw this up for us. And send word when you decide to care." With that, Lycus stood, pausing. "For the record, Galen, I never stopped caring."

Galen swallowed thickly. The words cut deeper than he had expected.

"Lycus," he called out, stopping the man as he opened the tavern door to leave. Lycus didn't look back.

"I quit!" Galen yelled, picking up his second tankard of piss-poor ale and finishing it in three long gulps. He slammed it back down onto the bar as Lycus left through the door, letting it bang behind him.

His heart pounding at what he'd just done, Galen stared at the door, half expecting Lycus to come storming back to try and talk some sense into him.

But Lycus didn't return.

The longer he watched the door, the more he realized he'd come to rely on Lycus helping him find his purpose again. If Lycus had given up on him...

Galen, feeling at a loss for what to do next, sank back into his seat.

Wordless, the bartender raised his eyebrows to ask if Galen would like a third, but he'd lost his appetite and shook his head.

"It ain't none of my business," the man hedged, wiping the counter next to Galen and clearing the now-empty cups and plates. "But you look like a man who could use another beer. Tell ya what, it's on the house if you'd like."

Galen glanced up at the barkeep, noting his red beard and bald head, the dirty white apron wrapped around his protruding belly, and the kind blue eyes sparkling amidst hundreds of tiny smile lines.

"I do not need charity," Galen said somewhat sharply, getting up to leave.

"Aw, now. Ain't no charity here," the man replied, nodding meaningfully towards the door where Lycus had disappeared. His intention was clear. Galen didn't know how much the bartender had overheard, but it had been enough to make the man feel sorry for him.

Galen suddenly felt angry that Lycus had cornered him in this way, humiliating him in front of people who did not need to be involved in this mess of a righteous movement he'd become tangled up in. Perhaps that was why he'd done it the way that he had; Lycus knew Galen's heart hadn't been in it for a very long time.

That, and apparently, someone on the inside hated Galen. Hated him enough to give him more reasons to leave.

Galen had a fleeting thought that he should have at least told Lycus before leaving his people altogether, that there might be someone in their midst without their best interest at heart, but he shoved the thought aside.

Lycus had lost the right to that sort of information the moment he stopped believing in his friend.

Galen decided he would no longer be involved in any way. He would find a quiet little home where he could live in peace from both the activists and the loyal subjects of Belrune.

"Alright, fine." Galen nodded to the bartender. The man smiled and poured two glasses, beginning their night of drinking together.

By the time Galen stumbled from the tavern, it was the small hours of the bionight, and he was so drunk that he could hardly walk, let alone ride his horse. Somehow, he managed to free the reins from their post, and he walked his gelding down the road until he came across an inn. It didn't matter what inn it was; it just happened to be the first one they found.

Thankfully, someone was awake inside, and they helped him settle his horse in the barn and get to his room. Galen locked his door and fell facedown onto his bed without even bothering to remove his shoes.

What a shit day.

Soon, he was fast asleep, plagued by dreams not of the events happening now but of the nightmarish image of the Founders walking around and wielding Ardors at him that he'd never seen before, despite still being made of stone.

CHAPTER 8
BRIATTA

They had left the Founders a few hours earlier, just after her Choosing, and Briatta was still trying to grasp all that had happened. Owena forbade them from speaking of it while they were in the carriage, as it was not soundproof and Petyr and their designated Air Ardorist might overhear.

So, Briatta remained in a stunned state of agonizing silence from the moment they left the site of the Founders until the second they shut the Belrose house's front door behind them.

"What in the name of the Founders?" Aden demanded, running a hand through his hair as he dropped his bag.

Owena cast a meaningful look in the direction of the kitchens to where Preida might be preparing their dinner.

"I think we will do some training tonight," Owena said emphatically, her eyebrows raised as she looked at each of her charges. "Perhaps an hour or so after dinner."

Briatta dipped her chin. "Alright."

Relenting, Aden picked up his bag again and took it to his old room, shutting the door abruptly behind him. He'd spent more time there in the last week than he had in the past year. It was both good to see him and strange to feel his presence as constantly as they once had.

Adjusting her own bag, Briatta headed upstairs with Ellery. As soon as Briatta entered her bedroom, her younger sister slipped in after her and closed the door.

"Can you do it again?" Ellery asked in a hushed tone, her eyes wide. "I still can't believe it."

Casting a nervous glance towards the door, Briatta set her things on the foot of her bed. She lifted a palm and stared at it, wanting to see her...was it even Ardor? No documented Ardor explained the powers she'd displayed in that circle of statues, and there was also no record of activity from the Founder who'd awakened it. In fact, none of the Silent Founders had ever been active—that was why they were called Silent.

Perhaps this was a new Ardor. Either way, Briatta was unsure and resolved to simply call it Ardor unless it was proven to be otherwise.

"I..." She felt suddenly nervous about trying to use her Ardor again so soon, even as she tentatively reached for that new channel that existed within her. What if she lost control and couldn't stop it? What if it spilled from her windows and someone saw it?

"Maybe later," Briatta said shakily, letting her hand drop. "El, what did you see? During my Choosing, I mean."

A flash of disappointment crossed Ellery's face, but she quickly wiped it away and sat on the edge of Briatta's bed.

"Well, at first, it didn't seem like anything was happening." Ellery's face took on a thoughtful expression. "Then, one of the Founders who isn't supposed to be active, his eyes lit up. They were glowing bright blue, like how the Founder of Fire lit up for Aden, remember? And then, well, I think you know the rest."

Briatta plopped down onto the mattress beside Ellery,

falling backward and letting her arms splay outward. "Do you think Owena has the power to wipe minds?"

"I don't know." Ellery frowned. "Whatever she did, it felt awful."

They fell silent, Briatta staring at her ceiling and Ellery playing with the fabric of the blankets on Briatta's bed.

"Alright, well, I am going to unpack and take a nap," Ellery said finally and a little too brightly. "I'll see you at dinner!"

"See you."

Briatta watched her go. For a long while, she was unable to bring herself to move. They'd arrived home mid-afternoon, so there were still a few hours until they'd be expected downstairs for dinner. At last, Briatta rolled onto her side and gazed at her wall just to look somewhere else.

She felt a mix of apprehension and excitement regarding her new power. Sure, she had manifested *something*, so all her hopes and dreams for this day had come true. But at what cost? There was more to it, or Owena wouldn't have gone to such efforts to hide it.

Then there was the matter of what Owena had done. Briatta hoped their aunt would give them answers when they met later under the ruse of training, but learning that Owena had hidden things from them made her feel even more uncertain about the entire situation.

Briatta and her siblings had been raised by the leader of a vigilante crew; they'd seen death firsthand and knew the fastest and easiest ways to end a life. She had always thought they were more well-versed in the trials and tribulations of life than anyone else their age, but now she wasn't so sure.

What else did they not know?

When it was finally time to meet her family for supper, Briatta dragged herself out of bed, going through the motions of eating and making pleasant conversation with her family, for Preida's sake. She even forced tears to well in her eyes when telling the cook that she didn't have Ardor and accepted a warm embrace from the woman.

A dark, slimy feeling grew heavier in Briatta's chest with each of her lies.

Yes, she had been dishonest many times before because of her association with the Night Roses, but never had she blatantly deceived someone close to her about something as important as the Choosing.

Preida had worked for Owena since before the Belrose children had moved in, though they had been fresh out of Ardor training at the time. They'd helped raise Briatta and her siblings. She and Petyr were so well trusted that they were even privy to some of the secrets surrounding the Night Roses.

Outside of her family, Neven, and other members of the organization, very few people knew everything about Briatta. She hoped Preida and Petyr would forgive the distortion Briatta now weaved if they were to ever discover the truth of her Choosing.

By the end of dinner, Briatta was angry about the entire situation. She'd dreamed of this day for her entire life; she'd wanted the chance to create good with her own Ardor and share it with her loved ones. Now, it had been snatched away.

Life wasn't fair.

Instead of returning to her room until the designated meeting time, Briatta changed into loose pants and a tight black top and headed to the basement early. She wanted to spend the time working out some of these feelings through physical exertion so she would meet Owena with a level head.

Briatta wrapped her hands with protective cloth and picked up a pair of daggers, going through her usual fighting stances to warm up. She moved slowly at first, speeding up as her body loosened.

At some point, she heard Preida leave through the back door, retiring to the guest house where Petyr would be waiting for her. Briatta paused and tilted her head as she waited for the click of the lock, then resumed her training.

An hour later, Briatta was drenched in sweat, and while her turmoil hadn't been completely tamed, she at least knew that she wouldn't be overwhelmed with emotion while discussing the dwindling options of her future. And...whatever had happened at her Choosing.

"Bria." It was Aden. He appeared at the base of the stairs, hair damp from bathing and dressed in his night clothes, a pair of soft grey pants and a white shirt.

"Aden," she answered, tossing her practice daggers onto the cushioned floor and unwrapping her hands.

"You should have told me you were coming early. I would have joined you."

Briatta glanced back at Aden, her expression flat. "I needed to think."

"You guys are annoyingly punctual." Ellery's voice echoed down the stairs behind Aden. "Why can't you ever be just a few minutes late?"

His brows creasing into a frown, Aden stepped off the last stair and into the room. "You should maybe consider being on time for once."

Owena appeared behind Ellery. "You're all on time as long as I arrive after you."

Ellery and Aden would find something to argue about even if they were facing the end of the world. Briatta was sure their aunt was already more than accustomed to it.

"Come," Owena urged, walking to the far wall of the basement. It was the only space where racks of weapons hung from the wall rather than being stored in bins. This wall was where Owena hung her most precious artifacts; the ones with stories, the ones she couldn't bear to wield again because of the associated memories.

The Belrose children were forbidden from touching them, and this was one of the few rules that they had unequivocally obeyed.

Owena reached up and wrapped her fingers around the hilt of a throwing axe that looked as though it had been hurled into the wall and then left there, lodged in place. She pulled the handle outward, and the axe's blade hinged smoothly through the wall, though it didn't pull free. Instead, there was a deep, internal click from somewhere within the stone, and Owena released the handle, allowing the axe to fall back into its usual position. Then, Briatta heard old gears grinding into movement.

"What is this?" Aden asked, his voice full of suspicion.

The wall swung open, revealing once-invisible seams and exposing a dark space that stretched beyond the edge of the basement.

"A secret room?" Ellery gasped, her face alight with excitement.

"Aden," Owena said. "A flame, please. If you will."

Still appearing apprehensive, Aden lifted a hand and lit a small flame in his palm, stepping hesitantly forward. Briatta, still channeling the calm from her exercise, followed her brother.

With Aden's small flame lighting the space, Briatta could see that they were inside a plain, circular room made of stone. She and Ellery shared a look of confusion, but neither questioned their aunt just yet.

Owena reached across them and pushed a small rock Briatta hadn't noticed protruding from the wall. It looked like a natural part of the stone, but responded to their aunt's touch, and the hidden door swung closed behind them. There was just enough space to avoid it, and as the first door shut, it unveiled yet another secret entrance.

Briatta had to admit it had been cleverly done; one secret door opening to reveal a seemingly meaningless den that would only lead to the real, clandestine vault if one knew to close the door first.

Briatta walked forward, moving in front of Aden and his fire. The room before them appeared to have once been a gathering place. Three large sofas were arranged in a semi-circle around a small table. Beyond the couches was a huge fireplace that had been built into the stone of the wall. To Briatta's right, the wall was lined with bookshelves. The volumes looked incredibly old, and Briatta couldn't resist reaching up and running her finger along the spines.

"What is this place?" Ellery's voice was quiet and full of awe.

Briatta turned to the other half of the room where there was a large table with a three-dimensional map of what appeared to be Belrune built into it, surrounded by a wide wooden border, though she couldn't be certain from where she stood. On the walls around the table were more maps, older maps, and images of unfamiliar Elfeans with large red marker drawn through their faces, crossing them out.

Most noticeable of all, however, was the thick layer of dust covering the entire room.

"This was once the war room," Owena said pensively.

"We've had a *war room* all this time?" Aden gaped, the flame in his palm flickering and betraying his surge of emotion.

A small smile creased Owena's lips. "Yes. It's soundproofed and a secure place to meet. We can speak freely."

Briatta approached the couch and looked longingly down at it. If it weren't so filthy, it would have been a nice place to sit and talk about the day's events.

"We can clean it up," Owena went on, correctly assuming the direction of Briatta's thoughts. "If you'd like."

"Maybe another time," Briatta replied, moving away from the sofas. Instead, she approached the wooden seating around the table and brushed the dust from one of the chairs.

Briatta wanted to speak, but she wasn't certain how she could even begin to start with all the questions circling in her mind. She took a deep breath and wet her lips. When she opened her mouth to try again, Owena raised a hand and pulled out the chair next to Briatta.

"I know you must have a thousand questions," she said. "Let me try to explain and clear up at least a little of what happened today."

Aden, who had been examining the posters of the crossed-out Elfeans, and Ellery, who had been looking at the bookshelves, drifted closer.

"First, I do not know much more than you do, I swear it," Owena spoke earnestly, her brows furrowed. Her right hand rested on the table, forming a handprint in the dust there as she leaned forward and looked into Briatta's eyes.

"Alright," Briatta formed the word slowly.

"We've been told there exists only six types of Ardor, but I know there are others. I know because Lila and I both had... strange ones." Owena swallowed. Briatta knew it was painful for Owena to talk about her mother. She didn't remember much of what had happened when they were little, but she had known that Owena had tried for many years to find their mother after their father said she'd been put into a home for the terminally ill.

"I prayed to the Founders that you would not, especially after Aden manifested one of the usual six," Owena went on. "But it would seem that we Belrose women have an affinity for attracting trouble."

"Mom had Ardor?" It was Aden who spoke, and his voice was a strangled whisper. Briatta wasn't certain if it was from the reflection of the fire in his hand, but his eyes seemed faintly rimmed in red.

"She did," Owena confirmed, shifting her eyes to Aden. "She summoned storms...thunder, lightning, all the worst parts of a squall. It happened mostly when she grew upset, and I think that made it difficult for her to remain hidden in the same way I could."

"Storms," Ellery echoed. The worst that ever happened in a biodome was when water fell from the sky, generated by Water Ardorists. Though as children they'd been taught about storms in school, they had no real concept of what storms looked like.

"Yes." Owena nodded. "She might have been very powerful if the crown hadn't condemned the manifestation of any Ardor that isn't one of the six."

"I don't understand." Briatta tilted her head. "Dad put mom into a long-term care facility before he sent us here."

"The crown is aware of other Ardors?" Aden asked at the same time.

Owena shook her head and answered Briatta's question first. "She was taken. That's why he sent you to me. So that he could search for her. I tried to help, to use my resources. But... she vanished. It was as if Lila had never existed." She turned to Aden. "And...yes. The crown is aware."

A wave of shock washed over Briatta, and she gripped the edge of her chair as she reeled, her fingernails digging into the wood.

"Why are you just now telling us this?" Aden's expression warped from sadness to fury as hot anger emanated from him.

Owena's mouth twisted as she tried to explain. "I...At first, you were all very young, and I didn't want to cause you any more distress than you'd already experienced. Allard had sent you to live with me until he could find her, and then...three cycles after, I lost contact with him. The years passed, and I didn't—couldn't—find hint of where they'd gone. The longer it went on, the less hope I had of finding them."

It had been a long time since Briatta had heard her father's name uttered in this house.

"What...what happened to him?" Ellery breathed, sinking into the seat on the other side of Owena.

"I don't know." Owena stared at the table, her fingers rubbing absently along the grain of the wood. "I sent my own people after him. There was...nothing. The same as Lila."

Aden paced the room; Briatta knew that if they weren't sequestered in the war room, he would have left the meeting entirely. The flame in his palm, still the only thing illuminating the space, cast his long shadow behind him as the table that Briatta, Ellery, and Owena sat around fell into darkness.

"What about your Ardor?" Briatta managed, trying to bring the conversation back to something that wouldn't rock the foundation of her world as much as the news about her parents had.

Owena exhaled. "Time. I can turn back time, but only by a few minutes, and it has limitations."

"So that's how the anchors and Horace forgot about my Ardor...but how can we remember?" Briatta almost laughed as the insanity of the entire situation threatened to bubble over inside her.

"You were all touching me when I used my Ardor."

"Do you know what Bria's Ardor is?" Ellery leaned forward. She seemed to be handling this ground-shattering news better than her siblings. Briatta straightened her spine and schooled her expression into passive neutrality as she observed her younger sister sitting cooly beside Owena.

"I do not." Owena sighed regretfully. "I fear we will have to figure that out together."

Briatta glanced at Aden's back, the glow from the fire in his palm flickering with the turbulent feelings still undoubtedly surging through his body like an unsettled sandstorm.

"What do I do now?" she asked helplessly, facing her aunt again. If she could not be recognized as an Ardorist, Briatta would live her life as a member of the disgraced, along with the other Ardorless. She would have the least desired work and have to fight for her job, unlike the Ardorists who were given comfort and security from the very beginning.

At least Ardorists' jobs made a difference in the lives of their peers. Briatta would be reduced to nothing.

Hurt flickered across Owena's features. "Living as a member of the Ardorless isn't that bad, Bria."

Shame welled in Briatta's chest, and she curled over herself, her elbows digging into the wood of the table.

"You've done something for yourself, though," Briatta said into the table. "You have a purpose. You lead the Night Roses."

Owena did *good* in her life. She contributed to Montclair's society in ways that even those with Ardor could not.

Owena placed her hand over Briatta's, the wounded look morphing to sympathy, clear in the crease of her forehead and the quirk of her mouth. Her aunt hadn't always been the leader of the Night Roses. At one point, she'd been in the same position as Briatta. While a Belrose had always led the vigilante group, the position had to be earned.

Her aunt's eyes suddenly lit up, and she sat a little straighter in her seat.

"Well." Owena cocked her head, and her brows lifted as the ghost of a smile appeared on her mouth. "There's always the Ackmanlee."

CHAPTER 9

Hours later, Briatta laid in her bed, unable to sleep.

The night's conversations swirled in her mind like the little whirlpools her younger self had liked to create as her bathwater drained, each thought passing behind her eyes, consuming her attention, and then being sucked into the depths of her mind as the next became too loud to think of anything else.

There was so much to unpack.

The Ackmanlee was a competition originally created by King Novak, but was now hosted annually by Lord Mallon in Montclair, because it was the closest city to the Founders. It was meant to be a consolation prize for the year's Ardorless, a way for them to still be an important member of society. Having hoped she would never need it, Briatta had only ever attended through the lens of amusement; participating in the entire affair was considered beneath Ardorists unless they were involved in the execution of it—but that was mostly because they weren't allowed to compete, and therefore, felt snubbed. However, it had become a large source of entertainment for the Ardorists of Montclair over the years, watching those they considered beneath them fight for a chance to be included in their world, and Briatta and her family had attended both the announcement ball and closing ceremonies each time they'd occurred.

Now, it might be her only way out of being associated with the other disgraced Ardorless of Montclair.

While Briatta and her siblings had not been raised fully amongst the revered Ardorists of Montclair, they had also never been entirely excluded from that social group. Owena was well known, and she regularly received invitations to the most important functions. None of her friends among the Ardorists knew what she did for a living, but after she'd won her place at the head of the Night Roses and became loosely associated with King Novak after he'd publicly hired her to help Lord Mallon 'manage affairs', she was included more out of curiosity than respect. This was a point that Owena had ensured all of the children understood; the Ardorists didn't actually care for them, they desired her connections.

Everyone wanted to know what King Novak had meant when he'd said 'manage affairs', and Owena's rehearsed answer was: "I assist Lord Mallon with ensuring the Ardorless of Montclair are taken care of. After all, I am one of them, and he does not have to dirty his hands."

This was mostly true.

Owena had inherited the Belrose Estate, passed down through generations of their family and not necessarily a source of wealth, and she'd worked hard for what she had now. Both the house and the underground organization were already doing well under their previous owners and leaders, but they had flourished and grown under Owena's management.

When people began to pry, Owena had taught Briatta and

her siblings that sometimes, simply letting people believe what they wished was enough of a lie.

Part of being a familial member of the Night Roses meant that Briatta had been raised to defend the weak, the people left behind by members of the Ardorists. The organization took these cases most frequently, as the Weilers would prioritize important cases but often allowed the ones they deemed lesser to fall through the cracks.

Briatta had grown up protecting the Ardorless, raised to ignore social standing, but she still couldn't bear the thought of being forgotten by her friends, of not being invited to the parties she enjoyed, and of no longer reveling in the privileges she'd had for most of her life.

She had grown accustomed to their lives and the access Owena's status had afforded them.

Briatta's thoughts turned to her brother, who had retreated to his bedroom without a single word to any of them. She knew Aden likely resented Owena for keeping such a large secret about their parents, for not even giving him the chance to try and help find them. She knew because the same begrudging feeling also brewed in her heart.

Allard and Lila. What would they say about her situation? Would they support her if she were to compete in the Ackman-lee? Briatta didn't think it was usually dangerous, but she really had no idea what it was about. From the little she'd cared enough to glean, it was related to gaining a ranked position amongst the Weilers, which were usually reserved for Ardorists.

Regardless of Ardor, the Weilers were well respected, and they *definitely* served a purpose in society. Many of them also received courtesy invitations to the societal events hosted by Ardorists where they were stationed.

It wasn't the life that Briatta had pictured for herself.

A small *plink* on her window jolted Briatta from her thoughts, and she sat straight up in bed, her hand going to the knife beneath her pillow. She waited as still and quiet as a mouse—a creature which had been brought back from extinction so medication refining Ardorists could experiment on them—until a few seconds passed.

Then there was another *clink*.

Briatta pushed her covers aside and, bringing her blade with her, crept to the window. There was only one person who would toss pebbles at her room, but she was careful each time just the same. There was always a chance that someone would observe the behavior and mimic it to lure her outside. Briatta didn't know who might care enough to do so, but doing the work that she did, it was possible she had invisible enemies.

It was dark in her room, and as Briatta approached the glass, the Ardor lights outside made it easy to see who was standing on the ground outside.

Neven.

An immense wave of relief swept over Briatta, and the tension in her shoulders since they'd left the Founders released. She unlatched her window and waved.

Neven climbed up the side of the house, using the established fingerholds in the painted bricks that had formed over the many years of Briatta sneaking out and Neven creeping in. Briatta climbed out of her window and pulled it almost closed behind her, stepping carefully to the spot on the roof where they'd spent many nights talking about their lives and staring up at the swirling patterns the Light Ardorists formed on the inside of the biodome.

The creation of the moving Ardor lights on the darkened biodome hadn't always been a regular occurrence. At first, the lights were dispersed evenly throughout the biodome in a mimicry of the story about the Founder of Light putting Ardor lights in the sky, so that they would not be completely blind when it was darkened for the duration of the Nocturne Sun's presence. The story went that one night, a Light Ardorist was bored with maintaining the static fixtures in the sky and decided to have some fun. It had been a simple design, just two smaller versions of the Polar and Nocturne Suns rotating around each other, but the response to it had been explosively positive.

The Light Ardorists started designing more complicated images for each bionight ever since.

"Bria," Neven said as he crested the edge of the roof, joining her and enveloping her in a hug. The rune on his brow, over his right eye, was a stark reminder of what he could publicly brandish that she could not.

"Hi," Briatta managed, her throat feeling suddenly tight with emotion.

"I'm so sorry." Neven pulled away, holding her at arm's length. "I heard what happened. I know how badly you wanted Ardor."

Briatta tried to reply, but the words wouldn't form between her lips. She and Neven had grown up as opposite—he a member of the Ardorless, she of neither—but they had been brought together by a friendship forged through the Night Roses and Owena. A few cycles ago, he had returned from his Choosing as a Light Ardorist and a new member of the welcomed and celebrated contributors to society. They had effectively swapped places, and while Briatta had never faulted Neven for his status, she didn't know how to verbalize her feelings to him without sounding like a spoiled and overprivileged little girl.

For a moment, Briatta contemplated telling Neven the truth about everything that had happened, but Owena's admonishment still rang in her ears. Her aunt had known that Neven was the one person Briatta would want to confide in.

"I..." She looked away, turning from Neven and sitting on the roof outside of her room, curling her legs to her chest and wrapping her arms around them. "I don't know what to do."

"Do as you've always done," Neven replied, taking a seat beside her. His left leg remained straight while his right knee bent up to his body, and he didn't take his eyes from her as he settled in. "Live like Owena and...me, before my Choosing."

His words were halting, and Briatta sent him a sidelong look, feeling a flicker or surprise at the gruffness of his tone. Perhaps he was experiencing the opposite of the emotions that were still bouncing around in her heart like crazed flutterflies. Maybe he also didn't know how to process their converse positions.

"You before your Choosing wasn't a bad thing," Briatta said softly, but even as the words left her mouth, she felt guilty because she did not believe the same thing about herself, and what did that say about her true feelings regarding Neven? Would he understand, or would he be disgusted by her hypocrisy?

Neven gave Briatta a tight, sad smile. "Bria...I know you. Probably better than you know yourself. You've always treated me no differently than anyone else, but I know you have no other friends outside of the Ardorists. I know you only help those beneath you when Owena makes you."

Briatta's guard was down, because this was her best friend; she wasn't expecting him to be so direct, and his words cut deep. They were unexpected, especially when Neven should have been offering her comfort. Abrupt, hot tears welled in her eyes, accompanied by indignation that burned up her chest and neck. Trying desperately to keep her tears from spilling, she looked away from Neven and took deep breaths, trying to rationalize what he'd said and form a response that wasn't rooted in fury.

"Bria, if Owena hadn't taken me in, I doubt you would have ever given me a second glance," Neven continued, his voice strained. "I know this was a blow for you in more ways than one, but I am also sure that you will come to see that it isn't so bad to be...Ardorless."

Why was he still talking? It was like rubbing the salty red dirt of Carceron in an open wound.

"Stop it," Briatta gasped, choking the words out as a sob racked her in response to his continued verbal assault on her person. She sucked in the air, wrapped her arms around herself, and pushed to her feet, rushing to the farthest edge of the roof away from Neven. Briatta tilted her face up, watching with blurred eyes as two desert cats formed by Ardor lights batted a tumbleweed back and forth across the underside of the biodome.

Neven remained where he was and, thankfully, was quiet.

Of everything he'd said, at the forefront of her mind was the question of whether Briatta would have turned away from a dirty little blue-eyed boy had she seen him on the streets rather than in the Night Roses.

A yawning pit grew in her stomach as she realized she likely would have ignored Neven if Owena hadn't introduced them. There had been many children on the streets when she was young—there still were—and Briatta rarely paid them heed unless she was working with her family or on a case.

She always assumed they would get help from someone else. She didn't need to waste precious time that she could be using to further herself both in school and at the Night Roses to track down every lonely child's missing parent.

Was she nice to other Elfeans when she spoke to them?

Always. But did she willingly spend her time with them when they were at their worst?

Never.

A small voice in the back of her mind whispered that, at one point, it had been Briatta and her siblings who had been the dirty, lost children. Thankfully, Owena had been willing and able to take them in, but not every child had family like that. Many didn't have any family at all.

An uncomfortable sensation rose in her heart. Briatta was well-read and highly educated like the children of the Ardorists, and the texts she'd been exposed to had all confirmed that even if she had tried to help every lost child, it wouldn't make enough of a difference.

But Neven thought she should have put herself out there anyway. She should have fought a repeated, losing battle and allowed her heart to be broken every time.

Briatta's chest tightened. The more she considered what Neven had said, the harder it became to take even breaths. His words were painfully true, forcing her to admit she had turned her back on her inner child, the younger version of Briatta who had been turned out by her father. Was she really so insecure that she feared her standing with Ardorists would have suffered for having been seen helping the Ardorless?

Apparently so.

Briatta had never even considered her beliefs were bigoted, or that they had negatively affected her closest friend, but the longer she stood there and pondered it, the clearer it became and the more her pain curdled into anger. A newfound resentment for her very best friend boiled within her as a response to Neven being upset by who she was.

Though the Belroses hadn't technically been members of high society, she'd never really considered herself as any other, and because high society was raised to believe they were better, maybe it wasn't her fault she thought the way she did. Or maybe it was, because Owena had tried to expose them to the Ardorless more often than they went to Ardorist events. But Briatta had, so, so badly wanted to feel important.

Founders, if she'd only manifested an acceptable Ardor— and that thought, that poisonous, terrible thought that confirmed she really was as terrible as Neven believed she was, was the final breaking point.

When Briatta could take a deep breath without hiccupping with tears, she wiped her cheeks dry and spun to face Neven.

"If you hate who I am that much, why are you here?" she demanded.

Taken aback, Neven rose to his feet. "Bria, that isn't what I meant at all."

"It obviously is," Briatta retorted bitterly. "Why else would you come here on what you know to be the worst day of my life and belittle me?"

Neven's expression grew dark. "I know you're upset, and I am sorry. I was only trying to point out that maybe you should try to establish yourself in the circles of the Ardorless. Otherwise, you'll be all alone."

"Oh right, because you're a member of the Ardorists now." Briatta's voice lashed like a whip. Her fury had calmed her, sharpened her focus, and she spoke with chilling clarity.

"I would never abandon you," Neven growled, taking a step toward her. Briatta instinctively backed away, glancing behind her as she was still close to the edge of the roof.

"Get away from me," Briatta snarled, glaring up at the boy who had once been her safe space.

"Bria, I am trying to help you." Neven scowled and crossed his arms. "Don't push me away, now."

"I don't want your help."

Hurt flickered across Neven's features, and he took another

halting step. Briatta pulled her dagger from its sheath and raised it against him. He stared down at it in shock before carefully smoothing his features into something flat and unrevealing.

"Fine." He turned his back to her, returning to the part of the roof where it would be easiest to climb down, and disappeared over the side.

Briatta stood, frozen, holding her dagger pointed at the spot where Neven had been. She immediately regretted her anger towards him. They'd grown up in different worlds with different rules. Neven would understand that she was only speaking from misplaced anger and stress regarding her new path in life. Surely, he would come back.

After a moment of stillness, the sounds of Neven's retreat having faded, Briatta allowed her blade to fall back to her side. She couldn't take her eyes from the spot where he'd been.

Briatta had reacted strongly and poorly to the words of her oldest and closest friend, possibly losing him in the process.

It had been a very long day.

She used to think she and Neven would end up together, despite their different societal backgrounds. But now that their positions were reversed and she had acted as she had, would Neven still want to even be her friend? Briatta would never be able to tell him the truth about her Choosing ceremony, and he knew her well enough that eventually, he'd figure out she was lying—if she hadn't chased him off entirely.

It was all going so wrong.

Briatta sourly thought about her aunt, her mother, and the fact that they—and now she herself—were forced to live in hiding as Ardorless because the king had deemed their powers as unacceptable.

Despite how late it was, Briatta was more awake than ever. She eventually climbed back through her window and closed it, sliding the latch into place, regretting the solid click it made as if it symbolized a distinct point where her friendship with Neven had fractured.

They may be alright in time, but it would take a while for Briatta to process everything Neven brought up. There were several points that she grudgingly admitted were true, but she had never questioned herself in such a manner until tonight.

She replaced her dagger beneath her pillow and crawled back into bed, lying on her back and staring up at the ceiling in the dark. Eventually, her eyes adjusted enough that she could make out the lovingly maintained swirling designs carved into the old wood of her ceiling.

Had her family always been included amongst the Ardorists? Or was that a newer development, because of Owena and her connection to King Novak?

Maybe if societal hierarchy hadn't always depended on a person's value to their survival on this hostile world, families might have been ranked in other ways. Maybe, at one point, there had been no structure at all. The idea was too strange to consider, so Briatta rolled onto her side and stared at her wall instead, hoping the plainness of it would calm her mind instead of prompting foreign thoughts like her decorative ceiling had.

When Briatta finally fell asleep, she had a nightmare in which she was desperately trying to enter a ball to join Neven to apologize, but she was not allowed through because she was not good enough.

CHAPTER 10

The next morning, life seemed to resume its normal pace without Briatta. The Belrose family received a missive at breakfast from the Mallon household that Lord Olrik Mallon, the resident of Malcalaire Manor in the middle of Montclair, would be returning. He'd been absent with his eldest daughter for most of the past year, having taken her to Srila to find her a husband.

Briatta was thankful that she was not the daughter of a lord and wouldn't have to marry when it was arranged. Owena believed that if one were to marry, it should be for love.

At least that was one thing she wouldn't have to worry about in the midst of her life being uprooted.

In celebration of his daughter's marriage, Lord Mallon was hosting a ball that would take place one week from today. The letter also noted he would announce and outline the rules and qualifications for this year's Ackmanlee during the event for the amusement of his guests, the Ardorists in attendance. Papers would go out for the Ardorless the following day, formally inviting them to compete.

THE NEXT AFTERNOON, Naius entered the Belrose house in a whirlwind of fabric and pins along with his entourage of young assistants, having already been notified of the event and ready for a call from his favorite clients. Briatta generally dreaded the days when Naius came because it meant hours lost to standing around, being measured, and listening to him talk about the poor fashion choices of Srila's Ardorists. It was of his opinion that those in Belrune's capital should be the most well dressed of any city, and he always had something to say about it. In *great* detail.

Briatta knew he was just upset that he wasn't the first to dream of those ideas, especially because those same fashion choices hadn't yet emigrated to the other cities due to lack of travel between the biodomes. As such, popular clothing trends didn't spread as quickly as Naius would have liked.

Today, however, Briatta was grateful for the distraction. Anything that pulled her from the depths of her mind—which seemed to be bent on dwelling upon Neven and on her Choosing—was a welcome diversion.

While she'd questioned Owena about whether she would be allowed to attend the ball given the result of her Choosing, her aunt had dismissed her with a wave of her hand. If Briatta wasn't allowed, she wouldn't be going either, and people desired connections with Owena and her ties to King Novak more than they cared if Briatta was present or not.

Naius and the Belroses met in the sitting room, as usual. The room was a dark-blue lounge by the front window. In the center of the space, two grey sofas faced each other with a grey and blue chair between them. The floor was dark hardwood, covered by a large white rug, with white curtains framing the windows that were tied open to allow the light of the afternoon Polar Sun to stream through.

On the small tables beside each of the couches were small stacks of coasters and a couple books. Along the inside wall were lamps containing Ardor lights and a long buffet where Preida sometimes set out hors d'oeuvres for visitors.

Naius brought an assortment of colored fabrics into the room—far more options than Briatta had thought possible—while she and her siblings were instructed to choose a style of celebratory gown and suit from a series of his sketches, as well as a preferred fabric and color scheme. It was Naius's favored way to work, and the Belrose family had never been disappointed by the results.

By the time Naius prepared to leave, dinner was nearly ready. His many assistants cleared the fabric, examining the floor to ensure no stray pins or needles had been dropped. Briatta stood dutifully out of the way, standing at the wall nearest the door through which she could soon escape, as she had grown increasingly agitated from having scarcely slept the two nights since her Choosing.

THE NIGHT BEFORE THE DANCE, Briatta was sent on a mission with Neven, who had requested her as backup. Zora had sent her a note in the usual coded fashion, informing Briatta she was not to accept the mission if she did not feel up to it. Briatta had seriously considered turning it down, considering their most recent conversation.

However, Neven had already done all the reconnaissance, so all Briatta had to do was be where he wanted her to be. She'd also accepted because, despite everything, Neven was still her dearest friend, and she felt horribly guilty about their last interaction.

The mission ended up being straightforward, and Briatta found herself wondering why Neven had needed her there at all. They reported directly back to headquarters, predictably skipping their usual Noodlegeuse outing, though not for being late.

While Neven gave his account of the evening, Briatta wandered the area. She walked by Owena's office and paused, considering her choices of remaining a full-time member of the Night Roses against competing in the Ackmanlee and becoming a Weiler. There wasn't anything wrong with staying with the Night Roses, but she also wanted to forge her own path rather than rely on her family's influence.

Feeling slightly better, Briatta decided it was time to go home; she hadn't slept well all week, and they were attending Lord Mallon's ball tomorrow.

Neven waited in the false break room, and Briatta eyed him warily as the wall opened and she stepped through. She was too tired to jump into their usual banter and wasn't sure if he would even want to talk.

"It's late. You didn't have to wait for me."

Neven's brows creased. "I always wait for you."

It was true, though unexpected unease bloomed in Briatta's belly where she usually would have been warmed by the gesture.

"You're...you aren't mad?" Briatta asked dumbly, standing frozen in front of the hidden entrance to headquarters.

Neven sighed and looked down at his feet. "I was hurt, but I'm not mad. Let's go."

A jolt of anxiety coursed through Briatta's veins. What was wrong with her? Besides their recent fight, Neven had never done anything but care for her. He'd been there for her while they were training, throughout school—even though he'd not been permitted to join her in public due to his societal standing—and had never hesitated to help when she'd asked.

"Are you ready?" Neven asked, drawing Briatta out of her thoughts. He'd halted halfway to the exit and turned when he realized Briatta was not following him.

Clearing her throat, she answered, "Yes."

Briatta followed Neven from headquarters, and they walked back to her house in silence. The roads were dimly lit by the bioluminescent plant life and the Ardor lights, placed so that pedestrians could see. Neven remained by her side for much longer than he usually did, only saying goodnight and peeling away into the darkness once the Belrose Estate was in sight.

Briatta watched him until his back disappeared into the shadows of the houses lining the street he walked, feeling confused about him and everything that had happened to her and her family. Finally, after staring blankly at the bionight-blurred spot from which he'd vanished, she turned to her house and took a moment to look at it—really look at it—for the first time since she'd returned from her journey to the Founders.

Petyr had planted a new flowering plant that glowed purple in the bionight beside the front steps on the left side, and the tree that stood to the right of the stairs had fluorescent moss that had taken root within the cracks in its bark, giving it a vaguely striped appearance. The house was otherwise just as Briatta had always known, blue-grey painted brick with white trim and a black double front door. It was quite charming under the Polar Sun's light, but in the darkness of the bionight —at least tonight—it looked intimidating.

Briatta shook her head. This was her home.

Maybe it was because Briatta had recently been peering

inward and spending more time examining her sense of self, but she didn't feel like herself anymore. The Briatta walking through the front door of her house wasn't a version of Briatta that she recognized.

The following day, Briatta slept in again. She hadn't slept well since her Choosing, and despite sleeping late every morning, she did not feel rested. When she finally cracked her eyes open, hours after her family had already eaten breakfast, she groaned at the light streaming through her curtains and forced herself out of bed. She wouldn't get to bed on time tonight, for it was the night of Lord Olrik Mallon's ball.

Going to balls was Briatta's favorite part of growing up as a sort-of member of the Ardorists. The only downside was that as she grew older, she realized the majority of her targets came from that world, and she was much less defensible in heavy skirts.

Thankfully, at Owena's request, Naius always made their gowns as light as possible for this very reason. Still, one could only fight so well in a ballgown.

Owena had thought of this, too, and Briatta's least favorite training sessions were ones where Owena put weighted petticoats on her and Ellery and forced them to spar. She used to pitch a fit every time Owena had announced it was time to practice their hand-to-hand combat while dancing, but now she was grateful for those lessons.

Briatta also considered Neven, who had yet to be permitted to attend these dances. Those Ardorless who were lucky enough to retain relations with an already powerful family were sometimes invited, but any Ardorless without connections were cut from all events.

Neven, however, had manifested Ardor at his Choosing. There was a chance he would be attending this ball, and Briatta had mixed emotions about it. Neven had never spent time with her while she wore the persona of a proper lady, though now she wondered if he had always seen straight through her.

A soft knock came at her bedroom door, and Briatta started from where she'd been staring out the window, enveloped in thought.

"Yes?"

"It's just me," Ellery announced as she entered, carrying a tray of food and tea. "I thought you might be hungry."

"Thank you." Briatta meant it. Her stomach growled in recognition of the food even as she accepted the tray and set it down at the foot of her bed. "I'm sorry I haven't been able to wake up for breakfast."

Ellery shrugged, sat on the bedroom bench, leaned against the mattress, and helped herself to a small piece of toast. "Aden hasn't been there either, so it's alright."

When Aden wasn't staying at the Belrose house, he was at his own place, so this wasn't outstanding news, but Briatta was still grateful Ellery thought of it that way. She nodded to herself as she took a bite of oatmeal, which was loaded with berries and cream the way she liked it.

"How are you, Ellery?"

Ellery tilted her head back and smiled, looking at the ceiling with a dreamy expression. "I'm excited for the ball."

Briatta took another bite to avoid answering, as she was not as enthusiastic about the evening's agenda as she normally would be. It wouldn't be long before the very people she'd dance with realized she was no longer their peer.

Ellery gave Briatta a sidelong look at her silence. "You aren't, then."

It wasn't a question.

"I...am afraid."

Understanding came over Ellery's expression. "Afraid of what people will think."

Briatta nodded, then changed the subject. "Have you received your first case yet?"

Ellery would turn eighteen soon, and Owena would allow her to work with a seasoned member of the Night Roses as an apprentice to establish herself.

Ellery raised an eyebrow. "Not yet, but Owena said it would be a gift on my birthday."

"Hmm." Briatta hummed. "She gave me my first case a week before."

Ellery straightened, indignant confusion all over her face, and Briatta wiggled her eyebrows mischievously.

"Founders, Bria!" Ellery cried, taking a pillow and swinging it at her sister when she finally understood that she was being teased. She laughed then, flopping back onto the bed and resting her hands on her stomach.

"If you like, I will help you," Briatta said, warmth filling her chest at the sight of Ellery laughing.

"I know." Ellery's voice was quiet as she turned to look up at Briatta. "Why don't you like to dance anymore?"

The question came out of nowhere.

Briatta looked away. The truth was pretty simple. Any of the handsome men with genteel upbringing who might sweep her off her feet could also be the subject of her next mission. It was a conflict of interest to enjoy getting to know any of them. Owena disagreed, stating firmly that it was better to know the person she was tasked to eliminate.

"I just don't," Briatta finally said in answer.

Ellery sighed and pushed herself up onto her elbows. "Do you want to spar until we have to get ready?"

Briatta finished her oats and examined the rolls, fruit,

bacon, and the small glass of juice next to the tea she'd been sipping.

"Why not?" she agreed finally, rejecting the rest of the meal. A good training session might help her feel better, and it would distract her from thinking too much about Owena and how little her aunt could help the situation.

Five minutes later, they were changed into their training clothes and in the basement training area. Ellery picked up a pair of twin swords and grinned wickedly at Briatta, whose favorite fighting method was with that very pair of swords.

Scowling, Briatta chose a short sword and a dagger instead. She moved to stand across Ellery on the mat, spinning the sword lightly to get a feel for its weight and balance.

Ellery moved first, charging at Briatta with a well-rehearsed series of movements that would confuse any regular opponent so she could either strike at the navel or the neck. However, they'd had the same teachers, and Briatta had been taught to guard against more than one weapon. In fact, all of them carried daggers on both sides of their bodies so they would always be able to defend themselves ambidextrously.

It was also why Owena had metal bracers forged for them to wear in the field; it might break their arm to block that way, but at least they'd survive.

Briatta easily parried Ellery's attack, guarding her throat with her sword and deflecting the blow aimed for her midsection with her dagger. She used the momentum to twist and thrust at Ellery's ribcage, the small blade angled upwards to pierce between the ribs and enter the heart, but Ellery had already moved away and was preparing another strike.

The sisters attacked and defended, becoming lost in their dance of blades. Despite using real steel, neither made a single mark on the other. Owena had taught them to strike true, but also how to not harm at all.

The next time Briatta pulled her blow, Owena's familiar words coursed through her mind: *Sometimes, all you need to do is frighten your opponent. If they know you can easily kill them but won't, that might work in your favor. It could also work against you. Fight the man in front of you, not the idea of one.*

It wouldn't work on Ellery, of course. But it was a mantra that had been repeated to them so often, it was practically a part of her.

Briatta's body moved in response to Ellery before her brain could even register her sister's motions. This was the part of fighting that she loved; it was as second nature to her as waking up and getting out of bed in the morning. Completely instinctual.

"Break!" Ellery called the word Owena had taught them to use before stopping a fight. Because the Belrose family fought at such high levels, if one person were to stop moving without telling the other, they might accidentally put themselves in true harm's way lest the other could not halt their blow.

Briatta lowered her sword and dagger, stepping back. Her breath was a little quicker than she'd realized while caught up in the fight, so she paced in active recovery.

"You did not hold back," Ellery said breathlessly, her brow glistening and a look of delight on her face.

"You did not need me to," Briatta replied, smiling. Ellery had been a proficient fighter for years and would have been able to hold her own in any bout on the street, but it had only been recently that her speed was developing.

Ellery returned her twin swords to their rack. "Thank you. I needed that."

Briatta nodded as she put her sword back, though she held onto the dagger. "Me too."

CHAPTER 11

B riatta sat in front of her mirror, watching as one of Naius's assistants worked on her hair. It was pulled into an intricate, braided updo, though a couple loose curls framed her face, and the remaining unbraided hair was piled on top of her head. It was tight, but Briatta liked how it accentuated the already-sharp angles of her face.

While most Ardorist households employed Ardorless ladies full time to help with daily hair and clothing, Owena had always felt that was a waste of money and time. Instead, Naius would proudly bring his creations to the Belrose Estate on the day they were needed and make last-minute alterations and adjustments as needed. His assistants would also help fix the Belroses' hair to Naius's vision. Briatta liked this arrangement the best because Naius rarely got it wrong, and she wouldn't have to plan for or worry about her hair.

When her hair was complete, Briatta left her room in a long black robe to join her siblings. Only Aden was downstairs as a young man circled him slowly, examining Aden's suit for any flaws before nodding in approval. His hair had been artfully shaved on the sides to mirror the rune on his temple, and the top was swept to one side. Briatta had to admit her brother cut a sharp figure.

Naius observed Aden's fitting with obvious self-satisfaction from across the room. When he saw Briatta, he turned and fiddled with the ties of one of the dress bags hanging on the wall.

"You look ready to take on a bunch of Ardorlites," Briatta drawled, smirking at Aden and intentionally using the derogatory term for Ardorists frequently used by the Ardorless. He rolled his eyes, tugging uncomfortably at the suit jacket. While Aden wore the fine clothes well, she knew he had never felt comfortable in them.

"I see you're adjusting just fine." Aden's eyes narrowed at his sister. He knew her well enough to recognize the front that it was.

Naius finally finished with the garment bag, pulling a dress and holding it behind him and over his head to avoid dragging it on the floor.

"Miss Belrose, here is your gown. Please take an assistant with you to put it on," Naius said, handing the dress to her. As with everything Naius created for them, the dress was much lighter than the gowns Briatta's peers—or ex-peers, she supposed—would be wearing to the dance. Briatta left with the dress in hand and headed upstairs without looking to see if anyone followed to help.

Ellery was on her way down, and they passed each other on the way.

"Oh, that's lovely," Ellery gushed, looking up at Briatta's gown when she paused at the sitting room doors.

"It's my favorite color." Briatta grinned.

She pulled the dress into her room, and when she glanced at the hallway behind her, the same young woman who'd done her hair was hurrying after her. Briatta closed the door firmly once the woman entered her bedroom.

As she slipped into the gown, which fell smoothly and comfortably against her body, Briatta sighed with pleasure. Although she was most comfortable in her combat black, she still loved getting dressed up and attending these parties. When she'd been younger, it had been the allure of the people, the jewels and imagining herself as a well-respected Ardorist that drew her in. As she'd grown older and stopped dancing as much, becoming more aware of the harsh realities of their world, she'd discovered a different sort of joy in keeping watch over unsuspecting young Ardorist women and knowing she could protect them from untoward behavior. Tonight, though, it was the old and familiar desire to be needed by the people of her world that weighed on her heart.

Though, it wasn't only men who were dangerous. The Night Roses had been forced to deal with women as well, so Briatta knew not to trust them, too. However, it was usually the men forcing affection where there was none and pushing the bounds of propriety.

"There you are, miss." The woman stepped back, clasping her hands together and smiling widely at the result of her work.

Briatta turned and examined herself in the floor-length mirror next to her wardrobe. The gown was crafted from shimmering lavender fabric; it had long, draping skirts over a wide petticoat and cream brocades both on the bodice and visible through the artful slits in the skirt.

It was a very proper-looking dress.

Paired with her hair, Briatta looked the part of a true Ardorist. The only thing missing was a rune on her brow. Subconsciously, she reached and touched a finger to the bare skin, and for a brief moment, wondered if there was a rune in the old dialect to describe shadows.

Maybe she would look it up later.

With a small smile of sorrowful satisfaction, Briatta spun to leave, though she hesitated at the door.

"Thank you," she told the young woman, turning her head so her chin nearly touched her shoulder.

Briatta headed downstairs, where Aden nodded as she entered the sitting room.

"Do I look good enough that people will overlook the fact that I am now one of the deprived?" Briatta asked, spinning so the skirts flared.

Aden frowned but did not reply.

Naius walked around her, scrutinizing the gown.

"Yes, this will do nicely," he said finally, though Briatta didn't think it was in response to her question.

Owena breezed through the door then, already wearing her sage-green gown. It sparkled at the bodice and at the hem, and she looked every bit the elegant, rich aunt she was.

"Oh, Bria, that looks wonderful," she commented, giving Aden an acclamatory nod.

Ellery reentered the sitting room after their aunt, wearing a velvet dress the color of an eggplant that fit her snugly and modestly. She looked regal and fair, which added to her image as the innocent youngest sibling.

"You look beautiful," Briatta told her sister, hugging her after Naius deemed himself satisfied with Ellery's dress, as well.

Ready to go, Aden grabbed their cloaks and ushered them out the door and toward the waiting carriage. As Petyr stood waiting, for a moment, Briatta saw the scene in the same way as the day the Belrose family had left for the Founders. If it had been brighter and cooler, it would have been the same. But for the purposes of the ball, Petyr had grown black roses, and they exploded from the back of the white cart, draping down to the road beneath and adding a layer of elegance to the otherwise average carriage. It had a haunting appearance, the bone-white against the ink-black flowers, but it was also starkly beautiful.

It struck Briatta how obvious it would be to anyone in the Night Roses that this was the carriage of the Belroses. There was irony in willingly traveling to the ball, to the den of vipers, in this cart. The family flaunted a clear symbol of their organization, practically declaring who they were to the Founders themselves if one only looked closely enough.

Briatta followed Ellery into the cart, Aden and Owena climbing in last and closing the door behind them. The four did not speak, for it was not a long ride to Malcalaire Manor, and there was no telling who might overhear while on the way to a public event such as this. Owena had taught them from a young age to be careful about what they spoke of at parties. The training was second nature at this point, and Briatta recognized just how well Owena had prepared them now that she faced the possibility of life with the Weilers, far from her family.

Petyr guided the horses to join the line of other carriages, and Ellery made small talk. She made a point to mention the names of several young and eligible men she might be interested in dancing with, as well as saying that she hoped to see her friends and catch up. Briatta slipped into the role of a tittering partygoer easily, agreeing with Ellery and commenting when necessary. The drivers for each house paid attention to and gossiped about everything, so if one needed to make a connection or wanted another family to know something indirectly, mentioning it now—before even entering the ball—made all the difference.

The Belroses were yet to be interested in finding a marriage partner due to their association with the Night Roses and the potential complications that might cause in a normal relationship, but they all made it a point to interact with those who *were* looking to blend in. And, because it could be fun to flirt. Besides, if any of them fell in love, they would find a way to make it work.

Their cart finally rolled to a stop at the main entrance to Malcalaire, and Petyr hopped down from his seat to open the door. This was a familiar—albeit social rather than physical—battlefield; one that had once been the delight of her childhood. She found comfort in the normalcy of it, but at the same time knew that this night would be fundamentally different. There was, of course, the matter of her public lack of Ardor, and the unknown factor of how the guests would receive her presence. Then, there was the issue of Aden and his impending bachelorhood, which was becoming an annoyingly prominent topic whenever they attended functions. Briatta took a deep breath, knowing she was about to embark on an evening of false pleasantries, sympathies, and countless inquiries from overbearing Ardorist mothers regarding whether Aden had begun his search for a wife.

Aden also appeared to realize this, for he looked as though he would rather bury himself early than walk into this party.

"Are you feeling alright?" Ellery asked cautiously as she peered up at her older brother.

Aden cleared his throat and nodded, smoothing his facial expression with what appeared to be quite a bit of effort. "I'm just tired."

Owena raised an eyebrow, her eyes sparkling. "Imply that you have other interests if it's really that bad. It worked for me."

Briatta's eyes widened, and she burst out laughing at the

unexpected insight from her aunt before fighting to collect herself and remain somewhat dignified.

"I can spread rumors if you like." Ellery smirked, catching on and hooking her arm through Aden's. The four of them made their way up the sweeping marble staircase outside of Malcalaire.

"Do not," Aden replied darkly. Owena hid her mouth with a hand, falling behind so he wouldn't see her.

The marble, which had gold veins like those of the Founders Halls and was a statement of wealth and the family's closeness to the Founders, were a striking image against the dark stone of the manor and the wrought iron gates. The groundskeepers had outdone themselves for Lord Mallon's return, planting vibrantly glowing flowering plants throughout the property, vining them up the manor's walls and leveraging their Ardor to help ripen the fruit-bearing trees. Staff were already stationed beneath those trees, ready to assist guests in picking and cleaning their own fruit should they want to.

On the walls, already lit for the evening, were the golden sconces marking a royal household. In Montclair, only Malcalaire had the honor of housing a royal family, so these were the only golden sconces in the entire city. Briatta always thought it odd that there were no others in a city the size of Montclair, even if it was considered small compared to the capital, but maybe Srila was where they all wanted to be.

At the top of the stairs, just inside the large double doors, a waiting pair of footmen took their cloaks. While the cloaks weren't necessary in the current warm evening air, they would be later as the biodome cooled. A third footman waited as they gathered inside.

"Please, if you will follow me," said the footman, leading them down the hallway—decorated to guide the unescorted—

to the ballroom, which was some ways from the main entrance.

Every sconce lining the walls was lit a dim, warm yellow with Ardor light. Between them hung brilliantly colored tapestries and paintings depicting the well-remembered deeds of past lords and ladies. The current Lord Mallon's father, the late Lord Valin Mallon, had died when he'd gone into a burning building to save children from the flames. The building had burned quietly, and the Fire and Water Ardor teams had not been called until it was too late for the Lord.

It crossed Briatta's mind then that Lord Valin Mallon was an unfortunate name, but the thought left as quickly as it came when she stared at the image of the man bursting through a flaming doorframe with a small bundle in his arms.

Beside the doors leading into the ballroom were the portraits of Lord Olrik Mallon and his wife, Lady Raynia Mallon. If Briatta had passed either of them on the street, she would not have paid them much attention, for Lord Olrik was an older man, perhaps entering his seventieth year, and appeared very much like most other older men. His face did look kind, but the artist could have fabricated it for the portrait. Lady Raynia was similarly unassuming with plain brown hair and a soft smile. The only difference between these people and others was in their clothes and titles.

The doors to the ballroom were already wide open and framed by their hosts and by large, flower-filled planters. Briatta bent to smell a rose as they passed, and then a server in a smart black suit appeared with refreshments. Ellery and Owena accepted after learning it was a variation of lemonade, and they all stopped just inside to take in the sight before them.

It seemed most of Montclair's finest were already here in their most extravagant outfits. While Lord Mallon hosted a ball at least once a year, he had been gone for a while, and the people were excited to resume posturing to gain the lord and lady's highest favor. Briatta rolled her eyes as one of the families performed a small, clearly rehearsed routine of curtsies and bows as they greeted Lord Mallon and Lady Mallon.

"People will pay us more attention than usual tonight," Aden reminded Briatta, though his lips were also curved upwards at the ridiculous display.

"Right." Briatta sighed, regretful that she would have to watch herself more than usual as she plastered a neutral smile onto her face. She must appear pleasant enough to greet others but not so happy that people might assume she was celebrating her disappointing lack of Ardor.

Aden joined the line of families waiting to greet Lord and Lady Mallon, turning in a slow circle to examine the room.

"The usual suspects," he commented, his voice low. "We don't need to be anyone tonight but the nieces and nephew of Owena Belrose. Easy."

"I'm right here," Owena said, sipping her lemonade.

"So easy," Ellery murmured with enough sarcasm to make the man in front of them look over his shoulder with barely disguised curiosity. She took a long drink from her glass; Aden reached for the beverage, sniffed it, and coughed.

"Go easy on those, Ellery," he cautioned. "Especially before dinner."

"Oh, this will be a fun night," Briatta said, a genuine smile blooming across her lips.

"*So* fun," Ellery said, snatching her cup back. She had just been allowed to partake in the drinks at soirees under Owena's supervision, and their aunt looked down at her youngest niece with bemusement. Briatta knew that her sister was no stranger to the effects of alcohol and Owena would be taking care of her, but she made a mental note to keep an eye on Ellery nonetheless.

The line moved quickly, and they were soon in front of Lord and Lady Mallon's dais. A steward waited expectantly for Aden's small, folded piece of paper, stepping back after scanning it and folding his hands behind his back.

"Mistress Owena Belrose with her attending nephew and nieces, Master Aden Belrose, Miss Briatta Belrose, and Miss Ellery Belrose," the man announced. He was tall and thin, his fingers long and bony where they clutched the paper.

As their names were spoken, the Belroses bowed and curtsied. Lord Mallon's face grew curious at the mention of their last name, and he leaned forward on his high-backed throne. It looked to be made of dark wood with intricate, runic carvings representing Ardor covering every visible surface, though they didn't appear to follow a specific order the way the Founders did, as Briatta spied two Fire Runes right next to each other.

"I extend my sympathies to you," Lord Mallon said, finding Briatta's gaze. "There is no greater shame than being unable to support our society's greatest trials. Our world is hostile, and we require all the help we can get."

Briatta looked down at the floor, her throat constricting at his pointed, targeted words. Her body went cold and then warm, the heat of humiliation burning up her neck and cheeks. She clenched her fists, her nails biting into her palms as she took a deep breath.

"Indeed," Owena said, though her tone was dry.

Not soon enough, they walked away from the room's attention, and Briatta exhaled with relief. Aden squeezed her arm with barely concealed disgust in his expression.

"Don't think I've ever wanted to punch royalty quite so bad as I did back there," he said under his breath. Briatta snorted at the brotherly defense, smiling gratefully at him.

"*Now* we can have fun." Ellery's eyes glinted mischievously as she swept away, disappearing into the crowd after briefly clasping Briatta's other hand. Briatta watched her go only long enough to determine her trajectory before pivoting to a table laden with food; it wasn't dinner, but there were enough options that she would not go hungry tonight.

Aden took up a post along the wall beside other young and eligible bachelors, leaving Briatta to wander by herself.

"Bria!" exclaimed a young woman's voice just as Briatta bit into a curried chicken sandwich. Briatta turned to see Morenna Kildenbar, a young lady of the Ardorists, approaching swiftly in her light-orange gown, which looked elegant against her smooth olive skin as the skirts swept behind her. Morenna's golden-brown hair was curled and pulled back in a way that looked both messy and graceful, and her hazel eyes shone warmly as she looked at Briatta. On her temple, the rune for Flower Ardor was still healing from her Choosing a few weeks before during the last Cycle of Silence.

"Morenna." Briatta smiled at her friend, though she was suddenly riddled with nerves. How would Morenna handle the news of her lack of Ardor? Her forehead felt glaringly bare, and Briatta resisted the urge to touch it.

The two young women had met in school, later finding companionship at the balls and parties they were required to frequent as young potential Ardorists. Both had loved the events as children but found themselves sticking to the outer edges of the dancefloor of late, though Briatta knew Morenna had started regarding the present young men more seriously than she had in the past.

"I was ever so sorry to hear about your Choosing," Morenna said, true sympathy filling her eyes. She reached out and took Briatta's hands. "Please, don't hesitate to tell me if you need anything." Then, she leaned in closer, lowering her voice. "Don't worry. I won't abandon you. It's happening more and more, you know, and Mother and Father have always found the disdain toward Ardorless distasteful, anyway. We are all people."

That was news to Briatta, but perhaps Morenna hadn't felt comfortable confiding in her before, despite Owena not having Ardor. Uncomfortably, Briatta wondered if she'd appeared to be as prejudiced to Morenna as she evidently had to Neven, and she swallowed. All the same, a sense of relief lightened her heart, and she smiled thickly.

"Thank you." It was likely the only time this evening someone would speak to her about her Choosing without condescension. Morenna was a good friend, and Briatta would never take it for granted. With a pang, Briatta realized that perhaps, despite having had a secure childhood and never knowing loss the way Briatta had, Morenna was a better person at her core.

Occasionally, especially at times like this, Briatta felt a prick of regret about the second life that she would never be able to share with Morenna. Sometimes, she dreamed about what it would be like to have a friend who was not part of everything but could still be aware of it.

"Now, how shall we occupy ourselves tonight?" Morenna asked, changing the subject and grabbing a small sandwich from the food table and popping it in her mouth.

Briatta looked around the room, finishing the last of her food and acting as though she were deep in thought. "Perhaps we shall find someone handsome to flirt with?"

It was mostly a joke; a question they'd asked each other when they were younger and had found the idea of a man and woman liking each other to be quite novel. Briatta and Morenna usually spent the night commenting on social faux pas and acting out conversations between suitors and their targets. But sometimes, at the very beginning of the night, before everyone became too deep in their drinks, the girls would try talking to some of the men to see how the others suffered. At least, that was what they told each other.

Morenna grinned devilishly. "Now that does sound fun. Shall we make it a game? Whoever can make the man blush first?"

"You have yourself a bet," Briatta replied as they set off towards the wall of bachelors.

CHAPTER 12

"Oh dear, and the chicken did...what exactly?" Morenna asked, the picture of polite confusion.

"Well, you see, it had gotten into the basement and knocked over the jars of plant slime—that's another long story—and then it tried to fly away and splattered the nasty stuff everywhere." The man paused to laugh, lifting his cup to his mouth as he watched Morenna and Briatta for their reactions. Briatta observed, keeping her face plastered with mild amusement; the man's chuckle, as well timed as everything else he did, sounded as expensive as the clothes that he wore appeared to be.

He was either immune to their lack of interest in his stories, or he enjoyed having someone listen to him talk so much that he didn't care. Briatta was doing her best to pay attention to this never-ending tale about a chicken, but it was the third in a series of similarly unfortunate events that seemed to plague this family.

"I could tell you the story about the plant slime, too, if you'd like," the young man continued, oblivious to the epidemic of boredom he was causing.

Morenna looked at Briatta and widened her eyes slightly, a silent plea for an exit plan. Briatta smiled at her friend and scanned the throng of people for Ellery—perhaps Briatta could use her sister as an excuse to leave. She was still searching for the telltale purple dress when someone cleared their throat behind her. Briatta sent a quick apologetic look in Morenna's direction before turning to see who had joined them.

A tall man wearing a dark-blue suit waited patiently with his hands behind his back; he had black hair cut short and slicked to the side, and dark, slanted eyes that crinkled as he smiled at Briatta. On his temple was the rune for Air Ardor, and he gave a short bow at the waist as he nodded sharply.

"Might I have the honor of a dance?" he asked, lifting his eyes to Briatta from under his lashes.

Briatta was slightly taken aback, as no one had asked her to dance at a ball for a long time. Perhaps she and Morenna had gained a reputation for being unreceptive in marital pursuits, even though they participated in the flirtations and chatter.

"Of course," she managed, her heart skipping a beat as the man's lips quirked up. He straightened, and she blinked to gather herself for the coming waltz. "You are...?"

"Simeon," the man said, holding out his hand.

"Very well, Simeon. I am Briatta." She took his hand, and he started towards the dance floor. Briatta cast one last glance over her shoulder and saw Morenna's openly curious face watching them leave, the chicken man trying to regain her interest by embarking upon yet another tale.

"Sorry," Briatta mouthed to her friend, but Morenna merely looked delighted by the turn of events, giving a little shooing motion with her hands.

"A pleasure, Miss Belrose," Simeon said as she turned back to him. Briatta must have appeared surprised at the mention of her surname, and the use of the prefix given she hadn't introduced herself that way, because he added, "I overheard someone mention your family name when you arrived."

"When I arrived?" Briatta echoed, regarding her new dance partner with more calculation. It was curious that he had noted her arrival, though she supposed that it wasn't completely out of the ordinary at these events. That meant, however, he might be the sort of person she should worry about. "Can I ask where you are coming from tonight, Mr. Simeon?" Even as she said his name, awkwardly adding a title because he had, she realized she had no idea whether it was his first or last name. "I do not believe we have met before."

"We would not have," Simeon affirmed. "I am visiting from Srila for the current cycle."

They arrived at the dance floor, and the musicians began a new song. Simeon placed his hand on Briatta's waist and took her right hand in his left, pulling her smoothly into the dance as the music picked up cheerfully. She was pleasantly surprised at how accomplished a dancer he seemed to be from the first few steps.

"Are you here on business or pleasure?" Briatta asked as they moved, already thinking it was likely the former. People scarcely moved between biodomes. Simeon spun her away and tugged her back into him, his hand gentle but firm on the small of her back. His strength was immediately evident in the easy way he swung her. If Simeon meant her harm, it would be a brutal fight.

Owena had taught Briatta and Ellery never to be so naïve as to believe they were physically stronger than a man, even one who appeared weaker. Instead, they needed to be wiser. Quicker.

"Business," Simeon answered predictably, turning her and bringing them toward the front of the room.

"And what do you do?" Briatta probed.

Simeon smiled down at her. She was surprised her stomach fluttered a little at the curl of his lips, which revealed straight white teeth, though she was also unnerved that she found it difficult to read him, as she had become adept at perceiving her peers. She tilted her head as she watched Simeon for any signs that hinted at his thoughts.

"It is not important," Simeon replied, piquing Briatta's interest further.

"And what is important, then?" Briatta asked.

Simeon's smile widened as he released his hold on her waist and spun her again. When he drew her back to his chest, he held her a little closer than he had before, his fingers spreading over her back. A tingle traveled down her spine, and Briatta fought the instinctual urge to stiffen and pull away as she became acutely aware of how small she felt in this man's arms.

"This dance," Simeon replied. Then he dipped his chin so his mouth was by her ear and said in a softer voice, "You are quite light on your feet."

"I had dancing lessons," Briatta answered breathlessly. Though she kept her tone casual, she felt increasingly guarded. For the first time in a very long time, her foolish body had abandoned its senses. Just because a man could dance and was strong did not mean he was safe or...whatever else her heart might think it wanted.

"Of course," Simeon murmured. Abruptly, he pulled his head back, looking down at her while gently walking them backward on the dance floor. "This may be none of my business, but I heard your Choosing did not go how you wished."

Briatta couldn't stop herself from stiffening that time, and he must have felt the change because he loosened his hold on her.

"You are right." All possible desire for this stranger abandoned her the moment he brought up her Choosing. "It *is* none of your business."

Simeon did not answer. Instead, he twirled Briatta to the music alongside other dance partners. When he spun her back to him, he appeared more melancholic—the first noticeable change in his expression besides those small smiles that might reveal an ounce of what he felt.

"Forgive me for saying so then, but I hope you will consider the Ackmanlee." He dipped her. "I will leave it at that."

Briatta looked up at him, her brows furrowing as he lifted her. Multiple warning bells clanged in her head. Why would a stranger suggest that she join the Ackmanlee? To most of society, she had cultivated the image of a soft, young, rich girl. The public shouldn't see why she would be an asset to the Weilers.

"And why would I do that?"

"It's not important." Simeon flashed a teasing smile. Briatta realized her visceral reaction to his request might have given away more than she wanted, so she forced herself to relax.

"And what *is* important?" Briatta plastered a soft smile onto her lips as she repeated her earlier question, but a small stone of anxiety formed in the pit of her belly. Who was this man?

"You're quite astute." Simeon swept her away again. "You tell me."

Briatta was silent as she reconsidered everything he'd said, filing through each statement, and searching for clues. While travel was possible between cities and their biodomes, each location was entirely self-sufficient, since transportation of goods took tremendous effort and many people. If someone were to journey for business, it was more likely to do with politics or a crime terrible enough to warrant outside assistance.

"You are a king's man," Briatta said finally. It was a broad statement, as technically, everyone at the ball could be called a king's man or woman, but it could also refer to someone who worked closely with the crown.

Simeon raised an eyebrow, though he did not comment.

"And you are here for Lord Mallon's announcement of the Ackmanlee," Briatta continued slowly. "You will have some part in that."

The song slowed and ended, and Simeon stepped away from Briatta and bowed once. The sudden removal of his hand from her back felt wrong; she felt cold and empty without its presence, and Briatta shivered. Again, her body had taken leave of every survival instinct she had carefully cultivated over the years. Simeon grinned knowingly when he straightened and folded his hands behind his back.

"A pleasure, Miss Belrose." Just like that, he was gone, disappearing through the people.

Briatta was at a loss for words, watching him walk away for just a heartbeat before shaking her head and clenching her hands. She turned to find either Ellery or Morenna to distract herself. The latter was still trapped in discussion with the chicken man, so Briatta walked the room's perimeter to see if she could spot Ellery. Aden stood against the wall, trapped in conversation with two older mothers, and she nodded to acknowledge him as she passed by. Normally, she would have laughed, but Simeon had flattened her mood.

"Briatta spotted Ellery and Owena standing in the corner of the room with a few other women, appearing consumed by their conversation. Briatta sighed and approached the beverage table, reaching for a glass of brambleberry lemonade, when someone tapped her left shoulder. Briatta turned, sipping her drink, then froze.

It was Neven, dressed in a slate-grey suit and smiling

nervously down at her. He had trimmed his hair and brushed it back. It was the first time Briatta had seen Neven dressed so finely, and her heart flipped a little in her chest. Founders, what was wrong with her? Seeing him in this place was such a shock to her system that she beamed, almost completely forgetting any of the strangeness she'd felt about their disagreement and lying to him about her Choosing.

"Neven, you look amazing!" Then, she wilted a little, unsure of how he'd respond.

"You're radiant yourself," he answered, bowing. "I have been watching for you all evening."

"I wasn't certain you'd attend," Briatta admitted, her chest turning uncomfortably at the thought that Neven had eyes on her but hadn't approached her until this moment. "But I am so glad you are here."

Neven moved around Briatta to the table, asking for a whiskey with one ice cube.

The server returned quickly with the glass, and Neven took it and thanked them.

Briatta watched her friend with wonder; from the little she'd seen, he handled his first event with the grace of a man who'd been attending these events his entire life. Guilt crept back into her chest. For a few blissful moments, she'd completely forgotten that her closest friend had no idea of the truth of the past week.

She wanted so badly to tell him everything, to be a part of his journey in mastering his Light Ardor and he a part in hers with her...darkness, or whatever formal name it had.

What harm could come from it? Neven had practically been a member of the family since he was nine years old. The likelihood he would have an ulterior motive or betray the Belroses was simply inconceivable. Owena had always been overly cautious. While she had only just started realizing, now more than ever, how well Owena's habits had protected her over the years, this was *Neven*.

Briatta took another drink from her fruity beverage, watching the dancers flow gracefully through the motions as Neven stood at her side like he always had, the worlds of their childhood colliding. She came to a decision. She loved Neven deeply, and while she was still confused as to whether the love was that of a friend or more, she didn't want to feel strange around him any longer.

"Neven, come with me," Briatta said, grabbing his hand and pulling him through the crowd. They left the ballroom and hurried down the hallway, past the portraits and back towards the entrance.

"Where are we going?" Neven asked, smiling widely. His blue eyes twinkled in the shadows of the Ardor lights on the walls.

"Somewhere private," Briatta answered.

Neven made a choking sound behind her, and Briatta glanced over her shoulder.

"Not for that," she scolded, and Neven's cheeks flushed. Briatta faced forward and pretended not to notice, though she smiled to herself despite everything.

When they arrived at a doorway on the left, she cracked it open, peering inside to a small, empty room.

"Can you light it up?" Briatta asked Neven.

He stepped into the room, a look of concentration settling on his features as he raised his hands. An Ardor light appeared in each palm. He lifted his arms to send them floating toward the ceiling to reveal they were in a small sitting room with a few chairs and a couple bookshelves crammed with leather-bound tomes. It was, blessedly and thank the Founders, empty and appeared infrequently used, based on the layer of dust on the chairs.

"So, why are we here?" Neven asked curiously after he pulled the door closed behind them.

"I need to show you something. And tell you something. I can't stand it anymore," Briatta said, holding up her hands.

Briatta hadn't tried using her Ardor since that day at the Founders. She had wanted to honor her promise to Owena to never use it where it might be discovered, and her family had been too busy to help her begin training. So it was now, in this odd little room in Malcalaire, that Briatta finally used her Ardor again.

It was reckless. There were so many people nearby. Anyone could walk in at any second.

It exhilarated her.

Shadows bubbled from her palms and spilled onto the ground, and a sense of intense relief filled her as something within her relaxed, both from using her Ardor and from finally sharing this part of herself with Neven.

Neven's eyes were wide with shock as he watched Briatta.

"What is this, Bria?"

Briatta cut the contact with her Ardor and lowered her hands. "It's my Ardor."

"You said—you said you didn't manifest," Neven said slowly. His face had drained of color, and she could see his hands were fists at his side while trying to process what she'd just shown him.

"I lied, and I'm sorry," Briatta rushed to say. "It's a long story. Can I tell you everything now?"

Neven hesitated, then nodded, and Briatta launched into the tale, starting from the morning of her Choosing ceremony. She told Neven all the details that she'd seen, including the strange man, and continued until the part where her Ardor had flooded the circle of the Founders, and Owena had made all the

Belrose children swear never to discuss this phenomenon with anyone, not even Neven.

"I wanted to tell you," Briatta said as she finished. "It felt so wrong not to tell you."

"If Owena thought it wasn't safe to tell anyone, why are you telling me now?" Neven demanded. Briatta was surprised to hear a note of anger in his voice. "Owena is right. You must be extremely careful, Bria. This could get you killed."

"Killed?" Briatta repeated, stunned by the vehemence in his voice.

"Yes," Neven said. "People fear what they don't understand, and...this is new."

He paced, running his hands through his hair.

"We are going to have to be extremely careful." Neven shook his head.

Briatta swallowed nervously, her mouth having gone dry as the implications of what Neven was saying began to sink in.

"I can never tell anyone else," she whispered.

"Exactly. And we're going to have to train you in secret so that you can control it," Neven said. He moved to one of the chairs and plopped into it, ignoring the small cloud of dust that puffed up around him.

When he looked back at Briatta, she smiled sheepishly.

"Have you trained at all?" Neven asked.

"No, there's been...too much happening," Briatta said, her voice solemn.

Neven nodded. "I understand. We'll have to start as soon as possible."

He was serious, rubbing his chin in thought as he leaned forward. Briatta wanted desperately to lighten the mood in the room again.

"You know what the great thing is, Neven?" she asked, brushing off the other chair before taking a seat on its edge.

"What?" Neven was distant.

"You are light, and I am dark; we are complementary. Maybe we were always meant to be friends," Briatta said, leaning forward slightly.

A slow smile spread across Neven's face. "The light to your dark."

Briatta grew quiet then, the levity fading as she realized she and Neven were alone in a private room during a ball, sitting close to each other.

"We should return to the dance before anyone notices that we've been gone for too long," she said, standing and backing away.

"Right." Neven stood and opened the door, checking the hallway to ensure it was empty before pulling Briatta out of the room. Quickly, he twisted his hand to extinguish his Ardor lights. They winked out of existence, and the pair hurried to return to the dance. Before entering, Neven looked back at Briatta.

"You know, I should have known that you were lying," he told her, a strange look on his face. He appeared perplexed—perhaps at having ever believed she didn't have Ardor. "I've known you for years."

"Maybe a part of you did," Briatta replied, taking his elbow as they stepped through the doors to the party, which was still in full swing. "Have you seen everyone else yet?"

Neven shook his head. "No, you were the first Belrose sibling that I found." He nudged her teasingly, a dimple appearing on his cheek.

"Let's walk the perimeter, then."

Neven nodded and led the way, allowing Briatta to pay attention to their surroundings instead of where they were walking. They passed the table of finger foods, which was notably emptier than earlier. Briatta hoped tonight was one of the nights Preida had set aside some snacks in the kitchen for when they returned.

The room was as crowded as it had been all evening, and the noise level increased in conjunction with the amount of drink that was served. Owena typically liked to leave around this time, though with the Ackmanlee being announced, Briatta was unsure what they would do. Even if they didn't hear it at the ball, it would be in the papers the next day. Regardless, if they left now, the Belroses' early exit wouldn't be unusual, as she had established this reputation long before her nieces and nephew had come to live with her.

They made their way past the now-empty wall where the men often gathered in the beginning, strolled by the drink table, and finally, past the wall of older women watching their younger charges dance and drink and mingle.

"Bria," Morenna said as they passed, having joined her mother. "I've been looking for you!"

"Sorry, Morenna," Briatta pulled Neven to a stop, smiled, and looked between her two friends. Friends from both halves of her life. "Have you met Neven?"

Morenna looked up at Neven, seeming to just realize Briatta had a man with her. She smiled shyly. "No, I don't believe I've had the pleasure."

Briatta's eyebrows lifted as Neven removed his arm from hers and bowed shallowly to Morenna.

"The honor is mine," Neven said smoothly, and a pretty, pink flush rose in Morenna's cheeks.

Founders, this evening was steadily growing more bizarre.

Aden materialized, glancing from Neven to Morenna with similar confusion but masking it well. Gathering himself, he looked beyond them to his sister. "Bria, Owena will be ready to go as soon as the Ackmanlee is announced."

He pretended to notice Neven then, and a look of delight

overwhelmed whatever other emotions Aden had been feeling. "Ah, Neven! I'm so glad that you're here. Maybe I will stay later after all and show you around, introduce you to some people."

Aden pulled Neven away as he spoke, his hand settling on the younger man's shoulder as Morenna watched them leave wistfully.

"Your family is friends with Neven?" she asked curiously.

"Ah...yes," Briatta said, trying to think of an explanation. It was rare that families of Ardorists and Ardorless to mix and socialize before a Choosing elevated an Ardorless into the same status as the Ardorists. Though, because Owena was Ardorless, it could be more understandable. Given Aden's familiarity with Neven, Morenna was rightfully curious that Briatta had never mentioned him before, and Briatta was at a loss for words. Morenna's reassurance to Briatta also meant she might not think anything of it, but Briatta wanted to make sure she got it right. "It's a...um, long story. I can tell you next time I see you?"

"Alright." Morenna sighed, giving Briatta an odd look. It disappeared as quickly as it had appeared, and she leaned in to hug her friend. Sometimes, Briatta thought Morenna was just as good at playing games and getting information as Briatta was.

It was just a different game.

CHAPTER 13

Briatta watched Aden and Neven for a long stretch of stillness once Morenna had pushed her way back through the crowd and reached Lady Kildenbar. Her brother and her friend arrived at the group of men with whom Aden usually passed the time at these functions when he wasn't being cornered by mothers; they seemed to make introductions as Neven politely bowed his head.

With each greeting, Neven appeared more cordially removed, as though he paid attention only to please Aden. This would create appeal for the others, who would wonder about this quiet and distant man, and Briatta wasn't entirely sure that it was accidental. Neven seemed completely at ease despite never before having been to a ball. At least not that Briatta was aware of.

He would fit in well.

Perhaps their training with the Night Roses had prepared him better than she'd realized.

Or maybe there was another explanation for his comfort;

Briatta only ever saw him when working and on the occasions he'd visited the Belrose Estate.

Briatta considered what she knew about how Neven spent his free time as he nodded courteously to another man and said something that must have been a question, because the other man cocked his head and lifted his gaze to the ceiling as if in thought.

When they were younger, their time had been spent either training or finishing assignments from their respective schools, with Briatta often helping him when he didn't know something. She knew of his adventures wandering through Montclair and the people he'd observed through his stories as they grew.

In more recent years, however, Briatta couldn't recall a time when Neven had shared details about what he did when they were apart. What had changed? Did he no longer trust her the same way that he used to? Did nothing he do seem interesting enough to share? Or was he hiding something?

Briatta stopped momentarily and shook her head, nearly laughing out loud at the direction of her thoughts. Neven was one of her most trusted friends. Maybe the reason she wasn't aware of what he did in his downtime was completely innocent, like perhaps he'd found a girl he liked and was courting her. That would certainly be an awkward enough topic. Briatta definitely wasn't privy to everything Neven thought and felt—especially regarding potential romantic partners—just as she wouldn't tell him how dancing with Simeon had affected her tonight.

Founders, Briatta had never had much interest in men aside from the passing thought that Neven would make a good life partner should their friendship ever head in that direction. She fought the urge to search the ballroom for Simeon again and brushed her hands on the front of her gown with determination.

Finally tearing her gaze from Neven and Aden, Briatta made her way towards the rest of her family near the exit. Just as she reached the entrance drink table, the musicians stopped playing, and the room fell as silent as it could when filled with people well into their cups.

Briatta slowed, her head swiveling at the sound of metal ringing against a glass from the front of the ballroom. On the dais where Lord and Lady Mallon still sat pompously, a young herald was doing his best to gain everyone's drunken attention, holding the clear goblet high in front of him as he banged it relentlessly with a spoon.

When it had quieted enough, he cleared his throat. "Welcome, honored citizens of Montclair. Your presence tonight in celebration of Lady Raya Mallon's marriage is greatly appreciated, and we are most thankful. Now, here are a few words from the host. Lord Olrik Mallon, if you please."

The herald stepped back, slipping behind the curtains on the side of the platform and disappearing.

Lord Mallon pushed to his feet with what appeared to be a great deal of effort. He was neither a young man nor a strong one; his great belly protruded, and it was a surprise that the buttons holding his jacket didn't burst, despite it appearing to fit well. His thinning, plain brown hair had become unkempt throughout the night, and beads of sweat glistened on his brow that Briatta could see even from her position nearly all the way across the room.

"It is nearing the time of night when some of you will take your leave," Lord Mallon said, approaching the front of the dais and gesturing at the crowd, which had finally stilled. The goblet in his hand sloshed dark-red wine over the side with the jerky movement. Lord Mallon pulled the cup back to him, glancing down at the liquid on the ground with an irritated frown before clearing his throat and looking at his guests.

"There are a few announcements I must make before you go," the Lord continued. Briatta could have sworn he looked pointedly at Owena, who was respectfully watching from the opposite side of the ballroom, though that might have been paranoia from her interaction with Simeon. "Firstly, I must bring up why we are all here tonight. My recent journey to Srila has resulted in my eldest daughter, Lady Raya Mallon, making a wonderful match and marrying her new husband, Duke Ezio Valenka."

Clapping and cheering appropriate for the Ardorists of society—subdued and restrained—filled the room, and Briatta raised her hands to join in the soft applause.

"Thank you, thank you," Lord Mallon beamed, waving his chalice-free hand dismissively. Though he seemed to act as if it weren't a big deal, the marriage of a young lady to a Srilan duke would lift the Mallons' social standing even further— despite already being at the top in Montclair. He waited for the adulations to die down as he sipped his wine, then turned his beady eyes back to the crowd before him.

"There is one other matter of business that I am obligated to bring to your attention. This year's Ackmanlee."

The room went deathly still. The Ackmanlee did not affect most of the guests, but some surely had family to whom they would take this information. If what Morenna said was true, and the Kildenbars didn't agree with the discrimination, perhaps there were other minds changing. Maybe a family wouldn't discard their own the way they might have once.

Her own assuredly wouldn't. But, that was different. Wasn't it?

Briatta straightened, her gown suddenly feeling tight and

hot, and her mouth drying with anticipation. For some reason, her eyes flitted around the room in search of Simeon. She silently cursed herself for turning in that direction and snatched another brambleberry lemonade from the table behind her, squaring her shoulders to the dais and Lord Mallon as she downed the contents.

"Nasty business, and it won't apply to most of you, though it will be amusing to observe, to be sure. Applications will open starting tomorrow morning," Lord Mallon said. "They may be dropped off at your local Weiler station. While it is always an opportunity for someone to accomplish greatness where they might not otherwise, this year's Ackmanlee is looking for a particular sort of young man or woman. I am told that a special position in the Weilers will be available to the winner, should they prove themselves worthy. I will leave you with this warning: It will not be easy, and it will not go to just anyone."

Briatta could have heard a pin drop in the silence of the room. Then, the excited whispers began as people turned to each other, their curiosity aroused by the mysterious words and the implication that this year's Ackmanlee would be different from the previous.

A rope of nausea turned in her belly, and Briatta placed a hand on her stomach, immediately regretting the drink she'd just consumed.

Of all the years Briatta could have turned twenty-one, it had to have been this one—the one where the Ackmanlee sounded far more selective and far more complicated than usual. Though Briatta was physically skilled and capable, she had always been riddled by anxiety with tests; even those administered by the Night Roses would plague her with the concerns of failure right until the moment she was on the mat or breaking into the testing house.

Still, Briatta couldn't help the thrill that traveled down her spine as she finally turned and closed the distance to her aunt and sister. This was precisely the sort of thing she'd been raised for—if only she could succeed against the mental blocks.

"Wonderful," Owena said, realizing that she now had both Ellery and Briatta with her. "Where did Aden go?"

"He's introducing Neven to some of his friends," Briatta supplied. "He said he'll come home later."

Owena nodded and walked with purpose through the halls and outside after retrieving their cloaks, where Petyr was already waiting with their cart. The pair of horses stood placidly, swishing their tails against the few bugs that had been permitted to exist within the biodome for their necessary contribution—the animal conservation department based in Srila only allowed the most essential life to be preserved in the biodomes.

As if summoned by her thoughts of bugs, a flurry of small pink flutterflies, glowing in the bionight, swarmed the great flowering bush behind the cart by the circular landscaped section comprising the center of Malcalaire's driveway.

Briatta watched the vibrant little insects for a heartbeat before following her aunt and sister into the carriage. It lurched forward as soon as she closed the door behind her, and once again, Briatta wished she hadn't had that last drink as her stomach turned with the motion.

Owena eyed Briatta curiously with a strange expression, though she didn't speak until they cleared most of the commotion and were on a quieter street. One with fewer eyes and ears, though Briatta knew her aunt would still refrain from talking about anything confidential. Owena just lived her life that way.

"You haven't said anything about the Ackmanlee," Owena finally said, folding her hands in her lap.

Briatta shifted awkwardly under her aunt's piercing gaze, turning to look out the window and watch the glowing plant life instead.

"It sounds...intriguing," she muttered without looking at Owena.

"Intriguing? I thought the announcement was rather cryptic and foreboding." Ellery shivered in her seat next to Briatta.

"I'm inclined to agree with Ellery," Owena said, though her tone was emotionless.

Briatta shrugged, lifting her gaze to the biodome that flashed each time a star-shaped Ardor light fell to the edge and exploded. The light show honoring Lord Mallon's ball was mesmerizing.

"I thought it seemed exciting." Briatta faced her aunt, tearing her gaze from the window.

Owena's face creased with disapproval, but she said nothing.

"Exciting? You've *always* hated tests." Ellery frowned.

Unexpected emotion surged within Briatta. She was both angry that she even had to consider the Ackmanlee as an option at all and frustrated that support from her family was now unforthcoming despite the competition originally being their suggestion.

"Well, what choice do I have?" Briatta snapped, gripping the skirt of her gown. "I am disgraced if I do not, useless as the newest member of the Ardorless. You heard Lord Mallon."

Owena's eyes flashed, and her lips thinned. Briatta realized too late that what she'd said also applied to Owena, so she drew back in her seat, her blood chilling with shame. Ellery bit her lip and looked between them, her brow furrowing with concern.

"You think the Ardorless are useless?" Owena asked, her voice dangerously low.

A flicker of uncertainty flared in Briatta's chest, but she steeled herself and barreled on. The alcohol wasn't doing her any favors. "We are a burden on those who have the Ardor that keeps us alive," she retorted. "I might as well be dead weight."

Owena's jaw clenched, her knuckles white as she gripped the edge of her bench. "I hope you do not mean that."

"I do." Briatta lifted her chin. Founders, what was she doing? Even as she recognized the cruelty of her words, she couldn't stop. Everything flooded from her as though some emotional dam had violently burst within her.

A long silence passed in the carriage, Ellery glancing nervously between them.

"Bria, are you certain?" Ellery inquired timidly, breaking the tension.

Briatta swallowed. "All we hear about in school and everywhere we go is how difficult it is to sustain life with the growing amount of Ardorless in every city. I don't *need* to believe it because everyone else already does. I am *nothing* without being able to declare my Ardor." Her voice broke with the last sentence, and she was breathing hard.

Ellery's face turned sorrowful, and Briatta immediately felt terrible. She should have kept these feelings to herself; Briatta was setting a horrible example for her younger sister and how Ellery should feel about herself when it came time for her own Choosing.

"It is not *bad* to be a member of the Ardorless," Owena said, her words clipped. "I am shocked and immensely disappointed that you think so lowly of us. I thought I had raised you better."

Briatta flinched, the earlier indignity deepening into something endless and black as she folded her arms over her chest, feeling like it was about to cave in.

She knew the right thing to say would be an apology, but it was difficult to force one out because, at the end of the bioday, she didn't think she could mean it. Owena would be able to tell if she were insincere, and the punishment would be infinitely worse than merely keeping her silence.

"Alright then. Here is what's going to happen. You will get a job tomorrow," Owena bit the words out. "I do not care what you do. But you are going to do something other than wallow like a spoiled rich girl, which you apparently are. I have worked long and hard to give you the life that I have, but it is clear to me now that you have no appreciation for it. You will work and pay rent to stay in my house until the Ackmanlee. At which point your fate will be your own."

The cart rolled to a halt in front of their house. Briatta's head spun, both from the alcohol and the stinging rebuke. Without another word, the Belrose matriarch exited the cart and walked up the house's front steps.

Briatta fought to keep calm. She was enraged and upset, and her breaths came quick and hot. She gripped the edge of her seat as if she would fall out of the cart without it, glaring after Owena and trying to form a single coherent thought as her aunt disappeared into the house.

"Bria," Ellery said, her brow creased with uncertainty as she placed a hand on Briatta's free one.

Briatta closed her mouth and took deep breaths through her nose until some of her anger dissipated, though it would be a long time before she would come to terms with their exchange.

"El," she managed.

"I'm sure that Owena didn't mean that." Ellery's voice was

soft, though she avoided Briatta's eyes. "Maybe you can speak with her in the morning when you've slept the drinks away. You can apologize, and it will be alright."

Briatta forced a nod, but she didn't feel certain. Owena rarely lost her temper with them as children and certainly never as adults. She was a level-headed woman who preferred a quiet conversation or even physical combat to resolve a disagreement, which was why Briatta was experiencing the maelstrom of emotion within her chest.

For the first time, Briatta wondered if Owena had given up more than she'd shared in order to give them the life that they had.

Ellery wrapped her fingers fully around Briatta's hand, and Briatta roused herself enough to follow her younger sister out of the cart and into their home. Owena was nowhere to be seen, but the dim glow of light was visible beneath her bedroom door.

"Goodnight, Bria." Ellery squeezed her sister's hand before letting go, quietly closing her door behind her. Briatta's hand felt cold and empty without her sister's in it, and she flexed her fingers as she faced her room.

Something about going to bed felt wrong, as if the normalcy of Briatta's life had been wiped away in a single instant. It wasn't just that Owena had ordered her to do something other than school or work for the Night Roses for the first time in her life; it was...everything. It was her Ardor, her position in society, and her desire to do anything that would make a difference so she wouldn't be viewed as a burden by her fellow Elfeans. Briatta honestly had no idea how they lived with themselves every day, knowing so many of their peers had to put in extra effort to keep them alive.

She didn't know how she would live with herself.

And she certainly didn't understand how Owena didn't feel

that way, too. Or...maybe she did, and it was a closely guarded part of her heart that Briatta had accidentally pierced tonight.

Briatta resolved to go back downstairs and drink some water before she retired for the night. If nothing else, it might help her clear her head and stave off the headache that she could already feel blossoming at the front of her skull.

CHAPTER 14
GALEN

It had been weeks since Galen had left the Founders and quit Kalaiden. He'd spent most of it searching for food and water for himself and his horse, which had become progressively more difficult. For a long time, he'd stopped in Verowen —a city between Montclair and his destination—and worked odd jobs to increase his stores before returning to the road to the eastern edge of Belrune.

Galen had ridden as far east as possible to create more distance from anyone who might recognize him and identify him as some traitor—or whatever the members of Kalaiden were considered when they left. He knew that others didn't have the freedom to leave as easily as he had. If he'd ben anyone else...Lycus wouldn't have let him leave that bar.

Now, Galen was seated at yet another bar in a tiny little town called Isa, sipping on the worst beer he could find and resting his elbows on the counter. He'd only just arrived, and thankfully, the journey there—aside from his extended visit to Verowen—had been entirely uneventful. Boring, even. In some ways, this unsettled Galen. In his soul, he felt it should have been much harder to leave Kalaiden behind. He knew a lot of information about them; shouldn't someone have come after him to silence him?

But no. That wasn't the way Maverik operated with those who were his friends, and Galen knew it despite his oldest friend having once announced to all of Kalaiden that it would be death to leave. It was a necessary threat for anyone Maverik didn't personally know; the community of Kalaiden members in Belrune was growing and it was becoming too vulnerable to allow people to leave the organization. Someone would reveal something eventually, regardless of intention.

Maverik didn't kill the ones who deserted, not really. He just tucked them away where they wouldn't be able to divulge sensitive information. They'd be safe until things improved, and if things didn't, the defectors were probably better off hidden anyway.

Which was why Galen felt it had been far too easy getting to Isa. Travel between biodomes wasn't specifically restricted, but because it was usually Weilers and families traveling for Choosing ceremonies, Galen should have stuck out like a sore thumb.

But no one had challenged him.

Having made it to his destination without incident, Galen wasn't going to push his luck and question it, but it did put him on edge when not a single Weiler had behaved as if they were suspicious of him. His cautious side warned perhaps they all knew who he was, and they were allowing him to pass, thinking that he would lead them to information regarding Kalaiden. His logical side dismissed the theory, knowing it would be difficult for every Weiler to memorize faces. After all, there were far more Kalaiden members than any of them realized.

Until this point, Galen had always used false names, especially when working for Maverik. Since arriving in Isa, he had not given anyone a name at all, even at this bar. He was tempted to simply use his own name. It had been a long time since he was able to just be himself.

Perhaps it would be healing.

Maybe he could even get a normal job. Isa seemed quaint enough that he could possibly convince someone to take him on as an apprentice in a trade. Galen really had only a few skills, all of which were more suited to working for a rebellion than life as a civilian in a town like this. He was adept at hand-to-hand combat, spying, pretending to be anyone but himself, and manual labor. The finer things in life were not where Galen excelled, but maybe it was time to change that. He took another swig of his shit beer.

"Need another, friend?" the bartender asked in his deep, gravelly voice. He was a large man with a big black beard, a bald head, and a belly that spoke to how often he indulged in his own stores.

Galen pushed his empty glass across the counter and nodded. The barkeep filled it, tilting it and pouring the amber liquid down the side of the cup to prevent too much foam. Then, while Galen watched curiously, the man filled a second tankard and pulled up a stool across from Galen. There were only a few other people in the bar at this time of day, and they were all still busy with the food or drink in front of them.

"Mind if I join you?" the man asked, already seated. Galen shrugged. "We don't get many new folks in. I know just about everyone under the dome around here. What brings you to Isa, son?"

Before he answered, Galen lifted his fresh beer to his lips and took a large drink. It was so satisfyingly terrible. "Trying to start a fresh life, I suppose."

"Something wrong with the old one?" The big man chuckled, the sound resonating deeply in his chest.

Galen smiled slowly into his beer. "You could say that."

"Well, you don't have to tell me why. Just don't bring anything bad here, you got that? There are good people in Isa." The bartender took a sip of his beer. "The name's Brat."

Lifting an eyebrow, Galen looked up. "Like the sausages?"

Brat laughed heartily this time, as though it were the best joke he'd heard in years. A little uncomfortable with attracting attention, Galen shifted in his seat and glanced around.

"Sure, kid. Like the sausages."

"I'm Galen," he said without thinking. The second his name passed from his lips, an immense sense of relief flooded him. It was easier without worrying too much about who he would be in Isa. He was used to adopting an entirely new persona, even going so far as to change how he walked and held his shoulders so he would be more challenging to recognize. Not anymore.

"Galen," Brat said, setting his beer on the counter and absently reaching for a rag to wipe the surface between them. It seemed habitual. "That's a solid name. Knew a young lad by it, once."

"Did you?" Galen asked politely, but he wasn't really interested.

"Sure as shit. Young couple came here with their kid. Kept to themselves, they did. Only ever got the boy's name. Or, maybe it was Kalen..." Brat trailed off.

"Huh." Galen's fresh beer was almost halfway gone.

Brat seemed lost in thought about the young family and the child who might have shared a name with Galen, so Galen took the opportunity to polish off the drink and take the rag, which had been sitting forgotten to the side when Brat had started the story. He wiped the counter where he sat and stood.

"I'd better be off," Galen said. "Might be back later."

Brat grinned. "I'll count on it."

Leaving the tavern and stepping into the bright light of the midday Polar Sun was somewhat of a shock to Galen's senses. Blinking to adjust his eyes, he shoved his hands into his coat pockets and gave himself a tour of Isa. While small, it was fairly spread out, and he was already feeling more at home than he ever had on the western side of Belrune. For the first time in a long time, he walked straight and relaxed, with his own swinging gait, taking deep and untroubled breaths.

The roads in Isa were all dirt, and there were not as many carriages here. There were only horses and good, honest folk. Each house that he passed seemed more different from the last. There was a house with a yard filled with Ardor lights artistically laid throughout the plants. Then there was a home artfully overrun with flowers, done in such a way that it looked like a cottage from a fairytale where a little old lady would offer cookies to an unsuspecting child—Galen's mother had told him such a story once.

One of the most interesting things about Isa was how close it was to the edge of Belrune; Galen could see the drop-off from the easternmost side of town. The drop-off was, until now, something he'd only heard of in passing. Belrune, which was both the kingdom and the name of the land it sat upon, was a large area of land that stood higher than the rest of Carceron, its edges falling away sharply. The bottom could not be seen, as it grew darker the further one tried to look. Galen had yet to see that part for himself, but he planned to make his way there at some point. He imagined Belrune as a flat piece of land on long, spindly legs, standing on Carceron like a table.

The other places he might have seen the drop-off were by

Seradan and the Founders, but they were far enough from the precipice that it was more difficult to get there than here in Isa.

When Galen passed a house with a blazing fire—though he could only see the smoke rising over the back—he heard the clanging of a hammer against metal, and he paused. It could have been anyone hammering nails, but the scent of hot metal was in the air, and Galen couldn't help himself. Even as a very young boy, if there was a chance to see a blacksmith working, Galen had wanted to watch. Something about the craft had always fascinated him, holding his attention like nothing else did. From the road, however, Galen could not get a good view into the smithy. While he wanted to avoid any spy-like behaviors in the new life he was determined to create, old habits did die hard.

Intrigued, Galen crept around the house's exterior, staying close enough to the wall that he could duck beneath windows and avoid being seen by anyone inside. Finally, the stone building behind the house came into view. It was open to the elements, with only a roof to provide shade from the relentless heat of the Polar Sun. The smoke from the fire billowed through the chimney in the roof, placed just over the forge. There was only one man working the hammer, and he must have been a Fire Ardorist because there weren't any bellows. Still, the flames burned white against the molten metal that he was shaping.

Fascinated, Galen checked to ensure he wouldn't be spotted from any angle then settled in to observe. Galen was a Fire Ardorist as well and was quite good at it. However, he'd always hated that fire was perceived as more destructive than constructive. For this reason, along with his childhood fascination, Galen remained enthralled by blacksmiths throughout his years. They used the heat to craft the most beautiful things, and a small part of him yearned to do the same thing.

The only artistic thing he could do with his Ardor was create little animated flaming images in the air. It had worked a few times to intrigue women, but it was more complicated than he'd expected to find work as a Fire Ardorist when he'd never finished school. Those pricks who grew through the king's finely tuned funnel to become Ardorist socialites preferred their employees to be disgustingly educated. Not that being learned was bad, but Galen had never had the privilege, at least not in the sense that was expected. He'd been raised under...different circumstances.

The blacksmith lifted the object of his focus and examined it in the light. From this distance, Galen could only see that it was some sort of sword.

What did they need a sword for, all the way out here?

It was extremely difficult for Galen to draw himself away, as enraptured as he was. Perhaps he would return the next day to continue watching. Or maybe, if he were brave enough, he would approach the blacksmith and ask if there was a chance he could learn. Until then, however, he would continue as he always did. Slinking in the shadows, making his way through life with scraps and leftovers.

CHAPTER 15

BRIATTA

"If you compete, I'm coming with you."

Briatta clenched her jaw as she turned, pushing shadows away from her to conceal the weapon rack that Neven had moved to the middle of the Belrose basement.

He'd told her to hide it, to cover the rack with her Ardor and hold the shadows there, and she was trying, after having finally mastered accessing her Ardor. Most of this first lesson had been learning to summon it by reaching for that new funnel of power within her and opening the channel. She learned to recognize it as it filled her body, her fingers tingling with the itch to use it, to let the shadows escape.

Briatta ignored Neven's comment as he leaned against the wall in her peripheral vision, watching her vibrate with focus. The shadows still slipped away from her nearly as quickly as she generated them. With a huff of frustration, she dropped her hands, and the darkness that had gathered around the swords dispersed slowly, fading into the existing shadows of the room.

"I still don't know if I *will* do it." Briatta sighed. "Besides, you're an Ardorist. You can't compete."

Neven nodded towards the rack. "Again."

Groaning, Briatta faced the hanging assortment of forged steel and raised her hands.

It had been two days since Lord Mallon's ball, which meant there were four more days to submit an application to her local Weiler station. At the time, Briatta had been confident the Ackmanlee was her next step, but after what had transpired on the drive home...

Of course, Aden did not want Briatta participating in the competition. He felt that if she were to join the ranks of the Weilers, her life would be more unpredictable and more dangerous than it already was, and she would never again be close to where her family could protect her.

Neven remained steadfast in his insistence that Briatta could do whatever she wished, with the caveat that if she were to enter, he would go out on missions with her, even though he couldn't compete himself. Briatta felt strongly that if she were to join the Ackmanlee, she wanted to complete it herself and on her own terms. If she were to receive help, how would she ever survive on her own out on this secret mission for which they were hiring a special position?

Unsurprisingly, yet also out of character, Owena had remained silent and absent while Ellery quietly continued to encourage them to speak to each other without getting involved in any decisions regarding the Ackmanlee.

Instead, Aden, Neven, and Briatta talked in circles for the past two days.

Aden and Owena had been furious upon discovering that Briatta had told Neven about her Ardor. For Aden, it had been predictably short-lasting. He had sighed dramatically and claimed that nobody ever listened to him, even though he hadn't even been the one Briatta had promised. Owena, on the other hand, had gone white with fury and disappeared. Her silence—coupled with the fight still hanging over their heads —might have been one of the worst things to have ever happened to Briatta, and her heart clenched with the desire to make things better.

But they were both very stubborn women, and this time, it wasn't just Briatta's ignorance standing between them. Now, it was also her disobedience.

The only good thing that came from this was Neven's reinforced determination to ensure Briatta was equipped with the appropriate knowledge needed to use her Ardor. He claimed he could not let her join the contest with a good conscience without being completely sure she could defend herself.

Still, Briatta had argued she could defend herself with an exaggerated eye roll while Neven eyed her reproachfully, as if she'd hurt his feelings just by claiming she didn't need his help.

And so, they were in the basement of Briatta's house, practicing the most basic motions of controlling Ardor. Because hers was one that hadn't been seen before, they were also testing the limits of what she could do. Without the ability to even maintain control, however, they hadn't gotten far.

Briatta pushed the darkness forward, attempting to stop producing more and only focus on what she'd already generated. Unfortunately, everything vanished, instead.

"I'm never going to get it," she growled, kicking at the floor.

"You've only been trying for two days. It took me weeks to get the hang of just producing light. I'm still shaky with the more advanced stuff, and there are things I haven't even begun to learn," Neven said gently.

Disappointingly, Briatta's connection to her Ardor already

felt drained, so they stopped for the day and left the Belrose Estate to go check in with the headquarters of the Night Roses. As Owena had locked her office door and ordered her assistant against allowing Briatta or Neven through, the pair asked Aden if anything needed to be done. Aden waved them away, mumbling something nearly incoherent about how all the day's tasks were already filled.

When Neven and Briatta left the headquarters side by side, as they so often did, it hit Briatta that during the Ackmanlee, and if she were to win and be stationed somewhere else, they might not have any more missions together.

Neven walked ahead, reaching up to touch the fire escape where he liked to sit as they passed beneath it.

"What should we do?" he asked, glancing back at her over his shoulder.

Briatta shrugged. "Do you need any more clothes? Since you haven't been an Ardorlite for long?" She nudged his shoulder with her own and smiled playfully, even as the word stung in her mouth. Once, she would have given anything to be included. Now that Briatta would never be an officially recognized Ardorist, the derogatory term didn't feel quite as satisfying.

Neven rolled his eyes, but he turned at the following street corner, and they headed toward the center of Montclair.

They passed Noodlegeuse, and it was Neven's turn to bump her with his shoulder, an eyebrow lifted in question.

"Maybe later," Briatta said, smiling warmly. It did sound good, but it was a little early for noodles. "On the way home?"

Neven nodded.

As they drew closer to Parkette Street, the main shopping avenue in Montclair, the number of pedestrians increased steadily. Some folks rode their horses with large bags attached to the backs of their saddles, some drove carriages, and there was even a prototype of motorized carts that were being researched as Ardor weakened with the decreasing number of Ardorists. The motorized carts were reported to run on vaporized plant matter that contributed to improve the biodome's air quality as it burned. Still, they were noisy and relatively new, so most looked upon them with firmly grounded dislike, and this was the first one Briatta had seen in person.

Maybe Kalaiden had a point.

Briatta considered the rebel group as she watched a motorized carriage rumble by. Despite knowing they were good for their little ecosystem, the black cloud bubbling behind the car smelled terrible, and she wrinkled her nose.

Thankfully, Owena still preferred to go by horse.

At last, Briatta and Neven turned onto Parkette, where Briatta was almost shocked at how much busier it was compared to the corner around it, especially because it wasn't Seren. The Weilers had blocked off the ends of the street so people could walk up and down it safely while perusing the shops, carrying their bags, or hiring someone to follow them. Horses were tied at many storefronts, swishing their tails against bugs and resting one of their hind legs as their lower lips drooped while napping.

"There's the shop," Neven commented, nodding across the street to where Mont-Clothes stood. The door opened as they approached, and a young woman exited the building with an armful of bright, turquoise fabric. It shimmered slightly in the light of the Polar Sun.

"Let's go." Briatta grabbed Neven's arm and pulled him towards the shop, but he planted his feet and shook his head.

"Oh no," Neven said. "I agreed to come, but I'll shop alone. I'm only going to get a few things, anyway." He held up the purse of coins he'd brought along; all of his savings from his new position as an Ardorist as well as money he'd made from the Night Roses.

Briatta frowned. "Why?"

"Can't have you seeing my outfits before I wear them." Neven smirked and gently pried her hand from his forearm.

"That wasn't in the fine print of our friendship."

"Oh well, it *was* in the bold. Off you go," Neven replied, walking towards the door of Mont-Clothes and waving over his shoulder.

Briatta rolled her eyes but didn't follow him, turning to the next nearest shop and pulling the door open. It was cool and dim inside, and as her eyes adjusted, she studied the wares artfully displayed by the front door.

It appeared to be a bookshop, but other odd trinkets were also shelved on the walls. Maybe a used goods store? There didn't seem to be any pattern to the inventory.

Briatta mindlessly reached up to play with the timepiece around her neck as she browsed, picking up a shining white rock from a shelf.

"Ah, now that's an interesting thing. Came from the moon, it's said. When we had a moon." A voice like dry paper came from Briatta's left, and she pivoted, startled. It was a very small, very old woman who had spoken. Her black hair, streaked with white, was braided with gold chains woven in. Wrinkles lined her face in a way that had Briatta suspecting she'd spent most of her life grieving.

"The...moon?" Briatta asked. The word felt strange on her tongue.

"Yes, well, no one would know about that anymore, would they?" The woman turned with a hefty sigh, returning to her work with tiny ceramic teapots.

Briatta thought the woman was odd as she set the rock down and looked through the other available wares. Finally, she settled on an antique ring with similar metalwork to the one on her timepiece and went to purchase it at the desk the woman sat behind. Glancing toward the front of the store through the windows, she still didn't see any sign of Neven.

The old woman sorted mismatched buttons into piles organized by color behind the register. She smiled as Briatta approached, setting the ring on the counter.

"That's a lovely piece," the woman said, picking it up between her fragile, cracked fingertips. "There is a story behind it if you're interested."

She peered up at Briatta, her rheumy eyes shining even in the low light of her store.

"Uh, sure," Briatta said, starting to feel strange about this place. Of all the shops that she could have walked into, it had to be this one? What even was this store? She didn't remember seeing this shop in all her previous times walking down Parkette Street.

"Alright, then." the woman settled in her seat, placing the ring back down on the counter and writing its cost on a small piece of paper. "Long, long ago, a young man from the Polar House fell in love with a young girl from the Nocturne House. They were...balanced, you see. A good match. But in our world, there are good matches, and then there are *great* matches. No matter how hard they tried to make it work, this couple was not a great match. Balanced though they might have been, they clashed when it was most important. Instead of bringing greatness to the world, they cultivated terrible danger."

She pushed the paper across the counter to Briatta, who accepted it and reached for her purse.

"Despite it all, they decided there was no one else for them in this life. On the day before their wedding, the young woman was out riding when she discovered a cave amidst an oasis. At first, it seemed ordinary, although it was a beautiful spot.

Sparkling blue waterfalls, trees like you've never seen, and birds flocked to nest there. The girl enjoyed going there to read, but as time passed, she began to dream about it. Something drew her to the cave again and again, pulling her further into its thrall, until she ventured deep inside it and did not return. The man went after her, and no one is sure what transpired within, but when they finally escaped, it was with a stolen crown and a curse, and it would eventually destroy this world. This ring is the very same one that the young woman wore on her right hand."

The old woman coughed as she finished and reached for a miniature porcelain teacup, taking a long drink of the dark liquid.

"That's...quite a story," Briatta said, setting her payment down on the counter as the woman seemed to be done. "Thank you for sharing."

"Thank you for listening to an old woman." She chuckled dryly, still holding the teacup. She did not reach for the coins. "Urban legends have always been my favorite. I wonder, though, how much truth there is to that one. Regardless, I hope that ring brings you more joy than it did its original owner."

"Of course," Briatta said, hesitating before taking the ring. "Well, have a lovely day."

"You too, dear." The woman nodded, smiling placidly as if she hadn't just spewed the strangest story Briatta had ever heard. A Polar and Nocturne House? Named after the suns, perhaps? Briatta shook her head and frowned, turning from the counter and the woman.

The feeling of something being off about the store faded as Briatta made her way to the exit. She was just a harmless old woman; missing a few spare parts in the head, but friendly enough. Briatta put the ring on her right hand as she walked. It fit perfectly on her fourth finger, and she smiled in satisfaction as her apprehension disappeared.

A small bell rang as she pushed the door open and stepped onto the sidewalk.

In the light outside the shop, Briatta held up her hand to examine her new purchase. Under the Polar Sun, the dark gem set in the ring glimmered ever so slightly, and there might even have been some pale graining in its depths. It was lovely.

Briatta looked back at the gently swinging sign hanging over the door behind her. It was faded and worn, which seemed out of place compared to the other stores; their signs were kept freshly painted and frequently replaced. This one read: Callyra's. Maybe the old woman's name? A family name?

Briatta made a note to look it up later in the Belrose library. Owena owned some copies of Montclair's ancient ancestry books, and they were stored there in the cooler, dry environment that suited them and kept them in the best possible condition.

She walked through the people crowding Parkette Street and stepped down from the sidewalk. Neven would leave Mont-Clothes when he was done and find a nearby frozen cream store, as it was their usual meet-up spot for missions when they were separated.

On the way, Briatta entered a few more stores, purchased a lovely brown coat for Ellery, and eventually stopped at the sweets store. Neven was already sitting out front, finishing the last of his peppermint frozen cream.

"You took your sweet time," Neven said, standing and throwing away the empty bowl and spoon.

"You were faster than I expected," Briatta returned smartly. "Naius is normally quite thorough."

"He wasn't there," Neven replied. "I was sent away almost

as soon as I went in. They told me to return in three hours; that's when he's expected back."

"Did they tell you where he went?"

Neven shook his head. "Just that he is out on house calls."

Briatta sighed, shifting the coat she'd bought for Ellery to drape over her shoulder. "Ah well, you'll just have to get new clothes another time."

It wasn't odd that Naius was away from his shop in the middle of the day; he was frequently called to his wealthier clients in the comfort of their own homes, leaving his seamstresses to handle the shop work while he was away.

Neven glanced at the sky, where the Polar Sun sank lower as it neared bionight. He looked back at Briatta with a spark in his eyes.

"Noodlegeuse?"

Briatta grinned, and they left Parkette Street for their favorite noodle shop.

After they were seated and happily scooping up noodles and broth, even the savory dish couldn't stop Briatta from thinking about how she still hadn't met Owena's conditions. She had not found a job, she had not paid rent, and she had not submitted her application for the Ackmanlee. Worst of all... she'd disobeyed Owena's one request of secrecy regarding her Choosing.

Briatta had no idea what she would do for a job. She had known there was the possibility she could be Ardorless, but she'd still grown up believing that she would be an Ardorist and be assigned work. Applying for one—*searching* for something she'd enjoy doing—had never truly been in her thoughts, and she didn't know where to begin.

"Neven," Briatta started, setting her spoon on the table beside her noodle bowl.

Neven swallowed his bite and lifted his napkin to his mouth, patting it dry. "Yes?"

"Owena, um..." Briatta swallowed. This was more difficult than she thought it would be. "Well, she told me I have to get a job."

Lifting an eyebrow, Neven leaned back in his chair. "Why?"

Briatta looked away, guilt rising as she recalled the conversation that had led to this. "I was a huge ass. Let's just leave it at that."

"You? An ass?" Neven asked, sarcasm dripping from his tone.

Briatta threw a bean sprout at him, trying to frown and failing.

"Alright, alright." Neven smiled. "So, what is it? You need help finding a job?"

Grinning sheepishly, Briatta nodded. "Will you help me?"

Neven sighed. "I'll help you."

Neven walked Briatta home when they finished their dinner. He stopped at the base of the front steps and waited until she was through her door before leaving, his hands in his pockets and an unreadable expression on his face.

What could possibly have him so worried to be walking her all the way home so consistently before going home to D'ivory? It wasn't as if anyone knew what her Ardor was, and she wasn't working a mission for the Night Roses where she could be discovered. If anything, Briatta was safer than usual.

Just inside, Briatta saw a flash of movement as Owena shut her office door, and she flinched at the click of the lock a second later.

Tomorrow, she would face that battle. She swore it to herself.

CHAPTER 16

Briatta sat on the roof, the window to her room left cracked open behind her as she watched the opaque biodome fade, allowing the Polar Sun's light to filter through. She held her hand out and summoned shadows, trying to match them to the shapes cast by the morning light around her. The Ardor did not come easily, and the darkness slipped from her control more often than she succeeded in forming any semblance of the shapes she was trying to mold.

With her position no longer disguised by the bionight, Briatta ceased the flow of her Ardor and leaned back against the wall, tilting her chin up as the Polar Sun warmed her skin.

As soon as she woke this morning, she'd decided to submit her application to the Ackmanlee. It was no longer a question of whether she would do it; it was a matter of when.

Until then, however, she would still need a job.

What kind of job would Neven help her get?

A tiny flicker of frustration flared in her belly when she considered her inability to even accomplish this task on her own, though she quickly squashed it and pushed to her feet.

Briatta had dressed in her casual combat clothes, the ones reserved for on-duty public appearances with the Night Roses when the need to fight might still arise. While they were relatively standard in appearance—a long-sleeved light-green shirt and black pants with boots—they had been carefully tailored to disguise her daggers and throwing knives.

She wasn't anticipating a fight, but if she was going to participate in the Ackmanlee, it would be wise to begin establishing a reputation with appearances now. Most people wouldn't recognize her clothes as being different from theirs, but a well-trained fighter would see that they were easy to move in, to spar in.

Briatta returned to her room and latched the window shut, picking up a hair tie from her dresser and reaching back to braid her hair as she entered the hall. When she arrived at the bottom of the stairs, she caught a glimpse of Owena's back just as her aunt swept into the dining room.

Founders, Briatta had been hoping to be earlier than Owena.

Taking a deep breath and tying off her braid, Briatta paused at the entrance, her gaze flickering toward her aunt.

Owena looked up from where she was pouring her tea. Her brows furrowed instantly in disapproval at Briatta's outfit, but she didn't say anything.

At her aunt's silence, Briatta wondered whether her recent lack of missions with the Night Roses was part of her punishment, too. Briatta rarely had downtime from them. If she wasn't working on her own case, she was supporting another. A week of nothing was...unusual.

Hurrying to leave the room, Briatta snatched a scone and a cup of tea and fled without even adding sugar or cream to her drink. She went directly to the library, closing the great door behind her and sinking into one of the large, plush chairs of the room.

Repairing her relationship with her aunt was at the top of her list for today, but Briatta still couldn't quite find the words. She knew she needed to mean them, or Owena would see through her apology. And letting down that woman wasn't something Briatta could bring herself to do.

When she'd finished her measly meal and set the empty teacup aside, Briatta stood from the chair and laid on her back in the middle of the library, right in the center of the enormous rug. As a young girl, the library was where she'd spent hours of her free time reading between training and school. She'd found immense comfort in the company of the books and in gazing at the mural on the ceiling. Now, trying to think through her feelings about Owena and what Briatta logically knew she *should* feel about the matter, that same comfort wasn't coming to her.

Remembering the odd shop she'd entered the day before, Callyra's, Briatta stood and went to the section of the library reserved for familial history and ancestry trees that dated back to before the Binding. They were kept in a large metal, temperature, and climate-controlled safe powered by Ardorists who regularly came to recharge and service it. When they'd been younger, Aden and Briatta liked to pick random names from the ancient books and pretend to be that person during those days' battles. They'd stage wars between the upstairs and downstairs of the house, though the downstairs had a significant advantage as it was next to the kitchen, and whoever held the bottom half of the home could simply starve their sibling into submission.

Smiling at the memories, Briatta ran her fingers down the spine of *Elfean Ancestry of Carceron, B.B.* It was the book they'd most often reached for.

The double 'B' stood for Before Binding. Although many

years had passed, it was still the most pivotal event in the history of the world as they knew it. The book was bound in dark-blue leather, which had held up remarkably well throughout the years that had passed since it was written.

Briatta, temporarily forgetting about Callyra's, picked the book up and carefully flipped through the pages. They were hardly brittle, nearly the same as she remembered when she'd turned these pages as a child under Owena's supervision.

There was one family Briatta had particularly loved to play as a child, but which one had it been? If she remembered correctly, it was somewhere towards the middle of the book.

The Rosenbergs. Her heart jumped with delight as she found the page. That's right, it had been the Rosenberg family that she'd always wanted to be. She'd liked them so much because they had so many daughters, and each of them had been titled something important sounding. Even as a young girl, Briatta had wanted so desperately to be important.

Trailing a finger down the page and reading through the family tree, her heart nearly stopped at the name *Callyra Rosenberg*. Momentarily frozen, her pulse raced, and she tried to remember whether she had ever noticed the name as a child. Taking a slow breath, she reminded herself that a connection between this Callyra Rosenberg and that odd shop was unlikely. It was probably just a coincidence.

"What in the name of the Founders," Briatta mumbled.

There was a short description at the bottom of the page about the Rosenbergs, as there was about every family tree, and Briatta ran her finger across the words as she read.

The Rosenberg family was a powerful Elfean line that was among the first to cross over to Carceron, along with the Gallitin and the Zardoth families. They primarily had daughters, which was unusual for Elfeans as, typically, the children would be well-balanced, as with all matters of life and Ardor. Unlike many Elfeans, the Rosenbergs were known for coming into rather unique powers that were kept well concealed by anyone close to them. This author was not able to uncover any more information. The Rosenbergs, unfortunately, disappeared just before the Binding.

BRIATTA'S FINGER drifted back to the mention of the Gallitin and Zardoth families so she could look them up as well.

And...what did the book mean by 'cross over to Carceron'? She had never learned about anything like that in school. In fact, their schools had taught in great detail of Carceron's lengthy history, including theories about what had happened before the Binding based on physical clues. There was no way they had *arrived* here. Wouldn't there be remnants of some form of transportation or...other evidence?

No, it just wasn't possible.

"Ah, that old thing." Aden's voice startled her from her thoughts, and she whipped around. He lifted an eyebrow in confusion. "What? Hiding secrets in there?"

"No." Briatta frowned and shook her head. "Just didn't hear you. Did Owena send you to enforce her will?"

"You wound me," Aden said, pretending to have been stabbed in his side as he stumbled forward and leaned on the library shelf to his right.

Despite herself, Briatta's lips quirked upwards. "Sorry." She returned to the book and flipped the page as though she was reading through it—as if the page about the Rosenberg family *hadn't* just made her question everything she thought she knew.

"I was just coming to check on you, to see if you'd decided to compete in the Ackmanlee."

Briatta turned the page again without looking back at her brother. "I will submit my application today."

If she didn't know her brother as well as she did, Briatta might have thought Aden had slipped away for how quiet he became.

"I think that is the right decision," he finally said.

A little surprised by Aden's concession about her participation, Briatta paused; he'd been so adamantly against it only a few days before. "That is an understatement."

Aden studied her. "Listen. I knew that you wanted to help society in some way, but I didn't realize how badly. I still feel like it's important to say that you don't need to have Ardor to help. And..." He lowered his voice. "I know you know already, but you really hurt Owena. She has given everything to care for us. Can you at least say sorry to her?"

All the rawness and frustration that had coursed through Briatta's veins since her Choosing rushed to the forefront of her senses. Her vision blurred, and her throat tightened. She fought to swallow, her tongue thick and heavy in her mouth. When she finally took a few deep breaths and the tears no longer burned behind her eyes, she faced Aden.

"I cannot," she said. "Not right now, at least. I would say things I would regret, and I do not want to make it any worse before I..." She trailed off, unable to finish the sentence.

Aden's face creased with understanding and concern. "It would be better to say something now. The longer you wait, the more it will fester."

"I can't give her an apology that I don't mean. And that's the problem. It would be an insult to her."

Something like grief passed over Aden's features. "You are worth more than your role in society, Bria."

Briatta couldn't look at him. She knew he meant well, that her brother was only trying to help. He was just doing it so *kindly.* She didn't deserve that sort of gentleness, not after she'd discovered such a foul part of her soul. She gently closed *Elfean Ancestry of Carceron, B.B.* and placed it back on the shelf in the safe, resisted the urge to throw her empty teacup at the wall, and instead returned to her original supinated position on the floor, glaring up at the intricately painted ceiling.

Taking the hint, which would have been more appropriate if she'd been five years old, Briatta heard Aden leave the library.

Briatta had always loved the ceilings of the house, and she had practically memorized every stroke of paint from all the times she'd lain on this floor. Now, as her eyes traveled over the artwork, she saw it as if seeing it for the first time.

It was an illustration of people walking on the surface of a planet without buildings or headscarves; plants grew in such abundance, they nearly covered the entire ground beneath the traversing people. More importantly, the sky in the background was dark and glittering with thousands of little Ardor lights. Briatta had always thought it the product of an artist's wild imagination—probably one who had been well into their drink—but now she wondered whether there was such a world out there.

A world where plants could grow anywhere.

For the first time in her life, this room offered no reprieve. Instead, Briatta felt worse than she had when she'd woken this morning. She questioned herself, her childhood, and even the history of her people. Why were there Ardors—she now knew of at least three—that the monarchy was aware of and condemned? Why did they keep it a secret?

Briatta glanced at the timepiece around her neck and sighed. It was time to go to the Weiler station.

Heaving herself to her feet, Briatta went to the stables to saddle a horse. The Weiler stations were more scattered throughout the city than the Founders Halls, so even the closest one was farther than walking distance. With a white headscarf to protect against the sun, she was soon mounted and trotting away from her house.

Briatta was still so consumed with her thoughts that she didn't observe her surroundings with her usual diligence. In fact, she only realized she had arrived at the station because of the incredibly loud crowd surrounding it; they were also directly in her way.

Briatta pulled her horse to a halt and surveyed the scene. The people appeared to have formed a line that gradually made its way into the Weiler station.

"Excuse me," she addressed the person closest to her—an older man resting his weight against the staff in his hands. "Is this all for the Ackmanlee?"

The man nodded emphatically. "Indeed, it is. Been waiting all morning to get in."

Briatta groaned inwardly. There wasn't a good spot to tie her horse, so she dismounted. How could so many Ardorless want to compete in the Ackmanlee? Surely, there weren't *this* many people who needed the Ackmanlee and its reward. Briatta looked around again before sighing and tugging the gelding with her. The horse would have to wait with her, then. She led it to the back of the line, folded her arms impatiently, and settled in to wait.

Within minutes, the Polar Sun was already beating down on her, and as she sweat beneath her headscarf, Briatta peered around the people in front of her to note with dismay that there were still too many to determine how long it might take to reach the front.

Perhaps this was part of the test.

A tingle of awareness raised the hair on the back of Briatta's neck, and she swiveled to scan the roofs around her. She froze when she saw a cloaked figure crouching above the crowd and observing the mayhem. They were broad-shouldered and heavily armed; Briatta could see the sheaths lining their legs and hips even from where she stood.

The person—some sort of dropper, or assassin, perhaps—sat where anyone could see them. A quick look at the people around showed that either no one noticed the figure, or those who did notice did not care.

Was *this* part of the test?

Uncertain, Briatta positioned herself to see the Weiler station on one side and the veiled figure on the other. For hours, while she waited, she maintained her surveillance on both. The entire time, the person on the roof never moved an inch, and she began to wonder whether they were actually real when, at last, the front of their right boot shifted ever so slightly.

Ah, the dreaded pain of a stakeout. Briatta smirked, practically feeling the needle-like prickling the figure was undoubtedly experiencing. She could sympathize with that.

By the time lunch passed, Briatta's stomach rumbled. Cursing herself for not thinking of bringing food in her horse's saddlebags, she watched as a few people waiting gave up their tireless shift and left the line, claiming they would be back the next day.

This was *definitely* part of the test. Surely, the Weilers were looking for people who would not give up on a job just because they were missing one measly meal. They'd also want candidates who were resilient enough to wait in the heat of the Polar Sun to finish the task they'd set out to complete.

Between those who had left and the scant few who had disappeared into the station, Briatta, her horse, and the man she'd initially spoken to had only moved a few feet.

"Has it been like this every day?" she asked. Like her, the

man had remained quiet and vigilant, and he'd eventually caught sight of the watcher on the roof, as well. Though a few others had also noticed, they had taken nearly all Founders-damned day to do so. Owena would have never allowed such ignorance.

The man nodded solemnly. "I haven't participated until today. But I've passed by."

"What in the Founders sort of job do they need someone for?" Briatta muttered, turning to examine her horse. She felt bad that he hadn't had hay or water since they'd left their house this morning. Thankfully, he still appeared bright-eyed and content with one back leg cocked and his lower lip drooped in relaxation.

"Not certain," the man admitted. "But I heard a rumor it has to do with the movement."

"The movement?" Briatta echoed.

The man nodded. "The climate rebels."

Briatta didn't have a response, so they fell silent as she glanced again at the person on the roof.

It wasn't until the Polar Sun had begun setting that suddenly, the mysterious watcher slipped away and disappeared. Briatta watched, trying to see which direction they'd gone and what they would do, but there was no other sign of them.

A short while later, the doors to the station opened, and a group of Weilers came out to take the names of those who remained.

Briatta gave her name to a young woman, who wrote it down. When she turned to leave, Briatta stopped her. "Wait."

The woman looked back.

"Is there anything else I need to do? For the application?"

The woman shook her head. "No, we have everything we

need already. You'll receive notice in about a week if you've been accepted."

Briatta frowned, letting the Weiler go and glancing back up at the roof where the cloaked figure had sat for most of the day. She led her horse to the post at the front of the station, where enough people had cleared for her to offer her horse some water. He drank deeply as she leaned against the wood.

"You took long enough to apply," a familiar voice drawled.

Simeon.

Briatta looked up, swallowing at the sudden nerves jolting through her.

He stood in the doorway of the station, a half-smile on his lips, dressed in an officer's uniform with captain bars on his shoulder. She tried keeping the surprise from showing on her face.

"So, you *are* a king's man," Briatta said, returning her attention to her horse but rotating her body so she could see Simeon.

"Indeed," Simeon replied. Before he could say more, one of the Weilers who'd been in the square taking names approached and pulled him aside to speak quietly.

Briatta's horse finished, and she glanced at Simeon once to confirm he was still occupied before leading the horse away and mounting, starting in the direction of home.

She didn't like the unexpected flares of unease when she was around Simeon, and she'd only met him twice. The sensation that every part of her was bared when he was present made her feel ungrounded and like a foal floundering for its legs. Yes, it was best to avoid that.

Briatta had more significant problems at home.

CHAPTER 17

N even came by again the next day to help her train, as Briatta knew he would, and he brought a list of job options for her to choose from.

"Pick a few that sound interesting. We can go visit them tomorrow, and you can introduce yourself," Neven said before making her run through a series of Ardor drills that left her exhausted and drained. It was barely midmorning when they finished and went upstairs.

By that point, Ellery was the only one at home, saying— when Neven asked—that Owena had gone out on surveillance for a mission that no one had told Briatta about. They joined Ellery for breakfast, and then Neven left, reminding Briatta once again to be ready the next day. While Briatta felt a slight prickle of irritation that Owena wasn't there, she knew she hadn't done anything to fix the situation, so she didn't have a right to be upset. Ellery behaved normally enough with Briatta throughout the rest of the afternoon, but she could tell that her baby sister was bursting at the seams to ask questions about the previous day.

"Out with it," Briatta said finally at the dinner table. It was just her and Ellery, and Preida had opened a bottle of their favorite pink wine. Both sisters were already on their third glass, and a pleasant tingling was spreading on Briatta's lips and cheeks.

"How did the application for the Ackmanlee go?" Ellery gave Briatta a sly grin, reaching for a chunk of sharp cheese and a string of grapes.

Briatta stared at her glass as she swirled the wine by holding the stem and rocking it around the circumference of the base on the table. Her plate was mostly empty, having already eaten the roasted potatoes, marinated chicken, and squash that Prieda had served.

"I don't really know," Briatta mused. "It was...uneventful."

"Aden wasn't sure how he felt about it," Ellery commented. "He wouldn't shut up yesterday."

"Why not?"

"He's worried that he won't be able to keep you safe if you win and join the Weilers and leave Montclair." Ellery sighed. "Weilers get to visit so many places. I think getting stationed out of this biodome sounds like a grand adventure. The only reason anyone ever really gets to leave is for their Choosing, and we don't even get to stop in other cities like people coming from the south or the east do."

Briatta smiled. While she still had mixed feelings about the entire situation, wishing she didn't have to enter the Ackmanlee in the first place, seeing other parts of Belrune did sound exciting.

"I can write letters and tell you all about it," Briatta said. "If I win, that is, and travel to other biodomes."

"Good." Ellery grinned, and then her smile faded. "What about Neven?"

"What about Neven?" Briatta raised an eyebrow.

192

Ellery looked down, picking the grapes off the vine she'd pulled onto her plate. "I guess I always thought you'd end up together one day. That's all."

Briatta pointedly turned her gaze to the wall art behind Ellery. It was a painting of a young Belrose woman. Owena had told them that the woman was the founder of the entire familial line, and her image had been passed down to every eldest daughter, but her name had been lost to the wine Briatta was drinking, and she frowned, momentarily bothered that the name didn't come to her. What was it? Loretta, maybe?

"Even if I thought so, too, I am no longer sure what's meant to happen," Briatta replied slowly.

They sat silently for a while, and then Ellery picked up the bottle of wine, her glass, and gave Briatta a fiendish look. "Maybe *I* will seduce him, then. Neven is a *catch*."

Briatta grabbed a cookie from the platter that Preida had left out and threw it at her sister. Laughing, Ellery batted it away and shrieked playfully, tossing her grapes across the table.

"Alright, alright," Ellery said, still giggling. "I won't do that."

Briatta smirked, though confusion regarding Neven and their friendship weighed uncomfortably in her stomach. If she didn't love him in the way he deserved, she didn't have a right to keep other people from pursuing him.

That was yet another moral dilemma she'd have to face eventually.

"Have you found a job yet?" Ellery asked, leaning back in her chair.

Briatta shook her head. "Neven brought a list to choose from this morning. There are a couple that sound interesting."

"Good." Ellery tilted her head and stared up at the painted

ceiling. "Whatever you do, Bria...if you leave, just don't let yourself leave on bad terms with Owena."

Briatta took a large swallow from her glass of wine. "I won't," she said quietly.

~

THAT NIGHT, she had trouble sleeping as her mind filled with all the thoughts she'd had about herself since her Choosing—the constant internal debate about whether she was a good person raged within her.

Somehow, at some point, she had managed to fall asleep, though it was fitful and plagued with faceless people demanding whether she was a good person or not. The next thing she knew, she woke to Neven gently shaking her shoulder.

"Huh?" Briatta lifted her head. Founders, it felt like she hadn't slept at all.

"Training," Neven told her. "Then job hunting."

"Ugh." Briatta rolled over, squinting at her ceiling.

Neven folded his arms and lifted an eyebrow. "It's not like you to sleep in when you're working. Or, supposed to be, anyway. I think we can all agree I've done most of the heavy lifting here."

"Couldn't sleep." Briatta rolled her eyes and flung her legs out from under her covers, forcing herself to sit, her hands braced on either side as the movement made her head spin. She shouldn't have had so much wine. "I'll meet you downstairs."

Briatta splashed cold water on her face. Her head felt like it had been stuffed with cotton, and her eyes were puffy and tender. This was going to be a very long day.

When she was dressed in casual combat clothes, Briatta

braided her hair and went downstairs, braving the dining room for a cup of tea and a scone. Thankfully, no one was there, and she wondered briefly where her family was before going down to the basement, where Neven waited for her.

As it turned out, using her Ardor was especially disastrous when she was exhausted. After several attempts at training, Neven shook his head.

"We'll come back to this tomorrow."

Relieved, Briatta dropped her slightly shaking hands as Neven picked up her empty teacup to head upstairs. She cast a glance at the false wall at the other end of the basement. She still hadn't told Neven about it, but this was a secret she hadn't betrayed, and she was determined not to mess anything else up with her family.

Leaving the Belrose house felt like taking a breath of fresh air, and Briatta relaxed and felt a little better as she and Neven started the tour of the job opportunities he'd compiled for her.

First, they stopped at an orphanage, where the children screamed and ran around, ripping at each other's hair. The woman in charge—the headmistress—had massive bags beneath her eyes, and her hair stuck out at odd angles. She told Briatta that if she were to accept a position there, she'd take care of sick children and help as needed so the woman could manage the ones who were fine. It would be many unpredictable hours a week, and Briatta could practically see her life fading away.

Caring for children was important. It just wasn't what Briatta wanted to do.

During her training with the Night Roses, Briatta had seen blood; she could handle basic injuries. But...vomiting kids? There was no fathomable way that she could deal with that.

In the end, Briatta politely told the headmistress that she would consider it.

The second job was located at a free clinic for those who could not afford to visit a proper healing center. Because Briatta did not have any formal training in healing or caring for wounds or illnesses (she couldn't begin to understand why Neven had brought her here), she would help provide food and sanitary care to the patients who could not do it themselves.

Once more, Briatta politely told the clinic that she would consider it.

There was only one more that she'd picked from the list, of which there had been far worse options, and Neven and Briatta made their way to one of the poorer districts in Montclair, where Neven lived, as she understood it. It had, over time, become known as D'ivory because it was a sector without Ardorist inhabitants, and there was little sign of Ardor. Rather than lush gardens framing the houses, fountains, or decorative Ardor lights—of which were diminishing anyway—there were rows and rows of plain white houses. They looked, from a distance, like teeth. A long time ago, someone began calling the area The Ivories as a joke, but it had stuck and eventually been shortened to D'ivory.

As they entered the neighborhood, Briatta felt less like these houses reminded her of teeth and more like they were skeletons. This was the place no one wanted to be; to anyone raised in a home with Ardor, it was devoid of life. Briatta shuddered at the idea that she might have to tell Morenna she was frequenting a place like this. But no, Morenna might understand. Briatta reminded herself of the conversation they'd had at Lord Mallon's ball and tried to shift her mindset.

Swallowing thickly, Briatta glanced up at Neven. His hands were in his pockets, his shoulders relaxed, and he appeared completely comfortable.

Was this the life he'd known? Since her Choosing, Briatta

had been realizing she did not know the people around her nearly as well as she'd thought.

As they made their way through D'ivory, they saw more Elfeans going about their day. Some left their little white homes with bags, perhaps leaving for work. Others walked with their families. A few were playing in the streets, tossing balls to each other with small, colored handkerchiefs tucked into their belts to indicate what team they were on, their headscarves askew from running around. Nearly all of them stopped and greeted Neven by name, and he, in turn, asked personal questions.

Every single person was smiling and happy.

Briatta watched wide-eyed and silent, taking in this side of Neven that she'd never seen before, wondering why he'd kept it from her all these years.

Was her prejudice so apparent that he hadn't shared this with her out of fear of her behavior?

Briatta felt sick. Not only with herself but because of how obvious it was now that Neven had never fully let her in while she had bared herself to him since the day they'd become friends. Or, maybe she hadn't. In her mind, Briatta had fully convinced herself she was being honest with him, but it was becoming increasingly clear that wasn't the case.

Eventually, they reached a larger building where smoke billowed from a chimney, and something smelled mouthwateringly wonderful. Neven opened the door, and Briatta numbly followed him inside, thinking someone should fix the loud squealing of the hinges.

Briatta's eyes adjusted to the dim interior as she realized they had entered some sort of community kitchen. It had few Ardor lights, and in some places, flickering torches instead. The room was filled with long tables, and the far wall had a window that revealed a full kitchen bustling with people as they cooked and brought meals to the counter for those waiting in line.

"Neven," an older woman said joyfully from where she ate at the nearest table. "What brings you here today?"

"Leah," Neven said warmly, sliding onto the bench across from the woman. "I brought my friend Briatta with me. She's looking for a job, and I thought that you might be able to use the help."

Leah turned an assessing gaze to Briatta, looking her up and down. "A job, eh? I suppose we are a bit short out back. Can't pay much, is that alright?"

Briatta forced herself to swallow again, glancing at Neven for support before gingerly lowering herself to sit beside him.

"That's alright," she said.

Leah nodded. "Let me finish my food, and then I'll show you around and explain what you'd be doing."

Briatta shot another look at Neven, uncertainty welling. She cleared her throat awkwardly. "Don't you, um, want to interview me?"

Leah's brows shot up, and she laughed with delight. She reached across the table to pat Neven's hand as though there was a joke that Briatta had missed.

"That's a good one," Leah said, still chuckling. "No, dearie. Anyone that Neven brings in is good enough for me."

Had Neven brought others to work here?

Confusion replaced the uncertainty, and Briatta frowned, looking between them. Neven didn't meet her eyes, though he did reach down and take her hand, squeezing it once in reassurance.

"I heard you have Ardor, now." Leah smiled at Neven after swallowing a spoonful of soup, her eyes going to his Ardor-mark. "Congratulations, boy. You've come a long way."

For the first time in her life, Briatta watched as Neven

shrank into himself, visibly uncomfortable. He seemed smaller under Leah's scrutiny.

"It's nothing, really," Neven said. "Don't worry, I'll still come by as often as I can."

Leah shook her head emphatically. "It isn't nothing. You earned this. And I know you will."

She finished her food, scraping the bottom of the bowl with her spoon before standing and adding it to a bin of dirty dishes beside the door.

"Alright, come on," Leah said, leading them through the building, the kitchen, and then out the back door.

Behind the kitchen was a small white barn with fencing that stretched from the back corners of the building. Several chickens scattered when the door opened, clucking in indignation and ruffling their feathers.

"While a lot of our ingredients are donated or sourced from markets when they're about to go bad at a lower price, we also have some livestock that we harvest from and care for every day," Leah explained. "We have a few dairy cows and some goats in addition to the chickens, and they need to be milked every morning. The guy who did it for us just broke his arm, so we've been struggling to find the time to manage this and prepare breakfast for folks around here."

Briatta followed Leah and Neven into the barn, which was surprisingly spacious and clean, and noted that the cows were penned together on the left side while the goats were on the other.

"What I'd have you do, if you agree, is come before bioday each day to milk all of them and collect the eggs. Afterward, clean their pens and make sure they have food and water. We don't need much help otherwise, and it'd only be a few hours in the mornings," Leah continued, stopping in the middle of the barn and placing fists on her hips as she surveyed the animals.

Briatta frowned, momentarily surprised and irritated at the job's hours, the measly pay Leah kept implying, and the work that would be expected of her. This...was an Ardorless position. Yet, that was the reality of her life, now, and it was something she would need to learn to be okay with. Besides that, Briatta wanted to prove to Neven that she didn't care about being seen as Ardorless, even if deep down, it still stung. She wanted to show Owena that she was not just a spoiled, young, rich girl. Most importantly, this was a job that would help others, not that the other two hadn't been, they just weren't a good fit for her. But helping people, she could do.

Neven watched her, his face a mask, and Briatta knew she couldn't turn down this job, too. Of the three they'd visited, this was the one—despite all her frustrations—she was most likely to manage. She'd cared for horses; how difficult could milking cows and goats be? The idea of collecting eggs each morning even sounded a little fun.

Briatta also knew she wouldn't be able to bring herself to ask Neven for more help. He'd gone out of his way already.

Facing Leah, Briatta took a deep breath. "I'll help you."

Leah beamed, nodding approvingly at Neven. "Wonderful. Can you start tomorrow?"

Briatta nodded. "Before the biodome lightening?"

"Yes, a couple hours before will be perfect. The building will be locked when you get here, but you can come around the side and enter through this gate. I keep a lantern here and a metal lighter that you can use for light. By the time you finish, I should be here, and you can bring everything inside." Leah showed them the gate and the lantern and then led them back inside through the kitchen and to the main cafeteria. "I'll pay you when I can, but I'll try to have a bit for you every day."

"Thank you," Briatta murmured.

Leah bid them farewell, saying she needed to return to work in the kitchen. Briatta watched her go before leaving with Neven. There was an awkward silence between them as they made their way through Montclair back to her house. Briatta felt raw and possibly even worse than after her argument with Owena.

Every person they'd seen today was happy despite not having Ardor, living in a poor district, and being unable to contribute to the wellbeing of their neighbors. Briatta struggled to understand how they could ever be content with their lives the way that they were. Were they ignorant of the difficulties the Ardorists faced in upholding the biodomes with the steady decrease in their numbers? None of the Ardorless were doing work that really mattered—at least not in the way that Briatta could see.

And Neven...these people knew him. They loved him, and he clearly loved them.

"Neven," Briatta said as they turned onto her street. "Can I ask you a...strange question?"

Neven gave her a quizzical look but nodded.

"Did you ever feel like you were part of why Ardorists are having a harder time maintaining a livable space for us? Before you had Ardor?"

Neven stopped and stared at Briatta incredulously, his eyes widening slightly. "Of course not. I mean, that's certainly what the Ardorists want the Ardorless to believe, but just because we didn't have Ardor didn't mean we deserved any less to live than they did."

Briatta looked at her feet, her throat constricting. Whether the Ardorless should live had never been a question for her; it was a matter of self-worth.

"Why else do you think they call themselves Ardorists

while calling everyone else the Ardorless?" Neven continued, his tone softening. "Anything they can do to break us down and make us feel inferior, they'll do it."

"So...you never felt like a burden?"

"Founders, no. In fact, I don't think it's actually gotten to the point where the biodomes could have even a small chance of failing." Neven started walking again, glancing down at her.

A small sense of relief, just a bead, bloomed in her heart. But something he'd said had stuck with her.

"Gotten to the point? So, you believe it's heading in that direction?"

Neven sighed as they reached her house. "Listen, you aren't a burden. No matter what Ardorists say about Ardorless. And little do they know, you'll be able to take out most of them when you're fully trained."

He'd changed the subject, and while she regarded him curiously, she didn't feel like pushing the issue. She was still processing their day and how it had altered her perception of the reality they lived in, whether she still believed the things she'd said to Owena, and still dreading how early she'd have to get up every day from this point on.

"Thank you," Briatta said finally.

"Always, Bria." Neven gave her a small smile and watched until she entered her house.

CHAPTER 18

For the week following her application to the Ackmanlee and her job search with Neven, she woke up in the mornings, saddled a horse, and rode to the community kitchen—she'd since learned it was called Sour Soup—to care for the animals.

Leah paid her each day, and while Briatta grimaced inwardly at how little she made, she tried not to show it. If the Ardorless hardly made enough to eat, Briatta wanted no part of this life. It made her uncomfortable to be so keenly aware of the disparities between how she lived and how these people did, and she avoided greeting those in D'ivory. The shame was overwhelming.

After work, she met Neven to train her Ardor (which was still going terribly), then returned home to work through her combat training exercises.

A few times, Briatta went into the secret room to browse the shelves of books; she'd been curious to know if they were similar to or different from what was available upstairs. She recognized a few titles, but many sounded like odd romance books that she'd never heard of or had any interest in reading.

Owena had indeed cleaned the room as she'd said she would, and without the layers of dust and cobwebs, it looked more like the majestic space it had once been. Briatta almost thought of it as a space she could escape to and cozy up with a book she was actually interested in rather than the war room that it had originally been built to be. She had nearly laughed out loud when that thought crossed her mind, knowing that her ancestors would likely detest the idea of their war room being treated with such casualness.

Or perhaps they would be glad to see that it wasn't needed.

Aside from Briatta's continued exclusion from the Night Roses and rarely seeing Owena, her week had been relatively normal.

When six days had passed without having heard news regarding the Ackmanlee, Briatta grew restless. How would they let her know that she was accepted? Would they even tell her if she weren't chosen?

No, she couldn't think like that. The Ackmanlee was Briatta's only way out of this mess, and she wouldn't tolerate a reality where she *didn't* make it.

Ellery and Briatta were eating dinner when the front door opened, and Aden appeared. He breezed into the dining room and sat down across from them.

"Owena still isn't joining you for dinner?"

Ellery gave a pointed head tilt in Briatta's direction, and Aden frowned.

"You haven't apologized?"

"It isn't like she's been around to even try talking to her," Briatta grumbled, stabbing the beans on her plate with her fork.

"Well, that's fair, actually," Ellery said, popping a bite of steak into her mouth.

Aden sighed, and Preida appeared with a full plate for him. He thanked her and set about eating his dinner. Briatta glanced toward the hall, half expecting either Owena or a missive of denial for the Ackmanlee.

"Looking every five seconds won't make whatever you're waiting for appear faster," Ellery told her. She picked up the bottle of red wine in the middle of the table, reached for Briatta's glass, and filled it.

Briatta scowled, grabbing the glass from her sister and setting it on the table. Ellery shrugged and poured wine into her own cup, taking a drink and offering the bottle to Aden. He accepted it, looking between his sisters with raised eyebrows.

"It's been a week since she applied for the Ackmanlee," Ellery explained.

"Ah." Aden picked up his glass.

There was a knock at the front door then, and Briatta jumped so violently that she nearly spilled her freshly poured wine all over the white tablecloth, barely catching it before the glass tipped over.

"Founders, Bria," Ellery griped. "You need to go for a run or something."

Briatta frowned again, leaning to listen for who would be at the door as Preida hurried to answer it. A low male voice came from beyond the threshold, indiscernible from where the Belrose siblings sat in the dining room.

"Who do you think that is?" Briatta whispered, straining to hear.

Aden shrugged. "Can't think of anyone who was meant to call today."

Ellery widened her eyes. "Maybe it's someone here to tell you that you're already fired from the job you just got."

For the third time that night, Briatta gave Ellery a dirty look.

"You're really racking them up tonight, El," Aden commented, lifting his wine to his lips.

Ellery snickered.

Then, there were footsteps, and Preida appeared. "Briatta, there's someone here to speak with you."

Briatta's heart instantly raced. With shaking hands, she pushed herself to her feet and followed Preida from the room, giving her siblings one last look that she hoped would convey that they needed to stay put.

Briatta's tongue felt thick and heavy as she saw who was at the front door.

Simeon.

He stood on the porch, a bag slung over his shoulder and a folder tucked beneath his arm.

When he saw her, his entire face lit up with a broad smile. The flutterflies in Briatta's belly immediately took flight. One of her hands went to her stomach as if she were trying to settle them, and she swallowed.

"Miss Belrose." Simeon inclined his head politely.

"Mr. Simeon," Briatta said. Her mouth was dry. There was only one reason he would be here.

"Just Simeon will do."

Preida looked questioningly between them, hovering as though she weren't sure whether to stay or go.

"Thank you, Preida," Briatta dismissed her gently.

Nodding, Preida backed away and hurried toward the kitchen. There was probably something on the stove that needed tending, but being the wonderful woman that she was, she wouldn't have left Briatta to face this alone if Briatta had wanted her to stay.

"How can I help you, Simeon?" Briatta asked when Preida disappeared. The man smiled again.

"I am here on official business, as it were," Simeon said.

Briatta tensed, knowing what came next would determine her value to society for the rest of her life. "But first, congratulations on being accepted into the Ackmanlee."

He paused, smiling expectantly.

For a second, it felt like the floor beneath Briatta's feet had fallen away. She reached out and fumbled for the doorframe, her other hand still on her belly, because the joy that filled her was beyond anything she'd ever felt.

Thank the Founders.

The words repeated in her head over and over as she tried to steady herself.

"Thank you," she managed, making herself focus.

Simeon nodded curtly. "Weilers were sent out tonight to alert each contestant of their acceptance into the Ackmanlee and to give briefs on the competition. There are things that must be discussed in person, and we do not want competitors to know each other at the beginning of the competition."

That explained his house call. Briatta wondered if he'd been assigned here or if the job had been another Weiler's before he took it.

"Alright," Briatta said, still frozen to the door. Simeon raised an eyebrow, and she jumped as she realized she should have invited him inside. Stepping back, she gestured to welcome him. "Sorry, please come inside."

Simeon entered and tugged at the bottom of his coat, looking around. Briatta closed the front door and debated where to take him. Settling on Owena's office, as that felt the most professional, she led him through the door on the right of the hallway, and the Ardor lights within brightened as she went.

Once inside, and with the office door left cracked, Briatta moved to Owena's chair and sat down as Simeon took the seat across the desk. He pulled out a folded stack of papers.

"This is your contract for the competition. Acknowledgment of risk and all that. We're providing it beforehand so you can read over it, but we'll require it to be signed and turned in before you officially begin tonight."

Tonight. Founders.

Briatta accepted the sheaf with a jolt of panic at its size and the speed at which she would need to read, but she nodded. "Okay. Ah, tonight."

Simeon shrugged, his eyes traveling over the bookshelves in Owena's office. "Officially. We do recognize the time, however, and realize most people probably won't begin work until tomorrow."

A hint, perhaps, that she should not wait?

Briatta calmed from the high of acceptance and, slipping into her mask as a Night Rose, examined Simeon for any behavior that would reveal more than he was saying.

"The main reason you are allowed to compete is because you stood outside of a Weiler station waiting to apply to the Ackmanlee with the diligence we'd expect from one of our own," Simeon continued, becoming a more official version of himself before Briatta's eyes. "Also, you were among the few who noticed the threat we planted within the expected time frame."

Briatta recalled her day spent waiting in front of the Weiler station. "The mysterious figure."

Simeon nodded. "Exactly. Awareness of your surroundings and the ability to recognize and analyze threats is essential." He paused, shifting in his chair and putting one leg over the other. "The premise of the competition is simple. We have staged the kidnapping of a young individual by an organized group of perpetrators who have taken root somewhere in Montclair. The story is that many of the local vendors have been robbed, and it's creating unrest in the city, but the group hasn't done anything worse than that...yet. Your job will be to find the group, infiltrate their ranks, determine who was taken, and free them without revealing your cover. After that, report the location of the base to the Weilers so the criminals can be neutralized."

Briatta sat forward slightly, her heart lifting as it pounded with excitement. This was similar to missions with the Night Roses. Maybe she'd have an advantage.

"Now, there are some rules you will be expected to follow," Simeon continued. "You will not harm or kill any of the participants of the fictional group or the individual who has been taken. Your mission is to get in and out without any...hiccups. However, when it comes to your competitors, there are no restrictions. In the real world, you'll fight for your life more often than you realize. Therefore, should you encounter a contestant, your response is up to you."

Briatta frowned. "We're not allowed to see each other. How will we know whether we meet another contestant?"

Simeon folded his hands in his lap, the tips of his index fingers touching each other and remaining straight. "You won't."

Surprise rushed through Briatta, but she supposed it made sense. The Weilers would want to observe the way contestants handled a potential ally or threat.

"You may form teams if you can successfully recognize a fellow contender, though you will be penalized if you work with someone and betray them. We do not tolerate turncoats within the Weilers." Simeon leveled a hard look at Briatta, and she suddenly felt very small. This was a different man from the one who had spun her around the dance floor at Malcalaire.

Briatta swallowed. "Is there anything else?"

Simeon's expression turned thoughtful, and it warmed his presence so much that a slight shiver of apprehension traveled down her spine at how easily he changed his demeanor.

Simeon said. "You have one cycle to complete your mission. You will be judged based on how you interact with other contestants, whether you find the crime group, whether you manage to free the victim, and if you successfully deliver the information to the Weilers. There is no set point system, because we don't want to influence how you work; we want to see everyone in action, as they would be undercover without supervision. I believe that's all I have for you."

Only one cycle? Briatta felt as if the temperature in the office had dropped drastically. She was usually given as much time as was necessary to collect the required evidence against a case before she was allowed to take action, and while Briatta had always worked as hard as she could to close a case as soon as possible, it was sometimes difficult to do so within a single cycle.

Simeon reached into his bag and pulled out another folder, this one more familiar to Briatta than the contract she already held.

"Your case file," he explained. She accepted it, her fingers already itching to flip through it. Instead, she set it on her lap and picked up the contract.

"If you don't mind, I'd like to flip through this and sign it now, before I look at that." It sounded more like a question.

Simeon nodded. "Of course. I'm available for any questions you might have."

Briatta rang the little bell on Owena's desk. A second later, Preida appeared as if she'd been hovering nearby already.

"Will you bring us tea, Preida?" Briatta asked.

Preida bobbed her head and vanished. Briatta told Simeon

he was welcome to explore the library or the books on Owena's shelves while she worked, then she sat back in her chair and read through the contract.

It covered what Simeon had already told her in much greater detail and with the terminology Briatta expected of such an event. There were several disclaimers about injuries and statements claiming that winning the Ackmanlee did not guarantee the victor would be the right candidate for the job the Weilers were looking to fill.

When Briatta was a few pages in, Preida reappeared with a tray of tea and small sandwiches she'd made using the fixings from dinner. Simeon thanked her politely and poured himself a cup, happily taking a few of the sandwiches and eating them as he flipped through a book with a dark-blue cover from one of Owena's shelves.

The rest of the contract was pretty standard. Briatta was accustomed to signing them for missions, and she couldn't find anything unusual about it, though she would never claim to be an expert in that department. She reached for a pen on Owena's desk and used it to initial each required page, signing her full name on the back of the packet.

Wordlessly, Briatta passed it across the desk.

"No questions?"

Briatta shook her head. "I understand."

"That's it, then." Simeon smiled, popping the last bite of his sandwich into his mouth. He closed the blue book and lifted his teacup to his lips, downing the contents in one gulp. Briatta raised an eyebrow. That wasn't exactly polite behavior, but Simeon *was* a Weiler, and they didn't live the soft life Briatta was accustomed to, Night Rose position notwithstanding. Trying to ignore the implications of her potential future company, Briatta pushed herself to her feet and smiled.

She led him from Owena's office and nearly ran into Aden and Ellery, who were hovering in the hall. Both jumped at Briatta and Simeon's sudden appearance, though Aden's surprise was masked by a quickly darkening expression as he regarded Simeon.

"Simeon was just leaving," Briatta said before either of her siblings could say anything.

"A pleasure to meet you both," Simeon said, only slightly resisting Briatta's efforts to herd him towards the front door. She opened it and practically pushed him outside. He started walking away before hesitating.

"Oh, and..." he said, turning smoothly on a heel and facing her again. "Congratulations once again, Miss Belrose. Good luck."

Briatta couldn't help the grin that spread across her lips. "Thank you."

Then, Simeon really did leave. She watched him descend the steps and disappear into the darkness of Penrose Avenue. As soon as he was on the side of the road, Briatta shut the door and turned to her brother and sister.

Ellery and Aden were still standing in the hall, their faces open and curious.

"Who was that, Bria?" Aden asked, his arms folded.

"A Weiler," Briatta said. "I made it. I was accepted into the Ackmanlee!"

Ellery shot forward and grabbed her hands, jumping and shrieking as they turned in a circle. Briatta smiled so widely that her cheeks hurt, and even Aden cracked a grin, blurred as he was from her spinning with Ellery.

"I knew you would get in," Aden said, grabbing Briatta's arm, stealing her from Ellery, and pulling her into a hug. This time, he didn't tell her to be safe, or that she was worth more than her Ardor. She could tell he resisted the urge to say to her the things that an elder brother would. She hoped Aden was simply happy for her, because that was exactly what she needed from him.

Aden declared they were celebrating and opened a bottle of sparkling wine. The three of them crawled out of Briatta's window and sat on the roof, taking the case file with them and drinking straight from the bottle as they watched the decorative Ardor lights dance across the biodome. It was the first time in a long time they'd done this together, as they'd grown apart since Aden's Choosing.

Briatta found herself hoping they would return to spending time like this. That it was *her* unfortunate Choosing that brought them back together soured it only a little. She'd had enough time to adapt to the idea of the Ackmanlee and that she'd be helping her fellow Elfeans through service with the Weilers instead of as an Ardorist.

Even if it meant surrounding herself with people who were not as familiar with the politeness and expectations of Ardorists.

It would be enough.

It had to be.

CHAPTER 19

The morning after Simeon had briefed her on the competition, Briatta retreated to the Belrose library upon returning from her job at Sour Soup, asking Preida to bring her breakfast there rather than joining her family. Her head was pounding from the wine that she'd drunk with her siblings the night before, and the idea of facing Owena made her queasy.

A week at her job had given Briatta a greater appreciation for how hard the lower class worked just to live, but it hadn't pushed her in the direction that Owena had likely wanted it to. Rather than gaining respect for the people she toiled alongside and recognizing them as her equals, Briatta only felt more desperate to succeed in the Ackmanlee to find a way into the life that she wanted.

Shaking her head and resolving to return to the matter later, Briatta spread the Weilers' mock case file across the study table. With only one cycle to accomplish the mission, she didn't have time to dwell on anything but this—not if she wanted to win.

Case files were something she'd studied her entire life with the Night Roses, but this was particularly vague and nondescript. Briatta grudgingly supposed the Weilers wanted to see what the competitors would do with the small amount of information. She'd have to approach this as if she were building a case from the ground up, not as though there was already substantial material prepared.

She knew that a young Elfean named Tallor had last been seen a few weeks ago at a bar near Parkette Street called Allemor House with his friends, which they regularly attended in the evenings.

Friends. That was a potentially essential piece of information, and it had to have been included intentionally, given how little there was otherwise. Perhaps the Weilers had planted witnesses she could find and interview. Though, it was also possible that they would plant that information to try and lead competitors in the wrong direction.

She pulled a blank sheet of paper towards her and started taking notes.

Briatta knew of Allemor House. She'd visited several times on observation runs for targets that the Night Roses had neutralized, though she'd never once been there recreationally. It seemed she still did not have a reason to visit Allemor House for anything other than work.

With the mention of Allemor House, there was also a note about reports of missing medicine, food, liquor, and water supplies from sporadic points throughout Montclair. A map had been included, with each location circled in red, and Briatta consulted it before adding a few points to the list she'd begun. The connection between the cases had been confirmed —Simeon had told her as much—and they appeared to be supply runs. If one were running an organized crime group, they would need all the things that had been stolen.

There wasn't much else in the file, though profiles of Tallor and a few of his friends were also tucked alongside small sketches.

Briatta finished the dregs of the tea that Preida had brought, then packed a book and a notepad into a bag, checking to ensure she had all her daggers before tucking the case file safely away in her room. She wore her casual combat clothes to blend in.

Thankfully, no one seemed to be home when Briatta left the library, and she slipped out without running into either of her siblings or her aunt.

That was one small blessing.

When Briatta reached Allemor House, it was quiet and appeared to be closed, which was expected because it was early in the bioday, and the bar was best known for its evening atmosphere. Briatta moved to the rear entrance, pulling her lockpick set from her trouser pocket. The lock didn't take long to work open, clicking softly in response to Briatta's gentle ministrations. She tucked her picks back into her pants and opened the door, slipping inside.

Briatta swept the premises, checking every surface for possible hints and finding nothing obvious. She hadn't expected to find anything, because it would have been three weeks since Tallor had last been seen here, but she needed to ensure she had done her job thoroughly.

Double-checking that she hadn't left any evidence of her own, Briatta exited the building the same way she'd entered, locking the door behind her with her picks. She would return later to observe the servers and patrons, but her job here was done for now.

Briatta had memorized the locations where a theft had occurred, and she worked her way through Montclair, attending to each one. She questioned the Elfeans working in the stores, inquiring about the missing goods.

The people Briatta interviewed seemed ignorant of the reports and had no idea what she was talking about in regard to their stolen goods, and Briatta grew frustrated as the day wore on. If the Weilers expected her to build and crack a case against this imaginary group, why hadn't they planted more information for the contestants to find?

"What am I missing?" Briatta muttered as she left one of the marked locations after another fruitless discussion. She'd only made it to three so far, and it was already nearing the time when she should return to Allemor House.

Briatta could practically hear Owena's cool analysis of the situation in her left ear as she walked, fighting the urge to look over her shoulder.

They're probably testing the contestants' persistence, so it's likely only a few of these workers have been prepared, her aunt would say.

Shuddering at the thought of Owena's voice living in her head, Briatta tried to convince herself it was her own subconscious giving voice to the idea, because it made the most sense that it would come from Owena. And damned if imaginary-Owena wasn't right. If Briatta were the one trying to find a candidate to work on a complex case—which, based on the lack of information thus far, she was now sure was the reason for this entire competition—she would want to find someone who would work out all the evidence they could. No matter what issues they ran into.

Briatta sighed. One more stop, then.

Unsurprisingly, the last visit of the day was just as unsuccessful as the first three, and Briatta left the building as soon as it was clear that the young man working the store had absolutely no idea what she was talking about. Her stomach rumbled, and she glanced at her timepiece. She would get food at Allemor House.

As she walked back towards Parkette Street, Briatta's thoughts strayed to Owena. Her aunt had never shut her out like this before, and she couldn't help feeling irritated because it seemed like an extreme reaction. Sure, Briatta had drunk a little too much and had said some stupid things, but she was doing her best to make up for it.

If anything were to happen to her family, Briatta would go to the ends of Carceron for them. She would probably die for them. Probably.

Perhaps that was her one redeeming quality. Adjusting to change was difficult, but once she was there, Briatta would back up her friends and family with all the training she'd ever received and then some. Maybe she would even use her Ardor and expose herself if it meant her loved ones were safe.

It was just that even when Briatta had her friends' backs, she'd rarely done anything that hadn't also benefited herself in some way. Maybe that was why Owena had forced her to get a job, and why Neven had chosen the list that he had; none of them benefited Briatta outside the meager pay she received.

And of all the options, she'd chosen what she'd perceived to be the easiest one.

Briatta stalked down the sidewalk, exhaling sharply with the realization that she barely reaped anything for the work she did each morning milking the cows and goats and collecting the eggs. It was also a nuisance to rise so early every day and get to Sour Soup in time to take care of everything.

But it was a little rewarding.

Briatta found that she liked how Leah beamed whenever Briatta brought in the fruits of her labor and handed them over. It made her feel proud to see someone so grateful for the yield of such a physical task.

Every day, Leah told her what she'd be making with the ingredients that Briatta harvested and how many people it would feed, and Briatta had to admit that it was...nice.

Not that she would tell Owena or even Neven that yet. This tentative, fragile peace she was beginning to feel about her new life...that was hers. She wanted to keep it safe and tucked away for a little longer. Then, when she could face Owena and Neven knowing that she meant every word of her apologies, because they deserved nothing less, she would settle comfortably into this new version of herself.

Founders, it had only been a week. She really couldn't change that much in a week.

Briatta shook her head and returned to the task at hand. She'd mentally crossed out the locations on the map where people blatantly hadn't known anything and would physically write them out on a separate piece of paper when she returned home, in addition to listing the ones that she wanted to visit the next day.

Allemor House came into view then, and it was just opening for business. A few employees were setting up umbrellas that would protect people from the Polar Sun until the biodome darkened, and some Elfeans were already in line for an early evening drink or meal.

Briatta chose a seat outside and set her bag beside it. A few moments later, a server approached.

"How can I help you?" she asked, pulling out a notepad and looking at Briatta expectantly.

Briatta ordered cider and a meat stew, her stomach rumbling. The woman left, and Briatta noted no one from Tallor's staged friend group had arrived yet, as the case file had explicitly said evenings. But perhaps she could learn something else by being here early. Like the case file, Briatta had memorized the faces of each of Tallor's friends, and she mentally flipped through them, reciting the facts for each one as she observed the restaurant.

When she finished with that, she picked up the menu and searched for the list of suppliers to see if there were any connections between the restaurant and the thefts. There were a few, and she mentally made notes of that.

Briatta's cider arrived, and she took a sip. It was dry and semi-sweet—exactly how she liked it—flavored lightly with some of the dark berries that had been altered to survive more efficiently within the biodomes. They were supposedly more honey-flavored than they had been originally, and it lent a lovely accent to the crisp golden apples that Elfeans treasured.

Someone approached her table, and Briatta, noticing the movement in her peripheral vision, slipped the images of the friends back into her bag and looked up. Neven pulled a chair out and sat down, and Briatta felt a flicker of annoyance at his presence.

"Neven," she said. "What are you doing here?"

Neven lifted a brow and leaned back in his chair. "I'm here for the first meeting of your new art club."

Momentarily taken aback, Briatta's jaw slackened as she stared at him. And then, it clicked. Neven somehow knew she'd been accepted into the Ackmanlee. Even without knowing the competition involved a case file, he would have known she would immediately stake out any locations involved. And, as they'd done a hundred times before for Night Rose missions, he had just given them a reason to come back to this place without raising suspicion by announcing a fictional art club. The tension of his arrival abruptly shifted to irritation, and Briatta made a mental note to beat up whoever had tipped Neven off when she returned home.

"I don't need help." Briatta lifted her cider, taking a drink to avoid saying anything more.

"I know," Neven replied. "But I thought you might want some company while you're out studying for your *art*. Some say I'm inspiring."

He pulled out a sketchbook and a pencil, glanced around the room, and began to draw.

Briatta fought the urge to roll her eyes. She'd gone many places on her own when working a case, and Neven had never seemed to care very much about being separated. But that was when he'd been doing his own part to help. As Briatta looked around Allemor House, she noted that there weren't any other single patrons in the vicinity.

"Fine," she relented. "But just this once. I want to do this on my own."

Something like frustration passed over Neven's face, but he nodded without protest. The waitress returned with Briatta's food, and Neven eyed her stew before ordering a second bowl along with an ale.

As Briatta dug in, a young woman with long, smooth black hair entered the outdoor seating area with a cute leather satchel slung over her shoulder. As she moved, it was evident she was well muscled, and as she adjusted her bag, her arm flexed with the movement. She had slanted dark eyes similar to Simeon's and a pale, clear complexion. Pausing just inside the front door, she turned her head to take stock of her surroundings.

Another contestant?

Briatta watched as she took a seat near the bar. Like Briatta, she soon had food and a drink, but no one joined her. Glancing at Neven to see if he'd noticed, Briatta chewed thoughtfully.

"How's your job going?" Neven asked, a detailed sketch of the restaurant's interior taking shape on his paper. "Leah says you've been doing well."

Sighing, Briatta set her spoon down and leaned back in her seat. "It's...not what I expected. But it's growing on me."

Neven tilted his head in silent question.

"I guess I didn't fully understand how difficult Ardorists make life for the Ardorless," Briatta said slowly.

Neven's gaze remained steady, the tip of his pencil hovering over the sketchbook, but his eyes darkened almost imperceptibly. "They want Ardorless folk to suffer for making their jobs maintaining the biodomes harder."

It made more sense than Briatta cared to admit. Because she still hadn't fully adjusted to the idea of being an Ardorless member of society in the eyes of the Ardorists she'd been raised around, a terribly uncomfortable feeling swelled within her.

"I think...that's what Owena wanted me to understand," Briatta admitted after a long silence. Neven's food arrived, and he pulled it toward himself after tucking the sketchbook safely back inside his satchel, sipping his beer before looking down at his plate with a troubled expression.

"It might seem harsh, how she's treating you," Neven began eventually. "But I think she is trying to save you from the difficulties of realizing it later. When she wouldn't be able to help you anymore."

Briatta's heart clenched because it was so evident when Neven put it that way, a wave of tremendous relief washing over her. Owena had never been one to manage her charges with such rigidity; she'd cared for them far too much as her sister's children. Perhaps she had even given them *more* than she should have.

While Briatta still struggled to accept she was worth more than the Ardorists dictated, she felt a little less disgust with herself knowing that at least this, she could acknowledge.

Toying with her food, Briatta bitterly thought that if she'd been born to be such a bad person, why was she cursed with the knowledge that everything she said and did was wrong? At least the Founders could have allowed her to be terrible in ignorance. Then she wouldn't be constantly weighed down by this crushing guilt.

At that moment, a young man pushed his way into Allemor House. He carried his case file out in the open, and she straightened in her seat, watching as he tracked down a young bartender and pulled out the picture of Tallor.

"Do you know this person?" the young man asked.

The woman squinted at the image when understanding and something else—perhaps excitement—flashed in her eyes before she schooled herself. She, and likely other staff as well, had been prepared for this.

Well, of course, they had. The Weilers would have wanted to judge the performance of the contestants.

"He's a regular." The woman nodded solemnly. "Haven't seen him in a few weeks, though."

"When does he typically come in?" the man asked, tucking the picture away.

"Every first and third day of the week, always with the same group of people."

Shit. It was the second day of the week. At least this would not be a late night.

"Is there anyone here now?" the man pressed.

"Sorry, but no. If you come back tomorrow, I can point them out to you," the woman offered.

The man nodded curtly and left, vanishing through the door as quickly as he'd appeared.

Neven was listening with his head cocked, his interest piqued. Briatta turned back to him, sighing as she downed her cider. Then, she reached for her bag. She may as well play the part of being a member of an art club.

"Not what you hoped for?" Neven asked wryly, a corner of his mouth tilting up.

Briatta narrowed her eyes at him and didn't say anything. He shrugged and stuffed another bite of food into his mouth.

Someone else approached their table then, and Briatta twisted to see the young woman with raven black hair. Briatta looked up at her, unsmiling and chin high, waiting for the new woman to speak first.

"You're competing," the woman said. It wasn't a question.

Briatta studied the woman's clothes. They were well suited for combat, and there were definitely spots where weapons could be hidden.

"You are, too," she said at last, returning her gaze to the lady's pitch-dark eyes.

"I think that it may be in our best interest to work together." The woman's head tilted as she looked down at Briatta, waiting quietly for a response.

Briatta immediately stiffened. She loathed the idea of sharing the win and had already dismissed the thought of a team the moment Simeon had said that it was possible.

But another thought had occurred to her, one that she'd ignored at the time. Maybe working in a team was part of the test. They wouldn't have encouraged it if they hadn't wanted to see how contestants functioned in a group setting, especially when Simeon had specifically said there would be a penalty for betraying a team member. Briatta took a deliberate breath, exhaling slowly before nodding.

The woman sat down. "I'm Vydian."

"Briatta. What did you have in mind?"

CHAPTER 20

GALEN

"That's it, now hit the metal a little harder to the right," said Matty, the old smith. Since arriving in Isa, Galen had returned to watch him work from a distance every day. Well, he had only watched until the man's wife had caught him crouched in her brambleberry bushes, so entranced by Matty's work while snacking on the little red fruit that he hadn't noticed her approach. The woman, who Galen later learned was called Beryl, had snatched up a stick and chased him around the yard until Matty had come to see what was happening.

That was how Galen had found himself foolishly explaining how he had just wanted to watch the smith work because he admired the job and loved that the flames could be used to create such art. Then, at Matty and Beryl's disbelief, Galen had sworn he'd never do anything untoward ever again as long as he was allowed to watch Matty create something up close.

It had taken some convincing, but the smith had eventually taken pity on him. He'd miraculously put up with Galen's constant stream of questions while hammering away. When he'd grown tired of Galen's pestering, Matty just put the hammer in Galen's hands so that he could explain in more detail while still getting the job done.

As he'd been told, Galen shifted the point of impact slightly to the right on the blade of the sword he was working on, and Matty grunted in approval.

"Alright, let her cool," Matty said when the metal smoothed beneath Galen's efforts.

Standing back from the anvil and wiping his forehead with the back of his forearm, Galen grinned. This was the best that he'd felt in a very long time. Something about the manual labor and learning to channel his Ardor to create good had given him purpose again, even if it had only been for a cycle. Besides, he was growing very fond of Matty and Beryl.

"I think supper should be ready soon," Matty said, leaning against the low stone wall of his forge and glancing up at the Polar Sun low in the sky. "As always, you're welcome to stay."

Galen had stayed a few times, but he always felt terrible accepting food from the older couple. They certainly did well enough on the smaller and finer things that Matty created, but in a small town like Isa, keeping the local Weilers stocked with swords was probably Matty's most significant contract.

"Thank you, sir," Galen said. "I think I'll find something on the way home."

The truth was that Galen had taken a lot of coin with him when he'd left Kalaiden, and though his supply was running a little low, he still had plenty for the next couple cycles, even if he was buying food every night. Matty had offered to pay Galen, but he'd refused; he wouldn't take any money except for a commissioned piece he'd made from start to finish, including purchasing the materials himself.

"Alright then, boy," Matty said. "Clean up and get on home."

The older man stood, stretching his back before walking slowly, painfully, towards his house. Years of work at the anvil had made him unusually strong for his age, but he was stiff from the unbalanced muscles on his back, and the pain was evident in his movements. Galen watched him go, wishing he could do something to ease Matty's hurts, then tidied up the forge and put the fire out with his Ardor.

Leaving the smith always felt a bit like leaving behind the new and fragile internal peace he'd found, but Galen knew it would still be right there in the morning, so he went anyway. He'd made a few acquaintances in this little town, and it was starting to feel like some place he could put down roots and learn how to keep friendships that weren't built around an environmental justice movement that could crumble at any given moment.

He kicked his feet through the dirt on the road like a little boy, smiling down at his boots.

Isa. Who would have thought?

Truly, if only Maverik could see him now. Would he be pleased to see Galen smiling?

Even after he'd completely abandoned the mission they'd spent years working toward?

His good mood only a little dampened by thoughts of his best friend, Galen looked up at the biodome faintly shimmering in the low light of the setting Polar Sun. Maybe this world was too far gone to save, anyway.

Galen arrived at the fork in the road where one path would lead him to the inn he was staying if he were to turn right. He decided to take the left. There was no purpose to his wandering, which felt rather freeing. Galen could walk anywhere he liked, and there would be no consequences. No Weilers with his sketch on the wall, no Kalaiden members waiting to bombard him while he nursed a beer, no family to support even when he was failing himself.

The last one was a bit of a stretch, as Galen had never known his blood family. But he had friends. Friends who had relied on him and would probably never forgive him were they to ever see his face again.

Ahead, Galen could see the dirt road tapering into nothing, though there were a few residences on either side beyond the point where it disappeared. Past those buildings, the edge of the biodome was barely visible. Galen hadn't realized he was already so close to the outskirts of Isa.

Odd.

Galen paused at the end of the road before deciding to continue. After all, he was forging his own path in life now. He might as well create a literal one, as well.

Curious about the isolated houses that stood away from any roads, Galen drew closer. Two of them looked unoccupied with boarded-up windows and peeling paint lining the door-frames, their exteriors decrepit and unkempt. A thick layer of dust coated each of their front porches.

What sort of Elfeans had lived here? Were the houses empty because there was something wrong with them, or was it because their owners had left or died?

Perhaps he could fix one of them up and use it. It would be quiet out here near the edge.

The third house was painted a dark color, which was unusual, and Galen realized with a jolt of shock that it was occupied when he noticed a light was on in the window. There was a rocking chair on the front porch with a tiny old woman in it, slowly moving the chair with her left foot as she watched him silently with beady little eyes.

"Pardon," Galen said, taking several steps back. He was

closer to the house than seemed polite when its occupant was outside enjoying themselves. "I was lost in thought."

Turning to leave, Galen was still marveling at how long it had taken him to see the woman when she spoke.

"Galen Zardoth, I think. Unless my memory is failing me. It has been a very long time."

It was a statement, not a question, and Galen froze. It was the first time he'd heard his family name spoken aloud in... well, he couldn't remember the last time anyone had said it. Her voice was surprisingly solid for how old she appeared, and he slowly turned as the name continued ringing in his ears.

"Sorry, but should I have the pleasure?" Galen asked as casually as he could manage. He crossed his arms, putting his weight onto his right foot and resting his left leg. He looked closer at this woman to see if he'd ever seen her before, raking through every possible memory.

"No, you wouldn't have." The woman didn't elaborate. She just sat in her chair, rocking back and forth rhythmically using the tip of her left shoe, watching Galen with her steady gaze.

"Alright then," Galen muttered, unsettled as he turned to leave.

"You left your post at a very bad time, boy."

Sighing, Galen fought the urge to roll his eyes and again faced the house. She couldn't possibly know what she was talking about. This lady had to be senile. Or maybe she was a retired Weiler who somehow knew who he was. If that were the case, Galen would have to leave Isa. "With all due respect, ma'am, what do you want?"

The woman tilted her head. "I want you to explain why you left. I did not see this."

"You did not see...what are you talking about?" Galen demanded.

"Answer my question, and maybe I will answer yours."

Thoroughly irritated by the entire exchange, Galen stared up at the woman. She returned his gaze without blinking, without even appearing to breathe. Something about her felt off, and he shifted uncomfortably as he tried to identify it.

"I do not have to tell you why I left," Galen said finally.

The old woman's lips tilted upwards. "If you tell me, I'll tell you who I am."

Curiosity was warring with reason, and a sudden sense of rebelliousness filled him. Fine, if she wanted to play games, he would play games.

"I wanted to start a new life," Galen said.

"Liar."

"How would you know?"

"I know," the woman said, her voice smug. "Now tell me the truth."

Damn all the Founders, he *had* lied to her. How had she known? And, honestly, the more Galen considered why he'd left Kalaiden, the more he wasn't confident that he actually knew.

"I...I don't know. It was a spontaneous choice. I was...tired," Galen said at last.

The woman's head inclined in the other direction, and she blinked slowly. It almost seemed like it was the first time he'd seen her blink since he'd arrived.

"That was most of the truth," she said. "And it explains why I did not see. Now, as for the answer I promised you, I was once a young woman."

"That is not who you are," Galen argued.

"It is answer enough," she said. "Being a woman can be an identity in and of itself."

"Well then, who are you now?"

"Ah, see, you are learning. Now, I am an old woman."

"You mock me." Galen shifted so his full weight was back on both feet, glowering at the little old lady.

"You cannot blame me for having a little fun." She grinned, revealing two rows of yellowed teeth. "It is so dreadfully dull here. Why *did* you come to Isa, of all places?"

"Isa is not so bad," Galen retorted, growing increasingly frustrated. "It is quiet here. I can think."

"You can think anywhere, boy. You just didn't want to." The woman's smile vanished, and she seemed almost disappointed.

"What do you want?" Galen asked again.

"What I want is of no consequence. What I know, however, is that if you do not go back, something terrible will happen to your king. And then the world will likely end, and all that nonsense. Dire stuff, boy. I'd rather avoid it."

Galen burst out in incredulous laughter as she watched with an unamused expression, one eyebrow lifted. It only made him fall apart again.

"And how in the Founders do you know that?" Galen demanded when he finally calmed enough to speak, his tone now sarcastic.

The woman leaned forward, her hands steepling in her lap, and she sniffed down her nose at Galen.

"Tonight, on your walk back to the inn, you will see a dead man walking. Know this, Galen Zardoth, and you will also see the truth. Goodbye now." The woman abruptly pushed herself up from her rocking chair and picked up the cane leaning at its side. Painstakingly slow, the old woman hobbled towards the door of her home, leaning heavily on her walking stick.

"Why do you even care what happens to my king?" Galen demanded, his mind racing with the possibilities.

The woman paused with her hand on the door handle, though she did not look back at him. "I don't, really. But someone else does, and I've decided I quite like her. And, you know. The world and all that. I'd prefer to live."

The door to the dark little house slammed behind her, and the Ardor light inside went out almost immediately.

Galen was rooted to the spot, a whirlwind of emotions coursing through him. Anger was what he felt first, primarily directed at the tiny woman who had known things she couldn't have and had spoken to him like his grandmother had used to when he misbehaved as a child. It had made him feel small and like he didn't know the world as well as he should have.

Then there was the uncertainty that she'd planted in his mind. If something bad were to happen, Galen could not stay here. There was always the chance that she had lied, but what motive would a little old lady at the very edge of Isa have to put such notions in his mind?

He needed to clear his mind. Galen spun from the house and started back towards the road leading to the inn where he was staying. What did she mean by a dead man walking?

Paying more attention than usual to the emptiness around him with every sense on high alert, Galen kept his hand close to where he still wore his knives. Since he'd arrived in Isa, he hadn't needed to use them a single time, but it was a difficult habit to break as someone who hadn't left them behind since he was old enough to make his first kill. Before that, even.

The fork in the road came and went with no incident, and then he neared the part of Isa where most of the townsfolk were. The shops for food, the inns, the taverns, and even the clothing stores were all huddled together on one little street as though it were the physical manifestation of Isa's heart.

Each time a door opened, or someone turned his way, Galen jumped, unsure what he expected to see. When he passed the tavern to where he was likely to return after washing up in his room at the inn, he saw it.

A dark shock of hair tilted down towards a young woman who was picking through a bin of apples in front of the general store. It was the way the man stood, with the bearing of a soldier, his hand resting casually on the hilt of his sword. He was out of place here.

Galen couldn't move, but he needed to see the man's face. Then the woman laughed at something the man had said and walked around him, her apple selected, and she walked inside the store. As she moved behind him, the man turned with her, never taking his eyes from the bit of bare skin at her shoulders as he followed her through the door.

A cold shock flooded Galen's system as he registered who the man was. Why in the name of the Founders was he here? Of all places, why was he in Isa?

How was he alive?

Damn, that cursed old woman. Galen needed to leave, and he needed to leave now. Regardless of whatever bad thing would happen to his king if he didn't, he had to at least tell Maverik about what he'd just seen. *Whom* he'd just seen.

It wasn't possible, and yet, somehow, he was here.

Galen couldn't risk being discovered. That man would know him anywhere.

Hurrying to the inn, Galen paid the innkeeper extra to have supper ready for him when he returned downstairs with his things stuffed into the one small bag he'd arrived with. His Ardor masks didn't have much life left, but he had no other choice. He would just have to be very careful with how he used them on the journey back to Seradan.

As promised, the innkeeper had a bag of food waiting on the front desk, but as Galen picked it up, the front door opened and that black-haired ghost stepped through. Thankfully, the desk was far enough from the door that he didn't immediately look in Galen's direction upon entering.

"Pardon, but where is your back door?" Galen asked the innkeeper in a hushed voice, taking off as soon as the man pointed in the direction. He was careful not to appear rushed to avoid drawing more attention.

The back door was tucked around the corner of the hallway that led to the kitchens, and Galen thanked the Founders as he pushed it open and stepped outside. He'd made it out of there without being seen. The stable, built directly behind the inn, was perfectly positioned for him to get his horse.

Galen ran into the small barn, checking every stall as he passed without a care for his speed now. His horse was unfortunately at the very end of the aisle, protesting as Galen pulled the gelding out from the middle of his dinner.

"Come, we must go," Galen growled, finally getting the beast away from the hay and tying him to the stall door. Though Galen was an accomplished horseman, he swore tonight was the fastest he'd ever saddled a horse. Soon, he led his animal out of the back of the stable.

Galen mounted as he prayed that his papers would be enough to get him out of Isa at this hour and kicked his horse towards the biogate.

He raced from the town of Isa, back to where he knew Maverik was in Montclair as the biodome darkened upon the homes tucked safely within the borders of the city at his back. Along that road where he'd walked, where the little old woman had interrupted Galen's thoughts, were those three little houses.

The following day, long after Galen was gone, the Polar Sun rose. It shone upon three abandoned houses.

CHAPTER 21
BRIATTA

Later the same day that she'd met Vydian, Briatta laid in bed on top of her covers and stared at her ceiling. The woman had also overheard the man asking about Tallor and had noted Briatta's observation of the conversation as well. Vydian had appreciated that, like herself, Briatta hadn't outright asked the waitstaff either or waltzed around with case information visible.

Briatta had learned the uses of anonymity as a Night Rose, and she stuck to it with this case for several reasons. If she, a newcomer, had shown up at a bar where the associates of her target had frequented and had immediately made it known she was looking for that person and anyone who spent time with them, she could face challenges later. It was better to listen and gather information before approaching her subjects. Also, the art club. She grudgingly admitted that Neven had been right to start that.

Apparently, Vydian thought the same, though Briatta hadn't quite learned enough about the woman to understand her thoughts.

After the man had left, a few others entered Allemor House and asked different bartenders or staff members about Tallor and his friends. Briatta had found it most interesting that each person gave slightly contradicting answers.

One of the male bartenders had said that Tallor's friends were inconsistent patrons, showing up only to celebrate something, while the first woman had said that they came every first and third day of the week. Briatta would have to determine which of those statements was true; it would perhaps be as simple as making it part of her evening routine to pass by Allemor House each day, but it would be inconvenient.

Another female waitstaff had told an older woman that Tallor was abrasive to other guests on occasion, and she suspected he had some enemies among regulars. Tallor's file stated that he was a placid young man without apparent reason to be the target of a criminal group, implying he didn't usually cause problems.

If what the older woman said was true, it also meant that any one of the other customers could be a key witness. Or, none of them would be. There was no known connection between his friends and the crime group.

Maybe it wasn't necessarily the kidnapping that was the focal point of this investigation; Tallor was a victim of coincidence, and it was the crime group itself that needed to be brought to justice. Rescuing him would simply be a bonus.

Briatta rolled onto her side, exhaling with frustration as she considered what she'd discovered on day two of the contest. While it was completely normal to be without definitive leads this early in an investigation, she'd always felt a deep and overwhelming pressure to work harder and faster to solve the case before anything else could happen. In the Night Roses, the constant itch to make progress had become a regular companion due to the nature of her work. The people she'd tracked were the reason she trained the way she did, and it was difficult to tamp down the familiar, desperate urge to hunt.

She took a deep breath and reassured herself that nothing terrible would happen to Tallor. This was staged. It wasn't real.

Though Briatta was slowly realizing her incessant desire to press onward was rooted in something different. This case wouldn't just win her the Ackmanlee; it would save her own life.

Maybe she was being a little dramatic, and losing wasn't entirely comparable to dying, but still. Briatta had never wanted anything more than to win the Ackmanlee.

When she finally drifted off, she slept fitfully—normal while working a case. The only good part about struggling to stay asleep was being wide awake with plenty of time to make it to Sour Soup before the biodome lightened. Briatta was growing accustomed to her early rides through Montclair, and it quickly became a part of the day she greatly looked forward to. The city was still and peaceful, and the air was always at its coolest from having been mostly free from the light of the suns for several hours.

The sound of her horse's hooves was the only thing that Briatta heard as she entered D'ivory, arriving at the street where Sour Soup was a little earlier than usual. To her surprise, she could see from the end of the road that a light was already on in the central kitchen, but Leah normally didn't get there until just when Briatta was finishing up.

A bad feeling grew in her chest as she drew closer. She dismounted, tying her horse to the fence of a nearby house and palming a dagger while jogging down the sidewalk toward Sour Soup. As she approached, she heard banging from within that didn't sound like the normal cooking noises she'd become accustomed to with Leah's arrival in the pre-Polar Sun stillness of the biodome.

The front door had been left cracked open, and Briatta pressed against the wall. She leaned slowly forward, trying to peer inside without drawing any attention. She knew from experience that those hinges creaked.

From her position outside, looking into the sliver of the room, she couldn't determine what was happening. The kitchen wasn't visible from here, nor was the entire right half of the dining area.

Briatta, still holding her knife, crept around the exterior of the building and through the fenced-in yard. One of the cows lifted its head when she saw her, lowing with delight at the prospect of breakfast and having the pressure in her udder released with milking. Briatta cringed at the sound, freezing near the back door as the noises within Sour Soup paused before someone gave a hissed shout to ignore the damn beast and to keep working.

Having grown fond of the cows and Leah and this stupid little building, Briatta bristled. Whatever was happening inside was *definitely* not good.

The back door, unfortunately, led directly into the kitchens. Briatta would give away her position if she opened it then. Casting a glance around the small yard for something helpful, she seized one of the heavy wooden bars—used for keeping the barn shut during the winds scheduled for certain plants— and barricaded the door.

Satisfied that her quarry was trapped, Briatta returned to the front of Sour Soup. The opening was narrow enough that she wouldn't be able to avoid making the hinges scream, so she tentatively opened the channel to her Ardor, called the shadows to herself, and pressed against the side of the building, melting into the darkness as best she could with her still-clumsy use. Hidden by the inky black she'd created, Briatta reached out with her power and, concentrating, used it to shove the door.

Instead of swinging open a few inches as Briatta had intended, the door slammed open violently and bounced back towards the frame. Fortunately, it stopped with a gap large enough for her to slip through when she was ready. Unfortunately, the hinges had squealed louder than they had ever before, along with the thunderous bang it had made when hitting the wall.

She really needed to gain better control over her Ardor. Briatta felt a slight twinge of regret at having skipped her training with Neven yesterday to focus on the Ackmanlee and promised herself to work it into her schedule even as she held her breath, listening for what the people inside would do.

"Someone check that," a man barked.

Footsteps approached. An older man wearing a red headscarf around his face poked his head outside, his eyes wide as he tugged the door open a little further to scan the street.

"Th—there's no one there," he said, taking a halting step outside.

"Check around back. And keep watch when you come back," the man inside ordered. Red Headscarf seemed anxious; his eyes flitted about the street, but he obeyed, moving entirely out of the doorframe. His head swiveling nervously, then walked towards Briatta. She must have seemed normal while swathed in shadows, because he didn't notice her. She thanked the Founders for that small mercy.

When he was nearly upon her, Briatta darted behind him and lashed out with all her training, slamming the pommel of her dagger into the back of his head. He crumpled to the ground, and she slipped her arms under his shoulders to lower him quietly. Working quickly, she gagged him with the head-scarf, then cut a strip of his shirt to bind his hands behind his back before untying his boots and retying them together.

Confident he wouldn't be going anywhere for a while, Briatta returned to the door and peered through, this time with a much better view of the interior. There were only two other men inside; one was supervising the other, who was filling a sack with food from the cabinets.

With both of their backs to her, it was the perfect time to make her move. Neither appeared armed, but Briatta was wary of concealed weapons, and she especially eyed the man who appeared in charge as she stepped through the door and quietly approached. She released her hold on her Ardor, allowing the shadows to dissipate, as a large blob of darkness would be glaringly obvious in the dining area's light.

"You see anything out there?" called the leading man over his shoulder. He was now just in front of her though his eyes didn't leave the progress of the other man.

When there was no reply, the thief stuffing the bag looked up and locked eyes with Briatta over the shoulder of his boss a moment before she brought down the hilt of her dagger on his head.

For a long second, everything was still. Then, the working man dropped his bag and made for the back door. Knowing he wouldn't make it far, Briatta quickly took the scarf that the man in charge had also been wearing—though his had fallen around his neck rather than disguising his face—and used it to bind his own hands in the few moments she had before the escaping man would realize he was trapped.

She heard the rattle of the back door and profuse cursing. Then came a sound like drawers being opened, followed by loud and clumsy footsteps as he made no effort to be quiet now that they'd been caught.

He held a large butcher knife in one hand when he reappeared at the doorframe between the back and the dining hall.

It seemed there *could* be downsides to allowing a target to run free and unsupervised in a kitchen. Briatta couldn't even be mad at herself; she'd allowed it to happen.

"I'd advise you to put that down now," Briatta told him, drawing her other dagger so she held one in each hand. "Nobody wins in a knife fight. Except for, well, me."

The man's eyes were wide, glancing down to his leader and then to the front door, where his accomplice laid unconscious as well. But he didn't seem as nervous as before, and his hold on the butcher knife was steady. His gaze hardened, and he took up a fighting stance.

A fight it would be, then.

Briatta raised her knives easily as she stepped forward, and then, surprising him, she sat down at one of the tables.

"You can either come to me," she drawled. "Or we can wait like this for Leah to arrive, and she can fetch the Weilers."

An emotion that Briatta couldn't quite identify flashed across the man's face, and she tilted her head at him. Had that been...uncertainty? Or a sign of internal conflict?

Her question was answered a moment later when he lunged, knife first. She threw herself backward from the bench and onto the floor. Rolling to a crouch, she swung her left leg and kicked his feet out before jumping back to stand over him. His knife clattered to the floor. Briatta knocked it from his reach and knelt, holding her dagger to his throat.

For a second, she wanted nothing more than to make the cut.

Taking a deep breath as she stared down at the man, Briatta forced herself to pull the knife back so the blade wouldn't touch the flesh of his neck, her hand shaking with the effort.

This wasn't her. She'd never actually ended someone.

But this was personal.

They'd attacked something new and precious to her, something she was extremely protective of. More than she'd realized.

"You know, I actually thought you might know how to fight," she said with a tinge of regret. It had been a long time since she'd tested her abilities against a true criminal, one who didn't fight fairly and who was battling for their life. They always fought differently. While Briatta never relished the idea of battling against someone who truly feared for themselves and who was skilled, it would reveal her weaknesses. And that was important.

Besides, Neven had always been there to make the final blow or to help subdue the criminals so they would be tied and presented like a roasted pig next to all the evidence against them.

After securing and gagging all three men, Briatta dragged them and tied them to three separate tables by their arms so they wouldn't be able to free each other. Satisfied that she'd done everything she could, Briatta headed out the front and went around the building, removing the beam from the back door as she set to work milking the cows and goats.

When she'd collected everything from the animals, Briatta gathered it all as she always did and carried it into Sour Soup. She set it on the table nearest to the kitchen door and checked that her captives were still where she'd left them before taking a seat and settling in to wait.

Leah arrived on time, halting abruptly when she opened the door and saw what awaited her. Her hand went straight to her heart.

"Oh, my Founders," she gasped. "What happened?"

Briatta stood, gesturing to the still-full sack on the floor. "I caught them stealing food. I can go and fetch the Weilers now that you're here."

Leah's face crumpled with disappointment at the bag, and she regarded the men as if they were badly behaved children. "This is a community kitchen. If you were hungry, all you had to do was ask."

Shaking her head, Leah made her way toward the kitchen, picking up the stolen food and dragging it back to where it belonged, slowly pulling the contents out and organizing it. Briatta's heart clenched at the sight, and she glared at the men as she stalked toward the door. If they'd been targets of the Night Roses, and if this had been one of her missions, perhaps they would already be dead.

It was the first time that Briatta had considered death without hesitation. In the past, she'd never allowed herself to become emotionally invested in one of her cases because the things she'd seen and heard...well, it would have hurt too much.

These men had stolen from a woman Briatta had begun to trust and care for. Her reaction to them was so strong, so unexpected, that Briatta felt nauseated as she left Sour Soup and separated herself from the scene.

Briatta hadn't ever regarded a target in such a vicious way before; Neven normally handled the...dirtier aspects of their work. Did he think about it like how she was thinking about it now? For the first time, she wondered how he lived with himself for the acts he'd committed.

It only reinforced her will to maintain a personal distance from cases. She could not afford to lose control.

Briatta trudged her way back to her horse, the night of poor sleep and her early morning activities catching up with her already. When she arrived at the closest Weiler station, the lady at the front desk took one look at Briatta's face and offhandedly mentioned a delightful kavfe shop nearby and how she herself was going to fetch a cup soon. Briatta had never had kavfe, because it was a drink favored by the Ardorless, though Owena had never allowed them to partake because she'd claimed it would stain their teeth, and they would become addicted to the energizing properties it had. Though, as she'd grown up, Briatta hadn't wanted the association of being an Ardorless that came with it, either. Just that moment, however, she didn't care either way.

Fighting the urge to roll her eyes, Briatta requested assistance, explained the situation, and brought a small group of Weilers back to Sour Soup. They took statements from Briatta, raising their brows skeptically when she couldn't give them a straight answer on how the men had been apprehended, questioned Leah, and then led the three thieves away. Watching them leave, Briatta wondered if she should have told the truth. Publicly, she'd always cultivated a demure reputation. But for the Ackmanlee...would they hold it against her if she didn't admit to bringing down criminals?

If she won the Ackmanlee and became a Weiler, it wouldn't matter either way. She would have to train with her fellow Weilers, and people would know what she was capable of.

"I knew that Neven was involved with people who...helped others," Leah said uncomfortably as she emphasized the last word once it was just the two of them in the kitchen. "I hadn't realized that you were, too. Thank you."

Briatta turned from where she stood across the counter between the dining room and the kitchen and stared at the closed front door. "Neven told you that?"

Leah nodded, hesitating. "It was Owena who originally brought him here when she found him as a young boy, you know. She used to spend a lot of time in D'ivory before you three came to live with her, helping people, and at first, she would never let me feed her as thanks, but after a while...well, she had a lot of meals here at Sour Soup. Neven...told me a little. About what she does for us. I knew you were her niece, but I wasn't sure...well, sometimes parents don't want their lives for their children."

Neven must have held a tremendous amount of respect and trust for Leah if he'd even hinted at what the Night Roses did. Briatta had never told anyone, not even Morenna.

"Owena ate here?" Briatta felt chilled, and she took an involuntary step toward the kitchen.

"Oh, yes." Leah sighed and smiled, kneading the dough she'd started working on. "She still comes and helps out on occasion."

Not knowing how to respond to this new information, Briatta sank onto one of the benches. "I had no idea."

Glancing up from her dough, Leah smiled sympathetically. "She's talked a lot about all of you. She has a difficult time reconciling with the harsh truths of our lives. Owena wants you to have everything."

Briatta's heart sank, and her hands formed into fists. There was so much that she didn't know about her own family— both Neven and Owena—and the more that she learned, the more Briatta felt she hardly knew even herself. The person that Briatta had become, who she was, didn't align with the young woman she was beginning to feel she *should* be.

The lives that Owena and Neven had lived were the opposite of how Briatta had grown up, and she knew that her aunt had likely done that on purpose. But it had shaped Briatta differently. She was more separated from her family than she'd ever really known.

When Briatta left Sour Soup to find Neven for Ardor training, she was determined to better understand his relationship with her aunt and ask for his thoughts regarding the missions they'd worked on together. Apparently, Owena had shared more of her history with him than with her own blood relatives. Perhaps it would better help Briatta understand the punishment she was working through.

CHAPTER 22

A rdor practice went poorly again, but Neven nodded with approval at Briatta's marginal improvement. She still couldn't accomplish much with her Ardor other than enshrouding herself—though that had been a significant help at Sour Soup—making the room dark, and aggressively pushing things around. If she could learn to detect where people were in her shadows or control how hard she moved objects—and she thought that she could—then it would be a huge advantage. The only thing she'd become adept at so far was hiding herself, which was only useful in the dark.

The more she used it, the more she felt like her Ardor possessed a playful personality that she had to work with rather than control.

She didn't want to tell Neven just yet, because the concept of impish Ardor sounded ridiculous when she considered it, but it was also difficult to wrangle the power. It was less effort to...encourage it, instead. Maybe that was just how her Ardor worked.

Maybe she would practice her Ardor while they were out

working on the Ackmanlee case. She was still annoyed that Neven wouldn't let her do it alone, especially considering that he technically wasn't allowed to be involved and Vydian had joined, but Briatta had enough battles to worry about.

"That's enough." Neven watched her flop to the floor, his arms folded and then crossed the room to his bag. When he walked to her, he held out a packet of papers to her. "Here. Everything I could find on Vydian. There was only one file under that name—and not a whole lot. I'm assuming it's the same person."

Briatta had asked him to look into Vydian, to see if there was any information at Night Rose headquarters or in Weiler records. She hadn't wanted to risk her standing with the Ackmanlee, or face Owena. Blessedly, Neven had agreed, and she stared down at the file she held. *Vydian Lockwood.* Skimming through it, she read that the woman was from Seradan. She was Ardorless, which was obvious from her lack of an Ardor mark—though, Briatta considered, she could be hiding something the same way she was—and worked as a caretaker for elderly people. On paper, Vydian appeared harmless. But why had she traveled from Seradan to compete in the Ackmanlee? Not to mention she'd picked out Briatta and Neven immediately; that wasn't something any other competitor had done.

"Thanks," she mumbled. Then, closing the file, she looked up. "Neven." Thankfully, it was still early, though it felt much longer since that morning's events with the thieves in Sour Soup. "Why didn't you tell me that Owena brought you to Sour Soup before?"

Neven stopped in the middle of returning a sword to the rack on the far wall of the basement, his gaze turning to the floor. He was silent for so long that Briatta thought he might not respond at all, so she turned her attention to pulling on her shoes. She'd removed them in a desperate attempt to ground herself when she'd started to lose control of her Ardor for what felt like the hundredth time.

"It wasn't my place," Neven said finally, hanging the sword and facing Briatta. "I...it still isn't my place."

Briatta regarded him carefully. She saw her friend, but while Neven had always loved her and her family, this was a version of him that was surprisingly protective of Owena. While her aunt had helped him when no one else had, had given him purpose, education, and self-defense training, and had introduced him to an entire community that was still there for him in the D'ivories, Neven had always taken Briatta's side, especially as children.

But they weren't children anymore. That much had been made all too clear to Briatta in the recent cycles.

Now that she considered it, Owena had done the same thing for Briatta and her siblings as she had for Neven, but she'd been younger and didn't remember much about their lives beforehand, unlike her friend. If she'd been Aden's age when their father had left them...Founders, Briatta didn't know how that might have affected her life.

Briatta had often defended Neven to her aunt when sibling-like scuffles had broken out, and Owena had caught them fighting. She and Neven had kept secrets from their aunt, as all children did. But if there was ever a situation where Briatta and Owena had to hide something from Neven— Choosing and Ardor aside—what would she do? Briatta honestly couldn't answer that question; she thought she might cave and run to Neven just as she had with her Choosing, even if she wanted to believe she'd be able to remain as loyal to Owena as Neven evidently was.

Founders, yet another issue she'd have to address eventually.

A part of her warmed with affection for Neven because he

was guarding Owena, allowing her aunt to be the one to share her life experience with her adoptive children. There was something special about that, something that would have otherwise felt stolen.

Now, Briatta and Neven were both older, and apparently, Neven was a little wiser. That aspect of character growth had skipped her entirely, Briatta thought bitterly. Maybe if she'd gained a fraction of the experience Neven had, she could have saved herself the trouble she'd caused.

It seemed Neven appreciated all that Owena had done for him because of his past, whereas Briatta took it for granted because she didn't remember enough of the hardships she'd endured, only taking in the lavish life provided by her aunt.

Or maybe she just wasn't as good of a person.

Briatta's gaze caught on her shoes again. "Alright."

Briatta saw the flicker of surprise surging through Neven, because she wasn't the kind of person who would let an issue like that drop. The *old* Briatta, anyway.

Pushing herself to her feet, Briatta forced a smile and looked at her lifelong friend. "Vydian wanted to meet at the next store that had been stolen from, right? In about an hour?"

Neven, still looking at Briatta with an incredulous look on his face, nodded slowly. "Right."

"Should we grab breakfast before we go? I'm starving," Briatta continued. "It's been a long morning."

"What, milking a few cows getting to be too much for you?" Neven teased, though he still regarded Briatta with suspicion. She was glad for the shift, grinning over her shoulder.

"No, actually," she said. "Sour Soup was being robbed when I arrived."

"What?" Neven's entire demeanor darkened as Briatta filled him in on the events of her morning as they headed up the stairs to the Belrose dining room. Only after they went through the doorway did Briatta realize she hadn't checked who was there before entering. Since her fight with Owena, she'd always peered into the dining room first, avoiding it if her aunt were there.

This time, however, the one time that Briatta didn't look, Owena was sitting at the table, absorbed in the papers spread before her. She looked up at the sound of Briatta at the door, her face lighting up.

What?

Briatta stared dumbly at the woman, confused at the scene before her. How could Owena be happy to see her after what she'd said in the carriage? After how Owena had punished her?

"Bria," Owena greeted her with a warm smile, shattering the thoughts tumbling through Briatta's head. "I'm sorry I haven't been home. How are you? How is the Ackmanlee going?"

Briatta was frozen, her stomach plummeting through her legs and all the way to her feet. She swallowed thickly, but her mouth had gone so dry, it felt like cotton.

"O-Owena," she stammered, both thrown by the friendly greeting and her presence. If Owena had been avoiding her all this time, Briatta didn't understand why she was glad to see her niece now.

Owena's smile faltered, her gaze going briefly to Neven before returning to Briatta, puzzlement blossoming in her eyes.

Wait.

Did her aunt not realize the emotional turmoil she'd put Briatta through when she'd disappeared after having given Briatta the list of requirements for how she was to live?

"I'm sorry I haven't been home," Owena went on slowly. "We have an...interesting assignment at the Night Roses. But

Neven has been updating me on your progress when he's dropped by. I hear that things have been good."

Only just having considered that all her anger and frustration toward her aunt may have been unreciprocated, Briatta's mind snagged on the fact that Neven had been reporting to Owena. She whirled to face him, her stomach dropping even further—if possible—at the betrayal. Neven, who seemed to have realized the same thing, shook his head and stepped back at the same moment Briatta opened her mouth to question him.

"I only told her you'd been doing well when I saw her at headquarters," he said. "I swear it, Bria. Keep me out of this."

Caught between her aunt and her friend, Briatta felt as though she would have rather been quite literally anywhere else on Carceron—even outside the biodome without protection.

Owena appeared to conclude that there was more going on than she realized, because her brows came together as she nodded slowly. She looked between Neven and Briatta, the thoughts clearly churning across her face. Finally, her mouth parted as she sucked in a sharp breath.

"Briatta," Owena started, her head tilting. "Is there something wrong?"

Was there something *wrong*?

Briatta stared with disbelief at her aunt, and so much churned in her mind that she couldn't find the words she wanted to say, her mouth hanging open like one of those aquatic animals in her history books, gasping for air where there wasn't any.

Of *course* there was something wrong.

"Is there something wrong?" Briatta finally managed to squeak. Owena's brows rose at the raw emotion in her niece's voice.

"Yes," Briatta continued. "There is, in fact. For starters, I know that I am totally fucked up, and I didn't turn out the way you wanted me to, and I know I shouldn't have said what I did, but you handed over the harshest punishment you've ever given me, and then you stonewalled me for two weeks!"

Now that she'd found her voice, the words wouldn't stop coming. Just like the day she'd damned herself in the carriage on the way home from Malcalaire, but this time felt different.

"Owena, I've been questioning *everything* about myself," Briatta cried, her arms waving. She felt like a child, flailing for control over her feelings, but everything was pouring out all at once, and she couldn't help herself. "I can't decide whether I was cursed with this Ardor because the Founders see how rotten I am inside, and I will fail the Ackmanlee and live in D'ivory forever as penance. Or if I will eventually destroy myself because I know that I *should* be okay with that life, but I am not, and I will keep fighting for something better because I am selfish, and that will be the end of me."

The more she spoke, the more frustration flowed, and Briatta suddenly felt empty and exposed as she stood there, facing the one person who truly knew who she was inside and out.

Briatta wasn't perfect, and she had a very long way to go before she would once again feel good about who she was at her core, but recognition was a good thing.

To her surprise, tears welled in Owena's eyes. Her aunt's beautiful features crumpled as she stared up at Briatta.

"No," Briatta breathed, her heart clenching. Any hesitation she might have still felt toward approaching her aunt evaporated, and she rushed to the table, crouching beside Owena. "I'm so sorry; I didn't mean to upset you again. Ever since my Choosing, I can't seem to say the right thing. I...what can I do? How can I make this better?"

Owena placed her hands on Briatta's cheeks, her skin warm and calloused as her index finger gently brushed some of Briatta's hair back.

"I am the one who has failed you." A tear escaped the corner of Owena's eye, trailing down her cheek. She gazed warmly at her niece. "I should never have scolded you like that and then left. You're right. I...I can't imagine what you must have been feeling after your Choosing, and the choices that you're now faced with for your future. You are not rotten, my darling girl. You are just young. Young people make mistakes; they're flawed, and they have prejudices that they must work through. From the sound of it, that's what you're already doing."

The words washed over Briatta like cool water, the shock of realizing Owena hadn't resented her this entire time coupled with the dizzying knowledge that she'd been tearing herself up over...what? Nothing? This wasn't what she had expected, and Briatta's emotions welled up again in response to Owena's, tears threatening to fall from her own eyes.

"Oh, don't you cry, too." Owena laughed and pulled Briatta into a hug, pressing her niece's head to her chest and resting her chin on Briatta's hair, stroking it the same way that she had when Briatta was a little girl.

"I'm sorry," Briatta said. The dam of emotion behind her eyes released as she heard Neven leave the room. Tearing herself from Owena, she glanced after him, wiping her cheeks with her sleeve.

Owena held her niece at arm's length, looking at her sternly. "I'm fairly certain you could do just about anything, and I would still forgive you, Briatta. Just because I steer you in a different direction—and I'll admit I didn't do it well this time —doesn't mean I do not love you."

Despite herself, Briatta's heart swelled again, and she

laughed as she shed more tears. When she finally collected herself enough to drink deeply from a cool glass of water, Owena tilted her head toward the hallway.

"I'm sorry. I don't think I've been able to make enough to pay rent yet. I don't even know how much it is, but it's got to be more than what I've made." Briatta realized she was rambling and closed her mouth.

Owena looked confused before throwing her head back, laughing. Caught off guard again, Briatta rocked on her heels and watched her aunt, perplexed.

"You do not need to pay me," she finally said, smiling at Briatta. "That was meant to teach you how little many of our fellow Elfeans live on each cycle."

Nodding with understanding, Briatta looked down at her feet. "I didn't realize how much we had. In comparison, I mean."

"You did, my dear," Owena replied. "You lived that way as a child, but I believe you blocked much of it out. We must never forget where we come from, no matter how much it hurts."

Briatta's eyes heated again, and she looked at the ceiling as she pushed the feelings back. "I know. I'd forgotten," she admitted quietly.

There was a long stretch of silence, and then Owena nodded as though she'd made a decision.

"You can come back in, Neven," she called. He appeared a moment later.

"Well, I'm glad that's resolved," he said, sighing dramatically and pouring himself a large cup of tea.

Briatta picked up a roll of bread and tossed it at him in playful annoyance. He caught it effortlessly, taking a bite as he sat across the table from Owena. Her face still felt hot and swollen, so she took a clean napkin and dunked it into the cool water on the table, dabbing it on her face.

"What is it you're working on?" Briatta asked casually, setting down the wet napkin to put together a small breakfast.

Owena sighed as she sat back in her chair, lifting her tea to her lips.

"It's classified," she told them over the rim of the cup. Briatta raised her brows, glancing up at her aunt. It was very rare that something was so classified she and Neven weren't permitted to know about it—at least not at this stage in their careers.

"I promise I'll tell you when I can." Owena set her cup on the table and smiled at them both. "Well, I've got to get back to headquarters. I'll hopefully see more of you in the next couple of weeks." She rose to her feet and swept from the room. Briatta and Neven watched her go and immediately looked at each other.

One of Neven's eyebrows lifted in silent question, and Briatta shrugged. Unfortunately, she'd been entirely too wrapped up in her own emotions and concerns about her moral dilemmas and life problems to involve herself with whatever Owena was doing. Now, though...maybe they'd be able to fit in some additional scouting if things progressed well with the Ackmanlee.

CHAPTER 23

S hortly after Owena left, Neven and Briatta followed. They were running behind schedule to meet Vydian, but it had already been an entirely too-eventful day, and it was only just past breakfast. Briatta hoped they wouldn't have to deal with much more, even if it meant things progressed a little slower with the Ackmanlee. After all, it was only day three, and between Neven and herself—despite still being more than a little irritated that he was helping—Briatta was perhaps overly confident in their abilities to win this competition.

Vydian waited on the street corner of the shop they were visiting first, leaning against the wall of the building with her arms crossed and a bored expression. They were in an area of town mainly occupied by warehouses and businesses that required either manufacturing space or storage. Some buildings in this area were run down and abandoned, their exteriors peeling and patchy from neglect. It was a section that wasn't often frequented by the average person.

When Vydian saw them, she pointedly lifted her wrist and pretended to check an imaginary timepiece.

"Sorry," Briatta said without really meaning it, her hand going to her own timepiece at her throat. "I had an unexpected...annoyance this morning."

"Got more action at a soup kitchen than we have since this whole thing started," Neven said jokingly, although it was all too real of a statement.

Vydian pushed herself off the wall, straightened the light-weight jacket that was only meant to protect against the Polar Sun, and shook her head slightly. Briatta could tell Vydian didn't believe Neven. Instantly, her friend stiffened beside her.

While Briatta didn't care whether Vydian believed she could defend herself—and perhaps it was better her new ally thought she couldn't—Neven had always been protective of Briatta. She couldn't afford for that protectiveness to be a problem, especially if he was going to insist on following her around.

"Let's go," the woman said, turning and flicking her shining black hair over her shoulder.

Neven avoided Briatta's pointed look before following. After a moment, Briatta started after them, too, her thoughts shifting to consider how much she could trust Vydian. While she had initially approached Briatta, apparently, she had little patience for tardiness and levity.

The store wasn't far, and Vydian held the door open for them as they squeezed into the small, dim interior. The tiny bell above the entrance heralded their arrival, and a moment later, a young man appeared behind the front desk from a doorway that presumably led to an office or back storage area.

"Welcome, welcome," he called brightly, looking over those who had entered his shop. "How can I help you?"

They hadn't discussed how they would interview clerks or store, so there was a moment of hesitation from all of them as the man observed his three patrons.

"Might I interest you in some brambleberry liquor?" he asked. "Can't keep the wares out front, unfortunately. Everything's in the back."

Even though it was only mid-morning, Neven brightened at the sound of something to drink. The man smiled and disappeared through the door.

"How much should we tell him?" Vydian hissed.

"Don't say anything," Neven said, his tone so surprisingly condescending that Briatta gave him a wide-eyed look she hoped conveyed he should shut his mouth.

"Let us handle it," Briatta whispered to Vydian with a placating smile. "We have a...thing we do. It works."

Vydian's eyes flickered with irritation, but it was quickly masked as she folded her powerful arms. "Fine."

The woman was an odd sight in Montclair. While Briatta was familiar with other young ladies who looked like they were trained to fight, it was rare to encounter one whom she didn't know, especially if she weren't a member of the Night Roses. Being that Vydian was from Seradan, this made sense, but...well, she was a mystery Briatta would tackle later, after the Ackmanlee.

A few moments later, the man reappeared, and Briatta exhaled slowly with relief at having figured out their strategy —flimsy though it may be—and that they'd been quick about it. He placed three small cups half filled with a dark-amber liquid on the counter and set the bottle down.

"It has a nice, smooth flavor with a sweet aftertaste," he said, slipping into his salesman act. Briatta was adept at recognizing when Elfeans adopted a persona they often had to portray, and this was one of those situations. The man in front of her wore a mask, just as she and her companions did.

Neven obediently stepped forward and picked up one of the cups, holding it under his nose to smell before sipping it.

He set it back on the counter for a heartbeat before taking a second, slightly longer, swig.

"I see." Neven nodded thoughtfully. "That's very nice. Founders, I swear I recognize that flavor."

The man brightened considerably. "You might know us from Allemor House?"

"Ah, is that it?" Neven asked, his head turning as if he were genuinely surprised. In reality, Briatta knew he already recognized the shop's name from the tavern's menu, as she had. "It's a real shame that. Allemor House has been in shambles ever since that poor man went missing."

The man shrank into himself. He glanced over his shoulder into the back room, though Briatta couldn't see or hear anyone else, before leaning over the counter conspiratorially.

"They're saying it might be connected to some robberies that have been happening," he said quietly. Briatta's ears perked. In the corner of her eye, Vydian's hand fisted slightly.

Neven nodded solemnly. "They are. You...you haven't been affected, have you?"

The shopkeeper's face hardened. "As a matter of fact, I have. They took a good portion of my liquor."

"No," Briatta gasped, stepping in. This had always been her favorite part in working with Neven. They were naturally good at complimentary roles in their investigations together, at becoming whomever they needed to be to get the job done. "I'm so sorry, that's terrible."

The man sighed, then took one of the two cups meant for either Briatta or Vydian and downed its contents. "Brutal. I've got to make a living too, you know."

"Perhaps we can help with that." Neven pulled a bag of coins from his pocket, and Briatta looked at him questioningly. As far as she knew, her friend didn't have much money of his own, but he *had* been training with the Ardorists since his

Choosing, so he might have been making more. Or maybe it was money from the Night Roses that he'd used on a previous mission and hadn't returned yet.

Eyes widening at the sight of the purse, the man looked between them suspiciously. "What is it you want?"

"Information," Neven replied.

"On the thieves," Briatta added.

"Alright," the man agreed readily, tipping back the last cup. Neven's portion, which he hadn't finished, was the only one with any liquor remaining on the counter. The vendor took the money bag and tucked it behind him. "I wasn't here, but they left a signature."

A signature? For thieves? Briatta hadn't seen that very often. In her experience, thieves wanted to be as inconspicuous as possible, but she supposed it could be different for the Ackmanlee. The man produced a small piece of paper and pushed it across the counter.

For a second, Briatta's heart skipped a beat, but the signature of the black flower wasn't a rose, though it was so similar to the one that she'd drawn for years. No, this flower was some desert flower; Briatta couldn't be sure which.

"May we keep this?" Neven already asked, voicing precisely where Briatta's mind had gone. She wanted to identify the flower. If it had even remotely the same significance that black roses did to the Night Roses, it would offer a considerable advantage in uncovering the false thieves committing these fake crimes.

"Ah, sure," the man replied. "Weilers ain't doing anything about it, anyway. No matter how many times I bother them." It was meant to sound convincing, but the man's voice was a little too excitable, as if he were more pleased to be talking with them anyway. Likely, he had a stash of the signatures behind his desk to hand out to any who came asking.

Of the people Briatta had met since the Ackmanlee had begun, this man was one of the better actors, even if he still wasn't that good.

"Thank you," Briatta told him.

"Was there anything else that they left behind? Do you mind if we take a look around?" Neven asked. The man, who seemed to regard this conversation as friendly, suddenly appeared suspicious.

"What are you guys, anyway? You ain't Weilers," he said, squinting at them over his bottle of brambleberry liquor. The suspicion was obviously fabricated, and delayed, like the man had just realized he'd confided in someone he probably shouldn't have and was now worried he wasn't playing his role correctly.

"We are...friends," said Vydian, speaking up for the first time. "We'll take care of this for you. You said the Weilers weren't helping, anyway."

"No, how do I know you aren't the thieves themselves? Come back to collect the evidence?" The man reached for the paper he'd set on the counter, but Neven snatched it up before he could grab it. "See? Now, that's odd. Why do you care about that signature so much?"

With each word, he became a little more confident, and a bit more convincing.

Briatta sighed. The man was decent, but the actors didn't need to be quite so good that they prevented progress. But wasn't this exactly how many inquiries had gone while on duty with the Night Roses? Almost nobody believed that she or Neven were actually there to help, because they didn't wear recognizable uniforms. They had to wear disguises to prevent themselves from being recognized by their peers and alter their voices in those cases, but otherwise, there wasn't much difference.

"We're here to help," Briatta reiterated. "Why would we ask you these questions if we were the original thieves? Wouldn't we be finding some way to silence you instead?"

The man paused, peering at them through narrowed eyes. "You could be just trying to feel out what I know before you dealt with me."

Fighting the urge to roll her eyes, Briatta looked at Neven. Occasionally, if a victim were a little too confused about who was the enemy and who wasn't, it was exceedingly difficult to reach them.

"Alright," Vydian said, stepping forward. "Ignore them. What if I told you that we were trying to catch the group who robbed you? We could deal with them. For a price."

Gaze flickering between the three, the man relaxed, though it was an exaggerated movement. "And...what? You want me to pay you after you've just given me a cycle's worth of income?"

Vydian shook her head. "Just let us look around the shop where you keep your inventory. That's all. We'll be out of your hair immediately after."

The man looked down at the counter for a long minute, his fingers tapping in thought before he sighed in concession. "Alright, fine. But be quick about it."

Rather than thanking him, Briatta set to work without checking whether Vydian and Neven did as well. Years of working alongside Neven meant she knew he'd go to every entrance and exit first, even the inconspicuous ones, for those were how vagrants often infiltrated the scene.

The back room was filled with barrels and bottles stacked neatly on shelves, and a woody scent overlaid with the stinging smell of liquor hung in the air. Having never been very fond of that stuff, preferring cider and wine, Briatta wrinkled her nose as she scanned the shelves. Most were fully stocked, but there was one section where it was obvious that three barrels had been taken. Briatta went straight there and examined the empty space.

The unfortunate part of a staged crime scene was that if there were any clues, they would be extremely specific to the case, meant to steer the contestants in an exact direction. It likely wouldn't be the usual information people accidentally left behind when they were indeed in a panic about being caught, like a scuffed shoe mark or a piece of fabric snagged on a sharp edge as someone passed through a door.

The entire building had been scrubbed clean. There was nothing. But didn't that itself mean something?

"Has anyone else come to look or collect evidence?" Briatta asked without looking back at the man. She knew he'd followed them.

"No," he said.

"Did you clean up after?" Briatta turned to face him, annoyance at the shopkeeper filling her bones. She folded her arms so her hands wouldn't go to her blades as they so often did by instinct.

"Oh yes." The man nodded emphatically. "They left the place a right mess."

Vydian, slowly scrutinizing the shelves across the room, turned and met Briatta's eyes over the man's shoulder, her brows lifted in incredulity. Briatta's fingers tightened on her arms as she kept a calm expression.

"Can you describe the mess to me, please," she ordered, slipping into the Night Rose version of herself because if she didn't, Briatta thought she might throttle the man.

Perhaps recognizing the lethal glint in her eye, the man hurried to comply. "They must have been in a hurry because only two barrels were gone when I arrived. The third had cracked and leaked liquor all over the place. Still reeks of it in here. Anyway, it was lying on the floor here." He pointed at the ground beneath the empty shelves. "The paper was pinned there. And there was a bit of fabric caught there." He indicated the corner of a shelf.

So, Briatta had been wrong. The Weilers had been thorough in their set-up.

Touching the middle shelf, the man frowned as if reliving the moment.

"Were there any details that you noticed as you cleaned? Hair, footprints?" Briatta walked around so that she was in his line of sight again.

The man shook his head. "Sorry. I still have the broken barrel and the fabric, though."

"May we see?" Vydian interrupted, stepping forward from where she'd paused across the room.

"Sure." The man led them to a small office tucked into the far corner of the storage room, where stacks of paper weighed down a desk and a logbook had been left open with a pen on one of the pages. The barrel was tucked beneath the desk, and the man bent to drag it out. Its metal bands squealed on the stone floor as he did, and Briatta grimaced, bending to help. The wood had cracked down one side. Though it was still held together by the banding around its middle, it was wide enough that all the liquor was gone.

At first glance, Briatta didn't see anything.

"May we take this?" She looked up at the man, who shrugged. At least he wasn't questioning or obstructing their investigation anymore.

"Don't see why not," he replied. Then, he handed them a small piece of rough grey fabric. "Might as well take this, too."

Neven still hadn't reappeared, so Briatta and Vydian each picked up a side of the barrel. Rather than dragging it to the front of the store, they left through the back. The man held the door for them but slammed it as soon as they passed through, and Briatta glanced over her shoulder, scowling.

"Either they paid him really well, or he missed his calling as an actor for the D'ivory theatre," Vydian commented dryly. "The crowd would have loved him."

Briatta grunted in agreement; with some formal training, the man would have fit in at the large white building just at the edge of the district, run by the members of the poorer community for the Ardorists looking for entertainment.

They set the barrel down on the sidewalk, looking for signs of Neven, who appeared a minute later over the top of the building. He climbed quickly down the fire escape, dropping smoothly to the ground.

"They definitely broke in through this door," Neven told them, nodding to the back entrance. "I couldn't find evidence of tampering with locks anywhere else."

Then he noticed the barrel. "What's this?"

"A broken barrel left behind," Briatta replied, and held up the fabric. "This, too."

"Where are we going to put that?" Neven stared at the barrel and shifted his weight to one leg, crossing his arms.

Once again, Briatta and Vydian looked at each other. Briatta had to admit the other woman wasn't bad at this. She'd been mostly quiet, but she worked efficiently and didn't question their methods.

The barrel was heavy, and Briatta didn't want to draw attention as a couple of young women lugging it through Montclair, but she also didn't know of any place nearby where they could leave it.

Finally, Vydian sighed. "I know a place. If you trust me."

Neven made a noise but refrained from protesting. This was not his competition, and Briatta could tell he knew he was already pushing the limits of the rules by helping with interviews and with searching the premises of the affected shops.

Briatta chewed on her lip before nodding. If they were going to make this team work, trust would have to come into play. Even if she didn't have much confidence in Vydian yet, she could at least make the woman feel as if she did. "Alright. Show us."

They picked up the barrel again, and Vydian led them a short distance away to one of the seemingly abandoned warehouses. It had boarded-up windows and smelled faintly of hot metal. Vydian went directly to the side door and pulled a key from her pocket, unlocking the padlock and pulling it open.

Inside, the building was dim, and Briatta could see motes of dust floating in the rays of light that streamed through the cracks on the boards over the windows. However, a clean mat was in the middle of the room with a few wooden weapons lying in neat rows at its edges.

"I occasionally use the place to train." Vydian shrugged. "Figured it'd be a good spot for the barrel. Inconspicuous and all that."

Neven nodded appreciatively, though he wore a perpetual scowl as if he didn't want to admit that Vydian could possibly be right or more helpful to Briatta than he was. "This will do nicely."

Once the barrel was hidden beneath a tarp and they'd swept their footsteps from the dust, the three young Elfeans relocked the building and headed towards the next store on their list. The plan was to finish interviewing all the shopkeepers who had been robbed before returning to Allemor House for its opening hours. Briatta stifled a yawn as they walked, still hoping it would be a slower afternoon. She'd had enough notable events for one day.

CHAPTER 24

B riatta lifted her brambleberry cider to her lips, grimacing as a whiff of the scent brought her back to the store that had reeked of a sharper, more sour version of the drink she loved. She set the beverage down on the table without taking a sip, as she'd done every time she'd attempted to drink since they'd arrived two hours earlier. This was usually her favorite drink to order, but it had been a very long day, and apparently, the memory of the harder stuff didn't sit well with her.

The paper in front of her remained mostly blank except for the beginnings of a sketch of the little desert cat sitting outside of Allemor House.

Briatta was so tired. And she still had to rise early the next day for her shift at Sour Soup. Even if things with Owena were better than she'd realized—and Briatta had momentarily considered quitting her job—she found the idea of leaving Leah to manage the place on her own to be distasteful. Briatta knew they would find someone else to take care of the animals in the morning, but what if the kitchen was robbed again?

Would her replacement be able to protect Sour Soup the way she had?

This was a foreign feeling for Briatta, but it felt good enough that she would not abandon the little soup kitchen.

In fact, she actually looked forward to seeing if Leah was alright after this morning. Briatta hoped that she was.

The animals would be glad to see Briatta, as well. They'd grown accustomed to her presence, fondly grunting when she appeared each morning, and Briatta had become rather protective of them. She'd even started sneaking the cows extra apple pieces when she could, snagging the fruit from the Belrose kitchen on her way out—to Preida's confusion, as the family had never eaten as much fruit as since Briatta began working at Sour Soup.

Neven swallowed the dregs of his third ale and put the cup down a little harder than necessary, the glass knocking against the table's wood and making Vydian jump.

"Founders," the woman muttered, glancing darkly toward Neven from the corner of her eyes and pulling her spiked brambleberry lemonade closer to herself as it wobbled slightly from the impact.

Briatta had unfortunately discovered today that Vydian and Neven did not get along. At all. Neven had pointedly contradicted nearly everything Vydian had suggested, and the woman had become increasingly irritated and verbally combative, arguing her point and disagreeing with all his ideas in turn.

Briatta found she liked Vydian more and more with each passing hour.

Being that Neven had been her best friend for most of their lives, Briatta thought maybe she should defend him at one point, but then he'd stuck his foot into his mouth by calling Vydian aggressive when the woman was just standing up for herself in whatever disagreement they'd been having. Briatta had immediately gone to her defense, instead.

From that moment onward, Neven had glowered, stalking behind the two as they continued their tour of the robbed stores without saying much more.

It was also possibly the reason he was on his third beer when he didn't usually drink much.

The biodome had darkened a few hours ago, making it feel much brighter inside Allemor House than it had earlier. The crowds were dwindling, and nothing related to the Ackmanlee case had occurred even though Tallor's staged friends had appeared for a while.

Briatta had successfully recognized and identified them based on their photos, but they'd been somewhat subdued and hadn't stayed long. They seemed more like they were showing up in honor of their missing friend than anything else, and Briatta reminded herself that this was all fake as she watched them go through the motions. This at least confirmed that the bartender who said they came every third day of the week had been correct.

At one point, a few people without Ardor-marks—all moving as though they were aware of every part of their bodies —entered the establishment, stayed for a while, then left. A few of them approached Tallor's friends, but nothing helpful came of those interactions. Briatta was beginning to feel more like the friends had been placed in the file to intentionally mislead them, but eliminating a possible lead was still progress, and so she stayed.

The way those people had also examined the place from corner tables and had spoken at length with the staff suggested they were competitors, and Briatta carefully noted their faces. She had yet to identify other obvious teams, but they would be more difficult to pick out than solo contestants simply because they would appear more natural than someone loitering by themselves.

Neven waved for a bartender, and one hurried over to refill his ale. Vydian watched darkly as the yellow liquid filled his glass, her gaze flicking to Briatta's.

"Shall we call it?" Vydian asked. She'd barely finished half of her drink, and Briatta knew that, like her cider, it was mostly for show. "I doubt anything more is going to happen tonight."

"You guys can if you want," Neven said, taking a large swallow of his fresh beer. "I can hang out for a bit longer and see if I find anything." Now, he pointedly looked at Briatta. "Some of the most important information is gleaned in the most unexpected places."

Annoyance flared in Briatta's chest at the implication she was failing in her duties by neglecting small possibilities like who might show up at the Allemor House after everyone else had left.

Vydian scowled, her internal conflict over that response plainly visible as it rippled over her features. She obviously wanted to be somewhere else, but it was also clear Vydian hated the idea of leaving Neven to do a job that she probably felt she could do better.

Briatta ignored Neven's stare because she knew he was intentionally needling her, wondering where Vydian would rather be as she waited for the outcome of this verbal sparring session. Finally, Vydian folded her arms and settled into her seat, the glare she sent in Neven's direction scathing.

"I'll call it." Briatta smirked, rising to her feet.

Looking down at Neven, she relaxed her face as if she were bored, lowering her voice so no one would hear her next words and leaned in slightly. "Unless the Weilers are more meticulous than we realize, I doubt anything that will make or break the case will show up tonight."

Picking up the drawing she'd started, Briatta folded the paper, pointedly dragging her fingers along each new crease without looking away from Neven.

Vydian's dark expression faded as she looked between the two friends, apparently reading the unspoken argument. She leaned forward with a look of resolve. "Actually, I'll stay with Neven until he leaves."

As if that wasn't already obvious.

For what felt like a suspended second in time, Briatta's eyes flitted between Vydian and Neven, neither of whom she'd wanted to work with on this case, yet here they were. Neven appeared unhappy with the realization that Vydian would stay and shifted in his seat, taking another swig of his ale. At the same time, the woman pulled some of her raven-black hair over her shoulder and twisted it between her fingers, smirking down at her drink.

Fighting the urge to laugh as it bubbled up in her throat, Briatta left her untouched cider and weaved her way through the tables to the front of Allemor House. They'd been seated near the back of the restaurant, which had been helpful in having a clear view of the entire room, but it had meant being unable to monitor the front patio or activity beyond it. Briatta had been so exhausted—both emotionally and physically—that she hadn't protested, though she had been surprised Neven hadn't said something. Perhaps he was feeling the same.

Just as Briatta made to leave, she caught the end of a sentence from one of the servers.

"—as many questions tonight as I did?" A young woman pulled her hair back from her face as she smiled up at her male coworker. Pink stained her cheeks, and her eyes sparkled as she looked at him. Briatta knew immediately that she was infatuated with the young man, but his disinterested expression spoke clearly of his feelings. He obliged her anyway, leaning to reply.

Briatta flinched internally, knowing that heartbreak was in store for the girl.

"More than I expected. I figured they would be more... subtle about it." The male server straightened and glanced away.

Interesting.

That meant more contestants had come to Allemor House tonight than they'd managed to mark. Briatta continued through the front door and into the cooling air of the bionight without hovering for too long to avoid attracting attention. Above, the Ardor lights on the underside of the biodome formed a large, winged creature that Briatta didn't recognize. It appeared to roar and spit something from its mouth across the sky, flapping its massive wings slowly, its tail swinging behind. Perhaps it was some artist's creation, and it was featured to draw the consideration of possible buyers.

Her walk home was uneventful until Briatta had to fight to keep annoyance off her face when she saw a young couple dart into a dark alley together. She didn't care what people did together as long as it was private. And both parties were willing. While it was already a core value of society, Briatta was exceptionally steadfast in her viewpoint. Perhaps it was due to the horrible things she'd seen in her line of work, the people she'd saved, and the villains she'd helped to bring down; those who blatantly defied the ways of their people.

Despite her annoyance, Briatta stopped near the alley, opening the channel to her Ardor to hide herself, and waited until she was sure both young participants did, in fact, want to be there. Shaking off the shiver of revulsion at what she heard, Briatta dismissed her Ardor and hurried away after encouraging the shadows she'd created to join the existing ones on the ground.

Only when she felt she was far enough from the alley did Briatta pause, take a deep breath, and try to wipe the all-too-fresh scene from her mind.

There were many dark memories in her head that she managed to suppress—for the most part—but they all decided to rush through her mind and haunt her at the same time. Apparently, this was a trigger for her.

Briatta waited where she'd stopped, breathing deeply and focusing on the physical sensations in her body.

The bionight was warm, and she could feel the heat in the slight swelling of her fingers and toes. With the Nocturne Sun beating down even on the darkened biodome, it would never really be anything but hot and slightly less hot. A bead of sweat trickled down her brow, and she zeroed in on the sensation of it tracking over her cheek and then dripping from her chin.

At last, when she felt grounded again, Briatta continued home. It would be a very long time before she felt comfortable giving that part of herself to someone else.

Some people were the opposite. There were members of the Night Roses who would likely never settle down or have their own families, but they were free spirits with their bodies and minds. Witnessing traumatic things affected everybody differently.

Briatta found herself wondering what must have happened to the members of Kalaiden to have encouraged them to join the cause. There was no reason to believe King Novak was deliberately leading them down a path that ended with the death of their planet, as Kalaiden was trying to get everyone to believe. In fact, all signs indicated that was merely the natural progression of life; everything had an eventual expiration date, no matter how long it existed.

Kalaiden and its members could very well just be delusional, being the Ardorless who were unhappy with their lives and had become fanatical about all the reasons everyone else should be, too.

Though, supply raids had decreased over time, implying the group was becoming self-sustaining. That couldn't be a good sign for anyone. But they had never caused harm, to Briatta's knowledge, so King Novak hadn't made a large effort to stop them. At least not yet.

Perhaps the job that the Weilers were looking to fill involved Kalaiden and their many failed attempts to bring down the resistance group. That would explain the Ackmanlee case.

Briatta turned onto Penrose Avenue, hugging herself with her arms, and nearly ran into someone walking in the opposite direction.

"Oh, I'm so sorry," she said, leaping nimbly out of the way even as her hand went automatically to her dagger. She fought the urge to call upon her Ardor and snap the shadows to hide herself once more; the more she practiced with handling her Ardor, the more natural it felt to reach for it when faced with potential danger.

Ironically, using it would be more dangerous than not using it all, if the wrong person were to witness her Ardor.

The other person, someone much taller than her, caught themselves easily as they stepped backward, a look of surprise registering on his face.

Briatta's heart flipped, and her fingers slackened on the hilt of her blade. There was no threat here. Or, at least, that's what every fiber of her being wanted to believe. The man before her was still a Weiler, and while he'd been kind to her, she could never trust him completely. Her other profession would never allow it.

"Miss Belrose," Simeon said. They stared at each other for a sickeningly long moment. Briatta glanced down the road to her house and gestured weakly at it.

"I was just heading home," she managed.

Simeon followed her gaze and then looked back at her. "I ah...yes, that makes sense. I'll let you get to it, then."

He started to leave but hesitated. "How is the case going?"

The shock of running into him—and on her street—wore off and her nerves settled a little. Briatta felt herself slip into her confident Night Rose agent persona. She gave him a small smirk, hoping that it appeared secretive. "Should you be asking me that?"

Looking at his shoes and pushing his hands into his pockets as if he didn't know what to do with them, Simeon huffed a laugh. "No. Probably not."

"Hm," Briatta hummed, watching him closely. "It's going well, then."

It was, after all. At least, it wasn't going poorly. They weren't very far into the Ackmanlee yet, so anything was possible, but Briatta felt good about her progress.

A shadow of relief flickered across Simeon's face. He nodded curtly, his mouth tightening at the corners. "Is there anything else? To...report, I mean."

Briatta tilted her head, frowning slightly as her brows creased. She wasn't certain what he could be referring to. "Um, no. Not really."

The barrel wasn't anything unusual yet. While Briatta had learned never to dismiss even the most minor evidence, she'd also learned not to travel down a path presented by a possible lead and allow herself to become consumed by one piece of the entire puzzle. If she did that, she might miss other critical information.

It was possible the imaginary criminal group had left the barrel behind just because it couldn't hold liquor anymore.

Other than the barrel, Briatta wasn't aware of a connection between the robbery at Sour Soup to the Ackmanlee, and they hadn't uncovered details about the signature that would help them progress in their analysis of the case yet.

Simeon looked like he wanted to say more, as if the words were bursting to be spoken, but he tapped a foot instead and looked over his shoulder. "Alright. That's good. Ah...good night, then."

Once again, he turned away.

"Ah, wait," Briatta blurted, and then swallowed. What was she doing? "Um, can you tell me anything about Vydian?"

Simeon's lips turned up. "I'm sure I don't know what you mean by that."

Right. Briatta couldn't know who else was competing; for all she knew, Vydian could be lying to her about her participation. She could have broken into a Weiler station and read the mock case files. Why anyone would go through that much effort just to trick her, Briatta had no idea. Maybe it was part of the challenge.

And Simeon definitely wouldn't be allowed to talk to her about it.

"Of course," Briatta managed, and Simeon's smile widened before he bobbed his head. He left without hesitation this time, hurrying from the corner of Penrose Avenue just fast enough that it seemed almost like he was fleeing. Briatta watched him go, confusion welling where nervous anxiety had been a second before.

Founders damn her, but she craved that man's approval. For whatever reason, every bit of common sense and social etiquette abandoned her the very second she realized she was in Simeon's presence.

Briatta groaned as soon as he was out of earshot, throwing her head back and grimacing. She kicked the ground as she turned to her house, forcing herself to keep walking toward it. What about that man made her turn into a blubbering idiot? Even embodying the ever-self-assured agent didn't work for her when he was nearby, and that worked almost everywhere else.

Maybe she needed another approach for talking to him. One that would prevent her from making a fool of herself every time.

And what did that last part of the conversation mean? Simeon had clearly wanted to say more, but he'd restrained himself, almost painfully so, with a completely strained expression.

The next time she ran into him, Briatta would work up the courage to ask him about it. Whatever Simeon had wanted to say was probably irrelevant to the case, especially because Weilers wouldn't be permitted to meddle, but...it mattered. It mattered more to her than she cared to admit to herself, let alone to anyone else.

Founders, she hardly knew the man. Maybe she shouldn't ask him anything.

Completely wound up by the entire interaction, Briatta sighed deeply as she reached her home and headed inside. Maybe she would never know what to do when it came to Simeon.

CHAPTER 25

The following morning, Leah greeted Briatta with a new level of respect. Before the robbery, Briatta had just been an employee that the woman had taken on as a favor to one of her dear friends. Now, there was a fragile sort of bond growing into something more than just employee and manager—something akin to friends. Briatta left Sour Soup feeling more fulfilled than she had in a long time.

Over the next couple of weeks, there was no progress in the case. Briatta took daily rides through Montclair, keeping an eye out for any odd behavior that might hint toward a lead or any other possible clues that could help her find Tallor. She observed the friends, both at the Allemor house and at their homes, to no avail. A few times, Briatta caught sight of the other potential contestants—she'd committed their faces to memory during their visits to Allemor House—prowling the roads, seemingly doing the same thing that she was. It reassured her to see them tracking the same paths, the same leads. It meant that while she wasn't ahead as she'd like to be, at least she wasn't behind, either.

Vydian and Neven met up with her at the restaurant occasionally, always accompanied by a sketchbook, but they didn't want to arouse suspicion by suddenly showing up every night and hanging around until most of the patrons left. After a few of those sessions and asking pointed questions about the case that would reveal whether Vydian had read the file or not, Briatta decided the woman was truly competing.

On the nights that Briatta went alone to Allemor House, she took up watch from a rooftop across the street and cloaked herself in her Ardor, which she was still training with Neven.

She'd hit a mental block, though.

Despite being able to call her Ardor and control it better than ever—in big and sloppy ways—she couldn't coax it to form specific shapes or manipulate it with more detail. This frustrated her to no end, and while Neven reassured her that he still could hardly manage his Light Ardor in those ways, it didn't help.

A few times, Briatta returned to the decrepit warehouse to examine the barrel as well as the piece of fabric. They'd left the barrel as it was, and she couldn't see anything on the exterior or through the crack that made it seem like anything other than just a barrel. But it gave her time to think and a place to stop on her rides. Vydian had even sparred with her on occasion on the makeshift training mat, and Briatta was pleasantly surprised to find her a worthy opponent, though she didn't fight to her full capabilities, and she suspected that Vydian did not, either.

In addition to the Ackmanlee case, Briatta still struggled with reconciling the person she'd once dreamed of becoming with the person she had become. This new awareness was torturous.

There were areas where Briatta had grown, and there were parts of her that were still far from who she should be. Despite her reconciliation with Owena, which had gone well, she wasn't sure she could look at her aunt without feeling as if every ugly part of herself was on display, so she was more determined than ever to become the best version of herself.

But there was the possibility she would never be that girl. That woman. And perhaps that fear kept her on her rides through Montclair, finding excuses to avoid being home.

Lost in her thoughts and the gentle sway of the mare she'd taken from the stables that morning, Briatta held the reins loosely with one hand and rested her other on the cantle of the saddle, leaning back and staring up at the sky through the faintly shimmering biodome. It was its usual pale blue, never filled with anything aside from either of the two suns because of the lack of weather outside the biodome except for the occasional desert storm—thankfully predictable by Air Ardorists who could sense them before they happened.

No longer paying attention to where the mare was going, Briatta squinted as she turned her head to look at the Polar Sun, tugging her headscarf back a little. Had their world always been like this? So hostile that the people on the planet's surface had to survive using the very Ardor that fueled it? Or had there been a time when the world was more forgiving? Had it once looked the same as the painting in the Belrose library?

The Polar Sun was getting low in the sky, and Briatta watched it for a while, twisted around in her saddle, before deciding to head back home for the night. She picked up the reins with both hands and looked around at the small courtyard of shops, some of which had been closed permanently and were boarded up, and others that looked like they received little to no traffic. This was a poor section of town on the city's outskirts, northwest of D'ivory, where many Ardorless attempted to make a living.

Briatta frowned as she examined the shops, pulling the mare to a halt. How had they gotten here, where most of the storage for the entire population was concentrated?

A flicker of movement in her peripheral vision caught her attention, and Briatta turned. Something disappeared over the roof of the building closest to them, and Briatta hesitated only for a second before leaping down from the saddle, smacking her mare's rump to set her running home and scaling the wall of that very building.

On top of the roof, Briatta flattened herself, scooting forward until she could see into the alleyway behind it. A tall, broad figure wearing all black—*familiar* black clothes—was creeping away from her, a headscarf obscuring their hair and any other identifying features. They paused before twisting to peer in Briatta's direction, and she ducked behind the apex of the roof, waiting several seconds before peeking over again. The figure was gone.

What in the Founders?

Briatta nimbly jumped, landing in a crouch, and gauged the distance to the rooftop across the alley before deciding it was easy enough. This was a particularly narrow gap, and the roofs were relatively flat. Glancing again towards the end of the row of buildings and still not seeing anyone, Briatta ran to the edge of the roof and leaped, landing as lightly as she could on the other side, running a few steps to help with her momentum, and then made her way to the end of the strip.

The back side of the courtyard was a wide road, and she caught sight of the figure vanishing around the corner of a large warehouse a second before she would have lost them. Briatta studied the warehouse and frowned—wasn't this one of the locations that had been marked in the case?

This definitely qualified as suspicious behavior, and it finally gave Briatta something to do instead of wandering aimlessly throughout the city. Lowering herself to the ground from the top of the buildings, Briatta darted across the road and pressed her back to the wall where she'd last seen her target, leaning until she could see around the corner. There were two of them now, the second person similarly clad in black and disguised but feminine in stature and figure.

There was no question about it. They were Night Roses wearing the dark uniform that was as familiar to Briatta as her own skin. But what were they doing there?

They seemed to be in a discussion, and the female drew a dagger from her thigh, gesturing with its tip for the other to follow. Before the first Elfean did so, they turned slightly to check behind them, and Briatta drew in a sharp breath.

Even though he was almost entirely covered, and even though she was far enough away that she couldn't see perfectly clearly, Briatta knew those blue eyes anywhere.

Neven. But what was he doing here, wearing his Night Rose uniform in the middle of the bioday? And who was he with? The woman was a Night Rose, which meant she couldn't be Vydian—that, and she was too tall, and the two basically hated each other—but who was she?

Briatta didn't know how she hadn't seen it sooner. Neven's movements were intimately familiar to her, and now that she knew it was him, she couldn't unsee it.

Feeling a gleam of annoyance that she still wasn't privy to the Night Roses' jobs and now curious to figure out what they were up to, Briatta pulled her own black headscarf from her pocket and wrapped it around her head after tearing her pale one off.

The female paused at a door to the warehouse. While Neven kept watch, she broke it open, slipping inside. A heartbeat later, Neven followed. Briatta gave them a few minutes to get ahead before running to the door, listening carefully. No sounds came from within the immediate vicinity of the building, so she crept carefully through the doorway, fighting the urge to draw her blades. She didn't want to accidentally startle Neven or the other agent and hurt them or herself.

A quick glance around the area she'd walked into revealed that she was in a massive, open warehouse. Towering shelves stocked with rows of boxes blocked any view she might have had, but there was a ladder up the wall and mesh metal walkways crisscrossing over the shelves. While they were fairly exposed, there was a corner just above where she might be able to remain inconspicuous if she used her Ardor.

Briatta accessed the channel to her Ardor, calling the shadows even as she climbed. She swathed herself in darkness and hurried, as she didn't know the mission objective and how long it would take Neven and his female companion to complete it. Sometimes, it was as easy as running in and knocking someone out to collect a piece of evidence. Other times, it was much more involved.

Briatta didn't breathe until she reached her chosen hiding place, tucking her Ardor around her to hopefully appear as if the darkness were natural as she willed herself to blend into the shadows already here.

From the walkway, Briatta had an excellent view of the entire warehouse. She wasn't high enough to see between all the shelves, especially the ones farther away, but she could see almost everything else. Satisfied, she settled in to listen and watch, waiting for any hint of movement.

For a long, drawn-out silence, there was nothing. Then, a shuffling noise came from the end of the building, and Briatta strained to hear, desperately wishing she'd been sent on this mission with Neven instead of whoever the woman was. Knowing her best friend was down there somewhere working, yet being unable to have his back as she always did, was a new kind of torture. Honestly, she'd assumed he wasn't working because he was helping her with the Ackmanlee, but she should have known that he was. He wasn't a competitor, after all.

To her left, Briatta sensed—rather than heard—a third person, short but broad in stature, emerge from between the shelves. They wore an entirely grey outfit with a headscarf that covered everything except their eyes and had a bag strapped to their back. This third person, creeping toward the exit, kept their movements silent and smooth, probably to avoid Neven and his partner, though the Night Roses were still hidden from her view.

Briatta straightened. The grey outfit...it was familiar. Like the fabric they'd found in the liquor store. But why would Night Rose agents be in the vicinity of a character for the Ackmanlee, if that was connected?

This man must either be their target, or the place was being robbed while they were working. Or...there was another explanation. As the Elfean drew nearer, Briatta could see the bag on their back more clearly, weighed down with something, but they vanished through the exit before she could study it further.

Briatta shifted her gaze back in the direction of Neven and the other agent. What were they doing? How could they have missed the man? She was torn between wanting to wait, ensuring Neven was alright, and going after this third person, who was an unknown. They could be Neven's target—all evidence pointed to that, aside from the color of their clothes and that one thread of doubt. There were other possibilities—an independent robber or someone totally innocuous. However, why would anyone without ill intentions hide their features and creep around in a warehouse?

Finally, Briatta silently cursed her friend and slid down the ladder, keeping her shadows pulled to her, and followed Grey Figure through the door. Thankfully, they hadn't made it too far, and Briatta set out after them. Under the dimming light of the darkening biodome, Briatta remained relatively well hidden as she tracked the Elfean's shifty movements.

They constantly looked over their shoulders while hiking the bag higher on their back. It was clearly meaningful, but for all Briatta knew, it could just be filled with perfectly fertilized soil that this Elfean was taking home to use on plants that were special to them.

Briatta followed them for a long time, winding through Montclair's back alleys and streets. They paused when other people passed, crouching out of sight before continuing south through the city, well past the northern point from where they had begun. The farther they went, the darker it grew, until it was fully bionight.

Thankful for the total cover of darkness, Briatta allowed her Ardor to entirely blanket her as well as spread out to experiment with feeling for others within the shadows as her mark passed Penrose Avenue and continued toward D'ivory. Strange that they would go this way, as D'ivory had been just southeast of them from the warehouse. This figure was leading her all the way around the city.

Looking at her home as she stalked past, Briatta could see her mare had indeed made it back but was happily grazing in the yard, still fully saddled. Where were Petyr and Preida? He was typically swift to notice anything abnormal about the property, and if he didn't, then his wife would.

That would be an issue for later. Briatta continued her pursuit of Grey Figure.

They made it all the way to the edge of D'ivory when her target veered right, following the district's stark white structures. Grey Figure was nearly at the end of the biodome, then they took another sharp right, disappearing into an alleyway. When Briatta caught up and looked around the edge, they'd vanished completely.

What? Where had they gone?

Briatta confirmed there weren't any doorways in the alley. Nothing. Running her hands along the wall, she felt for any seams or cracks that her eyes might have missed as she paced up and down. It was long, so she was sure that she would have seen the figure by the time she had made it to the start of the alley.

Feeling nothing unusual on either wall, Briatta stared at the cobbled ground, walking slowly and watching for any strange or particularly loose stones. There were plenty of those in D'ivory, but none that she turned over revealed anything suspicious.

Shit. She tapped her foot and placed her hands on her hips. Biting her lip as she looked around, she was unsure of how to proceed. Her mark had disappeared, and she had no clue how to find them, especially if she were to leave this area tonight.

But Briatta also wouldn't know if Neven were okay if she were to stay here. Every instinct warred inside her; the ones that had been drilled into her by the Night Roses screamed for her to find a perch somewhere and wait, while the part of her that cared for Neven cried to go to him.

At last, Briatta decided to return home. She'd wanted to stay and watch for Grey Figure to see if they were related to the Ackmanlee because of the fabric, but if they'd been out and about tonight, maybe they were still placing hints and clues. The case had become stale, and Briatta hoped this would be a new direction. There were now several places in the city she could patrol to watch for movements, which meant she didn't need to stay.

Tearing herself from the alley, Briatta pulled her headscarf off and folded it, grateful for the reprieve the biodome offered them, tucking it back into her pocket and making her way home. She spent most of the walk puzzling over how she'd lost her target; it rarely happened, as she'd developed her tracking abilities over the years.

When she turned back onto Penrose Avenue, she saw a dark outline sitting on the front porch of the Belrose Estate.

Neven.

When they were younger, he'd often waited for her after missions he did on his own. More recently, he'd stopped doing that, and Briatta hesitated at the sight of him on her doorstep now. But seeing the horrors they were frequently exposed to made them want to reach for something familiar, to ensure it was still there and still safe, and maybe that's all this was. As she drew closer, he looked up, his blond hair flattened from wearing his headscarf.

"Bria." He sighed as if seeing her was the answer to every question he'd ever had, exhaustion etched in every line of his body as he sat up straighter. "Your horse was here alone when Owena got home, so she sent for me. We were worried."

Ah, the horse. She'd forgotten.

"I'm sorry," she said. "I was out searching the warehouse district for anything that could help with the Ackmanlee. The mare got spooked, and I fell. I had to walk all the way home."

The lie slipped from her tongue as naturally as if she were telling the truth, which was strange considering she hadn't been able to keep the secret of her Ardor from Neven just a couple of cycles ago. But this part of the Ackmanlee, or so she desperately hoped, was something she'd stumbled upon by herself, and she wanted to keep it that way as long as possible.

Neven nodded, though the look on his face suggested that he didn't entirely believe her. She'd never given him any reason to doubt her, aside from the matter of her Ardor, but if he were smart, he should. Especially in this moment.

"Where's Owena?" Briatta asked.

"She's out searching for you," Neven replied, looking down at his folded hands. "I'll find her on my way back to my apartment and tell her you're home."

An apartment. He'd moved to D'ivory cycles ago, after his Choosing, and Briatta still hadn't seen it.

Briatta's gaze dropped, too, unable to look directly at him, though she wasn't entirely sure why. A small amount of guilt tickled her gut, but she pushed it aside easily. There was no way she was telling Neven that she'd spent the evening following him and then chasing after someone she assumed they'd been out to apprehend, only to lose them.

"Were you out on a mission?" Briatta asked, stolid and gesturing towards his black uniform as she tried to fill the silence.

Neven glanced down at himself. "Yeah."

"Did it...go well?"

Shaking his head as he stood, Neven brushed his pants. "No. I'd better get going. Goodnight, Bria. I'll see you tomorrow morning."

"Goodnight, Neven." Briatta watched Neven go until he disappeared around the corner. Something about the Ackmanlee had changed her friendship with him, and she wasn't sure that she liked the direction it was going.

CHAPTER 26

After returning from Sour Soup the next day, Briatta went down to the basement and entered the secret room before Neven arrived for Ardor training. She'd taken to stashing everything that she'd found for the Ackmanlee—that wasn't in Vydian's warehouse—in the war room after wiping the room free of dust. She pulled out the map showing the locations of the shops that had been robbed as well as the detailed sketches of Allemor House she'd made and settled down at the table to examine them. The Ardor lights in the room flickered to life, giving the closed-in space a homey feel.

Briatta placed a piece of blank paper over the map, picked up a pencil and began tracing the important locations. First, she circled the location where she'd first spotted Neven, drawing the path to the building that he and the Night Rose woman had entered, and then set to outlining the trail she'd taken when following Grey Figure all the way to D'ivory. When she finished, she stepped back and looked at the map she'd made. It revealed that the area where Neven had worked was where most of the stores with reported robberies were concentrated. And that warehouse they'd been in had indeed been one of the locations.

Briatta also noticed the alley where she'd lost her mark wasn't near any of the affected stores. In fact, the more she studied the map, the more she thought it might be the furthest point from all of them.

That was odd. Culprits typically committed crimes within a certain radius of their residence. D'ivory was far enough away that it didn't follow any pattern Briatta could discern.

Considering this was a test, perhaps that was the point. Maybe the orchestrators of the Ackmanlee wanted the competitors to think outside of what was expected and examine possibilities that would otherwise be missed.

Folding her arms, Briatta tilted her head. This would be like searching for a specific flutterfly in the biodome.

Time was growing short before Neven would arrive, and Briatta reluctantly abandoned the map to fetch tea from the dining room while she waited for Neven. He still didn't know about the war room, but she wasn't going to betray another of her aunt's secrets.

By the time she descended the basement stairs again, Neven was waiting in the center of the training mat.

How would she explain that they'd need to expand their patrols without admitting that she'd followed him yesterday? Maybe she would start with Vydian and have her bring it up. They'd grown closer over the past weeks, meeting up for tea while they were both out working. What exactly Vydian did when she wasn't working on the Ackmanlee, Briatta didn't know yet, but the woman had proven to be efficient and reliable, so Briatta hadn't asked.

As Briatta greeted Neven brightly, she decided to set aside the Ackmanlee for now, starting the daily exercises that had become their favored way to start Ardor training. She still struggled with the more difficult summons despite his advice and ideas, and it went just as poorly as it had every morning prior. Briatta left training frustrated and feeling as exhausted as if she'd just run around the perimeter of Montclair.

After having had breakfast, Briatta headed to the stables to pick out her horse for the day. The mare she'd ridden yesterday was lying in her stall, nose scrunched to the ground as she dozed. Definitely too tired for another full day's adventure. Briatta picked out a large, black gelding called Cobalt, instead.

Petyr grabbed Cobalt's gear from the tack room while Briatta groomed him, the big gelding leaning slightly into the strokes of the brush. When she finished tightening the girth of the saddle and led Cobalt from the stables, Briatta found Petyr waiting with a full pair of saddlebags. He handed them to her with a small smile.

"Preida prepared you a lunch," he told her. "She's noticed you going out every day and wanted to make sure you had something to eat."

Briatta gratefully accepted the saddlebags. "Thank you."

If she did move away from home at the end of all of this, Briatta would greatly miss Preida and Petyr.

After leaving the barn, she turned Cobalt toward the warehouse district and settled in for the ride, keeping her eyes sharp for anything suspicious. The big horse moved comfortably on a loose rein, his bouncing gait smooth and relaxed as they passed a tea place she liked that emanated the most tempting scent of freshly baked pastries. Briatta almost stopped for something but decided against it; hand-to-hand combat on a belly full of bread never felt good, and she was heading to Vydian's place first for a promised sparring session, which Briatta now regretted with the weariness in her bones after training with Neven.

Montclair was still waking up. Some residents were on

their way to their daily tasks, and others carried bags containing breakfast and the fixings to accompany it.

Briatta squared her shoulders and turned the gelding at the following street corner. An older gentleman tipped his hat as they passed, and she nodded in return. Most Elfeans were friendly enough, but it was especially noticeable in the mornings when everybody was freshly rested.

When Vydian's warehouse came into view, Briatta steered Cobalt to the alley behind it. She'd taken to tying her horses in the darkness between the buildings, using her Ardor to hide them and testing to see how long she could maintain it from within the warehouse. With the gelding secured, Briatta circled back around to the front, using her picks to release the padlock on the door.

Vydian had seen her do that once and insisted that they trade lessons—immediately offering up her warehouse for sparring with Briatta. Even though Briatta didn't think Vydian could teach her much about combat she didn't already know, the idea of having a friend who wanted to see the more secret part of her life was too much to resist, even if Owena's voice in the back of her head told her it was a bad idea to let a strange woman see how she moved.

Surprisingly, Vydian was quite an accomplished fighter, and she'd taken Briatta's skill in stride. Neither commented on the other's capabilities, and it became an unspoken agreement that they wouldn't acknowledge it. Besides, it was nice to know that Briatta would be able to rely on Vydian having her back should the Ackmanlee come to a point where they had to force their way free of something.

It was definitely something that made Briatta regard Vydian with a more critical eye, and while she questioned the validity of the file Neven had found on her, she also knew that she likely wouldn't find anything different if she looked herself. Once again, she promised herself that after the Ackmanlee, if Vydian gave her a reason to question her, Briatta would look more deeply into her friend. But as far as she knew, Vydian hadn't committed any crimes. Night Rose agents swore to bring down the worst of the worst, and if Vydian wasn't that...well, then why should Briatta doubt her?

It was a war within her heart, one that Briatta hadn't faced before.

So, while they learned from each other on the mat, Briatta taught Vydian all that she knew about the many different mechanisms that could be hidden within a lock. In fact, she had also arrived with a set of picks for Vydian today, having decided she was ready for her own.

The barrel had been long forgotten as it hadn't provided anything helpful, and Briatta cast it a glance as she passed it— useless, rotten thing. On the mat, Briatta stretched, warming up her muscles for the second time this morning.

Vydian arrived shortly after, slipping through the entrance silently.

"Morning," she called, setting a small pack down just inside the door.

"Hey," Briatta answered, lowering herself to a seat on the mat and leaning back on her arms.

Vydian pulled a sweater off as she approached, tossing it aside and rolling her shoulders lightly. "You have a look on your face."

Briatta grimaced. Vydian excelled at reading people, and for whatever reason, she was irritatingly good at reading Briatta.

"I found something yesterday that I need you to tell Neven about."

Vydian's chin turned as she eyed Briatta sideways, walking

to the mat and dropping easily into a cross-legged seat. "Why can't you tell Neven?"

"Because...he'll know that I followed him if I do."

At this, Vydian's brows lifted. "Spill."

Briatta told her mostly everything about the previous day, excluding the part about Neven entering the warehouse with the Night Roses. Instead, she made up a story.

Vydian nodded. "I see. So, let me get this straight. You want me to say that I found someone nefarious near *my* warehouse and followed them all the way to D'ivory, where they vanished completely. And because of that, we should expand our search parameters."

Briatta bobbed her head, leaning forward to rest her elbows on her knees.

Sighing as if Briatta had asked her to do the most difficult thing in the world—speaking to her newest arch-nemesis—Vydian's gaze dropped. "Alright. I'll bring it up next time we go to Allemor House."

Beaming and feeling a little guilty about how Vydian and Neven chaffed each other's nerves so severely, Briatta crossed her ankles and rocked forward to stand. Moving to Vydian's rack of training weapons, Briatta selected a weighted hatchet. Practicing with something like this would mean she would need to be more careful about accidentally hitting Vydian, but it helped prepare Briatta for true combat with heavier equipment.

Dragging herself to her feet and not at all looking as though she wanted to fight that day, Vydian picked up a wooden staff and stepped onto the mat, facing Briatta.

A staff and a hatchet. Interesting. But that was what Briatta liked so much about her sessions with Vydian. They were unpredictable and—in spite of her initial doubts—helped Briatta grow as a fighter. It also felt a little like having a friend who could see this part of her without asking too many questions. Likewise, Briatta didn't question Vydian. Though she was curious, and *should* probably look into her friend's background, it was...something like mutual respect that kept her from doing so. That, and it made sense for the Ackmanlee. So long as Vydian didn't dig too deeply into Briatta's life, she wouldn't either. At least not now.

After the Ackmanlee ended, it would be a different story.

She had a feeling many of the Ackmanlee contestants felt the same way. Being able to defend themselves was one thing, but moving like honed fighters when being judged was another. This was perhaps the one time the Weilers wouldn't ask questions about where they learned to spar, especially if whoever they were observing won. Losing, on the other hand, might get Briatta placed on some sort of watchlist.

Keeping this part of herself a secret was the one thing she'd always regret when it came to Morenna. Sweet Morenna, who had absolutely no idea the sorts of things that her best friend got up to when they weren't in school. Briatta made a note to visit her before the Ackmanlee ended. To explain why she hadn't come by in so long.

Maybe someday, Briatta would be able to tell her the truth.

Vydian stepped forward, spinning the staff under her arm and whipping it towards Briatta's chin. Briatta gripped the handle of her hatchet with both hands and raised it to block the blow while throwing herself backward to avoid hitting herself in the face with both the hatchet and the staff.

Vydian led, and Briatta followed. The two women whirled and thrust, blocked and advanced, pulling their blows at the last moment by sheer will and years of practice. They were well matched, and soon, Briatta fell into the rhythm of the sparring match as if she were dancing, her muscles warm and fluid.

Then Briatta's lips lifted at the corners, and she took charge instead.

Vydian backed up, ducking as Briatta swung with the hatchet.

Soon, it became clear that Vydian grew tired. Her movements turned sluggish, as if her body were half a second behind her mind, and Briatta eased the pace to match her friend. When they sparred, they usually sparred until failure, and it had sometimes even been a toss-up as to who would tap out.

The moment Briatta brought the hatchet down hard toward Vydian's staff, the other woman stepped back, saying "Done."

Briatta twisted her body awkwardly to redirect the axe's trajectory, but in doing so, she lost her grip, and the wooden hatchet flew through the air.

Staggering to a standstill, Briatta watched dumbly as it hurtled toward the barrel and lodged itself between two slats, splitting the already broken barrel further. The metal bands squealed, barely holding the wood together, and Briatta cringed at the horrible sound.

"Damn." Vydian laughed. "You just split wood with wood. Remind me to never get on your bad side."

Snorting, Briatta went to retrieve the wretched thing, bracing a foot on the side of the barrel to pull it out. It gave eventually, but the metal squeaked and rasped horribly, sending chills down her spine and making her shudder. When it finally released, Briatta stumbled backward with the force she'd used, dropping the axe on the ground.

"Last time I ever fight with that thing," Briatta said, glaring at the barrel.

Vydian smirked. "I don't know. In a real fight, you'd be an asset with that. Even a wooden one, apparently."

The barrel, seemingly having reached the end of its will to exist as a barrel, crumbled in a noisy heap of planks behind Briatta as if to confirm Vydian's thoughts.

Vydian set her staff aside and stood behind Briatta, placing her hands on her hips and examining the remains of their one piece of evidence.

"Would you handle all cases like this?" Vydian's tone was playful.

"What do you mean?"

"Destroying clues when the trail runs dry?"

Briatta scowled, crossing her arms. Laughing, Vydian nudged her with an elbow, making Briatta smile, too. It was the first time she had experienced a moment with Vydian that felt effortless. Like the many moments she used to have with Neven before everything got so muddled.

Crouching beside the remains of the barrel, Vydian sifted through it. She pulled the detached planks from within the bands that still stubbornly encircled what was left, examining each one before setting it aside. Briatta joined her by the wall, leaning against it and sliding down to a seat, watching the other woman work.

"Think you'll find something?" Briatta asked.

Vydian shrugged. "It's worth checking. Then, at least, I can get rid of this eyesore."

Briatta looked around the warehouse with raised eyebrows, and Vydian glanced up, noting the movement from her peripheral vision.

"Alright, I know the place isn't exactly a dream training center, but it's mine." Vydian laughed.

Briatta felt the strain on her Ardor then, feeling Cobalt shift restlessly within her shadows. She made a mental note of the time it had taken to feel drained. She was improving, but it still wasn't where she wanted to be. Briatta focused on feeling the horse's presence in the darkness. Now that was a skill she had definitely developed. In fact, she started to believe she would be able to sense where Elfeans were in a fight rather than watching them.

Maybe, when Neven judged that she'd improved with the smaller tasks, Briatta would ask about trying it; they could completely darken the basement and spar.

Vydian gasped, holding one of the barrel's panels closer to study it.

"What is it?" Briatta asked, craning to see over Vydian's shoulder.

Wordlessly, the woman held it out. Accepting the piece of wood, Briatta looked it over. At first, she didn't see anything that stood out, but then she turned it over and looked at the underside, the part that had been hidden within the barrel.

Lodged in one of the ends of the wood was something small and white. Briatta pressed her face close to the wood, squinting. It was chipped and cracked as if it had broken with the force of being hammered into the wood, but it was unmistakably a tooth. Briatta's heart raced, and her eyes widened; she looked up at Vydian.

"D'ivory," she breathed. "The grey figure. I knew it had to be connected!"

"You were right." Vydian nodded. "If this didn't get here by accident, anyway."

Briatta returned her eyes to the slat in her hands, turning it slightly as she continued studying it. "This feels a bit more like a scavenger hunt than a criminal case."

It was Vydian's turn to snort, and then she laughed out loud. "That's true. Well, maybe they want us to think even further outside the box than we realized."

Setting the plank down and rising to her feet, Briatta

smiled wickedly and returned the wooden hatchet to its spot on the weapons rack.

"Feel like taking a trip to D'ivory today?"

Vydian's answering grin was what Briatta imagined having a female partner in crime would feel like, and she felt a warm sense of belonging in her chest that she hadn't felt anywhere other than with the Night Roses.

"I'm always ready for a hunt." Vydian was already reaching for her sweater.

While she waited for Vydian to collect her things and prepare herself for an actual potential encounter with someone, Briatta performed an inventory check on herself. She dressed for battle every morning, but she still felt better with the reassurance that everything was still sheathed and where they belonged. Patting her thigh dagger, which was the one she usually reached for first, Briatta walked to stand by the door, listening for anyone who might approach the unlocked door as well as for Vydian's movements.

It wasn't long before the dark-haired woman returned to the entrance, clad in significantly more leather than when she'd arrived, her hands behind her head as they worked her shiny strands into a tight braid. Briatta's hair was already pulled back, and she ran a hand along the side of her head without thinking as she watched Vydian tie her plait off.

"Before we go," Briatta said, pulling the pick set from her pocket. With the excitement around the barrel, she'd nearly forgotten. "Here. These are for you."

Accepting the lock pick tools, Vydian's lips curled up. "You think I'm ready?"

"Let's find out." Briatta shrugged. "Lock the padlock with them."

Eyes widening, Vydian's mouth thinned into a determined line as she pulled the door open and waited for Briatta to step through before following. They'd only worked on unlocking things, so maybe it was cruel to set this challenge before Vydian, but Briatta knew that if Vydian truly understood the mechanisms of the lock, she'd have no difficulties.

The door shut and the chain slipped back on the arm of the lock, then Vydian set to work. Briatta leaned against the building and settled in to wait.

"I have to run home and grab my actual daggers before we go," Vydian said, glancing up as she worked. "Wait here for me?"

Folding her arms as she watched Vydian's fingers closely, Briatta nodded. She could put off the hunt just a few minutes longer.

Then, they would head to the only district on Montclair that resembled rows of teeth, built against the red, dirt gums of the planet. And they would hunt.

CHAPTER 27
GALEN

Galen and his gelding were exhausted. They'd traveled as quickly as they could from Isa, though it had taken longer than he'd anticipated to get all the way back to Montclair. Because he was primarily a field operator for Kalaiden— or he had been—Galen didn't know exactly where the base was, but he knew that Maverik wasn't there. He hadn't been for many cycles.

No, the base was somewhere in the Nalaran mountains east of Seradan. But Maverik was here, in Montclair.

He cursed then smiled grimly to himself at the irony.

He was still a fair distance from the dark biodome encasing the city, but Galen hoped there would be soldiers manning the biogate when he reached it. The Nocturne Sun was low in the sky, so it shouldn't be too much longer.

Galen's Ardor-infused mask had worn out about an hour before, and while he had trained to withstand low levels of oxygen, he was feeling its effects. As for his gelding, well... Galen would put him up in the most luxurious stable he could find. This poor horse had put up with his indecisive master for far too long.

Swaying precariously on top of his horse, who plodded eagerly along at the sight of the biodome ahead, Galen fought to stay conscious and aware of his surroundings. His sense of time was skewed; when he blinked, it seemed as though Carceron was experiencing that brief moment of calm between when the Nocturne Sun set and the Polar Sun rose.

Odd. Hadn't the Nocturne Sun been glaring down at him not a minute before?

Galen shook his head vigorously and poured the last drops of water from his canteen into his mouth. He *really* hoped someone would be at the entrance to let him through the biodome.

Why was he there again?

Shit.

Galen kicked at his horse's sides lightly, hoping a bouncier pace would help him stay awake. Obediently, the gelding broke into a brisk, forward trot. Galen intuitively began to post it, standing every other beat to make the gait more comfortable. The movement helped clear his mind a little, despite also causing his heart to pound, and Galen blinked furiously at the now quickly approaching biodome. His vision was fuzzy at the edges, and he was just lucid enough to understand precisely what that meant.

Seeming to sense his rider's urgency, the gelding sped up into an easy canter, and Galen sat deep into his saddle. The rocking motion of the lope made him a little queasy, which wasn't normal for him, but they were so close.

Finally, the edge of the biodome was there, and the horse stopped. The Polar Sun began to rise, and with it, the biodome lightened. Galen quickly removed the Ardor-mask and tucked it safely away.

"Thank the Founders," Galen said out loud, fishing for his papers. Producing them, he searched for a sign of life, and then...yes, there was a Weiler.

The horse stepped forward as they moved farther down the edge of the biodome. The soldier saw them and shouted something over his shoulder, though no sound pierced the Ardor that formed the dome before him.

Finally, a thinner, permeable section of the biodome formed before Galen, and he urged his horse through it. The first breath that Galen took within went straight to his head, and a wave of dizziness hit him as though he'd just smoked something powerful. Grabbing his saddle horn, he leaned forward and squeezed his eyes shut, blindly holding out the papers. Someone took the stack from him, and the woozy sensation was only abating by the time the Weiler returned his papers and waved him through all the way.

At the first tavern Galen passed, he dismounted his horse and fetched water for both of them. While the gelding drank deeply from the bucket Galen held, Galen dumped water on himself and into his mouth from his freshly filled canteen. It was the best water he'd ever had.

Once they were both satisfied, Galen continued walking through Montclair, though now he only held the reins of his horse rather than riding him any further.

As Galen passed the old tavern he used to visit regularly, an unexpected flood of contentment swept through him. He'd missed Montclair far more than he realized and was starting to regret his little sabbatical to Isa. Though if he hadn't gone, he wouldn't have met the old woman who had sent him hightailing it back. Whatever the case, Galen was here now, and that was what mattered.

But how would he get ahold of Maverik?

Maybe he would write to Lycus. The man *had* told him to

write once he'd gotten his shit together, hadn't he? Did this count as having collected himself sufficiently?

Uncertainty filled Galen. He knew that he should be here, but the idea of seeing his friends again made him replete with anxiety about how he would be received.

What in the seven levels of atonement was he doing?

Atonement. That was something he hadn't thought of in a while. Shuddering at the reminder, Galen stopped and looked at his surroundings. His feet, which he hadn't been paying attention to, had taken him directly to his old apartment building, where many members of Kalaiden maintained a presence. There were places like this in every city, though their biggest presence was in Seradan; Kalaiden's reach extended far more than the Weilers and King Novak realized.

And just ahead, standing frozen on the sidewalk looking as though she'd just seen a ghost, was Vydian.

Galen's stomach had already been uneasy, but at the sight of her, it fell as far as it could have possibly gone. He couldn't swallow the sudden lump in his throat, and he wouldn't have been able to move any of his limbs even if he'd tried.

They stared at each other, each seemingly unable to make the first step for what felt like an eternity.

"Where in the name of the Founders did you go?" Vydian asked at last, her voice flat.

"I..." Galen trailed off, unable to find the words. Before he could flounder for too long, he at least managed to say, "I'm sorry."

"You're *sorry*?" Vydian's voice rose to a pitch that had pedestrians glancing towards them with concerned expressions. "Is that all you have to say?"

Just like that, the spell that had been over Galen was broken, and he found he could move again. The words that had abandoned him were now desperate to be spoken. "Please, Vydian. Can we go somewhere private?"

"What, so you just come back after disappearing and want to go *somewhere* with me? What am I to you, a common whore?"

"Vydian, that's not what I meant," Galen said hurriedly, stepping towards her.

"Isn't it?" she hissed, becoming visibly more furious by the second.

"Please," Galen begged helplessly. "I need to talk to you."

Vydian glared at him, breathing hard as she fumed, her fists balled tightly at her sides.

"Please," Galen repeated, his voice breaking. He took another halting step forward.

The silence stretched on as they regarded each other, Vydian seeming to cool only slightly. While Galen had expected that he would have some explaining to do with her, he hadn't realized Vydian would be so upset by his disappearance. This was a relationship...no, he couldn't call it that anymore. It was a friendship, at the very least, that he did not wish to lose. At this rate, however, it was looking more and more like Vydian might not come back around.

At last, Vydian said, "I have to go. I'm late for something."

Turning away, she stalked down the street. Unable to make himself go after her, still stupidly holding his horse's reins, Galen stood there and watched until she disappeared.

"Well, I can't say I've ever seen Vydian that upset," someone commented. Galen exhaled before turning to face another friend.

"Mav," he said.

The other man, with black hair and dark eyes, was wearing a blue shirt with black pants, and he was standing on the stairs that led into the apartments just out of sight from where

Vydian had been. It was just as well; she would have been even more furious if she'd known her elder cousin was there. Likely, he'd been on his way to visit with her.

"Galen," Maverik said, stepping forward to pull his friend into a hug. "What happened, brother?"

Maverik and Galen were not really brothers, but they might as well have been, and Maverik tended to refer to people as brothers even if he didn't know them well; everyone was family to him, and he looked after those who stayed close as if they were.

"I don't know," Galen said, shaking his head. "I just had this urge to leave, to get as far away as possible."

They walked down the street, Galen pulling his horse along and keeping an eye out for a stable. He knew the city well enough that he could have taken them directly to a nice barn, but Galen wanted to see where they would end up as they talked. He didn't want to force anything about this first, fragile act towards reparation.

Well, it felt brittle for Galen—as if one wrong word might break everything apart—but Maverik seemed as calm as he always was.

"Did you find what you needed?" Maverik asked.

Galen looked at his oldest friend, a small wave of surprise coursing through him at the casualty with which Maverik welcomed his return. "Are you not mad?"

Maverik appeared vaguely bemused, and he put a hand on Galen's shoulder. "Should I be? You came back. It sounds as though you needed this."

"I left with no explanation. I abandoned you and everyone else," Galen said, overwhelmed by the need to insist that he'd done something terrible.

"You did do that," Maverik agreed as they turned at the next street corner. "But these are bad times."

"That isn't an excuse," Galen lamented. "And it isn't a good reason for me to have left, either."

"We have been fighting this war for too long." Maverik sighed. "I can't tell you how often I've wanted to give up, too. I don't blame you."

This caught Galen off guard. "You've wanted to give up?"

"All the time," Maverik said.

That was news to Galen, who had always considered Maverik a steadfast and unwavering leader. Unexpectedly, emotion welled up inside him, and he found himself choked up, his throat tight, and his vision blurred.

"I didn't realize," Galen said quietly.

"We are all just people at the end of the day," Maverik said. "But we've gotten away from ourselves. How was your time?"

Galen swallowed, the tears drying up nearly as fast as they'd appeared. This was something that he had been dreading. Telling Maverik what he'd encountered in Isa.

"I, ah, have some really bad news," Galen said, unable to meet Maverik's eyes.

Maverik, to Galen's surprise, chuckled softly. "It can't be worse than what I've been discovering here."

"No...I think it will be at least the same," Galen replied with skepticism.

"Now, that is a high claim," Maverik said. "Alright, Galen. I'm now officially dying to know what you have to say."

Resisting the urge to roll his eyes, Galen glanced away and, in the movement, saw the barn he'd known they were going to pass if they continued in this direction.

"Wait," he said. "Let me stop here to get my horse settled."

Maverik followed Galen to the barn, his hands in his pockets, where they met a stableboy who took the gelding and the generous pile of coins that Galen shoved at him before disappearing down the aisle of the stables.

The horse had been a massive part of Galen's life for the past few cycles, and he watched him go with some regret, hating to be separated.

"We'll take him back to base and keep him with the others if you like him that much," Maverik said, appearing to recognize Galen's hesitation to leave the horse.

"Base?" Galen said absently, turning back to Maverik.

"Yes." Maverik nodded. "I think you've done enough field-work. Though...I have one last thing to ask of you, and then you may finally settle in one place for a while."

"Anything," Galen said, and the pair of them walked through Montclair once more, this time heading towards the center of the city—near Parkette Street—where the food and drink were plentiful.

"You won't like it," Maverik warned.

Galen gave his oldest friend an incredulous look. "Maybe wait to ask me until tomorrow, then."

Maverik nodded, a knowing and slightly amused smile on his lips. The pair continued in companionable silence while Galen struggled with the truth of what he had to tell Maverik; he didn't want to be the one to bring it up.

"You should know that after Lycus met up with you, we tracked down who delivered the checkpoint location to you. They've been taken care of." Maverik gave Galen a sidelong look, and Galen's relief at that was staggering. Not only because Lycus had believed him, but his friends had defended him even when he'd abandoned them.

"Do you think Vydian will forgive me?" Galen blurted suddenly, feeling heat rise in his cheeks. He had no idea what had possessed him to ask, but it at least shifted the subject away from himself.

Chuckling, Maverik threw an arm around Galen's shoulders and steered him into a homey little tavern, pausing to order two ales at the bar before they found a seat at the back of the place. They chose a little booth tucked into the corner, where they would be able to observe everything that happened in the bar and have a semblance of privacy.

Taking a sip from his ale, Maverik finally answered, "I think she will."

Galen raised an eyebrow at the delayed reply, taking a long drag from his glass.

"I mean, it will take a lot of groveling," Maverik added. "A *lot* of ass-kissing and maybe some nice gifts."

Grimacing into his beer, Galen nodded slowly. "In other words, it's probably hopeless."

Maverik feigned shock. "Brother, you've never shied from a challenge before. Granted, I'm not going to talk you all the way through this one. I mean, she's my cousin. But you've got to at least try."

"Alright." Galen sighed and grinned wickedly, twisting Maverik's words. "It might not be that bad. Vydian *does* deserve some ass-kissing."

"Ew," Maverik said, making a face. "Please don't ever say that to me again."

Both men laughed, and the mood was significantly improved, though Galen still suffered through the itching thought at the back of his mind that told him he needed to share what he'd seen with Maverik. *Whom* he'd seen.

"Maverik..." Galen started after a long while, once more finding it difficult to look his friend in the eye.

"Yes?"

"It is not only your cousin that we need to be concerned with," Galen said.

"Oh? Is there someone else whom you've gravely offended?" Maverik's tone was still teasing, but Galen swallowed hard.

"Not exactly," he said. Then, he finally spit it out. "I saw your brother."

Maverik went so preternaturally still that Galen thought his friend might as well have turned to stone. The color drained from his face, and his knuckles turned white where he gripped his ale.

"That isn't possible, Galen." Maverik's voice was cold. Hard.

Galen finally looked at Maverik, feeling himself sweat a little under his friend's intense gaze.

"I didn't think so either," Galen said. "But believe me when I tell you, Mav. I know who I saw."

It was Maverik's turn to look away.

"You were right," Maverik said eventually. "This is terrible news if what you say is true."

Galen felt a flash of irritation. "You don't believe me?"

"I don't know what to believe right this second." Maverik's words were harsher than Galen was accustomed to.

Unable to say more, unable to possibly upset his friend further, Galen sank back into his seat and drank his beer. At least he'd done what he'd come here for. Now he could rest, and after this conversation, it seemed like he'd be on his own for that.

It was early enough in the bioday for the tavern to still be quiet except for the two men. While Galen would find some place to sleep after he left, Maverik would likely need to go to work.

What a terrible way to start the day. Galen felt awful bearing this bad news to his friend but simultaneously relieved to have it over with.

"Okay," Maverik said eventually when some normal coloring had returned to his skin. "Tell me everything."

Eagerly, Galen started from the moment that he abandoned watching that Belrose girl to take off and get as far away from everything as he possibly could. He spoke of how he had gone east, how he'd ended up in Isa and then taken an apprenticeship with the smith there to learn to use his Fire Ardor better. For too long, Galen told Maverik all about Beryl and Matty, and he hoped that he could return to them for a little while sometime soon.

"And my brother?" Maverik prodded gently.

Galen nodded and explained the day he'd left the smith, taken a walk, and ended up at the strange house. He told Maverik about the old lady and their frustrating conversation, told him that she'd left him with a truth that would come to pass shortly after. Then, he spoke about walking back to the inn where he'd been staying and about the young woman shopping and the man who'd been with her.

"He didn't see you?" Maverik asked when Galen finished.

"No," Galen said, shaking his head.

But the mood had already been entirely soured. Maverik and his brother had a very long history, one that was tightly interwoven with the past of the very planet they lived on, and almost none of it was good.

Regardless, Galen was glad to be back with his friends. The purpose that had led him here hadn't been good, but all that mattered now was what he did with that information. And from the sounds of it, Maverik already knew exactly what that would be. Resolved to spend as long as was needed making up to Kalaiden for his hiatus, Galen was ready for anything. While Maverik sat across from him trying to come to terms with his brother being alive, Galen was ready to help support him unconditionally.

They would get through this.

CHAPTER 28

BRIATTA

B riatta followed Vydian, keeping watch behind them as they crept down yet another back road in D'ivory. This time, they were thorough. They would miss nothing.

They'd left as soon as Vydian returned to the warehouse from wherever she'd gone. The woman seemed withdrawn and preoccupied, and though Briatta couldn't imagine what could have happened in the half hour they were apart, she didn't pry. They might be allies because of the Ackmanlee, maybe even tentative friends, but they hadn't spoken of anything deeper than the competition, so Briatta didn't feel it was appropriate to pry.

On the way to D'ivory from the warehouse district, they'd briefly considered whether they should try to let Neven know what they were doing. It took only a split second for them to meet eyes and shake their heads. Briatta and Vydian were now a cohesive unit, and Neven would only be a distraction. He wasn't even a competitor, after all.

As she backed around the corner that Vydian had just taken, scanning the path they'd already covered, Briatta reflected on how Neven had been the one with whom she had felt this way only a short while ago, and how they'd once trusted each other implicitly to have their backs and get the job done.

How quickly everything had changed.

From the warehouse where the remains of the barrel stayed, Vydian and Briatta had ridden Cobalt together, then brought him home to the Belrose Estate on the way to D'ivory. They'd been on foot since, keeping watch for any hint of abnormalities.

Rather than going directly to the alley where Briatta had lost the figure in grey, they started their sweep from the farthest edge of the search perimeter that they'd established on the way over. As an added bonus, Briatta had instinctively signed to Vydian with her hands that they were actively searching as pedestrians passed and discovered that Vydian understood everything. Vydian's face had lit up with excitement, and her hands had moved so quickly in response that Briatta almost couldn't keep up.

Being able to communicate silently made the hunt much easier.

As they drew closer to that damned alley where she'd lost her quarry, Briatta grew more restless. Some part of her had hoped that she'd been wrong the first time, and that they'd find new clues as to where Grey Figure had gone, and the other part of her believed she'd been entirely thorough and didn't want to doubt her work.

Still, with everything going on, Briatta couldn't squash the tiny flame of apprehension that burned in her gut. It was now a constant companion, whereas she'd never doubted herself before.

Returning to the main street, Briatta straightened and fell

into step beside Vydian to appear normal as they walked to the next gap between the rows of buildings.

"Nothing," Briatta murmured, keeping her head on a swivel and smiling at Vydian as if the woman had said something interesting.

"Nothing, *yet*," Vydian replied, her own eyes remaining straight ahead, headscarf loosely draped over her head, the edges fluttering slightly with her movement.

They were searching for seams in building walls, oddly patterned bricks in the ground, and anyone who might be heading somewhere they shouldn't. Briatta had, of course, grown up studying different variations of the aforementioned oddities, and because she wasn't certain of Vydian's history, she found herself rechecking the places that the other woman checked, just to be sure.

When they reached the alleyway and found nothing, Briatta felt only a small glimmer of satisfaction. Almost immediately, that feeling curdled into unease. She stopped at the end of the narrow, dark space and looked over her shoulder.

Vydian lifted her hands to sign. *"What is it?"*

"This is the alley I told you about," Briatta replied.

Vydian's brows creased slightly, and she began a second, more thorough sweep of the alley. Briatta turned her back to Vydian and followed, looking behind them the whole way. She could see absolutely nothing, but something felt wrong.

When she gently bumped into Vydian because the dark-haired woman had stopped, Briatta turned. Silently, Vydian lifted a hand and pointed to a tiny gap between two bricks in the wall of one of the buildings. It appeared to be normal wear of the material used to bind bricks, and Briatta's brows furrowed with confusion.

"Look closer," Vydian signed.

Doubtful, Briatta stepped closer to the wall and leaned toward it. The hole was rectangular and a little too smooth around the edges. It would have been more jagged if a piece had broken off naturally. Just above it was a tiny etching of the same flower that had been on the signature left behind with the barrel.

"*I see it,*" Briatta told Vydian. She felt a flash of irritation at how quickly Vydian had spotted the abnormality in the wall, while she'd searched seemingly every inch to no avail. But annoyance would get them nowhere.

The corners of her mouth tilting up in acknowledgment, Vydian slipped her hand into her pocket and drew the brand-new lock pick set that Briatta had given her. Briatta couldn't help her own smirk as she stepped back, folding her arms and nodding.

As Vydian knelt before the wall and gently worked her picks into the hole, feeling for a lock or whatever else may be hidden, Briatta turned her attention to the alley's entrances. She could hear the soft scrape of the metal picks against the stone and mortar, the distant chirp of a bird, and the pressing sound of silence.

Vydian worked for a while, her forehead lined in concentration and her lower lip caught between her teeth. Briatta was content to let her friend continue trying. A few weeks ago, she might have shoved the other woman aside and attempted to pick the lock herself. That was growth, she thought to herself.

When Briatta grew comfortable with the quiet, relaxing a little, she caught an odd sound above her and looked up just in time to see someone, their head entirely hidden save for their eyes, watching from the roof. The eyes widened as she made eye contact, and they pulled back, vanishing from view. Briatta braced and turned, launching herself halfway up the wall and grasping for the nearest fingerhold. As soon as she had it, her feet scrambled for purchase, and she dragged herself up the side of the building.

"What are you doing?" Vydian asked out loud, surprised.

"Stay there!" Briatta called, hauling herself over the precipice of the roof and catching sight of Grey Figure once more as they sprinted across the roof and leaped across to the neighboring building.

If Vydian remained at the door, Briatta wouldn't lose them again. Hopefully.

Briatta took off running. Another Founders damned chase. At least this time, the target was aware of her, and as she was no longer trying to be discreet, Briatta could put all her effort into catching this cloaked figure.

Reaching the gap, Briatta threw herself across it, rolling as she hit the other rooftop and rising back into her sprint. Grey Figure glanced behind, noted her pursuit, and veered left, dropping to the ground. It would be more difficult for her to keep an eye on them there, and Briatta snarled with frustration as she reached the edge and swung down, glancing back and forth.

They wouldn't have gone back to the hidden entrance—if that's what it was—and Briatta had to trust that if they did, Vydian would be able to handle it. So, she headed in the opposite direction after a split second of thought. Sure enough, Briatta caught sight of the figure vaulting over a fence and into someone's yard down the first row of molar-like D'ivory structures.

Briatta crashed into the fence a few short moments later, leaping to grab the top and haul herself up and over. She didn't hesitate, as she didn't want to lose the Elfean, and scuff marks of red dirt were on the white fence ahead of her, so Briatta followed.

The third yard, however, had no signs of someone passing

over the fencing, and Briatta paused briefly to assess it. The properties were very small in this part of town, and the yards had enough space to sit, but there wasn't enough room to do much more.

A crunch sounded to her left, and Briatta whirled, spying Grey Figure just as they passed through the gate, the gravel on the ground having given them away.

"Stop!" Briatta yelled, again taking chase. She flew into the road behind the figure, who shoved their way past people walking down the road. "Out of the way!"

Startled, the residents of D'ivory were thrust into a state of panic. Rather than moving aside, they shouted and ran into one another, scrambling to avoid danger. It quickly escalated into a screaming mass of confused people trying to escape from nothing.

"Founders," Briatta cursed, trying to push through. "Clear the road!"

Unfortunately, either they didn't hear her, or they were beyond the point of listening.

Briatta was losing sight of her mark. Shit, she had to do something. She couldn't lose them again.

Finally bursting from the group of frightened Elfeans and onto the sidewalk, Briatta drew her knives and ran again. The only good thing about the fear now wreaking havoc on the street was that Grey Figure also couldn't make quick progress. As she raced, Briatta flipped her knives so that she held the blades between her fingers, counting down the moments until they would reach a stretch of empty road. When she saw a space up ahead, Briatta's gaze flicked between her target and the gap in the crowd.

The second the Grey Figure tore free of the people and she judged that she had a clear shot, Briatta lifted her arm and, with a deep breath and a prayer to the Founders that her aim would be true, hurled her knife.

As if moving in slow motion, Briatta watched every turn of the dagger in the air as she sprinted after the Elfean. All the while, she called on every scrap of her Ardor training and willed the smallest amount of shadow, invisible to the eye, to pull the blade around at the last second. With a thud, the dagger's hilt cracked into the back of the figure's head and they crumpled, crashing to the ground and skidding along the stone until they came to a halt and laid still.

The dagger clattered beside them.

Some women screamed along with other shouts of alarm.

Briatta slowed to a walk and shifted her other dagger to her right hand. As she approached the figure, they didn't move, and she crouched beside them, holding her blade to their neck as she gripped their shoulder and pulled them onto their back.

"Gotcha," she said more to herself than anyone else, breathing hard.

The thief remained unconscious.

Briatta reached out and removed the headscarf from her target while keeping her knife poised to attack, just in case they were feigning unconsciousness.

A young man laid before her with shockingly red hair and freckles that were starkly visible against his pale skin. Briatta's heart sank in her chest.

"Rory," she muttered, her mind going entirely blank. *What was he doing there?*

Rory Donal remained motionless, and she reached out to feel for a pulse. He was still alive, just knocked out cold.

"I didn't know it was you," Briatta told him, even though he couldn't hear her as she sheathed her remaining knife and lifted his head to examine the wound she'd inflicted on her Night

Rose comrade. As she'd hoped when she'd thrown the dagger, she didn't think it was serious. Just a small bump on the back of Rory's head that would probably give him a headache. Any healer's station would be able to repair the injury, and Rory wouldn't even feel like anything had happened to him.

Taking Rory's headscarf and folding it into a length of cloth, Briatta placed it under his head and lowered him back down onto it, sighing.

"Why were you running from me, anyway?" she asked the unconscious man.

Rory was still, and Briatta rocked back onto her heels, waiting for him to come around. She didn't think she could take him to a healing center by herself, but maybe one of the bystanders would be willing to help.

Suddenly, firm hands wrapped around her arms, and Briatta was pulled back by a group of men. Surprised and struggling, Briatta kicked out, hitting one of them in the shin. He cried out and let go briefly but was promptly replaced by another. Someone tackled her, knocking the wind out of her.

"I've got her! Someone get the Weilers!" a man called. Briatta, with her cheek smashed into the stone of the road beneath her, fought the urge to scream.

On the ground across from her, Rory groaned and turned his head but didn't wake up.

This day had not gone at all as Briatta had pictured.

It didn't take long for the Weilers to arrive, and the men holding her down were replaced by shackles that bound her wrists behind her back. Someone hauled her to her feet, but she shook their hand off, glaring up at them.

And her heart stumbled in her chest.

Simeon folded his arms and, with a vaguely amused expression on his face, looked between Briatta and Rory, who was sitting and holding the back of his head with help from another Weiler. Rory glanced up at Briatta and snorted.

"Damnit. Why'd you have to hit me so hard, Belrose?"

"I'm sorry, I didn't know it was you," she told him, her tone sharper than she'd meant it to be. Being surrounded by the Weilers and the confusion of seeing Rory after following the hint about Tallor's kidnappers being in D'ivory was getting to her. She took a deep breath, trying to compose herself.

Rory nodded. "Okay, okay. That's...completely fair." He rubbed the back of his head, grimacing.

"Why were you running from me, anyway?" Briatta demanded.

A pained expression rippled across Rory's face, and he looked up at Simeon as if for help with explaining himself. Most of the other Weilers who had responded were calming down the crowd and shooing them away, though a few looked similarly puzzled at the scene they'd been called to.

"Do I need to ask what happened?" Simeon questioned.

Rory shook his head. "We're good here. I'm sorry you were called."

Briatta was at war with herself over what was unfolding before her. As far as she knew, Simeon wasn't aware of the Night Roses, and there wasn't an easy explanation for how she and Rory knew each other. But...why would Rory know Simeon? Because the way that he'd looked to Simeon for aid was definitely not the expression of a stranger. And why was Rory wearing a uniform in the same grey fabric that had been left at the crime scene?

Nodding curtly, Simeon turned to Briatta and unlocked her bindings. Despite wanting to demand what was happening, Briatta stayed still until she was free, doing her best to ignore how Simeon's fingertips felt against her skin. His hands were cool and gentle as they worked to pull the shackles free, and as soon as the restraints fell away, she jerked her hands to herself and rubbed her wrists, avoiding looking toward Simeon. If she did, she feared she might forget how to speak entirely.

"All good here," Simeon said, and she heard him walking away a moment later. Giving in to herself, Briatta turned to watch him go as he gathered the Weilers and assured the crowd there was nothing to worry themselves over. Before he left, Simeon glanced over his shoulder and locked eyes with Briatta. It froze her completely, and she was unable to look away until he dipped his chin. Then, he was swept away by his fellow Weilers.

Sucking in air, Briatta spun to face Rory, who was finally climbing to his feet, grumbling about his head pounding.

"What is going on?" Briatta hissed.

Rory's face turned red, and he gripped the grey headscarf in his hands, wringing it awkwardly.

"Rory," Briatta said.

"I'm sorry, I can't tell you," Rory said finally. Briatta looked at the ground.

Why wouldn't he be able to tell her? They were both members of the most secret organization in Montclair...unless, for some reason, there was another that she didn't know about. No, she was certain that wasn't the case. In fact, Briatta probably had higher clearance within the Night Roses than Rory did, so there was absolutely no reason he would have to keep something from her.

Unless...

Briatta tilted her head as she studied Rory, chewing on her lower lip as her mind raced.

Slowly, the pieces were beginning to fall into place. Owena had told her the Night Roses had been working on a big project, and Briatta hadn't been to headquarters since she'd entered the Ackmanlee. Granted, part of it had been of her own doing because she had been avoiding Owena, but perhaps her aunt being so harsh to her in that carriage had been orchestrated. Perhaps Briatta's behavior that night had merely been an opportunity for Owena to punish her and push her away.

And...Neven had been going on missions that she didn't know about. Neven almost always told Briatta about the cases he worked on because he liked to think them through out loud with her. Between the two of them, they'd always solved every issue they came across. It was unlike Neven to keep things from her, and he'd been acting so out of character lately.

Then, there was the warehouse that Neven had been at. Rory had been there, too, assuming he was the one in the grey uniform.

Maybe they hadn't been working against each other that night. Maybe Neven hadn't been chasing Rory. In fact, that wouldn't make sense at all.

It could also explain why Rory knew Simeon, though she doubted she would get any of that information from him at this moment.

Did Rory know Briatta was competing?

"Come with me," Briatta said, grabbing Rory's arm as he was wrapping his headscarf back on, and dragging him back in the direction of the alley where they'd left Vydian.

CHAPTER 29

R ory was silent for the entirety of the walk back to Vydian, sneaking glances towards Briatta as they went, apparently still shocked at seeing her and seemingly nervous about what would happen next. Vydian had remained near the door in the alley as instructed, jumping up when she saw their approach. Her dark eyes traveled over Rory and his unbound hands and then went to Briatta.

"What took so long?" she asked.

"I got arrested." Briatta fought the urge to roll her eyes, knowing very well that if she'd stumbled across a scene like the one she and Rory had caused, she would have jumped in to help the same as all those people had.

"Ah." Vydian laughed through her nose, a smile spreading halfway across her lips. "Damn Weilers."

"Listen," Briatta said, turning serious. "I strongly suspect this is the place we are looking for. Did you get the door open?"

Vydian's eyes widened almost imperceptibly, and she shook her head. "I think it's beyond me. Do you want to try?"

Glancing at Rory, Briatta dropped his arm and faced him as another thought crossed her mind.

"I'm sorry for this," she informed him before reaching out to frisk him. She felt for weapons and anything else that might be on his person and was rewarded when she felt something with a little weight to it. The item was in one of the inner pockets of the lightweight jacket that offered protection from both injuries and the Polar Sun. Briatta undid the top button and slipped her hand into the jacket, pulling out a strange, small metal rectangle with one end that was square and wide, the other flat and round.

Rory licked his lips nervously.

"What is this?" Briatta asked.

The red-haired young man said nothing, his lips pressed into a thin line as he looked straight ahead and avoided Briatta's stare.

Vydian stepped around them, stopping beside Rory. She lightly rested a hand on his elbow, giving him a warning look before shifting her focus to observe Briatta's movements.

Briatta returned to examining the small iron object sitting in the palm of her hand, running her fingers along the heavy, wide side.

"Would that fit in the hole?" Vydian suggested.

"Hmm." Briatta knelt in front of the stone wall and held the metal up to the hole. The rectangular piece of metal was roughly the same shape and size as the gap in the mortar, and as she glanced up at Vydian, her heart pounded in her chest.

"Try it," Vydian urged.

Before Briatta tried to unlock anything, she turned her head towards Rory, looking at him over her shoulder. "When we go in, you will tell whoever is on the other side that you recruited us. We want to join this organization. If you give us away, I will send Neven after you."

Rory's throat bobbed, and he rocked from his toes to his heels. He nodded shakily; he would know she'd never been able to finish a job in the same way Neven could, and he would also know how much Neven looked after her.

Facing the wall once more, Briatta pushed the key—if that's what it was—into the hole. It fit perfectly, but it went in farther than she'd expected. When it seemed to be seated correctly, she turned it. At first, nothing happened, and Briatta frowned, putting more force into twisting the damn thing.

At last, something gave, and there was a soft click as the wall shifted just enough so Briatta could clearly see the outline of the door. Pulling the key from the wall and slipping it into one of her pockets, she nodded at Rory. He would go first. If anyone were standing guard, seeing a familiar face enter ahead of two strangers would be less alarming.

Rory swallowed again and hesitated, his hands gripping the fabric of his pants. Vydian nudged him forward, and he finally moved slowly, haltingly, to the door. He lifted his hand, then rolled his shoulders as if he were steadying himself as he reached for the narrow edge of the door now protruding from the wall. With the tips of his fingers, Rory pressed a small divot in the stone that wasn't visible before the door was unlocked, and a narrow bar released and popped out right into his waiting hand. Gripping the small metal handle, Rory pulled, and the door swung open.

The door itself wasn't as large as it had originally appeared to be and was only a thin layer of stone compared to the wall it was part of. Beyond it was total blackness, and Briatta instinctively reached for her Ardor, opening herself to it just enough to feel for life within the depths of the darkness ahead. She couldn't sense anything, so she released her Ardor, resisting the urge to call it to herself in the light of the Polar Sun where it would be noticed; it was starting to feel like a protective blanket to be surrounded by her own darkness.

Looking back at them one last time, Rory stepped inside. Briatta hurried to stay close on his heels, but she couldn't adjust her vision until he closed the door behind Vydian, plunging them into complete darkness. Briatta's breath quickened even as she closed her eyes, finally accessing the channel to her Ardor, feeling for her companions. She felt Rory moving along a wall in front of them and Vydian standing still behind her.

A small feeling of triumph surged through Briatta; she could not only sense the others within the darkness but also identify them. She tried expanding her senses then, and could only vaguely detect an opening in the wall somewhere near Rory and nothing further than that. Opening her eyes again but holding onto her Ardor, Briatta took a timid step towards where she could feel Rory.

"Where are you?" Briatta said, despite knowing exactly where he was. She wanted Rory to think that she had no idea where he'd gone in case he decided to betray them.

"Just give me a moment, Belrose." Rory's answer sounded much louder than she'd expected, and Briatta jumped.

Tracking his position with her shadows, Briatta's hands formed fists at her sides. He didn't appear to be in a hurry, but he also didn't seem to be drawing weapons or calling for aid. It was difficult to relax even with her deep breathing.

Then, from the direction where Rory had spoken, came a brief flash of light as sparks flew before a flame flickered to life. Rory cupped his hand around the blooming fire and blew softly, encouraging the heat to grow. He held a torch in one hand and a metal fire starter in the other.

Holding the new source of light up, Rory beckoned. "Sorry about that. No Ardor lights on the stairs. Follow me."

Briatta was still taking in their surroundings as she stepped after him. From the hidden door outside, they had entered onto a landing of sorts. A staircase descending into the ground was in the middle of the wall before them, the only exit from the room aside from the door from which they'd come through. Rory took the first steps down the stairs, and the torchlight on the landing dimmed almost immediately. Briatta and Vydian rushed to follow.

Founders, if this was the hidden entrance to the base of the false criminal group, they had a much better disguise than the newspaper front that stood on top of the Night Roses' headquarters.

"What is this place?" Vydian asked, seeming just as awed.

It was cool in the dark, encased by stone that never saw the Polar Sun, and Briatta found herself feeling what she could only describe as chilled. It was a sensation she'd only experienced once before—at her Choosing bath—and she shuddered. Even if this was an excellent hiding spot, she wasn't sure she liked it.

"You'll see," Rory said without turning his head.

Briatta and Vydian exchanged a wary look but continued after him.

The staircase was long and steep, but Briatta caught a flash of movement over Rory's shoulder. Two people were a little farther down, standing on either side of a large black door. The only reason Briatta knew it was a door was because of the gold handle reflecting the firelight from the sconces.

"What does the sparrow sing?" a woman's voice called. The sound of metal on leather sounded as weapons were drawn. Briatta's hand went to her dagger.

"The song that puts the cat to sleep," Rory replied. Beyond him, Briatta could see the guards relax, lowering their blades.

"Welcome back, Rory," the woman said. "Who do you have

with you?" Her voice was measured, even a little curious. She didn't sound like a protective, suspicious guard of a crime group. Probably not someone with a strong call to acting, then.

Rory stopped as they reached the door and lifted his torch. Vydian and Briatta stepped behind him.

"New recruits," Rory told her. The woman looked them over with a strange frown on her face, and Briatta belatedly realized she was probably trying to look skeptical.

"Don't get many new recruits," she said, her thumbs hooking on her pant pockets.

"Saw them fighting with each other," Rory replied. "Looked promising." Rory, at least, was a little more convincing.

Shrugging, the woman reached out and turned the door handle. "Let me know how it goes."

Rory nodded and crossed the threshold through the door. Past his shoulder, Briatta could see a dimly lit but welcoming sitting room. Judging by the lights spattered on the ceiling, these false criminals had at least one Light Ardorist.

Laughter and voices bubbled out of the space, and Briatta entered after Rory, feeling yet another surge of confusion. This was the secret crime organization? Men and women, all dressed to fight in grey uniforms, lounged in various comfortable positions around the room. Some played games, others read books, and most had drinks in their hands or on the tables in front of them. This was too happy to be a criminal organization. Though, if it was a false one, maybe the actors weren't as committed to the bit as the Weilers expected. Or maybe they were bored with how long the Ackmanlee was taking.

As people noted the two strange women following Rory, the room fell silent. Someone at the edge of the room jumped up and held up their headscarf, hiding their face as they fled from the room. Briatta and Vydian glanced at each other.

"What's this?" A deep, masculine voice resonated from one

of the large armchairs. The giant who had spoken had a full, curly beard and long black hair that fell down his back. There was no Ardor-mark on his temple, and Briatta felt a small measure of relief. Unless, by some chance, he was like her. An unregistered Ardorist with Ardor that they'd never be permitted to use in public.

"Recruits, Canon." Rory gave a shallow bow, so Briatta marked him as the leader. The man—Canon—seemed completely at ease in this room, even with two strangers present. He looked her over with shrewd, narrowed eyes, then examined Vydian with the same scrutiny.

"Don't look like much." Canon's head tipped to the side as his fingers steepled in his lap.

"I can vouch for them," Rory said. Briatta's gaze traveled to the back of his head, where he'd tugged his headscarf down and she could still see the bump she'd given him. She cringed inwardly. After all of this, she was going to take Rory out for a meal as an apology.

After a long silence, Canon sighed. "Alright, then. We'll see what they've got. Take them to rooms, place a guard, and we'll interview them later."

Rory's shoulders visibly relaxed, and while curious eyes still remained on them, most returned to whatever they'd been doing before Briatta and Vydian had entered.

Because Rory was here, Briatta found herself searching the other faces for any she might recognize, but none stood out to her.

The attention no longer centered on them, Rory pulled Briatta and Vydian towards a door that led to a hallway.

Briatta did a second scan as they walked, looking for anyone who didn't fit in as well as studying the other exits leading to more hallways. Everyone here appeared happy and relaxed, and nobody looked as if they were being held against their will or pretending to be, meaning Tallor likely wasn't in this room. Perhaps there was a holding area where he was being kept, or would at least be planted there to wait now that competitors were present.

"This is crazy," Vydian muttered, leaning close. "Do you think we should have gotten Neven?"

Starting at the sound of her oldest friend's name, Briatta turned to Vydian, feeling guilty. "There wasn't time. Besides, he isn't...participating."

Vydian raised her brows in response.

Rory glanced back at them but didn't say anything.

"What is this organization called?" Briatta asked as they passed into the hallway. Briatta wasn't sure why he hadn't betrayed them immediately. There were enough people down in the front room to easily overwhelm her and Vydian if Rory had wanted to. But he hadn't, so that had to mean something.

Rory shrugged. "Canon's group, I guess. Nothing very official yet; we're quite new."

"Did you leave your other post?" Briatta asked pointedly, a brow lifted, knowing that Rory would understand what she meant.

Some of the color drained from Rory's face. "Ah, no. I didn't."

"His other post?" Vydian questioned.

"I work as an investigator for the Weilers," Rory told her. "Unofficially."

That was true in a roundabout way. Briatta huffed a light laugh. "How large is the base?"

Rory shifted uncomfortably, knowing all the questions she would have before she even asked them. "It's quite large. Most of us stay here except for when there is a mission."

"Can we see?" Vydian leaned and reached out a hand to touch the wall of the hallway, her expression open and curious as her eyes roved over the structure and the ceiling.

Again, Rory glanced around.

"You can look," he said. "No one will stop you. But now that you're here, you will be kept from leaving."

Well, that made sense. If strangers stumbled across the Night Roses' headquarters, they wouldn't be permitted to simply leave, either. It would make freeing Tallor more difficult, but Briatta hadn't expected anything less. They would just need to track guard shifts and determine a low-traffic route to avoid detection when escaping with Tallor.

Almost snorting at how much she'd simplified the process, Briatta sighed.

Casting another look around the hall, Briatta forced herself to pay closer attention to where they were going. They'd been walking for a while, and they'd passed several closed doors and a few open ones. It was a straight hall, however, so there was no need to memorize any turns. The people in most of the rooms she could see into were occupied with their respective activities, and no one showed them any interest.

Despite knowing she should be treating this like a real mission, Briatta couldn't help wondering what they all did outside of the Ackmanlee that allowed spending their time lying around playing games rather than their normal jobs. Maybe they were all being paid a significant amount to do so, considering the winner would be given such an important position.

Clearly, they'd been instructed to ignore newcomers who were accompanied by another member, because no one stopped them.

"I could use a nap. Will there be dinner later?" Vydian smiled sweetly at Rory.

Briatta's belly rumbled at the mention of food. They hadn't eaten since breakfast—since they'd begun their sweep of D'ivory.

"There will be a feast" Rory grinned. "We are celebrating. You'll be allowed to come, if you pass."

"Celebrating?" Briatta echoed.

Rory's attention switched to her. "Yes. You'll see. Just... listen to Canon, okay?"

Vydian covered her mouth as she yawned. "Excellent. I will be ready to party after I pass your little test."

They reached the end of the hall, and Rory led them through a door on the right. It opened into a long stone hallway with evenly spaced doors on either side. Ardor lights turned on as they passed, illuminating the hallway and casting their shadows behind them. Each door had a black stone plate with a name etched in white—none that Briatta recognized— and they eventually reached doors with blank slates.

"These rooms are empty," Rory said. "You can pick whichever one you like. A guard will be posted outside until Canon comes for you. Don't try to leave." He directed the last words very pointedly at Briatta, who gave him an innocent smile and shrugged.

Vydian thanked him and opened one of the doors, stepping within. She didn't even bother comparing the rooms before shutting the door behind her without a word. Briatta frowned slightly after the woman, wondering whether she really needed to sleep or if there was something else going on.

Rory turned to go, but Briatta caught his arm and halted him. He half pivoted to her, raising his brows in silent question.

"Rory," she began, then paused and bit her lip. "Why didn't you turn us in? It would have been easy for you to do it in that sitting room."

"You're kinda scary, Belrose." Rory smiled. "I believe you when you say you'll send Neven after me. Besides, I think you'll like it here. Even if you threatened your way in, that's how most of us got here in the first place. You'll fit right in."

With another smaller smile, Rory left. His footsteps echoed in the rock tunnel as he walked farther away, and Briatta waited until she could no longer hear them before opening a door with a blank nameplate and stepping inside. However, before she closed it as Vydian had, she searched for something to scratch her name into the stone so that no one would try to enter. Finding a small white stick of something phosphorus sitting on the narrow entry table, Briatta etched *B.B.* for Briatta Belrose onto the door and shut it to examine the living space.

Seconds later, she heard the footsteps that indicated the arrival of their guards outside, and then the door was cracked open as the man checked to ensure she was present. Ignoring him, Briatta continued her exploration, and the door shut once more.

The room was simple. Besides the table standing by the door, there was a single bed, a tiny wardrobe, and a desk with a chair. It felt more like a prison cell than a bedroom, and Briatta wondered if all the people in the common room lived like this for the duration of the Ackmanlee.

If this was what they had infiltrated. Judging by the acting skills and the uniform color and the location in D'ivory as was hinted at by the barrel, Briatta was mostly confident. They just needed confirmation.

There was a slim chance Rory had betrayed the Night Roses, and a real organized crime group had sprouted since the fabrication of the case file, which meant Briatta and Vydian were now caught in something entirely different and very real.

Briatta laid on the bed and closed her eyes. For now, the

least she could do for herself and the task at hand was to get a bit of rest. They could get more information from people at the feast later, assuming they passed the upcoming test, or it could even be a good night to execute the mission when everyone was distracted. Regardless, a little sleep wouldn't hurt.

CHAPTER 30

Briatta awoke suddenly and sat upright. She was immediately aware of Canon in her doorway, and as she blinked herself to full awareness, she stared up at him. The man was massive, nearly filling the frame completely as he looked down his nose at her, one hand resting on the door handle.

"You sleep light, at least," he commented, lifting one corner of his mouth. "That's good."

Scowling, Briatta pushed herself to a seat at the edge of the bed and reached for her shoes.

"Come," Canon said, turning. Without waiting for her to follow, he crossed the hall and opened Vydian's door as well. From where she still sat, Briatta could see that the woman was lounging on her bed, somehow managing to peer condescendingly up at the man from where she rested.

"Ah, finally." Vydian groused and stood, brushing her hands on her shirt. "I was beginning to think you'd never show."

Briatta widened her eyes and shook her head at Vydian.

Was she trying to anger Canon? Didn't she know all that rested on their passing of his test?

Wordlessly, Canon leveled a flat look at Vydian and then started back down the hallway. The two men who'd been posted outside of their doors waited until Vydian and Briatta left their rooms after Canon before stepping in behind them.

"Not much of a talker, is he?" Vydian asked, nudging Briatta with her shoulder. Her tone was playful. Briatta shot her a glare, still confused as to why she would want to irritate their ticket into this place, and didn't reply.

"Not you, too." Vydian sighed as if no one in this organization understood her.

Still, Briatta remained silent.

Catching the hint, Vydian finally fell quiet. The four of them followed Canon back to the main hallway, then through a door into a room with only a table and six chairs.

"Sit." Canon walked to the other side of the table so he faced the door and gestured with one meaty arm at the seats across from him.

Briatta obeyed, not liking having her back to the door where the two guards remained, but Vydian perched on the edge of the table and lifted her right hand to her face, checking beneath her nails.

"Can we get this over with? I hear there's a party," Vydian drawled.

"Vydian," Briatta hissed. What in the Founders had gotten into her friend?

Vydian lifted her eyes to meet Briatta's, narrowed them slightly, and made a quick sign with her hands, so swift it was barely perceptible. "*Trust.*"

Grinding her jaw, Briatta sat back in the chair, her knuckles white where she gripped the armrests, though she moved it so that she could also see the guards.

"You already know that we won't allow you to leave," Canon started from where he coolly observed the two women, his expression a little too stern to appear entirely genuine. Briatta lifted her chin as she listened, maintaining her composure. "So, there's no use in resisting or...whatever it is you're doing." His voice cracked at that, and for a moment as he looked away, Briatta thought she saw his composure slip.

The last part was directed at Vydian, who mocked offense, her right hand going to her heart. Was Canon amused by Vydian's act? Or was he just not as good of an actor as she'd initially thought?

Briatta thought about the people in her life who had no idea where she was. What if they failed this façade of a test? What would the Weilers do? Would they keep the two of them there in this mock criminal base? Or would Briatta and Vydian be released as failures of the Ackmanlee, banned from continuing the competition and helping others?

Briatta hadn't considered warning Leah she might miss some of her Sour Soup shifts. She hoped Neven or someone else would be able to help in her stead. Of all the things to be worrying about at this second, Leah and Sour Soup were probably the least important, yet it was still one of the first things she'd thought about.

Maybe Owena had been right to make her find work.

"Rory already told you that," Canon said as he observed their lack of reaction to his threat. "Or you expected it."

Vydian shrugged. "Can't expect to walk into a den of vipers and stroll right back out."

Canon's brows drew together. "No vipers here, child. Only people who want justice."

"We believe in justice." Vydian placed her hand on the table and leaned toward Canon. "Tell me, who deserves it?"

"Classified," Canon said smoothly, though he appeared faintly amused at her gall.

"What will it take to earn your trust?" Vydian asked plainly.

It was becoming clear now to Briatta the picture that Vydian was painting. Her friend wanted Canon to view her as a young woman desperate for him to mete out his judgment, as someone who wanted to be part of this organization. While Briatta had known, to a degree, what to expect when interviewing the store owners, she wasn't sure how these people had been briefed or what they'd been told to do.

Canon, for all she knew, could be an actual Weiler trained in interrogation methods and would see straight through them.

But thinking that way wouldn't help. Just because this was a staged event didn't mean that the people were infallible. And it didn't mean they hadn't stumbled upon something real, either. This could very well be a true interrogation, and if it was, then Vydian was risking everything.

"Who are you? Names, both of you," Canon said, completely ignoring Vydian.

Scowling, Vydian pushed off the table and eased herself into a chair next to Briatta.

"Briatta Belrose," Briatta said without hesitation. Anyone in Montclair would be able to verify her identity, and there was no use lying; she didn't have false papers to prove anything.

Canon nodded as if he already knew, then looked expectantly at Vydian. The dark-haired woman folded her arms.

"Vydian Lockwood."

Briatta noted Vydian's family name, because it was her first time hearing it out loud. At least it confirmed that the file Neven had found was the right one, though it didn't explain how someone caring for elderly people knew how to fight as well as Vydian did. She returned to the multiple instances when she'd considered looking deeper into Vydian since then, but each time had decided that since the Weilers deemed her worthy—even if they were historically bad at that—and because there were no criminal records of her in Night Rose documents, the woman didn't deserve her scrutiny yet. If there was anything clandestine about her, it would be revealed in time simply by keeping her close.

Besides, it was nice to pretend that she had a friend in this woman, who could spar nearly as well as she could, without feeling the constant urge to dig into her background. Yet.

If for no other reason than those, Briatta had wanted to focus all of her attention on the Ackmanlee, and she couldn't afford to be distracted.

Again, Canon dipped his chin.

"Thank you for your honesty."

Vydian's eyebrows lifted. Briatta hadn't been expecting that either.

"Now, I must ask what you were doing trying to get into our base?"

Briatta shifted in her chair, unable to keep entirely still. It was one of her faults. To others, she knew, this would portray her as untrustworthy. Owena had drilled it into her thousands of times, and yet she could never manage to heed her aunt's words regarding stillness. She opened her mouth.

"Wanted in on the action," Vydian replied smoothly. "Like you said, there's justice to be had."

Canon steepled his hands on his lap, tilting his head at Vydian. The question was unspoken, and yet it was more effective than if he'd held a whip.

"Listen, we've heard the stories. The things that man did. We've been tracking the friends, and how little they seem to actually care. We're in." Vydian leaned forward, her tone low and intense. She looked like a woman who was ready to fight; someone who would draw her blade against anyone aligned with Tallor.

Briatta was confused, but then it clicked. Of course—they'd heard mixed stories about Tallor. The Weilers had reported that he was unproblematic, but some of the locals had a different story. This was a classic case of the common people taking charge when the authorities would not.

How could she have been so blind? Why hadn't Vydian shared this with her before?

The answer seemed satisfactory. Canon's mouth tightened, and he blinked before turning his gaze on Briatta.

"And you? What were you doing?"

"I'm with Vydian," Briatta answered. "I've been following the case with her, and it's as she said. We're in."

A small part of that acknowledgment stung. Somehow, Briatta had ended up following Vydian through this, just as she'd always followed Neven. Apparently, she could only separate herself from life before her Choosing so much.

Canon regarded Briatta for a breath too long, as if he didn't entirely believe her, but then he nodded. "Alright, then. Why join us? Why not do it yourselves, if you've collected so much evidence on your own?"

Vydian started talking before Briatta could get a word out.

"Hah, as if you think we could do it on our own." She scoffed. "We have no delusions, here. We're two small women, and while we might be good at what we do, we're up against a whole group of men."

The two guards, who had followed them inside and stood on either side of the door, glanced at each other. They were both tall men, and they shared a small smile and a laugh at Vydian's comments. A ripple of disgust traveled down Briatta's back. She and Vydian were likely to best all three men within seconds, even without knowing how well they had been trained.

The possibility that they were as good as she and Vydian was just so low.

Briatta hated they had to demean themselves to confirm their desire in joining this group, but it was something that Owena had taught her and Ellery. To be faster and smarter than their opponent, but to never think that they could be stronger. To assume they were stronger would mean their death. One must always enter a fight thinking they are the lesser of their opponent and be prepared for every potential outcome, or they would be bested within moments.

Despite thinking she and Vydian could handle these three men only seconds before, Briatta forced herself to reconsider.

Canon watched Briatta with his dark eyes as if he could read every thought that went through her mind.

"Do you feel the same?" He asked.

Swallowing, Briatta nodded. They needed to infiltrate this group if they wanted to win. And if this wasn't a group that had been put together for the Ackmanlee, then their survival hinged on their success in this room. "I do."

Quiet fell like a soft blanket over the table. Briatta fought the urge to move, forcing herself to sit still, while Vydian absently picked at the wood of the table as if she didn't even care where they were.

"There is a price," Canon finally said. "All must pay. Call it... an entry fee."

"Name it," Vydian replied instantly, looking up at him from under her lashes. It sounded more intimidating than innocent.

"You must tell us a secret. One that we can verify. One that would have you thrown into jail by the Weilers if it were to get out." Canon tilted his head as he spoke, watching their reactions carefully, coming to some internal resolution.

Briatta and Vydian shared a look. If they had indeed found the Weiler-created criminal group, then it would make sense that the Weilers would want to know their secrets. They could assume that Canon would, of course, be reporting everything. And they'd want to know everything about the candidate they'd be hiring.

If their innermost darkness could end up damning the Weilers if they hired them the same as it could damn them.

Canon waited silently, as patient as a father with a young child.

Without thinking about it, Briatta knew what she'd have to say. There was only one secret she had that would put her in jail, and it was the Night Roses. Rory would be able to verify. She could only hope that some relationship between Owena and the Weilers actually existed, because otherwise, this would ruin everything—not just for her, but for the Night Roses themselves. And what if this wasn't for the Ackmanlee? What would revealing the Night Roses risk?

Briatta's mind raced for something else, but it was as if every other memory she had was gone.

A new fear wrapped its oily fingers around her heart; the fear that she would destroy herself and everything she loved now that they'd finally made it this far. Briatta was trying to pull herself together to speak the words into existence when Vydian sat up straighter in her seat and cleared her throat.

"I will give mine to you," Vydian said. "But not with anyone else in the room. And...I trust that my secret will cover her, as well." She nodded in Briatta's direction.

Briatta's breath quickened, her nostrils flaring as she stared at her friend. What kind of secret could Vydian have that would account for both their entries?

"I will hear it." Canon had made his decision as his eyes shifted to the two guards. They moved to flank Briatta's chair, and she hesitated, looking to Vydian for reassurance. The word her friend had signed earlier, trust, rang in her head, and Briatta made herself move even when Vydian didn't meet her eyes.

The three of them walked out of the room, shutting the door behind them, and then stopped to wait. Briatta wasn't sure what to do with herself, with her hands.

She still had her daggers, which was a bit shocking.

Luckily, however, Vydian's reason for wanting to join the group had helped them both. Canon now presumed they were defenseless young women against a man of his size and likely never even considered checking for weapons.

Fighting the compulsion to reach for them, Briatta made herself pace in front of the guards instead.

They were at the corner of the hallway that led back to the main room and the wing where their rooms were, and Briatta glanced restlessly down each of them with every turn she made. There didn't seem to be anyone else about, though she kept a vigilant watch regardless.

The two guards eyed her but remained stationed by the door.

Canon and Vydian stayed in the room for what felt like an hour, and Briatta eventually ceased pacing and leaned against the wall at the end of the hall. At the opposite side, through the door leading into the main room, she could see when people passed by. She stared at the door, taking a mental note of everyone she glimpsed, when she saw a familiar shock of blond. It happened almost too quickly to confirm, but Briatta knew that head of hair anywhere.

At first, her heart had leaped. Neven had made it here, too. Perhaps they could meet up and finish this together.

But then he didn't come this way. No one led him down the hall to a room, and she hadn't noticed anyone guarding him.

She waited, but he still didn't come.

Why would he be unguarded?

The answer was already there, in the back of her mind, but Briatta couldn't admit it to herself yet. Perhaps there was another reason. Maybe he'd already found the organization first.

But if he had, why hadn't he shared it with her and Vydian? He was on her side, wasn't he?

Wasn't he?

"Excuse me," Briatta mustered the courage to ask the guards. They looked at her curiously but didn't respond. "Are all new members watched and questioned? Or...is it case by case?"

They glanced at each other, looking unprepared for such a question. But there would have been a protocol established, because of the premise of the test.

"Everyone is watched and questioned," the guard on the right said, but he left it very open ended, to account for any possibility.

Briatta's heart sank. There were many reasons she could think of, then, why Neven would be here and not have told her. None of them were good.

The remainder of the time that passed until Vydian and Canon reappeared was spent in emotional turmoil over every possible scenario, though Briatta did her best to keep it contained. When the door finally opened and Vydian emerged, beaming, Briatta stared at her friend from where she still rested against the end of the hallway.

"We're in," Vydian declared.

An act. This was all an act that Briatta and Vydian had to maintain until they uncovered the truth of their situation.

Briatta plastered a smile onto her face that she hoped looked more real than it felt.

"For now," Canon acceded gruffly before Briatta could respond. Briatta sent a silent prayer of thanks to the Founders that she wouldn't have to fake a celebration with Vydian in front of the three men.

"So, the party?" Vydian asked, reverting to the original topic of the evening. She linked her arm through Briatta's and tugged her gently away from the wall, winking at her friend before jutting her chin out at Canon.

"You'll be welcome," Canon conceded. "And there will be no more guards. But know that everyone reports to me, so if you're thinking of anything, don't."

Vydian mocked surprise at this, the small sniff of indignation saying more than she could have if she'd tried. "You insult me."

To Briatta's shock, Canon grinned wickedly. "That's the name of the game down here, sweetheart."

With that, the three men walked back down the hall to the main room, leaving Briatta and Vydian alone. As soon as they were gone, Briatta grabbed Vydian's arm and pulled her back to her own room, shutting the door behind them.

"What did you tell him?" Briatta demanded. If it had anything to do with her, she wanted to know. More importantly, perhaps, if Vydian had a secret that could put her in jail, Briatta had underestimated her.

"A secret is a secret for a reason," Vydian replied, shoving her hands into her pockets. "Sorry, but I can't tell you this one."

While Briatta would have pushed the subject any other day, she let it go for now. Until this point, she hadn't felt the need to look into Vydian. She knew that if she pushed, Vydian would be less likely to tell her, and she also knew that she'd have more tools to figure out what Vydian knew after they were out of this mess. For now, Briatta didn't care how Vydian had gotten them in, only that she had, and they were that much closer to winning the Ackmanlee. This could wait until after they'd rescued Tallor. There were now more pressing things at hand.

"While you were in there with Canon," Briatta started, wringing her hands on her shirt. "I think I saw...I saw Neven."

Vydian frowned. "What? But how would he have gotten here?"

"That's what I've been trying to figure out," Briatta replied, looking away. "I...I think that maybe he is part of this."

CHAPTER 31

Rory had knocked on Briatta's and Vydian's doors before the feast, giving them time to refresh themselves. There were communal bathing chambers where Water and Fire Ardorists kept warm baths drawn as needed. Briatta had taken him up on the offer, splashing some water on her face and using the extra time to explore the other rooms of the living quarters.

Rory offered her clean clothes for the party, but not wanting to part with her favored sparring outfit, Briatta declined.

When it came time for the feast, Briatta noted it was massive considering the size of the hideout. More people squeezed into the main room than Briatta would have thought possible, and it seemed every table and chair had been brought out for the event. Almost every seat was full. Only Neven was absent. Or perhaps Briatta hadn't seen him at all.

The food hadn't been served, but the many scents of different dishes wafted in from the other door—the one they hadn't been through yet. Maybe that was where equipment for cooking and other necessities had been placed, if all the participants of the Ackmanlee were living here for the duration of the contest. Maybe that was also where they kept the prisoners.

A sharp ringing sounded as Canon lifted his empty glass and knocked a spoon against it, standing in the middle of the crew. When everyone fell silent, he raised his arms as if to encourage cheering, which the people in the room obliged with enthusiasm. When *that* had quieted down as well, Canon set his glass on the table and nodded to the man beside him, who took it and refilled it with wine.

"Tonight, we celebrate the successful apprehension of the Benson boy," Canon shouted amidst the rise of excited voices again.

Well, that answered at least one question. Tallor Benson. This was the hideout for the Ackmanlee. Tension released in Briatta's chest, and she sat up and clapped her hands a few times so she wouldn't stand out as the only one not excited.

But...that meant that Rory *was* helping. And if Neven... Briatta's mind whirled. Suddenly, it made sense. Everything she'd been suspicious of clicked. Owena's longer working hours. The classified information. Why Neven hadn't been as forthcoming or helpful as he normally was. Why he and Rory had been at the same warehouse.

Founders.

"You have all done well, and so you will eat well tonight," Canon told them all, and Briatta shook herself back to the present. "And tomorrow, we will move forward with the plan!"

The plan? What plan? Briatta sat up straighter, briefly meeting Vydian's eyes.

Unfortunately, Canon appeared to be done talking as he lifted his now-full glass to lead the room in a toast. The missing barrels of brambleberry liquor were rolled into the room along with countless bottles of wine and other spirits. Briatta watched the seemingly endless procession of drinks with some disbelief.

Then, the food arrived.

Platters of roasted meats and bowls of fruits and vegetables suddenly filled the room as a whirlwind of people swept in and plopped what they were carrying onto the tables in a disorganized fashion before leaving. Briatta reached for a slice of hot bread and slathered it with goat cheese and brambleberry preserves, her mouth watering as she tasted it.

Vydian copied Briatta, eyes widening as she tasted the bread.

"This is incredible," Vydian said through the mouthful of food.

Rory appeared beside her, dropping into the chair with a bottle of pink wine in his hand. He pulled the cork and seized Briatta's glass, filling it nearly to the brim. She accepted it and waited for the other cups to be full, then knocked her glass lightly against theirs and took a sip. It was sweet and light, and on any other day, Briatta might have drunk much more. But tonight, she needed to keep her wits about her.

All around them were the sounds of utensils scraping against dishes as people served themselves amidst laughter and conversation. Briatta scooped several slices of meat onto her plate and ate them alongside the bread and cheese. Across the table, Rory and Vydian were already halfway done with their wine, but Vydian was also eating a lot of bread to help absorb it.

A loud crack rang out as someone tapped one of the barrels of brambleberry liquor, and Briatta jumped in her seat, nearly dropping her fork.

"Ah, no need for that here," the woman beside her said,

giving Briatta a concerned look. "We may not be Ardorists, but we have each other's backs."

Briatta pasted a smile onto her face and nodded, turning back to her plate.

It would be a long while before most people were too deep in their cups to notice anything odd, so Briatta bided her time. Vydian had started pouring her wine into Rory's cup, who was delighted that his drink was seemingly bottomless.

Then, someone shouted for music, and a burly bear of a man shoved his way to the front of the room and picked up a lute from where it had been tucked into the corner.

The energy shifted, and people started to clear out the tables, making room for those who wanted to dance. The man tuned the lute, the notes twanging loudly and eliciting hoots of excitement from the crowd. When he played, the small instrument quickly filled the sitting area with song. Before long, shrieks of laughter were heard as men spun women on the makeshift dancefloor.

Somewhat amused, Briatta pressed her back to the wall and watched. When they'd been displaced from their table, she and Vydian had allowed themselves to be swept toward the door they had yet to explore, and they were now close enough to slip away when the opportunity presented itself.

"Did you find anything?" Briatta whispered into Vydian's ear, finally able to talk. While Briatta had bathed and explored their side of the base, Vydian had wandered elsewhere. The woman dipped her chin subtly, her black hair shining in the dim Ardor lights of the main room. A man stumbled up to them and stopped, his drink nearly sloshing over the rim of his cup.

"Either one of you ladies care to dance?" he asked, his words slurring slightly.

"Not tonight," Vydian replied, flashing a dazzling smile.

"Next time, then." He winked and stumbled away. When people stopped paying attention to them, Vydian backed up a step to join Briatta flush against the wall.

"Are you thinking now or later?"

Looking around the room, as she had been all night, Briatta bit her lip. If they moved now, the noise and chaos could aid in their escape. But there were still far too many people awake, and the chance of running into someone was too high.

"Later."

The party passed in a blur. For a crime base that had just allowed two strangers into their midst, the inhabitants were drinking far more than Briatta would have if the roles were reversed. People shouted at each other joyfully, loudly bragging about how they'd taken Tallor and how they were going to get justice. No one ever said what that meant, and Briatta rolled her eyes after she'd heard it at least ten separate times.

When the hour seemed reasonable, Briatta told Vydian that she was tired and crossed the room to return to the small chamber she'd chosen. Everyone still awake would have seen her leave and go in that direction.

Vydian followed a short while later, but instead of going to her own room, she joined Briatta in hers.

"What did you find?" Briatta asked when the door was shut and locked.

"Tallor is in a guarded room near the kitchen," Vydian whispered, removing her jacket and shoving it into the gap beneath the door.

"How many guards?"

"Just one." Vydian pulled the chair out from the desk and sat down, facing Briatta where she was perched on the bed. "And I saw them join the party, so I'm not sure if they were replaced or if they were drinking while on duty."

Nodding, Briatta looked down at her hands, folded in her

lap. She rubbed one thumb over the other, thinking. "Let's take watches until the celebration dies down. I can go first."

Vydian returned to her room.

A couple hours later, the feast was still going strong, so Briatta woke Vydian and attempted to get some rest. She wasn't sure she was going to be able to fall asleep, but as soon as her head hit the pillow, she found herself dozing off. It felt as though no time had passed when Vydian lightly shook her shoulder, and she sat straight up.

"What is it?"

"Things have quieted down," Vydian told her. "Now's our chance."

Rising from the bed, Briatta checked her weapons and clothing before reaching up to braid her hair. Similarly, Vydian bound hers into a tight plait. As soon as they were both done, Briatta nodded and signed for Vydian to lead the way.

The hallway was dark now, and the silence compared to the raucous noise that had filtered through the door was eerie. Briatta opened herself to her Ardor, feeling for any movement in the darkness, sensing only the sleeping Elfeans behind their respective doors. They made it back to the common area without incident and froze in the doorway when they saw that Canon had passed out at the table, his head back against the chair and a half-full bottle still in his hand. A moment later, he snored loudly. Briatta relaxed.

Vydian adjusted her steps to be nearly silent, and Briatta followed suit, creeping through the room. When they'd made it to the other side, Briatta let out a breath.

"Just ahead on the right," Vydian signed and pointed to the closed door. A guard was indeed posted there, but they were asleep, seated and leaning against the wall. Briatta nodded in acknowledgment. Hopefully, he'd drunk too much to rouse tonight.

Pulling her lock picks from her pocket, Briatta gently wiggled the doorknob to verify it was locked. Vydian stood guard behind her, watching the hallway and the door to the sitting room. It was a straightforward mechanism, and she quickly released it.

Briatta suspected this was too easy as she opened the door and peeked inside. A young man was curled up on a low cot with a threadbare blanket barely covering him.

"Keep watch," Briatta signed to Vydian before entering the room. She approached the man slowly, careful to avoid startling him as she visually checked to ensure he wasn't holding any daggers or other weapons. As a prisoner, she doubted he even had access to any, but she would rather not be stabbed.

Carefully, Briatta hovered her hand over the man's mouth before pressing against it suddenly, squeezing his shoulder with her other. Tallor's eyes flew open, and he jerked back. Briatta lurched to keep her hand over his mouth and then slowly released it, holding a finger to her lips.

"Do you understand?" she asked, signing quickly. Tallor watched, but his expression remained blank, and he narrowed his eyes in question.

"Let's get you out of here," Briatta said under her breath. Understanding dawned in Tallor's eyes, quickly followed by an expression of excitement. Briatta wondered if they'd kept him in this room for the entirety of the Ackmanlee in case anyone were to find the base at any time. If that was the case, she hoped he was very well compensated for it. After all, it had been a little over two weeks since the Ackmanlee started.

Vydian appeared in the doorway, beckoning for them to move. Briatta obeyed. They flanked Tallor, with Briatta taking the rear, and moved back to the doorway leading into the common area. The trickiest part of this escape would be the base's main entrance, where there had been two guards. While the Elfeans keeping watch inside had evidently been laid back and had taken breaks, Briatta doubted the ones outside would have done the same.

Canon was still snoring, and Briatta fought the urge to freeze with every lengthy pause between his breaths. Vydian carefully turned the handle on one of the doors and cracked it, peering out to check for anyone on the other side. Time seemed to stretch as she looked, but when she glanced back at Briatta, her brows were creased and she shook her head. No one was there.

This definitely felt too easy.

Briatta considered other possible ways the group would have prevented an escape but then squared her shoulders. They hadn't seen anything obvious on their way in. It was unlikely that anything new had been added in the time they'd been here. Whatever they might encounter, she and Vydian would be able to take care of it.

Nodding to tell Vydian they could move, Briatta watched the room behind them as Tallor followed Vydian through the door before joining the two and pulling the door shut, trusting that Vydian monitored their path ahead.

However, Briatta couldn't hear any movement from her companions. Vydian and Tallor weren't heading to the staircase as they should have been. She froze and listened carefully. She could hear them breathing nearby but not moving.

Briatta reached out with her Ardor and felt a fourth person on the steps, sitting just high enough that they wouldn't have been visible from the door.

Turning to face the stairs, Briatta's blood turned cold in her veins.

Sitting there, with a drawn sword resting on his knees, was Neven. He was staring at the ground, one hand wrapped around the hilt, the other rubbing the back of his neck.

Silence stretched out, each of them so still that confusion bloomed in Briatta's chest. While she and Vydian had every reason to feel guilty and stand there, frozen, shouldn't Neven jump and offer to help?

But...he had been in the base earlier. Briatta was sure of it. He'd been known. They hadn't questioned him.

And he was still just sitting there.

"Neven," Briatta finally managed to say, keeping her voice low and her tone optimistic. Perhaps they could still salvage this. "You made it. I'm sorry we didn't get you before we came. But now you can help us escape."

Neven's knuckles whitened where he clutched the hilt, and a muscle feathered in his jaw. At last, he dropped his other arm to his side and looked up. "I can't let you do that. I'm sorry, Bria."

If she'd had a bad feeling before, Briatta's gut was screaming now to get out of here. "Wha...why not?"

Why was Neven here? How had he known they would attempt to escape tonight? Why wasn't he helping them? Even if he had a part in staging this with the Ackmanlee's false group, he'd been on their side until now.

Exhaling slowly, Neven drew himself to his feet. "I can't let you win."

"Neven," Briatta said, stepping back and bumping into the door they'd just come through. Her heart was cracking open in a new and painful way that she couldn't comprehend. Briatta was both hot and cold, and her ears roared. "I don't understand."

"What are you doing?" Vydian hissed at Neven, drawing her blades.

Neven pointed his sword at Vydian. "You can go. Take Tallor and win. Bria stays."

Tallor looked between the three of them, his eyes wide and

inquiring, his complexion pallid.

"I'm not leaving without her," Vydian snapped, scowling. "I knew you were bad news from the moment I met you. Why in the Founders do you want her to lose?"

Narrowing his eyes on Vydian, Neven snarled. "So be it."

"Neven, why—" Briatta began.

"Guards!" Neven yelled. "Deserters!"

"What are you doing?" Briatta shouted.

Vydian looked between them, clearly torn between taking Neven down and helping Briatta. Then, something solidified behind her gaze.

"Sorry about this," Vydian told Briatta before charging at Neven. Ready for her attack, Neven blocked the first blows before they fell into an evenly matched cadence. Briatta was still standing by the door, rooted to the spot, even as Vydian and Neven fought like they might actually kill one another.

"Are you going to do something?" Tallor demanded, waving his hand to get Briatta's attention.

"I..." She stared at him helplessly. Behind her, she heard the sounds of people stirring as shouts came from the common room. Someone retched. Frantically looking for something to block the doors, her eyes landed on the sword in Neven's hands. He was distracted by Vydian, who fought with a veracity that Briatta hadn't seen from the woman before.

Briatta took a few quick, shaky breaths before forcing herself to move. She had to do this without thinking, or she wouldn't be able to do it at all. Darting behind Neven, avoiding his blade as he swung it, she lifted her dagger and brought the hilt down on his head as hard as she could.

He ducked, whirling to shove her out of the way, and she hit the wall hard, her shoulder exploding in pain and one blade falling from her grip. Vydian snarled and swiped at his gut, and he dove to the side. Gasping for breath and holding her arm,

Briatta watched her friends fight. Still, it was hard to comprehend what she was seeing.

"Hello," Tallor called from the other side of the fight. "Do something!"

Gritting her teeth, Briatta set her jaw. She could do this. She knew all of Neven's moves. His back was to her.

Pushing herself from the wall, she let go of her arm and raised her dagger once more. This time, Vydian spun so that Neven was forced to turn further away from Briatta, and her strike hit true, the dull *thud* of her hilt hitting his skull vibrating through her arm.

Neven crumpled to the ground, and Vydian pulled back her blow just in time to avoid hitting Briatta, who stared dully at her lifelong friend.

Sheathing her knives, Vydian picked up Neven's sword and ran it to the door, laying it across the handles so it might hold long enough for them to make it up the stairs and figure out how to open the main exit from this side.

"Briatta, are you good?" Vydian shouted as she collected Tallor, dragging him to the staircase.

Neven looked so pale, so small, lying on the dark stone ground. Why had he done this? How could he have tried to take this from her? He knew how important it was to her, what this would mean for her life. Was it...was it because he knew what kind of person she was at her core? Had he thought she wouldn't—couldn't—change?

"Briatta," Vydian said sharply, and finally Briatta looked up. "Come."

Moving as if in a dream, Briatta obeyed, starting slowly at first but then breaking into a run as she followed Vydian and Tallor up the stairs. Behind them, the banging had begun, and she pushed herself harder, hurtling after the others, praying the sword would hold.

When they made it to the top, Vydian cursed. They didn't have a light source and hadn't seen how Rory had shut the damn thing on the way in. Briatta reached out with her Ardor, closing her eyes and running her hands along the wall, feeling desperately for any abnormalities or differences in the stone.

A large crash sounded as the doors banged open at the bottom of the staircase, and Canon roared. Heart racing, Briatta's hands shook as she worked. In all her years as a Night Rose, never had she been so close to being caught.

"Here! I think I found something!" Vydian shouted, and Briatta hurried to her side. There was a dip in one of the stones that felt smoother than it should have, as if hundreds of fingertips had touched it over many years, though it had likely been manufactured to appear that way. Briatta pressed hard and felt something click. The outline of the door was suddenly visible, and she pushed without hesitation. It was lighter than she expected, and Briatta nearly fell outside with Vydian and Tallor right behind her.

They took off at a run, skidding around the corner at the end of the alley.

"Where to?" Vydian called, keeping pace easily with Briatta along with Tallor.

"The nearest Weiler station!" Briatta yelled.

Behind them, Briatta could see the first of the false criminals rounding the bend in hot pursuit. Tallor was still keeping up, but he'd started to slow.

"This way," Briatta said, turning down a side street that would cut a few minutes from their route. Thankfully, the station wasn't far, but if they slowed at all—Briatta didn't want to think about what would happen. This was all for the Ackmanlee, but these people apparently took their jobs very seriously. Would they take her back to the base if they caught up? Would she be immediately disqualified?

Founders, they weren't even supposed to make a disturbance. What had Neven done?

At last, the Weiler station came into view. When the guard out front saw Briatta, Vydian, and Tallor sprinting at full tilt towards the station, then the large crowd of angry people chasing them, he shouted into the building for aid.

Briatta and Vydian skidded to a halt when they reached the building, breathing hard. Tallor slumped over, his hands on his knees.

"What's this?" demanded a female Weiler, looking over their shoulders at the group still running towards them. She looked as if she weren't sure whether to protect Briatta and her crew or to leave them to the mercy of the mob.

Briatta pointed at the man between her and Vydian and, through her gasps for air, said, "Tallor."

CHAPTER 32

"Tea, Miss Belrose?" Preida was already holding a tray out to Briatta.

"Yes, thank you." Briatta stared out the library window as Preida set the tea down on a table beside her and left quietly.

It had been four days since she and Vydian had presented the Weiler station with Tallor, and Simeon had stopped by the day after to tell her that scores would be tallied based on both individual and group performance and presented in three days —today. Even though they'd been the only ones to make it into the fictional group's headquarters and rescue the target, they hadn't succeeded by doing it the preferred way, and thus neither her nor Vydian were guaranteed the win. In the end, it could only be one.

Today was the day the winner of the Ackmanlee would be announced. The ceremony would take place just before dinner in the gardens at Malcalaire, and then there would be food and drink to celebrate. The whole of Montclair was invited, as the Ackmanlee was one of the most entertaining events for the entirety of the year. While the details of the Ackmanlee were kept secret until the awards were presented, the people of Montclair were enthralled by the mystery and always curious about who would come out on top.

Despite being worried, Briatta was no longer consumed by it. In fact, she was at peace, and for the first time since her Choosing, she finally felt she could breathe properly. While there were parts in the past few cycles where she could have been better, what was done was done, and in the end, she'd given it her all.

Owena appeared in the doorway, smoothing the front of the fuchsia gown she'd chosen for the event. Her aunt looked stunning with her brown hair hanging in loose curls, part of it pinned back on one side with a plain gold clip. The pink hue of the dress made her big green eyes look darker than usual as she sat down across from Briatta and reached for the teapot.

"How are you feeling?"

Leaning back in her chair, Briatta folded her hands and tilted her head. "Better, now that I understand everything."

Owena looked up from under her lashes, a playful smile tugging her lips. "Figured it out, have you?"

Briatta nodded slowly as she watched her aunt pour tea for them both. "Next time you need to teach me a life lesson and keep me away from headquarters, would you mind choosing a kinder method?"

Owena added a small amount of honeyed milk into Briatta's cup and set it in front of her. "I am sorry about that. But I will also say that I am very proud of what you've done at Sour Soup and the person that you are becoming. And likely, there will never be another reason to keep you out of headquarters."

Lifting a brow and picking up her tea, Briatta shook her head but couldn't keep from smiling. "How much fun was it? Helping with the Ackmanlee?"

Owena paused just before taking a drink, her eyes twinkling. "Very fun."

They both laughed, and Briatta finally took a long sip of her tea. A moment later, Ellery breezed into the room in a pale-blue dress with a low-cut back. The small white flowers dotted the fabric as if they had been blown from a tree and had settled onto the gown as they drifted towards the ground.

"Ah, it finally feels normal around here again," Ellery declared. When she saw there weren't enough teacups on the tray for her to serve herself as well, she stole Briatta's, nearly finishing the contents in one gulp. Briatta rolled her eyes.

Regarding her youngest niece with a thoughtful expression, Owena flicked her gaze to Briatta and winked. Perhaps Ellery had some character growth in her future, as well. Fighting the urge to laugh, Briatta turned to look out the window. A messenger was approaching, carrying yet another bouquet of flowers.

Her laughter died on her lips.

"I can't believe he tried to keep you from winning," Ellery said sourly, noticing the flowers as well. "In a way, it's sort of sweet. He's obviously afraid of losing you if you win and get stationed far away."

Owena frowned. "I raised you better than that, El. What Neven did was selfish and wrong. It wasn't sweet in the slightest."

Unable to look at either of them, Briatta's heart twisted painfully in her chest. She still hadn't been able to reconcile the friend she'd known since she was nine with the man who had drawn his sword against her to keep her in Montclair. Neven had sent a floral arrangement from the finest Flower Ardorist in the city every day since, each one larger than the last, but Briatta still refused to speak with him.

She couldn't. Not yet.

"Are you going to get ready soon, Bria?" Owena asked her, leaning forward slightly in her seat.

Briatta looked down at herself. She wore her favorite sparring outfit: a long-sleeved blue shirt, black pants, and lace-up boots. On her thigh, she wore her sheath exposed, which she didn't normally do, but it felt fitting for today.

"I was thinking I'd wear this," she said.

Ellery pursed her lips. "At least let me braid your hair."

Without waiting for a response, Ellery stood and combed her fingers through Briatta's thick brown hair, gently tugging out the tangles. She pulled Briatta's hair into two braids, wrapping them around each other and pinning them into a bun at the base of her skull.

"There," Ellery said, stepping back and examining her sister with a pleased expression. "Now you look like a warrior."

Owena said nothing, but the gleam in her eyes and the lines that appeared beside them told Briatta enough. She was proud. The three women gathered up their things and headed to the front door. When they opened it, they were met by Aden, who looked as though he had just been about to enter.

"There you are, Bria." Aden grinned at her, lowering his hand to his side. "Are you ready?"

Taking a shaky breath and exhaling slowly, Briatta nodded. "As I'll ever be."

The next few hours would determine the trajectory of her life.

WHEN PETYR PULLED the white horses to a halt in front of Malcalaire, Briatta peered out of the small window and stared at the gathering crowd of Elfeans from Montclair; it was unlikely that they had visitors from the other cities of Belrune because of how difficult and expensive travel was between biodomes. There had been a desert storm just the day before, and it had been nearly as dark within the biodome as during bionight. Still, perhaps a few Weilers or traveling authorities could be expected.

Petyr opened the carriage door for them, and Aden stepped down first, standing across from Petyr to help his sisters and aunt. Briatta let Owena and Ellery exit first, frozen in her seat. Aden watched her expectantly, but she felt as if she were moving through sand as she grabbed the carriage frame, pulling herself through the door and stepping onto the ground. She gulped, looking up at the spires of Malcalaire Manor and the garden that sprawled before it.

"It'll be alright," Aden said, pitching his voice so only Briatta could hear. He reached out, squeezing her shoulder.

All Briatta could do was nod as she took a deep breath, swallowing thickly. Then she started towards the gardens. Ellery and Owena, having paused to wait, fell in on either side of her as she approached.

The garden, on the backside of the building and not visible from the front where they'd entered for the ball, was magnificent. Hedges framed the entirety of the gardens with evenly spaced gaps in the bushes to allow entry, and there were a few of the same fruit trees growing throughout amidst a glorious display of vibrant flowers and glowing mushrooms. There were Weilers posted at each gap—there were at least ten that Briatta counts—to discourage Elfeans with bad intentions from joining the festivities. They nodded in greeting as the Belroses passed but didn't move otherwise.

People gathered around the tall tables—decorated with freshly picked flowers—scattered on the flat green paths of the garden. Elfeans dressed in black serving attire weaved their way through the growing crowd, bearing trays of appetizers and drinks. One walked by Briatta with what he confirmed to be a tray of brambleberry spiked lemonade, so she snatched one, taking a sip to dampen her dry mouth.

Briatta immediately identified who had competed and who hadn't based on whether they'd dressed up or appeared ready to fight—though she was sure not all of them had come combat-ready. She spied Vydian lurking by a group of tittering young women across the garden, obviously eavesdropping, and smirked.

Leading them to a table with an empty plate, Owena waved over a server carrying a tray of food and selected several small servings, setting them down on the table and handing the abandoned plate to the server. The Belroses were fairly early, despite having arrived after the announced time; Briatta knew the gardens would be packed before the announcement was made, and dinner wouldn't be served until after.

"Bria!" a familiar feminine voice called. Briatta turned to see Morenna hurrying over to their table and grinned.

"Morenna." She hugged her friend. They hadn't seen each other in far too long.

"What's this?" Morenna said, holding Briatta at arm's length and examining her outfit. "Did you compete or something?"

Briatta smiled sheepishly.

"Oh, my Founders, you *did*!" Morenna gasped. "You'll have to tell me all about it."

Opening her mouth to reply, Briatta's words caught in her throat as she saw Neven over Morenna's shoulder. He'd been about to approach but stopped when he met her eyes, uncertainty rippling across his face. Confused by her silence, Morenna turned and followed her line of sight.

"Oh no. Are we no longer friends with him?" she whispered to Briatta.

"Um, it's a long story," Briatta managed. Morenna closed her eyes and bobbed her chin in understanding.

"It's alright. You don't have to talk about it now. Let's just have fun." Hooking her arm around Briatta's elbow, Morenna steered her pointedly away from Neven and dragged her into the crowd. Briatta waved halfheartedly at her family over her shoulder, who gave her big smiles and waved, encouraging her to go.

Vydian joined Morenna and Briatta a few hours later, and together, they finished several brambleberry lemonades. Briatta felt a pleasant buzz in her head but decided against another drink after recalling what had happened the last time she'd been drunk at Malcalaire.

While Morenna and Vydian, in another world and at a different time, were unlikely to have shared the same circles, they were now getting along famously well. Briatta listened to them talk, slowly growing more nervous with every minute that passed until the announcements would be made.

At the front of the party, actors had started depicting the events of the Ackmanlee. First demonstrating what the entries had looked like, then the selections, and then some fighting. There were barrels tossed and fake teeth thrown into the crowd. Some people in grey fought those in regular, unassuming clothing. Briatta watched a little of it, though the reenactment was mostly for the Ardorists and others who hadn't participated in attendance. She'd used to love watching the shows.

At last, Lord Mallon took the stage, heralded by the same stringy man from before. Lord Mallon wobbled slightly from drink, and it seemed his great belly had grown a few inches. His head was short several more hairs than last time, and he appeared to have aged more than part of the cycle that had passed since his ball. The difference was so stark, Briatta nearly forgot why he was about to speak even despite her nerves. She frowned, wondering what could have possibly happened in such a short time to have caused this level of deterioration.

"Thank you for coming to the thirty-first results of the annual Ackmanlee," he called to the gathered crowd, who responded with a roar of excitement.

Briatta shifted on her feet, rubbing her hands together.

"First, a few matters of business," Lord Mallon said when the noise quieted, pulling a small piece of paper from his coat and squinting at it. "I must announce the disqualified competitors before getting to the winner."

Vydian and Briatta shared a nervous look.

"Sara Sutcliffe has been disqualified for permanently disabling one of the volunteers who acted in the fictional crime group," Lord Mallon said, his beady eyes searching the crowd for reaction. Whoever Sara Sutcliffe was, she didn't make a sound to reveal herself. Disappointment flared in Lord Mallon's eyes, and he returned to the paper clutched in his hand. "And...ah, this is a strange one. Neven Alderbeck, who was not a competitor and could not have been due to his status as an Ardorist, has received appropriate punishment for pretending to compete, and then turning against his two team-mates. Turncoats are not tolerated within the ranks of the Weilers or Ardorists. Mr. Alderbeck also, against the knowledge of the Weilers, assisted the actors who helped put on the Ackmanlee this year, giving him knowledge of the program that compromised his credibility."

Vydian and Briatta stared at each other with wide eyes. Briatta felt as if she'd been hit by a brick. She'd guessed, yes... but the confirmation. It was somehow worse. A loud, rushing sound filled her ears, and her chest tightened again.

"Now, to announce the victor," Lord Mallon continued.

Not only had Neven tried to keep her from winning, regardless of his intentions, but he had lied to her and Vydian from the very beginning. He had joined the Ackmanlee and interfered at every step because he didn't want Briatta to leave. On top of that, Briatta was willing to bet he'd applied to compete because he didn't believe she could do it herself. And...he'd helped Owena the entire time. That was why he'd been at the warehouse that night. Why Rory had, too. It had been one of the locations that had suffered losses at the hands of the crime group, and Briatta was sure they were there to stage a scene. She'd have to confirm.

Around her, the crowd worked itself into a frenzy at the anticipation Lord Mallon was building. He rambled about the honor the winners received and how rare a talent they must possess to outshine their competitors.

"—Miss Briatta Belrose!" Lord Mallon cried.

But all Briatta heard was the cheers of the crowd through the thoughts swirling in her mind.

A hand grabbed her elbow, and Briatta turned, seeing Morenna's look of concern. "Bria, did you hear? You won!"

"I...what?" Briatta asked.

"You won! Go up there!" Morenna smiled softer now, more encouraging, clearly noticing the distress between the two other women; Vydian was pale and tight-lipped, and she looked frustrated. Briatta's heart skipped. Was the woman upset she'd lost?

The crowd had begun noticing that Briatta was standing among them. They swept toward her, ushering her toward the dais where Lord Mallon waited. She walked stiltedly up the stairs, and the crowd grew louder, their adulation nearly deafening. If Lord Mallon said anything else, Briatta didn't hear it.

Soon, she was being welcomed back into the crowd. Now, she was holding the little golden orb that signified her win.

Someone passed her a drink, and Briatta accepted it but didn't take a sip, trying to find her way back to her family and friends.

Finally, Ellery materialized by her side, grabbed her hand, and pulled her back to their table. The rest of the night was a blur. Briatta wanted to forget everything that had happened with Neven and enjoy her win, but she couldn't ignore the fact that her lifelong friend had plotted against her success.

At some point, Vydian returned to her side. "Congratulations. I was always rooting for you."

"You didn't want to win?" Briatta asked in surprise. Her own entrance into the Ackmanlee had been borne of a desperate desire to be needed, so she had a hard time wrapping her head around any reason less dire that might drive someone to join.

"No." Vydian reached out and squeezed her hand. "But I am glad we met because of it."

The end of the night drew near, and the crowd dwindled. Briatta observed her family from their table. Ellery wasn't walking straight anymore, and she and Morenna were doubled over laughing about something. Vydian watched the two women with a tiny smirk at her mouth. Owena had vanished to find Ellery some bread rolls, and Aden chatted across the garden with a group of friends.

"Bria."

Briatta stiffened, every nerve in her body tingling from the combination of fear and fury that rushed through her as unbidden tears pricked the back of her eyes. Forcing herself to relax her shoulders, which had risen of their own will, and blinking to clear her vision, Briatta schooled her expression into something neutral before turning to face Neven. She didn't greet him. Instead, she stared up at him, hoping he could read in her silence the depth of her hurt from this betrayal from her oldest friend.

"Bria, I know what you must be thinking," he said, his eyes searching hers. If he were looking for any hint of forgiveness, he didn't find it. His brows creased with what Briatta thought was with the realization that this gaping new wound between them wouldn't be easily repaired with an apology or whatever speech he was about to give.

Glancing back toward her family, Briatta suddenly wished they were in the process of leaving, so she could simply climb into the carriage and leave Neven behind without the confrontation she knew this would turn into. She was still angry, but she was past the point of words. Now, Briatta was just disappointed and tired. Tired of his lack of belief in her abilities. Tired of being held back by the people who should support her growth and encourage change.

While the lesson had been painful, it was actually Owena who had made the importance of growth clear to her in these past cycles.

Her growth was important. Necessary. With every day that passed, she worked through more of her systemic biases and prejudices, becoming a better version of herself than the day before. Before her Choosing, she'd been too self-absorbed to recognize that all of this had to happen. Now...she could never return to being that girl.

Maybe she and Neven had simply outgrown each other.

"Bria," Neven said again. She took a deep breath and gathered their empty dinner plates on the table, turning her whole attention to the task to avoid meeting his gaze any longer.

"I don't have anything to say to you," she said.

The grass crunched softly from the direction where Neven was standing, and she could practically sense as he reached for her arm, as he'd done a hundred times before. She turned at the last second, stepping out of reach and glaring at him. The plates, now neatly stacked on the table, were forgotten.

"Stop it," she burst out before she could think better of it. "Please, for the love of the Founders, stop it."

Neven's eyes widened, and his mouth hardened. Briatta looked away again and started walking back to her family.

"Briatta," Neven said, his voice breaking painfully. "I was only trying to protect you. I realize that I was wrong now, but—"

Briatta whirled to face him.

"You could not even let me do *this* on my own," she hissed. "I am perfectly fine without you, Neven. I don't need you to babysit me through life or be my bodyguard. And you tried to come between me and the one thing that could truly help me. I really can't wrap my mind around why my best friend wouldn't want me to have the thing that is best for me. Why, Neven? Why?"

Hurt flashed in Neven's eyes. He reached out for the table to steady himself, stepping back as if she'd pushed him.

Briatta only felt empty in the same way she had after she'd exploded at Owena. But this time, it was warranted, and it had come from a place of hurt.

They stared at each other, Briatta the picture of sad fury, and Neven in stunned silence.

"I—I'm sorry," Neven stammered at last. "I had to protect you. The world is not forgiving, and the thought of you out there where I can't help you, where I can't protect you...it was too much."

"You don't get to make that decision for me," Briatta said quietly. Now, she was deathly calm. All the emotion that had overwhelmed her a moment before—even the emptiness— had left. "You can care about me as a friend, but you crossed a line, Neven. I don't know if I can forgive that."

Pain creased Neven's features, and his shoulders slumped. "Please, Bria."

Briatta took a step back.

"Is there a problem here?" Vydian's voice drawled from behind. Briatta's cool anger warmed a little at the realization that she had other friends who would support her through anything, even in this.

Shaking her head, Briatta retreated again. "I was just leaving."

Briatta didn't look back, but she knew Neven would watch her go. She looped her arm through Vydian's, as her friend narrowed her eyes slightly at Neven before marching Briatta back to her family. The pair joined Ellery and Morenna, who had stopped laughing and watched her approach with guarded curiosity.

The next time Briatta glanced back at their original table, Neven was gone.

CHAPTER 33

The week following the awards ceremony for the Ackmanlee was uneventful, and Briatta found herself milling aimlessly around her house when she wasn't working at Sour Soup or helping the Night Roses now that she was welcomed at headquarters again. The sudden lack of direction, so different from the drive she'd had during the competition, left her feeling somewhat lost, and she found herself fervently hoping that whatever the Weilers had in mind for her would provide a purpose like the one she'd found in the Ackmanlee.

Before leaving the ball at Malcalaire, Briatta had been pulled aside to sign a paper acknowledging her as the winner according to the history of the Elfean people and of Carceron while formally accepting whatever assignment the Weilers would appoint to her. While this felt wrong and went against everything Owena had taught them, Briatta had to trust that she was doing the right thing. She wouldn't get a second shot at this. She'd been told then by the young bespectacled woman that someone would reach out shortly to review what her new job would entail, but first there was paperwork that had to be filed and clearances that had to be processed.

Now, it was nearly the Cycle of Water, and she was growing anxious to embark on her new life. A couple times, she'd gone to the Weiler station to inquire after the status of her job, but they'd cited paperwork and clearances taking an exceedingly long time as the reason she was still waiting.

There was a certain mystery to it all, especially with the aspect of added security, and Briatta spent a lot of time in the Belrose library and the old war room in the basement, imagining the different things she might be doing in the coming cycles while practicing her Ardor—now by herself—and going through her regular physical training.

Each time Briatta worked with her Ardor, she felt a small pang of something painful because she wasn't working with Neven. However, her powers were finally coming more easily to her, and that she was discovering new and more exciting ways to use them, which always made her feel better.

She was in the midst of lifting an axe with her darkness and throwing it, unsteadily, towards a target when the bell signaling someone at the front door clanged violently through the house. Briatta jumped, her control over the shadows slipping. The axe hurtled at an angle toward the map on the wall. Heart leaping into her throat, Briatta threw herself and her Ardor after the weapon, barely creating a wall of solid, inky shadows in front of the map before the axe hit it and clattered harmlessly to the floor.

A moment later, the door to the secret room swung open and Ellery appeared, pausing as she took in the scene before her. Her lips quirked up.

"Well, I *was* about to ask how you were doing, but it looks like the answer is 'not great.'" Ellery folded her arms and tilted her head at Briatta.

Exhaling through her teeth and fighting the urge to scowl at her younger sister, Briatta pushed herself onto her knees, rubbing absently at her elbow where she'd hit it against the stone floor. Frowning, she scanned the room around her. The bells had never been so loud before, even when one was right next to the front door, but perhaps when the room was built, the sound had been intentionally increased as an additional precaution, in case extra measures were necessary to either hide or exit the secret war room.

"Did you hear how loud those damned bells were?" Briatta asked.

"About made me jump out of my skin." Ellery nodded. She looked over her shoulder as if she could see the front door from where she stood, her brows furrowing. "Wonder who could be calling at this hour."

It was late, that was true.

Realizing then that the solicitor might be here for her, Briatta scrambled to her feet and pushed past Ellery, hurrying from the room and extinguishing the Ardor lights as she left.

"Where are you going?" Ellery hissed, jumping to join Briatta so the swinging rotation of the door wouldn't hit her.

"Maybe it's a Weiler," Briatta replied, guiding the door so it closed behind them as quietly as possible. Then, both sisters paused in the center of the training mat as they strained to listen for any clues from upstairs.

The sound of muffled voices echoed down the staircase and into the basement. Briatta glanced down at herself and up at Ellery, smoothing her shirt and running a hand over her hair before heading up to the main floor.

"—just upstairs, please come right in here and I'll fetch her for you," Owena was saying, and Briatta paused. If Owena told their guest that she was upstairs, it wouldn't do for her to suddenly appear from the basement stairs. Then again, only someone looking for something to find suspicious would think it strange. Anyone could go downstairs in their own home for any reason at any time. These were the thoughts and suspicions of the Night Rose agent inside her.

Briatta hovered anxiously where she stood, biting her lip and glancing down at Ellery, who had followed close behind her. When they heard the doors to the sitting room close, the pair scurried lightly up the remainder of the steps. Owena was starting up the main staircase, a hand lifting her skirt to keep it out of the way when she looked over her shoulder at the girls.

"Ah, there you are, Briatta." Owena's gaze snapped to them. "Captain Simeon is here to talk to you."

While she'd been excitedly awaiting this day, Briatta suddenly felt very nervous. Beyond the doors of her sitting room, her new life awaited. Whatever she'd be doing, wherever she'd be going, it was all right there. Her security net for not having a recognized and permissible Ardor. Briatta swallowed and wiped her hands, which had quickly become damp, on her hips.

Recognizing the fear in her oldest niece, Owena's expression melted into something of concern, love, and pride all at once. She stepped off the staircase and closed the distance between them to grab Briatta's shoulders.

"I am so proud of you," Owena told her in a fierce whisper. "You are going to do great things. You already are. You already have."

Taking a shaky breath, Briatta nodded and leaned into her aunt for a hug. "Thank you," she whispered.

Ellery's fingers brushed her hand in a silent show of support, but she didn't intrude upon the moment between Owena and Briatta.

Standing back from her aunt, Briatta braced herself, rolling her shoulders up and back, and then walked into the sitting room. She closed the door gently behind her as her eyes immediately found Simeon. He was standing by the window, his hands folded behind his back, though he'd turned at the sound of her entrance, a bright smile illuminating his features.

Briatta's heart hiccupped in her chest, and she reminded herself to smile back and say hello rather than stare mutely at him.

"Captain Simeon," she said. "How are you?"

Nodding in greeting, he took half a step toward her. "I'm well. I must offer my congratulations on your victory in the Ackmanlee, Ms. Belrose. I had you marked as my guess from the very beginning."

"Th-thank you," Briatta stammered, her mind focusing on the fact that Simeon had thought she'd win the competition since...since when, exactly? The application? Or did it go back even further to when they'd danced at the ball?

"I'm very pleased that you will be working with us this year," Simeon continued, his hands releasing from their hold behind his back.

"With...us?" Briatta's mind wasn't keeping up with the conversation.

"Yes, you will be on my team."

Founders. Was she going to be working closely with Simeon for the foreseeable future? Briatta felt a little faint and, to her dismay, queasy.

"And, ah, what will we be doing?" she managed to ask.

Simeon waved a hand, his smile widening. "We'll get to that shortly, don't worry." He strode to one of the sofas, lowering himself onto it. "Now, please, have a seat."

A stack of small folders waited on the small table between the couches, and Briatta sat near him on the sofa perpendicular to the one he'd selected. Feeling more self-conscious than usual, being alone with Simeon and battling the urge to run to the bathroom and throw up, she shifted awkwardly in her seat, trying—but failing—to find a comfortable position.

"I'm sorry for the delay in your assignment," Simeon apologized, his lips slightly grimacing. "We are required to conduct a thorough background search on applicants and...as it turns out, there was no plausible explanation for where you learned to fight."

Already dizzy from the shock of Simeon sitting in front of her, Briatta grabbed the edge of her sofa and swallowed.

"Not to worry though," Simeon continued. "We were able to resolve that discrepancy by having a conversation with Owena."

Owena had spoken with the Weilers?

Simeon winked at her, his eyes twinkling.

Did that...did that mean he knew what she was a member of...of what she'd helped facilitate in Montclair?

"That's good to hear," Briatta replied numbly, prying her hands from the couch and clasping them in her lap.

Simeon nodded and moved on as if he'd never implied that anything illicit had ever occurred in Briatta's life.

"Now, before I tell you what we'll be doing, I have to go over your performance in the Ackmanlee and outline why you were the winner." Simeon picked up one of the folders and flipped it open, clearing his throat. "You were one of the only competitors to team up with someone else and, for the most part, work well with them. There was the...unfortunate incident that got Neven in trouble, but you handled it well, considering your history. The ability to work in teams and deal with conflict, especially in the middle of executing a mission, is an essential trait for Weilers, and that was highly notable."

Briatta's throat constricted with the praise and the pain of recalling that moment in the dark staircase when Neven had turned against her. She looked down at her hands, fearing if she continued staring at Simeon, the tears that still pricked her eyes when it came to Neven would break free.

"We interviewed your family for this next part. The way you handled the case and all the investigative work was systematic and logical, leaving room for each potential path until you had solid evidence leading you in a certain direction. Very good." Simeon turned a page in the file. "Your hand-to-hand combat skills are also much more proficient than what we expected from any contestant. Maybe someday *you* will tell me where you learned."

Simeon glanced up, his eyes twinkling with mischief. Again, he winked at her, his mouth tilting upward on one side.

A pit opened wide in Briatta's belly, and the sinking feeling that he knew exactly where she'd been trained grew stronger. This man would be the end of her, should he tell anyone.

Wait...did others already know? He'd said *they'd* had a conversation with Owena, but had it just been him? Or were other Weilers present? Was there some sort of understanding between Owena and the Weilers, as was rumored, or was it something that was only just coming to light?

Briatta forced herself to smile at Simeon and raise a brow. "Maybe someday."

He met her gaze for what felt like a moment too long, and then, chuckling softly, he looked back at the paper.

"We also judged you on your ability to balance the case with your daily life, and you did an admirable job. You may be surprised to hear that the burglary of Sour Soup was actually a test we had planted for you. Since most of your time working on the Ackmanlee was spent with Neven and Vydian, we wanted to see how you'd perform on your own in an unrelated scenario. While you didn't necessarily follow standard Weiler procedure—and I know you haven't been trained—what you did was effective, and I have to admit, it was quite fun picking up my peers after you had tied them up."

Briatta started, surprised, and then a quick and hot anger filled her as he continued. What if Leah had shown up before Briatta that day? She opened her mouth to demand answers, all her new worries surrounding her position in the Night Roses forgotten, but Simeon put up a hand to silence her before she could begin.

"Don't worry. Leah was in on it, and after you left, we approached her and compensated her for the damages that occurred, covering the repairs and then some. It had to look real to you. Ms. Martella was more than satisfied with what we provided." Simeon watched Briatta's reaction, his tone soothing.

Relaxing slightly, Briatta's hands stayed tightened in her lap.

"Good," was all she could say. Leah had probably been asked to remain quiet about the whole thing to avoid altering Briatta's perception of the Ackmanlee. Still, she made a mental note to bring up the robbery tomorrow and ensure her boss had been well and fairly paid.

And, depending on where this assignment with Simeon's team would take her, she'd likely have to give Leah an end date for her job there.

"Now, do you have any questions for me about the Ackmanlee and the results before we proceed?" Simeon asked.

"Yes. Why did I win over Vydian?" The question had been bothering Briatta since her name was announced at the ceremony, even though Vydian hadn't been upset. They'd performed very similarly, in her opinion, and she wanted to know what was different about them.

Tilting his head, Simeon blew a small puff of air. "I can only share your results with you. Vydian's feedback has been provided to her, and she may disclose it to you if she wants to. But...for various reasons, you were ultimately the better pick for the job at hand. Do you have any other questions?"

That didn't clarify much at all for her, but Briatta also could sense she wouldn't be able to get more than that.

"No." she shook her head.

"Good." Simeon set the first folder down on the table and reached for the second. "There are a few more pieces of paper that you must sign, along with an oath that you'll need to swear, before I can tell you anything more about your assignment."

He pulled three sheets from the folder and set them before her, tugging a pen from his jacket pocket and handing it to Briatta.

"The first is the paper version of the oath that you will swear in just a moment. It basically states that you will uphold the honor of the Weilers and proceed in your job with all of the moral codes of the Elfeans in mind, and that you will protect the young and the old. You can take a moment to read through it first if you'd like." Simeon pushed the far-left sheet toward her. Briatta skimmed it, but it appeared exactly as Simeon had said it was, and so she signed it.

"The second is the acknowledgment of the clearance you've been given." Simeon tapped the paper's center. "It outlines the level of information you're permitted to access and the penalties that you'd be subject to should you disclose that information to anyone without the appropriate clearance."

Briatta picked that document up and read it more closely than she had the first. It stated she would have Arcane, the second highest level of clearance. Also listed for her reference was the top clearance, which was called Occult, and the bottom, which was Esoteric. According to the definition of her authorization, she would be privy to more knowledge regarding Ardor than was available to the public, the movements of Weilers, and any threat against any city in the kingdom of Belrune. She may even be called upon to speak directly with the king if needed.

Her mouth a bit dry, Briatta lowered the document back to the table and signed. What exactly was she getting herself into?

"Perfect." Simeon tucked the first two sheets back into the folder. "Now, I can tell you more."

Briatta forced herself to chuckle at the dry attempt at a joke, and Simeon smiled. Then, he reached for the final piece of paper.

"This last one is your contract. It does not state exactly what you're doing because it's not a classified document—this one will be in the public record of the Weilers, accessible to anyone who checks after you. Treat this as your cover. I've brought a copy for you to memorize, and then you can keep it or burn it, whatever you like."

Briatta picked this sheet up with curiosity, though she didn't read it too carefully, as it wouldn't cover her actual job. Eyes widening at the very fair wages and nice benefits of this position, she happily signed it and passed it over to Simeon.

After all three necessary documents had been read and signed, Simeon had Briatta raise her hand and verbally swear the oath that she'd already endorsed on the first paper. She'd have to do it again when she reported for her first official day of duty, but this allowed them to go over what she'd be doing for now.

At last, Simeon pulled the final folder out and held it in his hands.

"This folder does not leave this room with you. When you have read it, I will take it back to my Weiler station and return it to the Arcane level room. I'll give you plenty of time to look it over, don't worry."

Briatta's jaw tightened, her eyes flicking to the folder with new curiosity, and she sat up straighter.

"Do not read it out loud. Do not ask me questions about it out loud. Just read it over, and when you're done, give it back to me. Your first day and the location are listed on the first page. When I see you there, we can discuss this further."

"I understand," Briatta said. With slightly shaking hands, she reached out to accept the folder that he extended to her. It was cool in her hands, and she set it reverently on her lap before glancing back up at Simeon as she ran her hands over the front. He nodded encouragingly.

Briatta opened the folder.

The first page had only three words: Operation Desert Rose.

It sounded ominous. Fighting the urge to look back at Simeon, Briatta flipped the page and began to read. With every sentence, her heart beat a little faster, and her eyes grew wider. The nerves she'd had about Simeon exposing the Night Roses and her concerns for Leah were quickly forgotten. And suddenly...the structure for this year's Ackmanlee made a lot more sense.

Briatta wasn't just becoming a Weiler. She was going to help the Weilers and King Novak take down Kalaiden.

The End

ACKNOWLEDGMENTS

I can hardly believe I'm writing this.

First and foremost, thank you to my fiancé and number one cheerleader, N. When I said I wanted to write a book, that I've always wanted to write one, you said: "So, do it. What's stopping you?"

You were right.

To my dogs: C and then later J, who sat with me through every writing session, cuddled on the couch with me during edits, and got me out of the house for walks when I had been staring at the screen for too long. The best boys ever. C is now enjoying his pain free life over the rainbow bridge, but he was there from the beginning of this book, and deserves all of the chicken and popcorn that Heaven will let him have.

Thank you to my amazing beta readers: Jessica, Becca and Dave. The three of you were the first "strangers" to read my work, and all of your encouragement, excitement and feedback made this process so much more rewarding and fun. This story would not be what it is today without you, and I will forever be grateful for that.

Thank you to my editor, Minna at Aurion Edits, who went above and beyond. Your responses took my little story and nurtured it into something stronger that I can be proud of. Every little detail, character trait, and plot inconsistency that you found helped me more than you know! Some of those things, I never would have begun to think of on my own. I was truly blown away by the thought and effort put into your work, and I will sing your praises from the rooftops! Thank you, thank you, thank you.

And lastly, thank you to my proofreader Ayre from Virtually Ayre. As the last line of defense before publishing, you have truly made my story shine. Not only that, your reactions had me grinning from ear to ear!

This book has been a labor of love. I officially started it in 2023 when N was gone for a year, but I'd really been working on it off and on since 2020. I just couldn't get the right plot down, or the characters or the dialogue right. But all of that starting and then restarting, rewriting, editing, and over ten drafts eventually paid off, and boy have I learned a lot.

I hope you, reader, have enjoyed this story as much as I loved writing it, learning about indie publishing and working with everyone who helped bring this to life. Welcome to the Poleaxes. Let's hope it's a long, long ride!

From Binding until Burning.

Yours,

J.C. Cooper